SPECIAL MESSAGE T(

THE ULVERSCROFT F(
(registered UK charity number 264873)

was established in 1972 to provide funds for
resea , diagnosis and treatment of eye diseases.
  amples of major projects funded by
the Ulverscroft Foundation are:-

- Children's Eye Unit at Moorfields Eye
  spital, London
- Ulverscroft Children's Eye Unit at Great
  nond Street Hospital for Sick Children
- ding research into eye diseases and
  tment at the Department of Ophthalmology,
  iversity of Leicester
- e Ulverscroft Vision Research Group,
  titute of Child Health
- in operating theatres at the Western
  hthalmic Hospital, London
- e Chair of Ophthalmology at the Royal
  stralian College of Ophthalmologists

Yo   n help further the work of the Foundation
making a donation or leaving a legacy.
E   contribution is gratefully received. If you
v   l like to help support the Foundation or
ire further information, please contact:

ULVERSCROFT FOUNDATION
ıne Green, Bradgate Road, Anstey
Leicester LE7 7FU, England
Tel: (0116) 236 4325

website: www.foundation.ulverscroft.com

BAND OF GOLD

When dashing Irish sea captain and part-time gunrunner Rian Farrell spontaneously buys the deed to a claim at Ballarat, where reef gold has recently been discovered underground, his wife Kitty is dismayed. Not only is mining dangerous work for the crew, who are seamen rather than labourers, but the desolate goldfields are no place for their adopted fourteen-year-old daughter Amber. As the headstrong and passionate Kitty endeavours to embrace the challenge by opening a bakery and building a small community of friends, she still yearns for life on the sea. But disaster strikes when the Yarrowee River bursts its banks and Rian disappears in the flood. Believing herself widowed, Kitty's heart is left in tatters. Alone and grieving, she turns to Rian's long-time shipmate Daniel, who has loved her from afar for many years.

DEBORAH CHALLINOR

◆

BAND OF GOLD

Book Three of the
Smuggler's Wife Series

Complete and Unabridged

AURORA
Leicester

First published in New Zealand in 2010 by
HarperCollins*Publishers* (New Zealand)

First Aurora Edition
published 2020
by arrangement with
HarperCollins*Publishers* (Australia)

The moral right of the author has been asserted

A catalogue record for this book is available
from the British Library.

ISBN 978–1–78782–251–1

Published by
F. A. Thorpe (Publishing)
Anstey, Leicestershire

Set by Words & Graphics Ltd.
Anstey, Leicestershire
Printed and bound in Great Britain by
T. J. International Ltd., Padstow, Cornwall

This book is printed on acid-free paper

Dedication

This one is for Florence Kim McBride

Acknowledgements

The characters in this story are all fictional, except for the ones already in the history books. A few points to note about the history: Bendigo was known as Sandhurst in 1854, but I have called it Bendigo for the sake of clarity. There were only thirteen men charged with high treason after the uprising at Eureka, not fourteen as implied in this story. I have altered the shape of the Yarrowee River to fit the plot, and to my knowledge there was no flash flood in Ballarat at the beginning of February 1855.

This novel is not intended to be a fictional account of the Eureka uprising, although many of the events leading up to that — and the conflict at Eureka itself — do feature in Kitty and Rian Farrell's story.

Thanks are due to Siobhán McHugh, who gave me a copy of her excellent radio documentary, *The Irish at Eureka — Rebels or Riff-Raff?*, to help with my research. Sovereign Hill at Ballarat, naturally, was a great source of inspiration.

Thanks also to the team at HarperCollins New Zealand for doing their usual great job of getting the book ready to go and out there, and to HarperCollins Australia, and to Anna Rogers for once again polishing the hell out of it.

Part One

New Gold Mountain

1

As surreptitiously as he could, Daniel Royce gazed down the long table at the woman he loved more than anything else in his life. The woman he had silently but passionately adored for the past fifteen years, the woman his heart had bade him follow to the ends of the earth. The woman who, unfortunately, was utterly devoted to someone else.

She caught him looking and offered a quick, friendly smile. Some women lost their looks as they aged, while others seemed somehow to become more beautiful, and at thirty-three Kitty Farrell was most definitely one of the latter.

On her left fidgeted her daughter, Amber, the half-Maori, half-European foundling Kitty had rescued from the rutted and muddied streets of Auckland in 1845, now just turned fourteen and already threatening to rival her adoptive mother in looks. She had been a trial, Amber, and still was. But she was adored by her mother and father, and indeed by the entire crew of the schooner *Katipo II*, presently sitting around the table finishing what had been a very filling, if not terribly tasty, meal.

On Kitty's other side sat her beloved husband, Rian Farrell, captain of the *Katipo* and Daniel's boss for the past ten years. Daniel sighed, as he

3

had a thousand times before. He had developed such a liking and respect for Rian that he would also gladly follow *him* to the ends of the earth.

As the apparently sole serving girtl of the Old White Hart's dining room staggered past under the weight of plates of steaming stew and roast mutton, Rian stopped her and asked her to prepare the bill for their meals. Several minutes later, in a harassed fashion, she dropped a folded piece of paper onto the table before rushing off to attend to someone else.

Rian opened it, his flint-grey eyes widening. 'Good God, this is extortion! It's almost five pounds!'

Kitty glanced at the bill, unsurprised: everything in Melbourne seemed to be absurdly overpriced at the moment. She collected her reticule and slid the cord over her wrist. 'Perhaps you should just settle it. We've sat here long enough, and we've things to do.'

Rian looked shifty. 'Er, well, actually, I can't.'

The *Katipo*'s crew eyed him with amusement: none of them could pay the bill either, as they'd not seen wages since the schooner put into Port Phillip three days ago. But no one was concerned: their entire cargo of supplies from the California goldfields had been sold this morning, so their pay wouldn't be far away.

Kitty's brow creased in a frown. 'Why not?'

'Because I don't have the money.'

'But what about the sale this morning?'

Rian rearranged his knife and fork. 'Well, the fellow couldn't pay for all of it at once, so I've held half of the cargo back until he hands over

4

the rest of the cash.'

'But you should still have half of the money, shouldn't you?'

'Yes. Yes, I *did* have it.' Rian stopped fiddling with his cutlery and added cheerfully, 'Actually, it's quite a long story, but it's probably best if I don't tell it to you here.' He tucked the bill under the salt pot and looked purposefully along the table. 'So we'll have to do the usual, I suppose. Is everybody ready?'

Kitty stared hard at her husband, a bubble of wary suspicion beginning to form in her chest. Nonetheless, she swivelled daintily on the bench so she faced away from the table.

'Go!' Rian urged, and all nine of them leapt up and charged out of the dining room, scattering as they burst out onto the street.

Behind them Kitty heard a bellow of rage, then the heavy footsteps of the publican as he pounded out of the hotel. Perhaps assuming that Kitty would be the easiest to run down, he set off after her, his boots slipping and sliding in the mud of Bourke Street. Risking a glance over her shoulder, Kitty caught a glimpse of him, his apron flapping and his face scarlet, apparently determined to risk death by heart attack for a mere £5.

Her skirts held high, Kitty raced ahead of him, Amber beside her giggling with excitement, dodging puddles, people and vehicles as they swerved across to the other side of the wide road. On and on they ran, past Exhibition then Russell streets, then Swanston Street. But before they reached Elizabeth Street, Kitty and Amber ducked into an alleyway, negotiating crates and broken barrels and heaps of ill-smelling rubbish, then shot out the other end like corks from a bottle and sprinted along Little Bourke Street and into the shadowed elegance of Victoria Arcade.

'Is he still coming?' Kitty panted as she stood, bent at the waist, hands on her hips, chest heaving. Whatever must all those people in the street have thought?

Amber peeked out, then shook her head. 'Can't see him, Ma.'

Kitty rested for a moment longer and took a last deep breath to slow her heart rate. She straightened, stared up at the vaulted roof above the arcade's clerestory windows, watched the sun sparkle off facets of the chandeliers she suspected would look magnificent at night, then took Amber's hand.

'Come on, sweetheart. Let's go and see what your father's done this time.'

★   ★   ★

'You've *what*?' she exploded.

Hawk, his long black braids waggling, shook his head and rolled his eyes. Simon looked dubious, while Mick, Gideon, Daniel, Pierre and Ropata appeared merely philosophical: they'd all had plenty of experience of Rian's money-making schemes.

So have I, Kitty thought. She should have known — Melbourne was seething with incomers eager to try their luck on the Victorian goldfields.

6

'Apparently it's a guaranteed winner on a proven lead. See?' Rian handed her several documents.

Unconsciously wrinkling her nose at the windborne stink from the Yarra riverbank slaughterhouses, Kitty warily perused the papers. One was the deed to a claim at Ballarat, where the alluvial surface gold had quickly disappeared during the rush of '51, but reef gold embedded in quartz rock had recently been discovered underground. The other was a document signing over ownership of a 'dwelling' in the vicinity of the diggings.

'How much did you pay for these?' she demanded, and almost fainted when Rian named the figure. 'But that's everything we got for the cargo!'

'Well, no, we're still owed half, remember.' Undeterred by Kitty's very obvious disapproval, Rian looked very pleased with himself. He rested his booted feet on the verandah rail of the lodging house where they were currently accommodated. It was rather basic but it was cheap, and all they could afford when they'd put into port. 'Think about it, Kitty. We'll make ourselves a fortune!'

Kitty closed her eyes and sighed deeply. Rian's rather cavalier entrepreneurialism often did make them very tidy sums, but occasionally it left them in serious debt, which meant they then all had to work to their utmost limits, buying and selling and shipping cargo around the world until they were back in the black again. Really, what did Rian know about gold mining? What did any of them know?

'Are we going to be rich, Pa?' Amber asked as she ate a handful of dates she had pilfered on the way back from Little Bourke Street.

'Very unlikely, sweetheart,' Kitty answered for her husband. She turned back to him. 'If this claim is a 'guaranteed winner' as you say, why has the owner sold it? And his house?'

'Not 'he': *she*. A widow. Mrs Murphy. Her husband died a month ago and she was wanting to go back to Ireland.'

'Died doing what?' Kitty asked suspiciously.

Rian shrugged. 'She didn't specifically say. But it was too much for him anyway, apparently.'

Kitty frowned and thought for a moment. 'What do you think, Hawk? Should we do this or not?'

Hawk's copper-coloured face was a little more flushed than usual, as though he were trying to keep his temper in check, but he answered her with his customary steady demeanour.

'I assume that the odds are that we may be successful, and we may not. It is common knowledge that gold mining is a gamble. And it is too late anyway — the money has been spent,' he finished with a hint of disapproval. Rian Farrell was his oldest and most trusted friend, but sometimes he made decisions about things he would have done well to have taken counsel on.

'Could we not sell the claim on to someone else?' Simon asked sensibly. He swept his arm in an arc encompassing the busy street before them, filled with people almost certainly

8

hurrying to and from business associated with gold-mining enterprises. 'Surely there would be plenty of buyers.'

'But I don't want to sell it on,' Rian said levelly, his tone confirming to everyone that he had made up his mind. 'The yield is guaranteed. This is a once-in-a-lifetime opportunity.'

Having heard this before, Kitty sighed again. Rian was more than she had ever imagined a husband could be — generous, passionate, handsome, brave and extremely capable — but he was also stubborn, careless of authority, had a quick Irish temper, and was sometimes down-right reckless. But none of that made any difference to his crew, all of whom were devoted to him. And she trusted him implicitly, even if they had had rather a lot of narrow escapes over the past decade and a half.

Also, they had little better to do over the next few months. The *Katipo* was on her side on the banks of the Yarra having her hull scraped and being refitted, so they might as well at least go and have a look at Ballarat — and their newly acquired claim of untold riches.

⋆　⋆　⋆

We must look a sight walking all together down the street, Kitty thought as she lifted her skirts to step around a pile of fresh horse shit, then raised the hood of her cape against the rain. They were accustomed to being stared at, though, and it did seem that they were a little less conspicuous here in Melbourne than they had been in some other ports. So far today she had already seen half a dozen black-skinned men, although none had been as spectacular as Gideon with his enormous African physique and shining bald head. His appearance almost always rendered people who didn't know him very nervous, and it was a treat to see their jaws drop when he spoke in perfectly cultured English and behaved impeccably. Except when he was angry, of course. People were right to be nervous then.

Melbourne in fact seemed to be teeming with people from all corners of the world. As well as the black men, she had seen Chinese, Jews and Pacific Islanders, and overheard accents from all over the British Isles, Europe and the Americas. There were plenty of women, too — wealthy-looking ladies in fine dresses wearing fancy gloves and bonnets accompanied by equally well-heeled gentleman, as well as women who looked as though they were used to working hard on the land. And there were whores, beckoning brazenly from windows and verandahs, and wild young men dashing about on horseback, and here and there a drunk nursing a bottle slumped miserably against a wall, looking as though his entire world had collapsed. And perhaps it had. As Hawk had said, gold mining was a tremendous gamble.

But she had not seen any other American Indians, like Running Hawk. He was Seneca, a tribe of the Iroquois nation, and was conspicuous because of his copper skin, high-bridged nose, long plaits and the knife he habitually wore tucked into his silver and turquoise-studded belt.

Simon Bullock, on the other hand, with his neatly trimmed sandy hair, pale blue eyes and nondescript clothing, looked exactly like the lay preacher he was. He had been sailing with the *Katipo* for almost ten years, ever since he had turned his back on the Church Missionary Society in New Zealand. He had not renounced God, however, and still ministered to anyone professing an interest, although he never made himself unwelcome and he never pontificated. He was an outcast and he knew it — a man of God without a specific religious order, and also that particular breed of man for whom women held no attraction — and he had never been happier, sailing the world in the company of those who accepted him for who and what he was.

'What about this one?' Pierre asked, stopping in front of a busy general store on Elizabeth Street.

'Let's have a look,' Rian said, stepping onto the wooden verandah running the length of the shopfront.

The outstanding payment for the *Katipo*'s cargo had been delivered that morning, everyone had been paid, and Gideon had been dispatched to the Old White Hart Hotel to settle the dinner debt. They were now shopping for provisions for the trip to Ballarat.

At the store's doorway, Pierre bowed low and ushered Kitty ahead of him. 'Pearls before swine, *chérie*.'

Following close behind, Amber demanded, 'Am I a pearl, too, Pierre?'

11

'Of the most lustrous kind, *ma petite*.'

Kitty smiled. Pierre doted on Amber. He had children of his own, he had once said, but had not seen them for many years, and Kitty wondered if he saw in Amber the family with whom he had spent so little time. He was a very kind man, Pierre Babineaux, a bayou Acadian from Louisiana. He was small and wiry, with weathered skin that made it difficult to judge his age — which was about forty-five — dark hair peppered with strands of grey pulled back in a queue that came halfway down his back, a long wispy moustache and several gold teeth. He was the *Katipo*'s cook, and was incredibly loyal and extremely handy in a fight. Kitty loved him dearly.

Inside the store, he rubbed his hands together and said, 'Now, where will we begin?' He was in charge of the food side of the expedition and, as always, relished the prospect of shopping for edible provisions. He wandered off, picking up various jars and bottles and peering at the contents.

Rian slid his arm around Kitty's waist and whispered, 'Do you think we'll have room to squeeze in a mattress suitable for two?'

Kitty looked into his mischievously twinkling eyes and didn't know whether to laugh or punch him on the arm for this latest escapade. Try as she might, she had not been able to remain annoyed at what he had done, such was his zeal for their new venture. And the more he talked about it, the more enthusiastic the others became, until it was clear to Kitty that they were all now determined not to return from Ballarat until they had found gold.

'Well, that depends on the accommodation, don't you think?' she replied, raising an eyebrow. 'Surely it would be inappropriate in the middle of a tent surrounded by our crew?'

Rian looked momentarily appalled, then realised she was teasing him. 'Well, no, we'll have the house.'

'If it *is* a house. It could well be a one-roomed shanty with a dirt floor and an old blanket for a door, for all we know.'

'I suppose,' Rian agreed. 'But the Widow Murphy was living in it and she didn't seem the type to live in a hovel. Surely it won't be that bad?'

'We'll just have to wait and see, won't we?' Kitty replied more cheerfully than she felt, and turned away to examine a length of dress cloth. Would they sell such things at Ballarat? Or should she take all her clothing with her? Not her best, of course — she couldn't imagine she would have any use for fancy gowns on the goldfields — but perhaps it would be prudent to take her everyday things and one or two of her nicer dresses. Just in case.

They had been warned by several shopkeepers that everything was even dearer at Ballarat than it was in Melbourne. This could have been a ruse to make them buy here, of course, but nevertheless, they intended to take a good store of provisions with them. Rian had already purchased two horses from Tattersall's Horse Bazaar, a near-new thorough-brace wagon, and a team of six bullocks — all for an exorbitant sum — and had skimmed a few items from the *Katipo*'s cargo before handing it over to the buyer that morning, who evidently intended to sell it at either Bendigo or Ballarat anyway. As far as Rian was concerned, he had done the fellow a favour by saving him some of the cost of haulage.

He had also selected stout Wellington boots for them all, and other supplies, including pots, galvanised buckets, ropes, shovels and spades, candle moulds and oil cans — plus several barrels of lamp oil and kerosene, as they had been told both were very expensive and hard to get on the diggings — three kettles, American axes and tomahawks, hammers and trowels, two tents, and prospectors' belts. They always travelled armed, but as a precaution Rian had added rather a large cache of ammunition to the pile of provisions piling up in the hallway of their lodgings.

He had also found a reliable man, Charlie Dunlop, to keep an eye on the *Katipo* while they were in Ballarat; there was no point in paying good money to have her refitted only to find her stripped bare by thieves when they returned.

Kitty flipped a length of fabric off a roll and held it to her waist, admiring the sheen on the material, then sighed. She was still trim and her waist neat, but her hips had not become any smaller over the years. Her stomach had remained flat and firm because she had never given birth, and never would, but with the amount of running about she did aboard the

Katipo, you would think her flanks and bottom would have at least stayed narrow. Rian said he loved her backside, and that her thighs were like a vice in moments of passion, which he seemed to think was marvellous, but still, why could they not be a delicate, *slender* vice? But she was strong, and very fit and healthy, so she supposed she should be grateful for that.

'That is very nice fabric,' Ropata said at her elbow.

'Yes, it is, isn't it? Are you looking for something for Leena?'

Ropata nodded, and rubbed the material between his fingers, feeling its weight. 'But I was thinking more of jewellery. I have seen some earrings, made from Bendigo gold. I think she might like those.'

'Oh, I'm sure she would,' Kitty replied, smiling at him fondly.

He was a good man, Ropata, and handsome in the way that Maori men from Ngati Kahungunu on the east coast of New Zealand often are. He had married Leena, a tall, half-caste Aboriginal girl from Sydney, eight years ago. But she absolutely refused to sail on the *Katipo*, preferring to stay with her people, and he just as adamantly refused to give up his life at sea, for now anyway, so they lived much of their lives apart. However, the *Katipo* harboured at Sydney Cove regularly, so he saw her and their two children, aged six and four, quite frequently; but Kitty knew he missed them, and they him.

Ropata made up his mind. 'Ae, the earrings, I think.' Having written to Leena and asked her to

15

join him at Ballarat, he added, 'Do you have any letters you would like posted?'

Kitty opened her reticule. 'Yes, actually. One to my mother, and one to Haunui and Tahi.'

Ropata took the envelopes, tucked them inside his jacket and set off to purchase his wife's earrings.

'Ma, can we buy this?' Amber pleaded, holding a wriggling puppy in her arms. 'Look how sweet he is.'

'Where did he come from?' Kitty scratched the puppy under the chin. Its eyes closed in bliss.

'A basket at the back of the store. There's four more. The man said I can have all of them for the price of three.'

'I'm sure he did. I don't think so, sweetheart.'

'But Ma, they're *orphans!*'

'But what about Bodie?' Kitty countered. Amber was getting that look on her face that meant she was going to dig her toes in. 'How do you think she'll feel?'

Amber looked slightly chastened. 'Cross?'

'Yes, very cross. I expect her feelings will be quite hurt.' And the result of that, Kitty reflected, could be rather nasty. Boadicea, known as Bodie, was Rian's aging cat and reigning queen of the *Katipo*, and an ill-disciplined and overly enthusiastic puppy might quickly find itself missing an eye or an ear. Anyway, a ship was no place for a dog. 'Go on, love, put it back.'

Clearly considering whether to make a fuss or not, Amber finally shrugged and headed back towards the puppy's basket. Kitty watched her go, her heart swelling with love. Without a doubt,

Amber had been spoiled over the years, but she was such a delightful child that it was very difficult to deny her anything. Although Rian loved Amber dearly, he said that between them they had raised a right little madam, but Kitty didn't think so. Amber was what she was always meant to be — clever, headstrong, irreverent and a little bit wild. One day she would make some young man very happy, but would probably also exasperate the hell out of him. Kitty felt sorry for the lad already; not just because he would have to meet her and Rian's expectations for their daughter, but also because he would have to gain the approval of the *Katipo*'s entire crew.

The store's floorboards creaked as Rian approached again, wearing a voluminous oilskin coat. 'I thought I'd buy us one of these each. What do you think?' He did a twirl. 'Waterproof, and quite warm.'

'Well, I've no doubt we'll need them,' Kitty agreed. 'It's freezing today.'

'And for the next month or so, I gather. And wet.'

'Oh, good, so we're going to be cold, wet and covered in mud?'

Rian looked sheepish. 'Er, yes, probably.' From behind his back he produced a hat woven from some sort of palm leaf. 'I'm not wearing one of these, though. There *are* limits.'

Kitty had seen plenty of men sporting them about town. 'Yes, there are,' she agreed. 'I'm not wearing one, either.'

Rian laughed at the image of Kitty's lovely face framed by the drooping brim of a cabbage-tree hat. 'Where's Mick?' he asked.

Kitty nodded towards the counter running down one side of the store; Mick Doyle was leaning against it, chatting animatedly to a girl standing on the other side — the owner's daughter, judging by the dark expression on the face of the man hovering nearby.

Typical Mick, Kitty thought. His curly black hair, flashing dark eyes and wicked smile seemed to have the girl mesmerised, which was not an unusual state of affairs. His devastating looks and smooth Irish charm ensured that he literally did have a woman in every port, sometimes several — 'Why ration meself?' was his motto — but his true love was the sea and he showed no inclination to settle down and take a wife.

'I need some things from the chemist,' Kitty told Rian.

'Be careful,' he said. 'We'll be along in a minute.'

He was forever telling her to be careful, Kitty reflected as she located Amber and headed for the door. She very seldom wasn't, but now it had become a sort of talisman every time they parted, even if only briefly.

Daniel and Gideon sat on a bench on the general store's verandah, their collars up against the cold. Gideon was dozing, his hat pulled low over his face, but Daniel was idly surveying the street, his long legs stretched out in front of him.

'Does anyone need anything from the chemist?' Kitty asked.

Gideon wasn't asleep. 'Not at the moment, thank you.'

'I do.' Daniel stood, and rubbed at the dark stubble on his chin. 'A new shaving brush. Mine's only got about six bristles left.'

Amber giggled at the thought, then pulled her mother into the street. 'Hurry up, Ma, I want some barley sugars.'

'Your teeth will rot,' Kitty warned.

'No, they won't — I'll clean them afterwards.'

'May I come with you?' Daniel asked.

Kitty nodded. 'Of course.'

They walked the hundred yards or so to the nearest chemist, a small shop tucked between a butcher's and an auction room. As Daniel opened the door for Kitty, they smelled camphor and valerian, a distinctive but somewhat overpowering scent. Wiping their boots on the mat, they entered and a bell rang somewhere in the recesses of the shop.

A woman in a house cap appeared behind the counter, and smiled at them. 'Good day, can I be of help?'

'Good day to you,' Kitty replied, knocking the rain off the brim of her bonnet. 'I'm needing English soap — about five pounds in bars should suffice — tooth powder, antiseptic powder, half a pound of horse worm pills, and two good-sized bottles of laudanum. Oh, and two large jars of lanolin cream, thank you.' She glanced at the knots in the ends of Amber's rippling, rum-coloured hair. 'And a good comb and a packet of barley sugars.'

'Off to the goldfields, are you?' the woman asked over her shoulder as she scanned the shelves behind her.

'How did you know?' Kitty asked.

'Five pounds of English soap is a lot to buy at once,' the woman replied. 'You've picked very unpleasant weather for it. Will half a pound of antiseptic powder do you?'

'Yes, thank you.'

Kitty examined the long row of large glass jars lined up on the counter, containing every herb, powder and plant extract an apothecary could need, from oils of amber and aniseed, to mercurial pills and mustard seed, to strychnine, tannin and zinc sulphate.

The woman placed Kitty's order on the counter and skilfully set about folding the soap, horse pills and powders into separate paper packages, which she sealed with red wax. 'You can take the worm tablets, too, you know,' she said helpfully. 'They work just as well for people.'

'Oh, really? I'll keep that in mind.' Behind her Kitty heard stifled snorts of laughter — Daniel and Amber elbowing one another, no doubt.

She paid for her purchases and waited while Daniel bought his new shaving brush. She knew full well that he was infatuated with her, and had been ever since they'd first met. When he had stowed away on the *Katipo* in Sydney almost ten years ago, after having murdered a man, Walter Kinghazel, to defend her honour, she had been shocked. At the time she'd had a dreadful job calming Rian's fear that Daniel would come between them; but he hadn't, and he never would. But still, his ardour for her hadn't waned, and it worried her. He was an attractive man — tall, dark-haired with deep blue eyes, and a very appealing, if slightly introverted, character — and she was dismayed that his infatuation might preclude him from taking a wife. But he had proved his worth as a seaman and crew member, and had become a friend to all of them, even Rian. If he ever were one day to marry and leave the ship, he would be greatly missed.

In the meantime, Kitty would continue to behave towards him as she always had, with fondness and respect, and a little private compassion.

2

Rian stamped his feet and blew on his hands in an ineffectual attempt to ward off the dawn's chill. The heavy grey sky threatened drizzle, and Kitty suspected they were in for a cold and uncomfortable journey.

The wagon had departed before light, loaded with provisions, on top of which Gideon and Mick sat somewhat precariously, armed with muskets in case they encountered the highwaymen who roamed the roads connecting Melbourne and Geelong with the goldfields. Hawk and Daniel followed on the horses, while Pierre and Ropata had been perched on the driver's seat with a caged Bodie in the middle, looking very sour at her temporary incarceration, even if she was nestled on a piece of sheepskin. Pierre had been swearing at the bullocks even before they had passed out of earshot.

'Why are we waiting?' Rian complained. 'I'm getting in.'

There had been no room on the wagon, and Kitty was secretly pleased that she, Rian, Amber and Simon would be travelling to Ballarat aboard a Cobb & Co coach. They would no doubt pass the wagon on the way and would definitely arrive at the diggings before the others. And, what's more, they would arrive *warm*; it really was a very cold day.

She buried her hands deeper in the pockets of

her cape and eyed Rian, who was leaning against the big yellow rear wheel of the coach. This morning he had dressed in a blue flannel shirt, black canvas jacket, snug grey moleskins and long boots. His dark blond hair, silvering slightly at the temples, was pulled back off his tanned and weathered face and he hadn't bothered to shave. His eyes, bracketed by wry lines, were watchful. He looked devastatingly handsome and Kitty felt like bustling him into the coach, shutting the door and finding a way for them both to warm up.

'Come on, it's freezing out here,' he said, and offered Kitty a hand to board, then climbed in and sat beside her. Amber followed and settled herself on the bench seat opposite, and Simon came last, bumping his head on the lintel and uttering a mild oath.

'I hope it's just us,' Kitty said as she removed her bonnet and arranged her skirts.

Amber gave an exaggerated shiver. 'It's cold in here, Ma.'

In response, Simon unrolled all but one of the canvas covers on the windows, allowing just enough light to enter so that they could still see each other.

But Kitty had spoken too soon: a minute later there was thumping and scraping as several items were secured to the roof of the coach, then the door opened and everything tilted as a rather large man clambered in.

'Good day to you,' he said, as he removed his hat and made a small production of looking for somewhere to sit.

'Come over here, love,' Kitty said, and patted the seat between herself and Rian.

Reluctantly, Amber changed places.

The gentleman nodded in acknowledgement and sat down opposite, his knees creaking in protest. He produced a bright green handkerchief, honked into it, then called out, 'Come along, Mrs Harcourt — don't dally.'

The coach rocked again as a considerably overweight woman hauled herself up the step and squeezed inside. After a lot of manoeuvring and tsk-tsking, she thumped down onto the seat, squashing Simon rather violently into one corner.

'My wife,' Mr Harcourt said, to no one in particular.

They appeared perfectly matched. In their forties, both were rotund and small-eyed. His mouse-brown hair was cut short and he wore whiskers, but Mrs Harcourt's hair was invisible beneath an ornate bonnet with a pronounced brim and layers of pleated fabric and lace, the ribbons fastened beneath her chins with a small brooch. They both wore nicely cut clothes and good-quality boots. Mr Harcourt's waistcoat displayed a watch and chain of heavy gold, and his wife's fingers were adorned with several rings mounted with precious stones.

Mrs Harcourt wriggled about until she was comfortable, then dug into a large tapestry holdall on her lap and withdrew a ball of wool and a pair of knitting needles. In no time at all she had cast on a row. 'Inclement weather, is it not?' she said eventually.

'Yes, very,' Kitty replied, moving her legs so that her knees wouldn't touch Mr Harcourt's.

Silence fell, except for the clacking of Mrs Harcourt's needles. Outside the five horses stamped and blew air between their rubbery lips, then a window cover lifted and the driver peered in at them. 'All set? We don't want to get behind schedule. Keilor, Melton, Bacchus Marsh, then Ballan, Ballarat, and end of the line at Bendigo.'

There was a general mumble of assent and he disappeared. The coach rocked slightly as he climbed up onto the driver's seat, then came a slight jerk as the five-in-hand strained in their harnesses and set off. Beside them the Criterion Hotel, Cobb & Co's staging post, moved out of view, and they were away.

Presently, Mr Harcourt asked Rian, 'Setting out for the diggings, are you?'

Rian nodded.

'First time?'

'Yes. And yourselves?'

'No, I've travelled this cursed road many a time. But I retired from gold mining last year. Well, my health isn't the best, you know. Hellishly cold out there this time of year, on the diggings.'

Kitty gave Rian a pointed look, but he pretended not to notice.

'We live in Melbourne now,' Mr Harcourt went on. 'I have a small business there.'

'And a lovely little home,' Mrs Harcourt interjected, her knitting needles clattering away.

'And it was worth your while, was it?' Rian asked. 'The mining?'

'Oh yes, very worth my while. I'm a rich man now,' Mr Harcourt replied without a trace of humility. 'I went into partnership on seven or eight claims, all at Ballarat. We had a consortium. Didn't dig myself, of course. Too much like hard work.' He patted his considerable belly. 'And of course they're all deep-sinkers now, and a man of my stature isn't suited to that sort of toil. It's a younger man's game, deep-sinking.'

'Deep-sinking,' Kitty echoed. 'What's that, exactly? I realise it means digging into the ground for some distance, but what *exactly* does it entail?'

'Well, my dear, it's a trifle confusing. Lots of technical terms and all that,' Mr Harcourt replied patronisingly. 'You might not catch my drift.'

Simon winced inwardly, but Rian only smiled to himself.

Kitty stared at Mr Harcourt unblinkingly.

Mr Harcourt harrumphed. 'Yes, well, of course, if you'd really like to know. Deep-sinking is the technique by which a shaft is sunk below the surface of the ground to a distance of anything between twelve and a hundred feet, and sometimes even deeper. Some leads run further down than others, of course.'

'Leads?' Kitty asked.

'A line of ore, shingle and rock and the like, that contains the gold. They run all over Ballarat. Or should I say, *under* Ballarat — they're actually the beds of ancient rivers.'

'Don't they fall down?' Amber asked.

Mr Harcourt frowned. 'Don't what fall down, dear?'

'The shafts. On top of the men.' She turned to her father. 'You won't be going down the shafts, will you, Pa?'

Rian opened his mouth to reply, but Mr Harcourt said hurriedly, 'No, they don't fall down. Well, hardly ever. You see, the miners line the shafts with slabs of eucalypt to hold up the sides, which is why there are hardly any trees left around Ballarat. Then, when the shaft reaches the lead, and all the ground water and sand and mullock and what-have-you has been winched out, the extraction of the gold can begin.'

'I know what a mullock is,' Amber said triumphantly. 'It's a fish.'

Rian laughed. 'No, that's a mullet.'

'Mullock is the useless rock that lies above the lead,' Mr Harcourt explained patiently.

'How do the men working in the shafts breathe?' Kitty asked.

Rian hoped the man wouldn't go into detail — in his opinion, Harcourt was making the whole process sound a lot more dangerous than it was. And frightening his wife and daughter.

'Wind-sails,' Mr Harcourt said. 'Erected above the shafts to direct fresh air down them. Quite ingenious, really.'

'And they never fail?' Kitty asked.

'No, they don't.'

Kitty stared at him: he'd put an emphasis on the word 'they', as if other devices associated with gold mining *did* fail. But she let it pass.

Mr Harcourt shifted in his seat. 'You've not been involved with gold mining previously, Mr . . . er . . . ?'

Rian realised he hadn't introduced himself. 'Farrell, Captain Rian Farrell. And no, I haven't. But I've just bought a claim, so I thought I'd try my hand at it.'

'You'll need a lot more hands than just your own, then. It can take up to twelve men to work a claim these days.'

'I have my crew of seven.'

'Crew as in labourers, or crew as in seamen?'

'Seamen. Mr Bullock here is one of my men.'

Mr Harcourt turned to inspect Simon, who nodded politely. 'So you're a mariner, Captain?'

'Sea trader,' Rian corrected. 'My ship is in dock at Melbourne at the moment.'

'Ah. Well, then, I wish you luck. You'll need it.'

It was an ominous comment, and followed by silence.

'There are some surprisingly nice stores at Ballarat,' Mrs Harcourt remarked suddenly. 'A much better range of goods than you would expect of such a, well, such an uncouth settlement. Except for the town proper, of course, and the Camp.' At Kitty's raised eyebrows, she added, 'Where the constabulary and government officials are emplaced. But I must warn you, my dear, that there are not very many women on the diggings themselves. Thousands of men, but far fewer women.' She screwed up her face unbecomingly. 'And the Celestials, of course — one should always steer clear of their camp.'

'Why?' Kitty asked.

'Because, well, they're not like us, are they? They're immoral. They're *Chinamen*.'

Rian frowned — the *Katipo* had docked at Canton, Shanghai and Ningbo many times over the past few years, and they had never had anything but very cordial relations with the Chinese they'd dealt with.

'And are there many churches?' Simon asked.

'Well, not churches as *such*,' Mrs Harcourt replied, smoothing out whatever it was she was knitting and checking for dropped stitches. 'But there are certainly quite a few church *services*. The Anglicans and the Presbyterians have visiting clergy, not every Sunday I might add, but the Methodists and the Catholics are certainly well represented. The Catholics in particular, because of all the Irish. Are you a church-going man yourself, Mr Bullock?'

'Not if I can avoid it,' Simon replied, to Mrs Harcourt's faint shock.

'Well, you won't be alone there,' Mr Harcourt said. 'They can be a godless bunch on the diggings, especially with the liquor in them.'

'You can talk, Mr Harcourt,' his wife said sharply. 'You're partial to a drop of liquor yourself.'

'Yes, but never on a Sunday, Mrs Harcourt, and well you know it.'

Kitty and Rian exchanged amused glances while Simon carefully examined his fingernails. It could be a *very* long trip.

★   ★   ★

Kitty's backside was completely numb, her belly rumbled cavernously, her neck and back were sore from the lurching of the coach over ruts and potholes, and boredom had driven her almost to distraction. They had been travelling for nearly four hours now, and still had another five or six to go before they reached Ballarat. They had overtaken the rest of the crew on the wagon a long time ago, Amber waving madly out of the coach window and the crew waving back. They all looked very cold, and Kitty didn't envy them their long, and much slower, journey.

They had also overtaken numerous wagons — one on its side in a ditch and another mired axle-deep in mud, bullocks floundering and the bullocky shouting and swearing — and men pushing wheelbarrows stacked with supplies, others walking with nothing more than a swag or potato sack over their shoulders, and the occasional dray with a family balanced atop what appeared to be an entire house-lot of goods. And dogs — almost every traveller appeared to be accompanied by a dog. The traffic went both ways, and, though it did not constitute what Kitty knew to be a 'rush', it was certainly busy.

Mr and Mrs Harcourt had chattered con-stantly for the first three hours but had fallen silent almost an hour ago, as if they only had a certain number of words at their disposal each day and didn't want to use them up.

There had been a very brief stop at Melton, just enough time to stretch their legs and use the distinctly noisome facilities at the hotel there, and the next stop would be Bacchus Marsh, where at least there would be a hot meal. Amber was happy straining her eyes reading a copy of Mary Wollstonecraft Shelley's awful book *Frankenstein*, Rian was asleep, and Simon was slowly being crushed by the combined bulks of the Harcourts. It hadn't grown any warmer outside, but the coach was slowly filling again with the warm fug of six confined bodies.

Kitty lifted the window cover and peered out — still nothing but grey hills rising out of marshlands, eucalypts, scrub, a few sheep and leaden skies.

Rian snorted and woke himself, blinking and stretching. He checked his watch and groaned quietly. 'God, not even halfway there.'

'Bacchus Marsh can't be far away, surely,' Kitty said, with an edge of desperation. Travel by road was so tedious compared with the *Katipo*'s speedy flight across the ocean waves, leaving mile upon mile in her wake.

They lapsed into another long silence as the coach juddered and lurched along the muddy road. In the confined space Kitty awkwardly crossed her legs, then uncrossed them, remembering a long-ago warning from her mother that crossing your legs gave you bad veins.

Then, without warning, a dreadful smell began to permeate the interior of the coach. Pierre's highly spiced *bouillabaisse* had a lot to answer for in the confines of the *Katipo*'s mess-room, but this was *appalling*. Kitty looked accusingly at Rian, who made a don't-look-at-me face. Then she glanced across at their travelling companions: Mrs Harcourt was studiously bent over her knitting while Mr Harcourt stared fixedly at a point just above Kitty's head.

Simon surreptitiously flapped the cover over his window.

Then, ten minutes later, it happened again.

Amber giggled.

'Shush,' Kitty reprimanded her, noting that Simon had slid so far down inside his coat that only his eyes were visible.

Rian had his eyes closed, his face set in a very odd expression. Kitty couldn't decide whether he was grimacing or trying not to laugh. She breathed through her mouth, but not too deeply — God only knew what they were inhaling.

Almost immediately, another even more sulphurous wave assaulted them, and this time Mr Harcourt had the grace to mumble, 'Beg pardon.'

Amber erupted into laughter, closely followed by Rian, who quickly rolled up his window cover and exclaimed, 'My God, man — have a heart!'

Without a word Mrs Harcourt reached into her bag, withdrew a bottle of milky white liquid and handed it to her husband.

Mr Harcourt took a generous swig, wiped his mouth and stifled a burp. 'Thank you, my dear. Tripe and onions,' he said, as though this excused his behaviour. It certainly explained it.

Kitty allowed an interval of ten minutes to pass, then enquired politely, 'Are you and Mrs Harcourt travelling all the way to Ballarat, Mr Harcourt?'

Rian and Amber succumbed to a fresh

outbreak of giggles; Kitty gave them a very pointed look.

Ignoring them, Mrs Harcourt replied, 'Just to Bacchus Marsh, my dear. We're visiting my sister and her husband. They have a hotel there.'

Kitty held in check a sigh of relief and, soon after, they reached Bacchus Marsh. But as the coach slowed, Mr Harcourt released one final nauseating, and very audible, manifestation of his intestinal complaint. The coach stopped and Amber hurled open the door and staggered off laughing hysterically, followed by a grinning Rian.

Kitty glanced apologetically at the Harcourts and shook her head. It was Rian's fault, the lack of respect and propriety their daughter frequently exhibited. And Pierre's. And possibly Mick's, as well. She wondered not for the first time whether Amber should be enrolled at some sort of girls' school where she would learn manners and the sort of refinement befitting a young lady. But Kitty knew in her heart that she could never do that to her precious daughter, and knew, too, that Rian wanted Amber near him. As a result she could not help but be party to the crew's escapades, not to mention their occasional smuggling operations. Rian justified this by insisting that, although Amber might not be able to play the piano, or plan a dinner party, she was learning how the world worked, and how to negotiate all the things that life would throw in her path, and Kitty had to agree. Amber could cook, though — Pierre had seen to that.

★   ★   ★

After a very good hot meal at Flanagan's Border Inn and a change of horses, and having bid a heartfelt farewell to Mr and Mrs Harcourt, Kitty, Rian, Amber and Simon set off again, this time with only one travelling companion.

Warily, Kitty studied the woman from beneath her eyelashes. She was extremely striking, with dark red hair — hennaed, Kitty was sure — arranged not in the currently fashionable centre-part flanked by sweeps of hair secured in a chignon, but in the long ringlets popular some years ago. She wore no bonnet, but had simply raised the hood of her heavy velvet indigo blue cape, and her dress of burgundy brocade hugged the impressive contours of her body. Kitty felt positively dowdy in her practical travelling dress and black cape, and had an overwhelming desire to throw her own loathed bonnet out of the window.

The woman's skin was powdered to the colour of milk, and her languid eyes, an arresting moss green, were outlined with a hint of kohl. Her jaw was strong and her rouged cheekbones high, and her lips painted a rose pink. Judging by the lines bracketing her mouth and at her eyes, Kitty guessed she was somewhere in her early forties. Not a classical beauty, but definitely a woman to turn heads: Rian's had been turned in her direction since they had set off again.

They stopped at Ballan, just short of halfway between Bacchus Marsh and Ballarat, at three-thirty that afternoon.

'I suspect she might be a whore, don't you?' he remarked as they stood stamping their feet while the horses were changed yet again. The driver had disappeared into the Ballan Hotel, followed by the mysterious woman.

Kitty blew on her hands. 'A bit long in the tooth, don't you think?'

'I've seen plenty older. But not so well preserved, I have to admit. I still wouldn't touch her with a ten-foot bargepole, though.'

'You stared at her long enough,' Kitty said teasingly.

'So did you. But she is quite mesmerising, isn't she?'

Kitty nodded. 'And we could be wrong. She could just be the wife of some well-to-do prospector who likes to wear a lot of rouge and lip paint.'

Rian looked alarmed. 'The prospector?'

'No, the woman,' Kitty said, smiling.

'Well, if she is, she's either mute or very retiring. She hasn't said a bloody word since we left Bacchus Marsh.'

'I wouldn't think she's the retiring type — not with that amount of face paint.'

But the woman turned out to be neither mute nor shy. Her name was Lily Pearce, she said, leaning forward after they set off again and offering her hand to both Kitty and Rian, who in turn introduced themselves, then to Simon, who took it very gingerly.

'I own a business at Ballarat.' Her voice was low and seductive, her accent revealing a trace of East London. 'On the diggings of course, not up near the Camp,' she added, smiling enigmatically to herself.

Kitty said, 'That sounds very enterprising of you. And your husband helps you run this business?'

Lily Pearce gave a tinkling laugh. 'Oh, no, I'm not married, Mrs Farrell. Never have been, and never plan to be.' She turned her attention to Rian. 'Is Ballarat your destination, Captain Farrell, or Bendigo?'

'Ballarat.'

'Ah, I see. *New chums*.' Her eyebrows were raised in amusement.

Kitty felt her hackles twitch in response to the woman's apparent condescension. 'I'm sorry — new chums?'

'Yes, it's what the diggers call newcomers to Australia and the goldfields. *Are* you newcomers?' Again she directed her question at Rian.

He stared at her for a slightly unfriendly moment. Perhaps, Kitty thought, he has also sensed something vaguely disagreeable about Miss Pearce. 'Actually, no. We trade at Australian ports frequently.'

'Oh, a *sea* captain. And now you're going to make your fortune on the diggings?'

Rian held her gaze a little longer than was necessary. 'Who can tell? Other people obviously have.'

Touché, Kitty thought.

Miss Pearce smiled slightly. 'And who is this enchanting child?' she asked, inclining her head towards Amber.

'Our daughter,' Rian and Kitty replied simultaneously.

Miss Pearce looked from Rian's fair skin to Kitty's, then to Amber's caramel-coloured complexion, her face giving nothing away. 'You're a very pretty girl, aren't you?' she said. She tilted her head to one side. 'How old are you, dear?'

'I'm fourteen,' Amber replied.

'Mmm, very nice,' Miss Pearce said, somewhat speculatively. 'You will need to keep an eye on her, Captain. A pretty young face is a welcome sight on any goldfield.'

Kitty stared at her. 'What was it that you said you sold, Miss Pearce?' she asked, her voice as cold as the weather.

'I don't think I did, Mrs Farrell.'

Kitty slipped her hand into Amber's. They rode in silence after that.

★   ★   ★

Dusk was approaching when the coach began to rattle past clusters of small buildings, most of them hardly more than shanties. Both sides of the road revealed evidence of mining in the piles of dirt and the shadowed pits and dips, the ravaged land dotted with small tents and lean-tos, and strange sail-like structures thrusting upwards into the gloom. Half a mile on, a hotel with glazed sash-windows and a fancy lamp over the door appeared out of the dusk. Soon, the shanties were replaced by more substantial and permanent-looking buildings, and Kitty saw that interspersed with a number of well-built houses were stores, a boarding house, offices and various business premises. But still the diggings were evident, encroaching almost upon the rear of the buildings on both sides of the road.

The coach came to a halt outside a solid two-storeyed establishment, its signage proclaiming that it was Bath's Hotel. Miss Lily Pearce stretched elegantly, then gathered her cape around her.

'Well, it was lovely travelling with you all.' Her gaze lingered on Rian. 'I hope to see you again, Captain Farrell. I'm sure our paths will cross, aren't you?'

Then she opened the door and was gone.

Simon retrieved his hat from the luggage rack. 'She was certainly a piece of work, wasn't she?'

'Didn't you like her, Ma?' Amber asked.

'No, actually, I didn't,' Kitty replied tersely, gathering her things.

'Ma?'

'What, love?'

'I didn't like her either. She made me feel . . . strange.'

'Well, you're not strange, sweetheart,' Rian said, pulling Amber close and giving her a quick hug. 'You're just right.' But over her head, his eyes met Kitty's, his face expressing both offence and anger.

'Well, she's gone now,' Kitty said, 'and let's hope our paths *don't* cross again.'

She stepped down from the coach and onto the verandah of Bath's Hotel, where they intended to lodge for the night. While the coachman passed down their luggage to Simon and Rian, she wandered along the boards until she came to a gap between buildings, and paused to look south across the Ballarat basin.

Spread before her in the middle distance were hundreds of fires, the smoke rising upwards and mingling with the settling mist, the flickering flames throwing countless tents and rough little shelters into jagged relief. There was barely a tree left standing, and the ground illuminated by the fires looked as pockmarked as though from a fierce and sustained artillery barrage. On the cold night air came the howls and barks of dozens of dogs, the lonely, mournful lowing of bullocks, and the smells of smoke and sour earth, mouldering canvas and human refuse.

It seemed to Kitty that she was staring straight into Hell.

3

Kitty poked an experimental foot from beneath the bedclothes, then braved the chill to cross to the window. She rubbed a circle of condensation off the glass. The view was certainly a little less daunting than it had been the night before, but the scene was still one of organised chaos.

'Is there a frost?' Rian asked.

Kitty nodded. 'Quite a heavy one. I hope our new house isn't down there in the basin.'

'Actually, I think it might be,' Rian muttered, then groaned as he heaved himself out of bed. The frame was relatively sturdy, but the mattress left a lot to be desired. He glanced at the heap of blankets on the vacant mattress on the floor. 'Where's Amber?'

'Gone downstairs to wait for the wagon. She's worried that Bodie might have frozen to death overnight.'

Rian snorted as he reached for his trousers. 'I doubt it. Not while Pierre's still breathing.'

Kitty turned away from the window. 'They won't be here until after midday, though, will they?'

'Not if they stopped overnight at Bacchus Marsh.'

'Well, I'm starving. Shall we go and have breakfast?'

Rian slid his hand over Kitty's hip, the silk of her chemise sliding under his fingers. The skin on his naked chest was goose-bumped, and she set her palm against his hard, flat stomach.

'I'm starving, too,' he said, 'but not for food.' He nuzzled her neck, and she pushed him away, laughing. 'Can you think of nothing else?'

'Not really,' he replied cheerfully. 'But I suppose, if I absolutely have to, I can think about what we're going to do today.'

'We're going gold mining, aren't we?' Kitty said as she stepped into her dress, wriggled her arms into the sleeves and turned her back. 'Can you do me up?'

Rian deftly fastened her buttons. 'No mining today. There's a lot we have to do before that.'

'Such as?'

'We need to have a look at this house of ours. And the claim, and pay off the bloke who's been minding it. And when the others arrive we'll need to unload all the gear.' He turned her around and kissed her nose. 'And then we'll have to buy ourselves a licence. Apparently you have to repeatedly pay the government to break your own back digging out enough gold to make a living.'

'To make a living? I thought you said this claim is a guaranteed winner?'

'It is a winner. Or will be, according to Mrs Murphy. She said Mr Murphy had a nose for it.'

'A nose? Good God,' Kitty said. 'Is that what happened to her husband — he died from a broken back?'

'No, I gathered it might have been a heart attack.'

Kitty poked him in the chest. 'But *you're* not

41

going to have a heart attack, are you?'

'Hardly.' Rian flexed his muscles and struck a pose. 'Look at me, I'm as fit as a fiddle.'

'Yes, well, you'll also be late for breakfast if you don't hurry up and put your shirt on.'

⋆   ⋆   ⋆

Breakfast was fried potatoes, porridge and black pudding. Whereas Rian had two helpings, Amber refused to eat the black pudding, insisting that it looked like rounds of dog turd. Rian laughed, but Kitty told her to watch her language and keep her voice down — other patrons were looking at them.

After breakfast, they set out for the diggings that spread out on both sides of the main road heading south towards Geelong. The night before, they had come in along the Melbourne Road through the diggings that extended eastward, and there were other heavily mined leads to the north, but their claim was to the south of the town proper and the Camp. On the advice of the publican's wife they hired a cart: the going would be very mucky and wet, even on the road.

The going was indeed extremely muddy, particularly down the hill on the Main Road into the basin that was Ballarat Flat. The carthorse, though, was an enormous animal, and negotiated the greasy slope with a minimum of snorting and head-tossing. There was little room on the seat of the cart, so Amber and Simon sat on the back, holding grimly onto the sides. Once they reached the flat, the ride was marginally smoother, but still hazardous and slow, and the holes to be avoided in the road even larger.

It was immediately evident that the Ballarat basin was a swamp. But, despite this, the Main Road was lined with stores and hotels, and behind them and to the south, as far as the eye could see, was a vast number of tents, slab and log huts, and tiny bark-and-tin shanties. Above the long-dry underground rivers that threaded beneath the basin, the ground had been excavated into a barren and currently frost-rimed landscape of gullies and deep trenches topped with great heaps of soil and gravel, as though a giant mole had gone berserk, spanned by spindly-looking timber viaducts and criss-crossed with rail lines. And again, the odd sail-like structures Kitty had noticed the night before were everywhere, taut in the raw, cutting wind. The vista was one of hectic, mud-sodden industry.

The people they passed on the street — and they numbered in the hundreds — wore heavy layers of clothing against the cold and damp. Men, many sporting bushy beards, wore rough work attire and sou'westers or the unglamorous but evidently ubiquitous cabbage-tree hats. The few women looked little different from working women everywhere, in their shawls, bonnets and flapping capes. All, however, appeared to be wearing very sturdy boots or clogs, and their hems were noticeably shorter than those in Melbourne. Among the civilians were several mounted and foot police, distinctive in their dark-blue uniforms with red trim.

'Where exactly is this house?' Kitty asked, her ears humming with the cold.

Rian transferred the reins to one hand and dug a piece of paper out of his jacket pocket. 'According to this, it's near the Red Hill Lead and it's the fourteenth dwelling directly behind the saddlery on the left.' He glanced along the road and pointed. 'Just up there, I'd say.'

He steered the cart into an alleyway and down a short slope, then along a rough track past a dozen or so shanties. 'This must be it,' he said, reining in.

Kitty's heart sank.

The 'dwelling' was a timber-and-iron cottage, with a window in each wall, a chimney and a single door. The windows were glazed, with the exception of two boarded-over panes, the silver-grey of the slab door testimony to its never having been painted. Above it had been nailed a shingle that read *Lilac Cottage* — the work of the Widow Murphy, Kitty assumed — even though there wasn't a lilac in sight. The cottage was tiny, but she had to admit it was markedly more substantial than many of the bark huts and tents flanking it, their sides sagging with frigid rainwater. And, thank God, it wasn't near any butchers' tents, more than a dozen of which they had passed. With carcasses hanging in the open air and great piles of discarded offal and skins lying about, they would be a putrefying, reeking Mecca for flies in summer.

'You could ask next door,' she suggested, her

fingers mentally crossed that they had made a mistake.

Rian climbed down from the cart and rapped on the sheet of iron that served as the nearest hut's door. A harried-looking woman appeared, wiping her hands on her apron; there was a quick conversation, then Rian turned to Kitty and nodded.

She smiled resignedly, climbed off the cart and brushed the creases out of her skirts. 'Is there a key?' she asked as he came back.

He opened his hand. 'Your woman there was looking after it,' he said, and unlocked the door.

Kitty stepped inside, followed closely by an inquisitive Amber.

It wasn't *quite* as bad as she'd been dreading. It was bigger than it looked from the outside, and had three rooms. Two were bedrooms, one only just large enough to accommodate a narrow single bed, and the main room had a fireplace fitted with a sway to hold non-existent pots and cooking utensils. But no matter, because Pierre, as usual, would be preparing all the meals.

There was, however, a small table with two chairs, and a rocking chair, which wouldn't rock properly because the bare floorboards were uneven, and the larger of the two bedrooms held an iron double bed frame, but no mattress. A glance through the window of the back bedroom revealed that the sanitary facilities consisted of a small copper on a tripod over a brick fire-pit, and a rickety-looking privy.

The cottage was also damp, and Kitty knew she would have to keep a fire going constantly to dry it out and keep them warm. And she would need to buy fabric for heavy drapes, and perhaps a few rugs for the floor. *If* they stayed at Ballarat, of course: she still harboured a faint but undeclared hope that Rian's enthusiasm for making a fortune as a gold miner would wane and they could return to Melbourne.

'It's a bit cold, Ma, isn't it?' Amber remarked. 'And dark.'

'Yes, it is, sweetie, but a good fire should fix that.'

But a quick reconnaissance outside the cottage revealed that there was no firewood.

'We'll buy some,' Rian declared, then pointed to the southwest towards a series of wooded hills. 'Or we'll go and cut it ourselves. It'll be wet, though.'

Kitty made a mental account of what they had brought with them, and what they would need to purchase.

'Perhaps we should stay at the hotel another night, until we have everything we need,' she suggested.

'Probably not a bad idea,' Rian replied. 'Come on, let's go and have a look at our claim, shall we?'

Kitty noted the gleam of excitement in his eyes: he looked exactly like a small boy with a new toy.

* * *

Their claim was a hole in the ground. A deep one, granted, but just a hole nonetheless.

46

Worryingly, the sides did not appear to have been reinforced at all in the manner described by Mr Harcourt, but at least duckboards had been laid around the lip to counter the mud. Water dripped somewhere, and Kitty suspected the regular *plink* sound came from the hole itself. And it had taken them half an hour in the cart to get to it. The claim wasn't in any way isolated, however — it was only one of many on the Malakoff Lead near the Yarrowee River, and their trip had been accompanied by the hoarse shouts of diggers, endlessly barking dogs, the scrape of shovels, the rumble of barrows and carts, and the rhythmic din of many hundreds of cradles being rocked in the shallows of the river. Judging by the number of tents and shanties, many prospectors seemed to have set up camp near their claims, and Kitty wondered idly why the Murphys had chosen to live so far away from theirs.

Rian was talking to a rugged little man with grey in his beard who had pitched his tent almost on top of the shaft.

'Kitty, this is Patrick O'Riley. He's been keeping an eye on things. My wife, Kitty.'

Patrick O'Riley touched the brim of his hat. 'Mrs Farrell.'

'Patrick says there have been two attempts to jump the claim, and the winching gear has been stolen, but otherwise he's had no trouble.'

'Sure, you turn your back here for more than a moment and everything you could call your own has gone,' Patrick said ruefully. 'But Mrs Murphy gave me enough money to keep the licence up to date, so she did.' He shuffled his feet, looking awkward but managing to hold onto his dignity. 'She said the new owner'd reimburse me, and pay for me services as a caretaker.'

Rian produced his purse. 'Been down yourself, then?'

'Not likely. Not on me own.'

'I assume this will cover your time and expenses?' Rian said, handing Patrick a generous fee. 'Amber! Come away from that hole!'

Amber stepped back, looking only vaguely chastened.

Patrick counted the money. 'Ah, it will, and very nicely, too, Captain.'

'You worked for Mr Murphy, didn't you?'

'I did that, but I'm goin' in a syndicate with some diggers now that you've arrived.'

'Promising claim?'

' 'Tis.' Patrick waved a hand in a south-easterly direction. 'Just down the track there. We'll be neighbours, so we will.'

'Well,' Rian said, 'if you're ever looking for work, I'd be interested. I could do with a man who knows his way around.'

Patrick nodded in acknowledgement of the offer, although his expression suggested that as far as he was concerned his days of working for anyone but himself were over. He scratched at his beard. 'Seen the cottage? You bought that, too, I'm assuming?'

'We have.'

'Me own place is right next door.'

'Ah, yes, I think we might have met your good wife.'

Patrick nodded. 'She's a fine lass, my Maureen. If you're after needin' anythin' for the cottage, *you* come and see *me*. I've got the contacts,' he said, winking and tapping the side of his nose with a dirty finger. 'Could save the wear and tear on your purse, shall we say.'

'Thank you, Patrick, that's good to know.'

'Only right, seein' as you're from across the sea. There's a lot of us Irish here at Ballarat, so there are.'

They left him pulling up the pegs around his tent and drove back towards Lilac Cottage, sticky mud collecting on the horse's hooves with every step.

'I suppose we'll have to be careful we're not robbed,' Kitty said unenthusiastically.

But it wasn't robbery that Rian was worried about — it was the safety of his wife and daughter. He'd already noted how the diggers' eyes had followed them, and the thought of leaving them alone while he and the others were working on the claim gave him a prickle of unease.

Simon, who had said almost nothing since they'd rattled down the hill from the hotel, read the concern on Rian's face and suggested, 'We could set up the tents behind the cottage. Pierre will be there most of the time to keep an eye on things.'

Rian brightened. 'Yes, we could, couldn't we? And if he wants to try his hand down the shaft, someone else can stay behind. Yes, that's an excellent idea, Simon!' He tweaked Amber's hair. 'And you are *not* to go anywhere by yourself, do you hear? And nor are you, Kitty,' he added, knowing his wife's propensity for doing exactly as she chose.

But Kitty had also seen the men's eyes hungrily taking in Amber's lovely fresh face and her barely flowering pubescent body. 'You don't have to tell me, Rian. I have no intention of letting Amber wander about alone. Not for a minute.'

* * *

By the time they had returned to Bath's Hotel, the others had arrived and were sitting on the verandah with their backs against the wall, enjoying a warming drink. The horses and bullocks were spattered with mud up to their bellies, and Bodie was still in her cage, looking even more bad-tempered.

Rian brought the cart to a halt, handed the reins to the hotel's stable boy, and climbed down.

'Just arrived?' he asked, offering Kitty his elbow as she alighted.

Hawk nodded. 'About half an hour ago.'

'Safe journey?'

'*Oui*,' Pierre confirmed. ''Cept for my arse. The seat on the wagon, he is very hard.'

Mick knocked back the last of his brandy and belched. 'Seen the claim yet?'

'Yes, and all it is is a big hole,' Amber said disappointedly. She knelt next to Bodie's cage and crooned, 'And how's our kitty-cat? Did you have a nice sleep on the way?'

Bodie gave her a baleful look.

'Can we let her out yet, Pa?'

'Not yet. Wait until we get back to the cottage or she might run away and get lost.'

Pierre snorted. No matter how many times Bodie ran away, she never became lost and never failed to return.

'Is the cottage suitable?' Hawk asked. '*Is* it a cottage? Or is it just a shanty?'

'Well, it is a cottage, but actually it's smaller than the *Katipo*'s living quarters,' Kitty replied, 'and, I have to say, far less comfortable. But I expect we can make do.'

Amber tickled Bodie's head through the cage. 'Simon said we should pitch the tents just behind it, then Pierre can watch out for Ma when she hangs out the washing.'

Hawk shot a questioning look at Rian, who frowned darkly and said, 'Yes, well, there's a hell of a lot of men here . . . '

Kitty sighed. 'Rian, I'm perfectly capable of looking after myself. You know that.'

'Yes, but still, I don't want — ' He glanced at Amber, and modified what he had been about to say. 'I don't want anything untoward to happen.'

Amber opened Bodie's cage and let her out. 'Whoops!'

Bodie stretched luxuriously, clawed the boards of the verandah, then streaked off it and disappeared.

'See?' Kitty accused, wondering why Amber had to be so contrary. 'Your father told you.'

'She be back,' Pierre soothed.

'And we met this lady on the coach,' Amber

said, ignoring Kitty. 'She had dark red hair and a lovely blue cape. But, actually, I didn't like her, and neither did Ma. Did you, Pa?'

'No, I didn't. And if you see her again, I don't want you going near her, all right?'

'Why not?' Mick asked, his eyes twinkling. 'She sounds like she might be worth getting to know, so she does.'

'Er . . . ' Simon began.

But Rian interrupted. 'I suspect she'd charge you for it, Mick.'

'He means she's a whore,' Amber said cheerfully.

'Amber!' Kitty admonished.

To distract Amber from pursuing the subject further, Gideon unfolded his huge frame, stood, and said in his deep, rumbling voice, 'Where shall we unload the wagon?'

Grateful for the diversion, Rian explained the route to Lilac Cottage.

The journey down the hill was as treacherous as it had been earlier, but even more so with the extra weight of the loaded wagon. But they descended without mishap, and with Bodie, who had come scampering and had landed with a flying, scrabbling leap on the canvas securing the load.

The tents were pitched a hundred yards or so from the rear of the cottage, on relatively dry ground and not too close to the privy. The tents themselves were of a reasonable size and could accommodate up to four men, but were nothing like the size of the truly enormous circular structure they had noticed this time from the

Main Road. Amber had been intrigued, insisting that it must be a circus tent, although that seemed unlikely.

Some of the gear was unloaded into the crew's tents, while the equipment worth stealing was packed into the smaller of the two bedrooms in the cottage, as Amber had elected to sleep on the floor in the main room by the fire. By one in the afternoon the animals had been hobbled, fed and watered, Pierre had built a fire and was preparing a meal, and Amber was swaggering about in her heavy new 'gold-digger's boots'. Kitty had to admit she was grateful for hers; the lighter boots she usually wore were clarted with mud and would be ruined in no time.

After the meal, and leaving their daughter in the safe hands of the crew, Kitty and Rian prepared to set off on horseback for a tour of the diggings. The horses — a bay and a chestnut, named Finn and McCool by Amber after the famous hunter-warrior of Irish legend — were sound and fine-looking. Unfortunately neither of the saddles was designed for a lady to use, a fact neglectfully overlooked by Rian when he'd purchased them.

'Well, I'm not sitting astride in skirts,' Kitty complained. 'I think I'll wear my trousers.'

'You bloody well will not!' Rian exclaimed. It was all very well Kitty habitually wearing trousers on board the *Katipo*, where there was only the crew to see her, but here on the diggings it was a different matter altogether.

'But I won't even be able to get my leg over, never mind my modesty!'

'Then I'll help you up,' Rian said, through slightly gritted teeth. 'Daniel, hold the reins, will you?'

Daniel took a firm grip on Finn's bridle and held the horse's head steady, as Rian put his hands around Kitty's waist.

'When I lift,' Rian instructed, 'put your left foot in the stirrup and hook your other knee over the pommel.'

'No,' Kitty said, 'I'll slide off.'

'Not if you hold on, you won't.' Leaning closer, Rian whispered in her ear, 'Behave, or I'll throw you over the other side.'

'You wouldn't!'

'I would,' he said and lifted her with ease.

She landed in the saddle facing him, and quickly clamped her knee over the low pommel as he placed her foot in the left stirrup.

'I can feel myself sliding off already,' Kitty grumbled as Daniel handed her the reins.

'Then brace yourself with the stirrup,' Rian said as he mounted McCool. 'Don't worry, we're not going far like this, just to the saddler.'

'I wouldn't *have* to worry if I were wearing my trousers.'

'God, woman, why must you be so unendingly *stubborn!*'

'Why must *you* be so bossy!'

They glared at each other, then burst into laughter.

Neither noticed as Daniel looked away, his expression impassive but his heart smarting from the knowledge that he would always be excluded from any such intimacy with Kitty.

At the saddlery, Rian asked to see a range of women's saddles.

'Don't get much call for ladies' saddles in these parts,' the saddler replied.

'You don't have *any?*' Kitty said, hopefully.

The man pushed his cap back on his head. 'Didn't say I didn't have *any*, but I don't have what you might call a *range*, as such.'

'Well, how many do you have?' Rian asked impatiently.

'One.'

'We'll see that, then, if you will.'

The saddler disappeared into the back of his shop, re-emerging a moment later with a side-saddle slung over his arm. 'Top-grain cowhide. Not very prettified but serviceable, so I'm told. I could tool the safe and pommel for you, if you're interested? Leaves and flowers, perhaps?'

Rian raised his eyebrows at Kitty, who shook her head. 'No, that will do nicely, thank you,' he said as he opened his purse.

'Up on the hill, are you?' the saddler asked.

'Sorry?'

'On the hill, near the Camp? Where the swells all live? It's just that only ladies buy side-saddles, and the ladies here all live on the hill. In fact it's only ladies as can afford to buy and keep horses, now that I come to think of it.'

'No, we're down on the Flat,' Kitty said.

The saddler looked taken aback, but noticed the flash of indignation that crossed Kitty's face. 'Oh, well, beg your pardon, Missus. And I'm not saying as there aren't decent women on the Flat, of course. There's a good few hardworking, God-fearing wives on the diggings.'

Rian said, 'I'd like to leave a saddle here to be collected by one of my men later today. Is that possible?'

At the man's nod of agreement, Rian handed over the money and waited while the saddler counted out his minimal change, which he did with a flourish.

'Christ, that was expensive,' Rian said outside.

'It wouldn't have cost anything if I'd been able to — '

' — wear your trousers. Yes, I know — but you can't, not here, and that's all there is to it.'

They changed the saddles then headed off up the road, which had narrowed to a rutted street lined on both sides with stores. Kitty was surprised at the variety of goods and services on offer. But then there were a lot of people to service on the diggings — over 20,000, according to the proprietor of Bath's Hotel. Most of the business premises here were wooden and seemed relatively permanent, unlike the canvas stores out in the gullies, which drew attention to themselves with the aid of large, gaudy flags on tall flagpoles. Here they passed barber shops, doctors' and lawyers' offices, tent- and mattress-makers, drapers — one of which, Kitty noticed, had a particularly spectacular window display of laces, silks, satins and fancy hats — several chemist shops, a gunsmith, a confectioner, two jewellers, bakehouses, a bakery, a grocery, an assay office, a photographic parlour, a post office, two blacksmiths, a tinsmith and a candlemaker, a theatre, several stables, shanties advertising lemonade or coffee or ginger beer or all three, which Rian insisted were grog shops, and at least nine hotels. There was even an undertaker's parlour, with a selection of coffins in the window and a sign advertising the services of a monumental mason.

Verandahs or boardwalks fronted most stores, keeping shoppers out of the worst of the muck. Down the centre of the street a channel had been worn by animals' hooves, wagon wheels and rain, and along this trickled filthy water, mud and sewage. Melbourne's central business district might be grander and more established, but there seemed little on sale there that couldn't also be purchased here.

Further along the street, where the road widened again, were a sawmill, several timber merchants, a brickyard, a foundry, and a wheelwright and coach builder.

'I think we'll sell four of the bullocks,' Rian remarked.

Kitty adjusted her seat: already the high, curved pommel was pinching the tender flesh above her knee. 'Won't we need them when it's time to go back to Melbourne?'

'Yes, but we can buy another team. Otherwise we'll only have to feed them, and the price of feed here is ridiculous. We'll keep two, sell the wagon and buy a smaller cart. Perhaps two.'

'But we'll keep the horses?'

Rian nodded. 'I don't fancy walking everywhere, do you?'

Eyeing her filthy boots, Kitty agreed. 'We also need to buy a few things for the house. A bath, for a start.'

'Yes, well, you and Amber can go shopping tomorrow.'

'She needs a camp bed or something similar. I don't want her sleeping on the floor.'

'Well, get her whatever she needs.' Rian brought McCool to a halt. 'Amber was right: it *is* a circus.'

Before them sat the enormous round tent they had seen the day before. From this angle, the sign was clear: *Jones's National Circus*.

He sighed in weary resignation. 'We'll never hear the end of it if we don't bring her to see it.'

'Well, we will, then,' Kitty replied simply, noting the banners advertising trapeze artists, strongmen and acrobats. 'It could be quite an afternoon's entertainment.'

'Not for me, it won't,' Rian said. 'I don't hold with men swinging about in their undergarments. It's not . . . manly.'

Kitty laughed and tapped Finn with her heel to move him along. They soon came to a capacious chapel built from bush timber with a canvas roof, then even more hotels, a concert hall, assembly rooms and another huge tent, its sign proclaiming it to be the Adelphi Theatre.

'I'd no idea Ballarat was such a mainstay of culture,' Rian remarked drily.

'Or so tolerant,' Kitty added, inclining her head towards two men hurrying in their direction.

They were Chinese, immediately recognisable

by their loose tunics and trousers, and their conical, broad-brimmed straw hats. Behind them trotted five European boys, throwing stones and shouting insults.

'Little shites,' Rian muttered. He urged McCool forward until he was between them and the Chinese, glaring at one boy readying himself to heave another stone. 'Hey, you! Yes, *you*, boy. What the hell do you think you're doing?'

'Chasing the Chinkees,' the boy replied insolently.

'Well, don't!'

'Why not?'

'Because I *said* not!' Rian barked, then leant down as if to take a swipe at him.

The boy skipped out of the way and blustered, 'I'll tell my father!'

'You can tell who you bloody well like. Now bugger off!'

Sullen-faced, the boys backed away, then turned and ran. Rian watched them go, then glanced at the two Chinese men, watching from a safe distance. One of them bowed slightly, and Rian touched the brim of his hat.

The remainder of their reconnaissance was fascinating, if uneventful. The diggings were littered with prospectors working on claims staked mere yards apart, and criss-crossed with muddy tracks over which bullocks pulled carts piled with washdirt, and men laboured to push teetering wheelbarrows. Many of the tents they had seen yesterday appeared to house both miners *and* the shafts they were sinking, and dogs, bulldogs in particular, roamed everywhere, getting underfoot and barking aggressively at passers-by. Here and there women and children fossicked in piles of mullock, hoping, perhaps, to find a few flakes of previously undetected gold.

Stopping to talk to diggers as they went, Rian and Kitty discovered that the sails they had noted all around the diggings were the contraptions Mr Harcourt had spoken of, that the half-barrels filled with washdirt and water that men were vigorously stirring were called puddlers, that a cradle was a box on rockers through which washdirt was sieved with water to separate the gold, and that the largest of these set into the Yarrowee and its shallow winter tributaries were called long toms.

On the way back to Lilac Cottage, Rian finally admitted to Kitty that he had a lot to learn about mining.

4

August became September and the weather finally began to improve. The rain was no longer a daily occurrence, and the swamp that was Ballarat Flat began to recede slightly, as though it were gradually being sucked back into the Yarrowee, which, it was said, would itself shrink to no more than an ambitious stream in the summer months. The temperature could still be low, though, and there were still days during which puddles remained iced over until the sun rose to thaw them. But the mud, at last, was hardening off.

Between them, Kitty and Amber had transformed Lilac Cottage. They had bought drapes to keep the heat from the hearth in and the cold out, and heavy oilcloth and a carpet for the floor. A daybed for Amber had been 'delivered' by Patrick O'Riley, with more tapping of the nose and a discreet payment from Rian, and shelves had been built in the back bedroom so Pierre had somewhere to arrange his pantry and store his cooking utensils.

It was while she was out shopping — on her own, against Rian's wishes — that Kitty once again, to her distaste, encountered Lily Pearce. There was something about the woman that raised Kitty's hackles.

She was looking at the price of linsey-woolsey

when a voice said, 'Mrs Farrell, how *nice* to see you again.'

Realising to whom the voice belonged, Kitty reluctantly turned around. 'Good morning, Miss Pearce.'

Today Lily Pearce was wearing a bright Prussian-blue skirt and fitted jacket, and a tiny black straw hat decorated with velvet flowers. It was a much fancier outfit than her travelling costume, but equally well cut. Kitty felt an irrational pang of jealousy at the quality of the woman's clothes, even if the colour and style were rather unsuitable for day wear. But then they would be, in her line of business. She noticed with petty satisfaction that there was mud on Lily Pearce's hem.

Lily's rouged lips curved in a pleasant smile that did not reach her eyes. 'I hear you and your fine husband have settled nicely into Lilac Cottage. Silly name for a slab hut, but then Henrietta Murphy was quite a silly woman.'

Kitty hadn't even met the Widow Murphy, but still she bridled at the unkind comment. And how did Lily Pearce know they had taken over Lilac Cottage?

'Were you acquainted with Mrs Murphy?' she asked. 'I wouldn't have expected you to travel in the same circles.'

Lily flicked her bright curls over her shoulder. 'Not so much *Mrs* Murphy, no. More her husband. And how is your charming daughter?'

'Well,' Kitty said brusquely.

'And has Captain Farrell made his fortune yet?'

'No.'

Lily looked surprised. 'Really? I was sure that a man with such enthusiasm and . . . *passion* would have struck gold by now.'

Kitty didn't reply. She eyed Lily warily.

Lily smiled again. 'Of course, having been here for some time, I know quite a lot about mining. Why don't you tell him to come and see me? I could perhaps give him . . . a few tips.'

Over my cold and lifeless body, Kitty swore to herself, then suddenly became aware of a presence behind her.

Lily Pearce's gaze shifted.

Wearily, a woman's voice said, 'Go and tout your wares somewhere else, Lily. You're wasting your time with this one's man.'

Fascinated, Kitty watched Lily's face lose its veneer of amusement and her eyes narrow to obdurate slits.

'And you'd know, would you? Tried and failed already?' she said, her sudden venom coarsening her accent. She laughed unpleasantly, then swept out of the shop in a flurry of skirts.

But Kitty missed her grand exit, as she'd recognised the owner of the voice. She stared for a long moment, then felt the anger and the tension drain from her body. She smiled. 'Flora Langford. It's been *such* a long time.'

'Yes, it has, hasn't it, Kitty? Nine years? Or is it ten? And it's Flora McRae now.'

Kitty continued to stare at her old friend, realising she wasn't particularly surprised to see her here at Ballarat. There were shallow crow's-feet around Flora's blue eyes now, but her hair was still a rich, dark gold and her face as calm and pretty as ever. Kitty also noted her heavy, black grosgrain dress and discreet jet jewellery.

'Are you widowed? I'm very sorry to see that, Flora.'

Flora waved a black-gloved hand airily. 'Yes, five years ago. But I like black. You know that.'

Kitty nodded, recalling the day in Auckland when she had discovered several gowns at the back of Flora's wardrobe — one black satin and one scarlet, both too beautiful, and rather too *risqué*, for a girl employed as an assistant to a watchmaker.

'You don't wear scarlet any more?'

Flora laughed. 'Oh, no, *my* scarlet days are well behind me. But I am still in the business, and what better place to operate such a business than on the goldfields where a lonely man will pay almost anything for an hour with a soft, willing and perfumed woman?'

'You have . . . an establishment?'

Flora nodded. 'The finest in Ballarat.'

'And Lily Pearce? Is she also . . . ?'

'A madam, yes.' Flora made a disdainful face. 'A working one, however. And her house is nothing compared with mine. *My* girls are said to be the most alluring in all of Victoria.'

Kitty was sure they were — Flora Langford had always had a flair for business.

Flora eyed Kitty thoughtfully. 'I have some time to spare, Kitty. Would you like morning tea?

* * *

64

They seated themselves in the dining room of one of the Flat's more salubrious hotels. The table was spread with a white cloth, the carpets were a floral pattern, oil lamps gave the room a soft glow and a fire crackled in the grate beneath an ornate mirror.

'Very nice,' Kitty remarked as she untied the ribbons of her bonnet, wondering yet again whether she should just not bother with it. Flora wasn't wearing one. 'Quite 'genteel'.'

'It is. The menu is often passable, too.'

Neither said anything as a young girl took their orders, then bustled off.

'And Captain Farrell, is he well?' Flora asked.

'Yes, very,' Kitty replied. 'Exasperating, though. He's decided to try his hand at gold mining.'

Flora nodded. 'I'd heard about that.'

'Had you?' Kitty was startled. 'How?'

'There may be thousands of men on the diggings, Kitty, but more often than not they're poor souls pushing barrows all the way out from Melbourne and hoping to make their fortunes. There aren't many Irish sea captains. Word travels fast here. I heard the name and wondered, so I asked around. I was hoping our paths might cross.'

'Yes, well, he bought a claim while we were in Melbourne. In fact he spent a good portion of the money from our latest cargo on it,' Kitty said ruefully. Then she laughed. 'He's absolutely convinced we'll make *our* fortunes.'

'You might,' Flora said, leaning back so the serving girl could set down a tray of tea and cake. 'You're still sailing and trading around the world, then?'

Kitty nodded, and turned the teapot three times. 'Constantly, since the last time I saw you.'

'On the right side of the law?' Flora's finely arched eyebrows went up.

'Not always. You know what Rian's like.'

Flora had a fair idea. She had never met him, but Kitty had talked about Rian frequently.

Kitty said, 'And did Hattie marry her butcher?'

'Yes, six months after you left. And produced a child exactly nine months later. Each to her own, I suppose.'

When Rian had sent Kitty to Auckland to keep her out of harm's way during the Northern War in New Zealand in 1845, Kitty had boarded with a widow named Mrs Fleming. Hattie Whelan and Flora Langford had also been lodgers.

'And I left just after that,' Flora continued, transferring a piece of cake onto a plate and reaching for a fork.

This time Kitty's eyebrows went up.

'I had to,' Flora said flatly. 'One of my 'gentlemen' decided he wanted to marry me.'

'Not your Mr McRae?'

'No, not Mr McRae. I made it clear that I had no interest in being a married woman, but he was very persistent. And then he became rather unpleasant, pointing out that were our affair to become public, I would have more to lose. He was quite correct, of course. He was a single man, after all, whereas I would be revealed to all and sundry as a harlot. Which, as you know, I was. Not an ideal situation in a town as small as Auckland. So I left New Zealand.' Flora sipped her tea, then relaxed back in her chair. 'You're looking very well, Kitty. Married life must suit you. Or is it the bracing sea air?'

'Both. I do love the sea, but Rian is my life.'

'Still?' Flora looked surprised. 'How extraordinary.'

'Well, what about your husband, Mr McRae? Did you not love him?'

'Not really.'

'Then why did you marry him?'

'I know, I always said I wouldn't be a wife, didn't I? But he was *extremely* wealthy, if somewhat elderly.' Flora met Kitty's gaze steadily. 'And then, of course, he died. A tragedy.'

'And left you all his money?'

'Yes.'

Kitty fleetingly felt sorry for poor, deceased Mr McRae, then gave a mental shrug: Flora's business was her own.

'And how is that child of yours, Amber? Still wild? Or do you have a great brood of them now?'

'No, just Amber. And, no, she's not still wild. Well, not often.' Kitty smiled. 'I think you'd like her, Flora. She's very, well, shall we say, independent? And rather clever.'

'She wouldn't remember me, I'm sure.'

'I think she would. She remembers Mrs Fleming and Hattie. Why don't you come and visit us?'

'Perhaps. Tell me, Kitty, I've always wondered

this, how did your husband take to being told he had suddenly become guardian to a little street urchin?'

'Father, Flora, not guardian.'

'I would have thought it would be the last thing a dyed-in-the-wool sea trader and part-time smuggler would want to hear.'

'It was, and to be honest he wasn't pleased at first. But then there was all the other trouble and by the time that was over he'd decided he quite liked her. Now he adores her.'

Flora took a bite from her slice of cake, then made a face and put it back on the plate. 'Lard, not butter. What trouble was that?'

Kitty blew out her cheeks, not ashamed of what she was about to impart, but not exactly proud either. 'When we arrived back at the Bay of Islands, after we left Auckland, Simon, Amber and I went off to look for Rian. And Amber was stolen, by a woman who'd been our housegirl at Paihia when I first went out to New Zealand. Her name was Amiria. Anyway, I followed them and when I caught up with them I . . . well, I had to kill her to get Amber back.'

There was a short silence, then Flora said mildly, 'You do surprise me, Kitty', in a tone that suggested no surprise at all. 'Well, these things are sent to try us, I suppose. Oh dear, that was trite, wasn't it?' She dabbed at her mouth with a napkin. 'And what happened to Mr Bullock? Is he still in New Zealand filling native children's heads with religious rubbish?'

'No, he isn't, actually. He left the church and

he's been sailing with us since, well, since we last saw you.'

'As a seaman? Really? I'd rather gained the impression he wouldn't have the fortitude for that sort of life.' Flora held Kitty's gaze. 'But, of course, a number of sailors are perfectly happy with the company of other men.'

Startled, Kitty stared at her. 'How did you know?'

Flora gave a faint smile. 'Because when it comes to those who would rather love someone of their own sex, it takes one to know one.'

'Oh.' Kitty felt a blush creep across her face. She'd had no idea!

Flora laughed. 'I'm sorry if I've shocked you, Kitty. I'm normally more discreet than this. And I assume Mr Bullock also is?'

Kitty wondered if Simon's ears were burning. 'I've never been aware of him pursuing a . . . liaison. And the others, the crew, think the world of him. I wouldn't imagine they would if he . . . you know.'

'Yes, I do,' Flora replied.

'Simon is just, well, Simon. A good, decent and loyal man. And a friend.' Kitty paused, embarrassed and wondering how her next question would be received. 'Flora, if you . . . well, being the way you are, how did you manage to . . . go with men?'

Flora drained her teacup, and placed it precisely back on its saucer. 'Money is a great motivator, Kitty. But back to Mr Bullock — you say he left the church entirely? I must say I'm quite surprised by that.' She thought for a moment. 'No, actually, I'm not. He *wasn't* your usual sanctimonious, self-righteous pedant, was he?'

'No. But he hasn't lost his faith. It just doesn't, well, rule his life any more.'

'I'm pleased to hear it. So, how long are you expecting to stay at Ballarat?'

'I don't really know. Until either Rian becomes rich beyond his wildest dreams, or he gets sick of it and gives up, I suppose.'

'You'll get very bored here, Kitty. There isn't a lot to do. Unless you're interested in fossicking?'

Kitty recalled the women and children she had seen scratching almost desperately in the dirt left behind by the miners. 'No, I'm not. I'll leave the prospecting to Rian and the crew.'

Flora looked thoughtful. 'Well, you might want to consider finding yourself something to occupy your time. A small business, perhaps?'

'Such as?' The thought had never entered Kitty's head.

'There's a bakery for sale just down the street. You could look at that.'

Kitty laughed. 'But I don't know how to cook! Well, not to a standard that people would be willing to pay for.' But a spark of interest had flickered within her. 'Pierre does, though,' she said slowly. 'But I don't think we could come up with the money to buy a business. We've spent most of it on the claim and the mining equipment.'

'Mmm. Well, as it happens, I'm looking for an investment. I've more money than I know what

70

to do with. *My* business is flourishing,' Flora said wryly.

'You would put up the money?' Kitty asked, astounded.

'I would. I trust you to make a success of it. You're an intelligent woman, Kitty, and I know you have the drive to do whatever you put your mind to.'

'And what would you expect in return?'

'A percentage of the profits, and when it's time for you to move on the business would revert solely to me.'

Kitty had to admit the proposal sounded far more interesting than the prospect of sweeping Lilac Cottage's floors and hanging out laundry for the foreseeable future. 'It's a generous offer, Flora. Very generous. But I would have to talk to Rian about it.'

Flora inclined her head in acquiescence. 'Of course.' Then she looked amused. 'But there is the possibility that he may object to his wife engaging in the sort of work that involves getting her hands dirty. Well, floury, at least.'

Kitty recalled the many times she'd helped on the *Katipo*'s deck when the weather became rough, or occasions when the schooner had had to leave port with the utmost haste. And there had been plenty of those. She smiled, almost to herself. 'He's not that sort of man.'

'No, I didn't think he would be. Otherwise he wouldn't have married you.'

At that moment three men entered the dining room, removed their hats and sat down, their rough work clothes, unshaven faces and shaggy hair incongruous against the crisp, white cloth draping their table. As one, they stared at Kitty and Flora.

Flora stared stonily back, until one by one they lowered their gazes. She sat back, satisfied.

Kitty said, 'Flora? This Lily Pearce, what sort of woman is she?'

'She's spiteful, Kitty, and has very few scruples. Watch out for her.'

☆   ☆   ☆

Impatiently, Rian looked at his watch: they'd been standing in this queue for almost an hour now.

'Is it like this every bloody day?' he muttered to Hawk.

They were lined up outside the office of the gold commissioner, waiting to pay the compulsory twenty shillings each for a monthly licence to 'dig, search for, or remove gold from Crown lands'. It was enforceable by government officials via the police, and the inability to produce one could result in a hefty fine or even imprisonment.

Rian thought the fee was outright extortion, but he couldn't risk not having a miner's licence: Sir Charles Hotham, Victoria's new governor, had announced that licence searches would increase from once to twice a week. Apparently it wasn't enough to have one licence per hole in the ground — every digger working said hole had to pay for the privilege. The rest of the crew would have to come in tomorrow for theirs. He waved as he caught sight of Patrick O'Riley hurrying up the street. The Irishman waved back, and mimed the raising of a glass to his mouth. Rian signalled his agreement.

Forty shillings grudgingly handed over and their licences finally procured, Rian and Hawk met Patrick in the nearest saloon. It was only eleven o'clock in the morning, but already it was crowded, noisy and thick with pipe smoke.

'Holy Christ,' Patrick complained as he sat down, clamping his hands to the small of his back. 'The rheumatiz, so it is, from workin' waist-deep in cold water for nigh on a year. Got your licences, I see?'

Their glasses of hot brandy arrived. Hawk thoughtfully turned his around on the scarred table top, and remarked, 'It is busy in here for the time of day. Is this usual?'

Evidently there was no rheumatism in Patrick's elbow: he lifted his glass and half-emptied it in one draught. He nodded in approval. 'There's usually a good handful of diggers keepin' the seats warm in these places any time you care to go in, but I have to admit there's a fair few today, so there is.'

'Any reason?' Rian asked, his eyes watering from his first sip of brandy.

Patrick tapped the side of his nose, and Rian wondered whether one day he might actually wear a hole in it. 'Trouble on the diggin's,' he said conspiratorially. 'This Hotham business, the diggers aren't too happy about it.'

'Well, I'm bloody well not, either,' Rian said hotly. 'Twenty shillings a month!'

'Sure, and La Trobe, the fellah before Hotham, was a fool as well. Introduced the licence fee in the first place, then was after raisin' it to three pounds a month. Three pounds! Nothing but a tax, pure and straight! But the chums organised and the fee stayed at thirty shillings. And, to be fair, it did go down to twenty shillings in November last year. But La Trobe wasn't just a fool, he was blind as well. Must've been, not to have known what a drunken, corrupt pack of Joes he had running around on the diggin's makin' an honest digger's life a misery. And they still do, the thievin' heavy-handed bastards.'

Rian raised his eyebrows. "'Joes'?'

'The peelers,' Patrick explained. 'Coppers. Now Hotham's supposed to be investigating' — and here he affected a braying upper-class voice — ''goldfields disputes and grievances'. Couldn't investigate his own arse, if you ask me.' He hoicked in disgust and aimed at a spittoon. 'Oh, the bloody fanfare when he turned up here, I tell you. Just before you came, it was. People were thinkin' he was Christ risen, the way they were carryin' on. But that soon changed, I can assure you.'

'And the disputes, what is the cause of them?' Hawk asked.

'Well, claim-jumpin' and claims overlappin' — or should I say *under*lappin' — and the like. 'Tis a real problem with deep-sinkin'. The trouble is the way the gold commissioner, that's Robert Rede, settles the disputes. Very arbitrary, so he is, and not often fair. The *grievances* now, that's all about the fees and the vote and the land and the like.'

'So this Hotham's not popular among the diggers?' Rian said.

'You could say that.'

Rian looked thoughtful. 'Is there any organised resistance to what he's doing?'

Patrick looked at him in surprise. 'Course there is, and why wouldn't there be?'

'Is it widespread?' Hawk asked. 'And *how* organised?'

Patrick took a moment to shred some tobacco and tamp it into his pipe, light it with a Lucifer and make himself more comfortable on his stool. 'It's been goin' on for nearly three years. It all started before I got here — with the monster meeting at the Forest Creek diggin's, up north of here, in '51. They were agitating for the cursed licence fee to be reduced, and the right to vote — except for the blackfellahs, of course — and to purchase land. That led to the Red Ribbon Rebellion last year in Bendigo. A mass meeting, it was, more like a carnival. All the nationalities had their flags flyin', so they did — the Americans and the Germans and the Danes, and the Irish, the Scots, and the Welsh, and the English. There was a Diggers' Banner, and pipes and a brass band. And they all decided that they were only goin' to pay ten shillings for their September licences. A lot did, and wore red ribbons in their hats to advertise the fact. After that they took a petition — over forty feet long, it was! — to Melbourne in a dogcart. Not that it did much good, mind.' He drew mightily on his pipe and was rewarded with a mouthful of smoke that dribbled out as he spoke. 'These days, because of that eejit Hotham, things are getting *very* interestin' here. 'Specially now that the Gravel Pits — '

Rian interrupted. 'That's the leads on the other side of Bakery Hill? To the north?'

' 'Tis. Now that them leads are payin' well, the Tipperary mob, who've staked most of the claims there, are gettin' stirred up. And rightly so. Claims allotted are only eight feet square, as you know yourselves, and if you hit a payin' lead beneath one, that's all and good, but if you don't it's a lot of hard work for bugger-all. Bigger claims would mean more chance of strikin' gold. 'Tis an awful waste the way it is. The tension's becomin' terrible. And you know what a crowd of Irishmen are like when they get riled, and there's thousands of them on the Gravel Pits. Plenty on this side, too.' Tap, tap, tap went Patrick's finger against his nose. 'You mark my words, there'll be trouble on these diggin's before the year's out. Serious trouble.'

Rian hoped not. He was itching to get stuck into his claim, which had only been driven to a depth of around fifteen feet below ground by the unfortunate Mr Murphy. Especially as two days ago, as he had been idly kicking at the mullock piled around the shaft, he had, to his utter amazement, uncovered a nugget the size of his thumbnail.

★ ★ ★

'Rian?'

'Mmm?'

'I need to talk to you about something.'

'Good,' Rian said, who wasn't listening. The firelight flickered on his face, sharpening the planes of his cheeks and jaw.

'Can you put the paper down, please? It's important.'

Rian folded the *Ballarat Times*, then scooped Bodie from his lap and plonked her on the floor. 'There, you have my undivided attention.'

Kitty wasn't sure where to start. 'Well . . . you remember when Simon and I went to stay in Auckland that time, when Hone Heke was campaigning against the British in the Bay of Islands?'

Rian nodded cautiously. He certainly did remember it — he'd almost had to physically force her to board the ship that would take her to safety.

'And you know how I stayed with Mrs Fleming? And Hattie and Flora, and Flora turned out to be a prostitute?'

Rian nodded again. When Kitty had told him about it, he'd laughed his head off imagining the quiet, bespectacled girl who worked for a watchmaker during the day transformed into a seductive *demimonde* by night. He'd enjoyed the story immensely.

'Flora was the one who procured the horses for you, wasn't she? So you could come back up north against my *express orders*, and be abducted by Hone Heke's warriors and then almost drown, along with our daughter?'

'Er, yes. Well, I ran into her today.'

'Really? Here on the diggings?'

'Yes, here in Ballarat. She was out shopping, and we had morning tea together.'

Rian grinned broadly. 'And what's she doing in Ballarat? Repairing watches?'

'No, making lots of money running a bordello.'

'That's a surprise.'

'She had a business proposition for me.'

'She wants you to go and work for her?' Rian looked shocked. 'But you're *my* wench! No, I *refuse* to share.'

Kitty gave him a withering look. 'She has money she would like to invest. She suggested she buy a business here in Ballarat and that I run it for her. A bakery, actually.'

Rian looked crestfallen. 'But, sweetheart, you can't cook.'

She had known he was going to say that. 'No, I know — but Pierre can.'

Rian looked at her for a long moment, his face gentle with concern. 'Come here, love. Come and sit on my knee.'

Kitty sat in his lap, flinching as the rocking chair gave an ominous creak. Rian put his arms around her and rested his chin on the top of her head. 'Are you bored?'

Kitty nodded, her face brushing against the fabric of his shirt.

'Already?'

Another nod. 'Yes, and I miss the *Katipo* and the sea terribly. I need to do something, Rian. It's all right for you, armpit-deep in mud, but what do I have to occupy my time?'

Rian rocked for a moment, enjoying the warm weight of Kitty's bottom on his thighs. 'Are you asking me for permission to accept Flora's offer, or telling me you've made up your mind?'

'I've already made up my mind. I want to do it.'

Kitty felt, rather than saw, Rian smile. 'That's my girl. I would have been quite shocked if you were asking me. So out of character. I have one proviso, though.'

'What's that?'

'That you don't sample everything that gets baked.'

Indignant, Kitty sat up. 'Are you saying I have a big appetite?' She did, actually, but it never seemed to have a negative impact on her waistline.

'No, I just mean you shouldn't eat all the profits.'

And he began kissing her. Slowly at first, then with increasing passion.

'Where's Amber?' he murmured.

'Out somewhere with Daniel and Simon.'

'Good.'

5

One evening in the first week of October, as Kitty and the crew ate supper around Pierre's cooking fire, a horse and cart emerged from the shadows and came to a halt near the rear of the cottage. For a second no one moved, then Ropata, his piled plate forgotten, shot to his feet, grinning wildly.

'Who is it?' Rian asked, his fork halfway to his mouth.

Kitty, smiling broadly herself now, exclaimed: 'Leena! It's Leena and the children!'

Ropata hurried to the cart and helped his wife down, then swung her jubilantly around so that her mass of black hair fanned out around her head. His children jumped off the cart and leapt around him, swinging on his trouser legs and demanding to be picked up.

Kitty crossed to Leena and embraced her. 'You came! I'm so glad you did. Ropata has been missing you terribly.'

'And I have missed him,' Leena replied in her low, melodious voice. She met Kitty's gaze, and Kitty noted that between Leena's full brows was a vertical line that had not been there a year ago. And, as always, she reminded herself of how lucky she was never having to live apart from Rian.

'You look well,' she said, and it was true. Leena's tall figure was as willowy as ever, and her dark eyes sparkled in the firelight. 'Will you stay long?'

'We will stay until we go again,' Leena replied in her relaxed, philosophical manner.

'And how are you?' Kitty asked, stooping to address the younger of Ropata and Leena's children, four-year-old Molly.

Her curls bouncing with a life of their own, Molly shouted, 'Good! I am good! We've come to see Papa!' and clapped her pudgy hands with excitement.

'And what about you, Master Will?' Kitty asked.

Six-year-old Will, his own curls rivalling his sister's, opened his mouth but his intended reply became a shriek of laughter as Ropata snatched him up and dangled him by the ankles.

'Me, too, Papa! Me, too!' Molly demanded.

Then someone else climbed down from the cart, stretched stiffly, and ambled over.

Kitty grinned, delighted. 'Mundawuy! What a *lovely* surprise! How *are* you?'

Leena's uncle, Mundawuy Lightfoot, a full-blooded Aborigine of the Cadigal band, held a special place in Kitty's heart. It was he who had offered to inter the body of Kitty's closest friend, Wai, in his people's burial cave in Sydney after she died in childbirth, and it was he who had taken Kitty back to the cave five years later to collect Wai's bones so Kitty could take them back to New Zealand for burial.

Mundawuy clasped Kitty's outstretched hands. 'Good to see you, too, eh?'

'It was nice of you to bring Leena and the

children down, Mundawuy,' Kitty said.

'Maybe, eh? But safer, too.' He hoicked up a gob of phlegm and fired it irately at the ground. 'Bloody police troopers and their bloody pet blackfellah trackers.'

Kitty nodded, aware of how unsafe it was for an Aborigine to travel alone, especially a woman. 'Will you be staying?'

Mundawuy shook his head. 'Got things to do. Gotta go back in a couple of days.' He looked past Kitty, his face lighting up as Gideon approached.

Mundawuy thrust out his hand. 'G'day, black man!'

Gideon, grinning from ear to ear, shook it energetically. 'Good evening, friend Mundawuy.'

It was a ritual they'd shared since they had first met years ago, when Gideon had gone to the aid of some of Mundawuy's people in Sydney.

Rian appeared, full of *bonhomie*, followed by Pierre, who urged the travellers to come and sit by the fire and allow him to feed them.

As the last morsels of extremely tasty stew were being mopped up with thick slices of fresh bread, Rian asked Mundawuy if he'd seen any of the New South Wales goldfields.

Mundawuy nodded and said through a mouthful of bread, 'Been out to Hargraves and Ophir. And Turon.'

'Did you try your hand?'

Mundawuy swallowed and wiped his mouth on the back of his hand. 'Yeah, had a go, but us blackfellahs not popular on the goldfields, eh?'

Rian grunted.

'What about you? You rich yet?' Mundawuy asked.

'Not quite,' Rian said, 'but the claim's showing promising signs. We're down forty feet now, to the basalt, but we've to get through the main drift next, and it's absolutely saturated with water. Christ knows how deep that'll go before we get down to the lead.'

'You got it all slabbed up and rendered? Don't want a cave-in, eh?'

Rian nodded, his aching back and shoulders testimony to the number of eucalypt slabs they had cut and carted to the claim, then laboriously lowered and secured into place.

'No, we certainly do not,' Kitty said. She quickly changed the subject. 'Leena,' she asked, 'how are you at baking bread?'

★　★　★

Rian, Mundawuy, Patrick and the rest of the crew sat in the Eureka Hotel. At half past twelve in the morning liquor had been crossing the bar for quite some time, and no one was sober.

The Eureka Hotel, on the Melbourne Road between Bakery Hill and the Eureka diggings, was hard to miss. James Bentley, the publican, was an ex-convict who had made money and, it was rumoured, influential friends in Melbourne, and had arrived in Ballarat with what many saw as a somewhat suspicious friendship with the police magistrate and chairman of the licensing bench, John d'Ewes. But, as Patrick pointed out, no one cared about any of that on the nights when he chose not to close his hotel's doors until one in the morning.

The hotel itself was two storeys of weatherboard with a shingle roof and costly sash windows, a fancy lamppost outside the front door, a detached dining room, a livery stable and horseyards, and a canvas-covered bowling alley, the whole precinct covering half an acre. Nearby were stores, auction rooms and professional offices. The hotel was always well patronised. Sly-grogging was prohibited on the diggings, although in fact it was rife, but it was better to be fleeced in a hotel than to continually pay the fines demanded by corrupt police, even when you were innocent — and even when it was common knowledge that those in their cups at the Eureka Hotel were frequently robbed, set upon and thrown into the street by Bentley's henchmen. And this in spite, or perhaps because, of the fact that the goldfields police and the commissioner's troops also drank there. The Eureka might have had a fancy lamp lighting its entrance, but to many on the diggings it was known as the 'slaughter-house'.

'I'll be buying the next round,' Mick said with the magnanimity of the pissed, even though he didn't have a penny to his name.

Rian opened his purse and peered into it, noting that there was very little left inside. He was fast running out of money, and if they didn't strike gold soon the whole endeavour could end in embarrassing failure and they would all be forced to return to Melbourne, penniless.

'One more round, lads, then that's it, I'm afraid.'

The last round was duly purchased and imbibed and, just as Rian was returning his empty glass to the table, there came a rattling at the front door, now locked.

No one took any notice. The rattling became more frenzied and eventually a front window shattered and a slurred voice shouted, 'Can ye no' let us in? We're wantin' a drink!'

From the vantage point of Rian and the crew, little could be seen of what happened next, but it seemed that Bentley, surrounded by his bullies and accompanied by his wife, crossed the room to the broken window and began to quarrel with someone outside. Insults were traded and threats made, and suddenly a hand gripping some sort of weapon emerged from the crowd, and struck out at a figure just visible beyond the glass.

Rian decided it was time to leave and they slipped out through a side door. For some minutes they walked through the darkness, skirting around the hotel's stable, doing their best to avoid a pungent stream of steaming horse piss, then headed down the hill towards the Flat.

Rian said, 'Perhaps we should have lent a hand. Poor buggers.'

'No, we should not,' Hawk countered. 'It is not our business. We cannot help every lame duck we come across.'

Rian tsk-tsked. 'You're a hard man sometimes, Hawk.'

'No harder than you. But I perhaps have a little more common sense.'

'I think you'll find you're the only one favouring that particular point of view.'

'I think you will find I am not.'

Behind them, Mick expressed his opinion of their drunken bickering by letting out an enormous, rumbling belch.

★   ★   ★

Late the following afternoon, Patrick told Rian that the man who'd been set upon the night before — a digger called James Scobie — had died. He'd been kicked mercilessly and suffered a fatal head wound. His inquest had just been held, and James Bentley had sworn that he'd been retired upstairs at the time that Scobie had been attacked.

'The jury found there wasn't enough evidence against Bentley. It's a rum business, so it is, Rian,' Patrick said, packing fresh tobacco into his pipe. 'A bloody rum business.'

★   ★   ★

After much haggling over the price, the deed to the bakery had finally been transferred to Flora and the astronomical £50 fee for the shopkeeper's licence paid. Until then Kitty and Pierre had been busy planning what they would sell, having decided to operate as a bakery only, not a bakehouse. Kitty favoured plain loaves and buns, because they were the only things she thought she could bake successfully, but Pierre had other ideas.

'Non, chérie, we will make this the best boulangerie this town has ever seen, n'est-ce pas? We can't be doing with just the breads and the buns! The other bakeries, they do the breads and the buns, but we will make the money. We will sell the baguettes and pains de seigle and brioches.' His eyes lit up with enthusiasm. 'Oui! And the macarons and perhaps even the petits choux!'

Kitty hadn't eaten brioche in ages. 'You hardly ever cook anything like that for us. Except for baguettes.'

Pierre waved his hands theatrically. 'To waste on sailors? Pffit! Who would?'

Kitty was doubtful. 'You don't think, well, you don't think petits choux and what-have-you might be a little exotic for prospectors? Mightn't they just prefer plain bread?'

'Oui, but they can get plain bread up the street. At Kitty Farrell's Fine Foods, they can buy something special, a treat for the midday meal. A reward for the hard work. And what about all the wives, hein? And the swells from the town and the greedy officers from the Camp?'

Pierre had a point there, and Kitty knew it. There were several bakeries on the Flat and in the town itself, but none of them sold anything particularly fancy. And she knew Pierre was an excellent bread and pastry chef. 'Well, all right, on one condition. Actually, two. The first is that we make croissants instead of petits choux, providing we can find a source of butter that isn't too outrageously expensive. And eggs. I think finding a source of cream for the *petits choux* might be more trouble than it's worth. And the second is that we call the business Pierre's Bayou Bakery. You'll be doing most of the cooking, remember.'

Pierre's swarthy face went pink with pleasure. 'It be *baking*, not cooking. *Mais oui*, I like that.'

Then came the day for them to inspect the vacated shop, a wooden building wedged between the *Ballarat Times* office and a drapery. Towards the rear wall sat an enormous bread oven made of solid brick, its dome peaking several feet below the ceiling, in which an opening had been formed for the chimney. Shelves for ingredients lined both side walls, several wide work tables stood before the oven, and a counter and bread racks bisected the shop, leaving an area at the front for customers. The floorboards throughout were unvarnished, and the store window bore the painted legend: *Golden Bakery*.

'We'll have to change that,' Kitty remarked.

The shop, unsurprisingly, smelled strongly of bread and yeast, and needed a good clean as smoke stains had accumulated on the walls and ceiling around the oven. Leena lifted the hatch in the counter and they moved through to the business end of the shop.

Standing before the oven, Kitty admitted sheepishly, 'I don't actually know how one of these works, Pierre. Aunt Sarah had a very small one in our house at Paihia, but I have to confess I never used it.'

Pierre flapped a hand dismissively. 'It is easy. The fire, he goes inside the oven, *oui?* Then, when the oven is white hot, we rake the fire out and wait until the oven cools a little bit. Then in go the doughs!'

Kitty eyed the oven's wooden door. 'Won't the door catch fire?'

'*Non,* we leave her open until the fire comes out, then we douse her in water.'

Kitty nodded.

'The hard part is getting up at the fart of the sparrow to prepare the breads and the pastries. Before, even. And we will be needing two of us — she is not a one-person job. Of course, I will have to be one of those persons, as I am the only one with the special recipes. *And* I will be having to prepare the breakfasts for the others, remember.'

Kitty felt vaguely guilty that Pierre would have so much extra work, but he'd insisted he didn't mind. Anything, he had admitted confidentially to Kitty, to avoid going down the shaft: he had a morbid fear of being underground.

'I do not mind rising early,' Leena offered.

'No, Leena.' Kitty was adamant. 'You have the children to tend to. I'll do it. You can come in later.'

Leena had already arranged for a local Aboriginal woman — a pleasant, pipe-smoking grandmother named Binda — to mind the children two or three days a week. And when Binda wasn't available, Amber had volunteered to look after Will and Molly, or to take Leena's place at the bakery.

Leena thought for a moment. 'I will come to the bakery and take the morning meals back to the crew, then I will start work.'

Kitty beamed. 'Yes, that will work beautifully, won't it, Pierre?'

He nodded, pleased. He hadn't wanted to leave his precious breads to finish rising on their own, and if Leena was in charge of ferrying the breakfasts, he would be free to get on with his pastries. Because, as everyone surely knew, making pastry properly was a complex process that could only be achieved successfully at the hands of an accomplished *fabricant de pâtisserie*. Which, of course, he was.

⋆　⋆　⋆

On the morning that Pierre's Bayou Bakery opened, no one came into the shop. Eight o'clock came and went, and nine o'clock, then Pierre lost his temper.

'Why are they not coming to buy the beautiful breads, *hein? Mon Dieu*, what a crowd of Philistines!'

Kitty was also feeling increasingly uneasy: you would think that hungry prospectors would be falling over themselves to buy good, quality baked goods. 'Perhaps we should have advertised? Should I have gone next door to the *Ballarat Times*?'

'The *Ballarat Times*, to hell with it,' Pierre said huffily. 'If they cannot appreciate my magnificent baking, then what is the likelihood they will have the brains enough to read?'

'We could put a sign outside,' Leena suggested.

Pierre stopped stamping his foot, and eyed her speculatively. 'Non, not a sign — we will put the fabricant de pâtisserie outside!' he declared triumphantly.

Grabbing a basket, he carefully arranged a selection of his pastries, two baguettes and two pains de seigle in it, and strode out onto the verandah. Kitty and Leena followed him to the doorway, wondering what he was about to do.

What he did was march up and down the street outside the shop, bellowing about the excellent quality of his goods and accosting everyone he encountered, almost forcing them to sample his baking. At first people gave him a wide berth — and who could blame them, presented with an angry little Cajun with a King Charles goatee and gold teeth — then a few stopped and tentatively sampled his offerings, then a few more, and, finally, they began to come into the bakery.

By the time Rian wandered in at eleven o'clock, the shop was crowded. Eating four macarons in quick succession, he looked around and remarked to Kitty, 'You're very busy. You must be pleased.'

She was more than pleased — she was ecstatic. Not to mention relieved.

★   ★   ★

A week after that, the shop was busy from the minute the door opened until it closed at two in

91

the afternoon, leaving Pierre, Kitty and Leena exhausted, tomato-faced and sweaty from the heat of the huge oven. The work, however, didn't end then. There was the oven to be cleaned out, the tables and the cooking utensils to be washed, and the bread dough prepared for the next day and left to sit, covered with damp muslin, to rise for tomorrow's baking. They had added meat pasties and savoury pies to their menu, and these were also proving very popular, but the fillings had to be partially prepared the day before to save time the following morning.

By the time Kitty returned to Lilac Cottage in the afternoon, she could do little more than collapse on Amber's daybed and contemplate her aching back and red hands, raw from washing so many bowls and pots. Pierre had assured her repeatedly that it would get easier once they got into a regular routine, but Kitty wondered. The only day they didn't open was Sunday, when everyone on the diggings observed a day of rest. Or, more likely, a day of drinking, sport or playing cards.

They were, however, making plenty of money, even after the extremely costly ingredients for the baking had been purchased twice a week. Some customers paid with cash, and some bartered, but many offered gold which had to be measured out on the set of brass scales kept under the shop counter.

Binda was turning out to be an excellent nanny for Will and Molly, who had taken to her immediately, which left Leena free to work in the shop whenever she chose. And when she didn't,

Amber was always more than happy to step in behind the counter, greeting each customer with a smile and a surprisingly professional line of patter about how delicious Pierre's pastries were. She was friendly to the wives and children who came in, and could charm even the roughest, hairiest, most pungent-smelling prospector into walking away with a hatful or a handful of treats.

One man in particular took a fancy to her, a miner named Mr Searle. He was a cheerful-looking fellow of around forty, Kitty guessed, with receding, nondescript hair and a ready smile. Every day he came in and purchased the same thing — a *baguette* and a *macaron* — and, leaning on the counter, spent so long talking to Amber about the wife and three daughters he'd left behind in Cornwall where he'd been a tin miner that Kitty had to remind her to serve the other customers. But she looked so sweet in her white apron with her thick, shining hair pulled back beneath a ruffled white cap, and it wasn't often that anyone left Pierre's Bayou Bakery in a worse mood than when they had come in.

One day, though, Lily Pearce swept into the shop and Amber immediately walked away from the counter and stood sulkily near the oven.

Kitty, rolling out dough, asked, 'What are you doing there, sweetheart? You should be at the counter.'

'Not while *she's* in here,' Amber answered tersely, her arms crossed over her chest.

Kitty followed the direction of Amber's gaze, and her heart sank.

'Good morning, Mrs Farrell!' Lily called, the

note of cheer in her voice flagrantly insincere. She pushed her way to the front of the queue. 'Working your fingers to the bone, I see!'

She was wearing another of her flamboyant gowns, her hair done up in a twist from which tumbled the usual cascade of ringlets.

Oh God, Kitty thought, irrationally irritated. Why does she have to go about looking like a parakeet? Surely even a madam can dress discreetly? Look at Flora.

'Good morning, Miss Pearce,' she said curtly, wiping her hands on a cloth.

Pierre, chopping vegetables for the next day's pasties, eyed Lily Pearce impassively, then split a fresh onion with devastating force.

'I would like some of those little things,' Lily said, pointing. 'What are they called?'

'*Brioche.*' Kitty wondered why the wretched woman hadn't addressed Leena, who was standing directly behind the counter.

'*Brioche?* That's a French word, isn't it? How cosmopolitan of you. I'll take half a dozen, thank you.' Then Lily suddenly looked at Leena, as though noticing her for the first time. 'Oh,' she said loudly. 'Oh *dear.*'

Kitty closed her eyes, waiting for whatever unpleasantry was sure to come.

'Is that a *myall* you have working for you?' Lily said even more stridently. 'Aren't you worried that she might, well . . . ' She left a deliberate gap for everyone listening to interpret as they chose. 'After all, you never know where her kind have been, do you?'

There was an uneasy muttering among the

customers waiting behind her. Leena flushed to the roots of her hair, but said nothing.

Kitty felt the heat of anger rise in her. No one had commented on Leena working in the bakery before, but now that Lily Pearce had drawn attention to the fact, customers would likely start considering whether they really wanted to purchase food handled by an Aboriginal woman, even if her skin was relatively fair.

Biting off each word, Kitty replied, 'She is the wife of a crewman on board my husband's schooner. And she is a very good friend.'

'But that's not much of a recommendation, is it?' Lily countered, shaking her head as though in genuine regret. 'No, I don't think I will take any of your *brioche* after all, Mrs Farrell. I always think it's better to be safe than sorry, don't you?' And she turned and departed the shop with a self-satisfied smirk on her painted face.

There was a moment of embarrassed silence, then Kitty said, 'Ignore her, Leena. She's taken against me for some reason.'

Pierre banged his knife down on his chopping board. 'She was insulting both of you. *Chienne!*'

And when Kitty turned to apologise to her customers, half of them had gone.

⋆ ⋆ ⋆

The seventeenth day of October started out more or less like any other day on the diggings — except for the mood of the diggers themselves. As a result of their intense lobbying of goldfields authorities, six days before James

Bentley and two of his associates, William Hance and Thomas Farrell, had been subjected to a judicial inquiry regarding James Scobie's death, although, to the diggers' dismay, the inquiry had been led by Commissioner Rede, Police Magistrate d'Ewes and Assistant Commissioner James Johnston. The diggers had fully expected a guilty verdict for Bentley and his associates, but all three men had been exonerated and discharged by d'Ewes and by Rede. Only Johnston had dissented.

A public meeting to discuss what to do next was arranged for the seventeenth. The same committee of diggers and others who'd pushed for the first inquiry was now pressing for a more thorough, and less biased, investigation, one that included a jury. The gathering was to be held at midday outside the Eureka Hotel, and it was hoped that a large crowd would attend.

Like plenty of other diggers, Rian and the crew had packed up for the day and come into town with Patrick and his chums. A conspicuous number of placards and bills advertising the meeting had been posted around the Flat and on Bakery Hill, the Old Gravel Pits and at the Eureka diggings. Even if the injustice of James Scobie's demise wasn't at the forefront of your mind, Rian reflected, you'd be very tempted to attend just to see what developed. Especially as it was rumoured that Bentley was so frightened of what might happen that he'd gone bleating to his mate d'Ewes and there were foot soldiers hiding behind the furniture inside the hotel.

Rian noticed that many of the meeting's

organisers were Scots: Patrick pointed out that several of them had been jurors at Scobie's inquest. Decisions were made: they would petition Governor Hotham for a fair trial, form an official committee to carry on the work, and begin a subscription list to provide a reward for the apprehension of Scobie's murderer.

Towards the end of the meeting, a party of mounted police arrived and stationed themselves at the rear of the crowd.

'That fellow over there, the one just voted onto the new committee,' Rian asked Patrick, 'who is he?'

'That, me boy, is Peter Fintan Lalor,' Patrick replied proudly, as though he'd personally raised the man from infancy. 'Went to Trinity College, da's an MP and strict anti-Union; here to make his fortune like everyone else. Got a good head on him, isn't afraid to speak out.'

Rian nodded — he'd heard of Patrick Lalor. 'He'll get the job done? Get justice for Scobie?'

'Sure he will. The poor bugger can rest easy in his grave then.'

Simon appeared at Rian's elbow, accompanied by Mick and Daniel. He inclined his head at the large crowd, for some reason suddenly getting bigger now that the meeting had ended. 'I thought there'd be a bit more argle-bargle than this. It's been a very civilised sort of meeting, hasn't it?'

'And where would the thousands of enraged diggers be?' complained Mick. 'I was looking forward to a good stoush, so I was.'

'I'd say there are well over a thousand here,'

Rian observed. 'But you're right, they've been pretty quiet.'

But he'd spoken too soon. A moment later, just after the mounted police began moving through the mass of people, a brick flew through the window of the Eureka Hotel, followed by a crash as James Bentley's lovely lamppost toppled to the ground. A great roar went up from the crowd — still growing by the second — the police horses reared in alarm, and hundreds rushed forward, brandishing spades, sticks and any makeshift tool they could lay their hands on. In a matter of minutes, every window in the hotel had been broken and the weatherboards were being systematically torn away.

Rian and Hawk, well away from the *mêlée*, watched as Commissioner Rede hurriedly arrived and climbed onto the sill of a broken window. His voiced drowned out by the clamour, he was forced to dodge as he was pelted with various missiles. He gave up, his place taken by another official, who also soon stepped down, and then the looting started. Clearly at the end of his tether, Rede signalled his troops to move into and around the hotel, amid a barrage of catcalls, jeers and small projectiles.

It was then that the faint smell of burning drifted through the air above the crowd. Heads turned in the direction of the bowling alley adjacent to the hotel, and a jubilant cry went up as ribbons of smoke could be seen curling around its canvas roof above tiny tongues of flame. In no time, the wind had made passengers of the sparks and deposited them among the shingles on the hotel's roof, and soon the hotel was ablaze. Half an hour later, James Bentley's pride, joy and golden goose was a smoking heap of charred timbers.

6

At Lilac Cottage, two evenings later, Rian was lovingly cleaning his pistols, the mahogany case open and its contents spread all over the table. The smells of oil and polish permeated the air, making Amber sneeze.

But her next sneeze became a scream as the door flew off its hinges and a stream of policemen burst in, pistols drawn. Bodie, startled out of her wits, shot under the daybed as Kitty, her own heart thumping madly, hurried to calm Amber.

Rian leapt to his feet. 'What the hell do you think you're doing?'

A sergeant barked: 'Thomas Farrell, we are under orders to arrest you for the murder of James Scobie.'

Unable to dismiss the diggers' strength of feeling against the Camp officials, Charles Hotham had ordered the re-arrest of those under suspicion for the Scobie killing.

'Oh, for God's sake, I'm not Thomas Farrell,' Rian said, and sat down again.

The sergeant, his eyes beginning to bulge in an already alcohol-reddened face, kicked the leg of Rian's chair. 'Get up! You're under arrest. You're being taken to the Camp!'

Rian shrugged. 'Suit yourself, but I'm not Thomas Farrell.'

'He's not!' Kitty protested. 'He's my husband,

Rian Conor Farrell. He had nothing to do with James Scobie's death!'

'Shut up!' the sergeant ordered.

'Don't tell my wife to shut up!' Rian shouted.

Hawk appeared in the doorway and pushed his way in. 'Rian, what is happening?'

A policeman attempted to shove him back outside and Hawk punched him, sending him flying. Another jumped on Hawk's back and they fell through the door, rolling in the dust outside. Then Pierre appeared, roaring like a man possessed, followed by Gideon, followed by everyone else.

★   ★   ★

Rian sat in the wagon, holding a sodden kerchief over his bleeding nose. Beside him, Pierre squinted through an eye that had swollen almost shut, and Daniel dabbed repeatedly with the tail of his shirt at a split lip. Only Gideon had remained unscathed.

Behind them trotted six mounted police, battered and bloodstained but nonetheless looking smugly pleased with themselves at having captured what they clearly believed to be a ruthless, cold-blooded killer and his band of brigands.

The Camp, laid out on a grassy mound in front of the town proper and overlooking the Yarrowee, was surrounded by a wooden fence that encircled neat lines of military tents, stables, and a tall flagpole flying the Union Jack. The troopers guarding the gate saluted as the wagon entered and came to a halt outside a collection of wooden buildings.

The sergeant climbed down and ordered Rian and the crew off.

Looking around interestedly, Mick remarked, 'I've never been in here before.'

'Shut up!' the sergeant snapped. 'You, you and you,' he said, pointing at three of his men, 'keep an eye and I'll alert Mr d'Ewes.'

A short period of standing around, then they were 'escorted' inside to face Police Magistrate John d'Ewes.

He sat behind a large desk, giving off fumes of what smelt suspiciously to Rian like very good Burgundy, and didn't look pleased to have been disturbed in the middle of his evening meal.

He stared at Rian for some time, then turned to the sergeant.

'This isn't Thomas Farrell.'

Rian smirked.

'I believe it is, sir.'

'It is not, Sergeant Coombes. I should know. I've already had him in front of me once.'

Sergeant Coombes fumbled for a piece of paper in his uniform pocket. 'But this is the address I was given for him, sir. Lilac Cottage, near the Red Hill Lead.'

'Well, you've been misinformed.' John d'Ewes turned back to Rian. 'You won't be tried for murder, but I am fining you five pounds. Each.'

'What for?'

'Disturbing the peace.'

'*I* didn't disturb the peace. Your trained monkeys did that.'

The magistrate looked pained. 'Would you rather pay ten pounds each, Mr Farrell?'

'It's *Captain* Farrell. No, we wouldn't.'

'Then pay five, and go away. I have a dinner to get back to. Sergeant Coombes? Have Mr Buckley make the arrangements.'

When he'd gone, Simon, whose ear had swollen to the size of a Brussels sprout and was causing him a lot of pain, said loudly, 'What a supercilious turd.'

'Watch your mouth,' Sergeant Coombes growled. Then he smiled unpleasantly and said to Rian, 'You can't pay it, can you?'

'Yes, I can.' Rian opened his purse and counted out £40 and waved it in Coombes's face. It was an enormous show of bravado — it was money he couldn't really spare — but it was worth it for the satisfaction of annoying the prick. 'Now run along and find this Buckley fellow.'

Coombes glared at him, then spun on his heel and marched off, slamming the door behind him.

After a moment, Hawk remarked, 'I am not sure that was a good idea, Rian.'

★ ★ ★

A week after Bentley's fire, it appeared that Pierre's Bayou Bakery was being boycotted, at least by some. Leena was distraught, apologising to Kitty repeatedly. As though it were her fault, Kitty thought angrily.

Not everyone stayed away, but the shop was

no longer crowded every day and profits were down. Flora came in one day to talk to Kitty about it.

In a complete reversal of his reaction to Lily Pearce, Pierre whipped out from behind the counter, grasped her hand and bowed low over it.

'Mademoiselle McRae, to see you again is a delight!' he exclaimed effusively.

Kitty wondered if he fancied her.

Flora smiled graciously at Pierre, and shook her parasol free of a sprinkle of rain from a recent shower. To Kitty, she said matter-of-factly, 'I hear we are having some trouble.'

'A little,' Kitty replied and reached for the hatch to allow Flora into the back of the shop. However, she was beaten by Pierre, who almost gave himself a hernia heaving it up and ushering Flora through.

Flora waited patiently until the shop was empty. 'And I also hear it originated with Lily Pearce publicly humiliating Leena and you?'

Kitty nodded, grateful that Leena was not at work today. 'I could have slapped her, Flora. She implied that Leena was unclean!'

'I suspect that Leena is a great deal cleaner than Miss Pearce,' Flora replied curtly. 'And as a result, customer numbers are down?'

'They appear to be.'

'You leave Lily Pearce to me, Kitty. She's not a woman to cross. And I will do what I can about the customers.'

When Flora had gone, Kitty said to Pierre in a voice low enough for Amber not to hear, 'You don't feel your behaviour is a little, well, enthusiastic regarding Flora?'

Puzzled, Pierre looked at her. 'Non. She be a fine woman, and I admire the feminine beauty.'

'Actually, I think you might be . . . well, I'm not sure Flora wants . . . ' She trailed off.

Pierre shrugged. 'So? I am not wanting to marry her, only to look. And to respect.' He tapped his head. 'She be a very smart woman, Mademoiselle McRae. Such a thing is very admirable.'

Flora was indeed a very smart woman: several days later a new sort of customer began to patronise the bakery. Both Leena and Amber were serving when the first came in.

He was Chinese, and had smooth skin but lines around his eyes, suggesting he could be anywhere between thirty and his mid-forties. He wore the customary Chinese costume, and held the hand of a girl who looked to be about the same age as Amber. She had exquisite features, beautiful honey-coloured skin, and hair with the colour and sheen of onyx. She was the first Chinese child Kitty had seen in Ballarat, and she wondered where her mother was. But perhaps she didn't have one: Kitty hadn't seen any Chinese women on the diggings, either.

'Good morning,' she said brightly. 'What can I get you today?'

His face impassive, the Chinese man replied, in excellent English, 'You may not recall, but some weeks ago you and your husband Captain Farrell saw off some boys who were throwing stones at my companion and me. We are now in your debt. I am here to repay it.'

'Oh,' Kitty replied, not quite sure what else to say.

The man went on. 'My name is Wong Fu.' He rested a hand on the girl's head. 'This is my daughter, Wong Bao. I am told by a mutual friend that you require patrons for your business.'

Kitty opened her mouth, but nothing came out.

'So I will purchase one dozen of those long bread loaves, and . . . ' Wong Fu bent to his daughter's level and said something to her in his own language, to which she replied in kind. ' . . . And half a dozen of the little round confectioneries, thank you. What is it you call them?'

'These? These are *macarons*.' Kitty hoped the child wasn't going to eat them all — she'd be ill. She selected what Mr Wong had requested, set them carefully in the basket his daughter placed on the counter, then added up the cost.

He handed over the money, and bowed. 'I am pleased to shop here, Mrs Farrell. Be assured that my people will also, if it is convenient for you.' He smiled faintly. 'It seems that it is often *not* convenient for other shopkeepers on these diggings.'

Silently thanking Flora, Kitty replied, 'You are always welcome here, Mr Wong. And we are grateful for your patronage.'

Mr Wong bowed again, then whispered something to his daughter. Letting go of his hand, she moved down the counter nearer to

Amber and, in English almost as good as her father's, said, 'Good morning. I am Wong Bao. I am thirteen years old and I have come to Hsin Chin Shan to help my father find plenty of gold. What is your name?'

Delighted, Amber grinned. 'It's Amber. This is my mother, and this is my friend Pierre. And I'm here to help *my* father find plenty of gold. What does *sin . . . shin . . .* what you said, what does that mean?'

'In Cantonese it means New Gold Mountain.'

Bao's father said then, 'Come, daughter, it is time to go. You may talk to Miss Farrell next time.'

As they departed, Bao looked over her shoulder and, with a cheeky smile, gave Amber a little wave.

'You might have found a friend there, sweetheart,' Kitty remarked.

Eyes sparkling, Amber replied, 'Oh, that would be nice, wouldn't it?'

★ ★ ★

'And you're sure that *will* be good for business?' Rian asked dubiously.

Kitty moved the oil lamp closer, and smoothed fabric over her knee to better see the hole — yet another — that Rian had torn in his trousers. 'I can't see why not. And there are quite a lot of Chinese on the diggings.'

'I know, love, but if half the population of Ballarat has stopped buying their bread from your bakery because Lily bloody Pearce has decreed the buns are off because an Aborigine girl works there, are they likely to start again if the place is patronised by Chinese? You know how they're viewed.'

'Well, I don't care what other people think — I'm happy to serve them in my shop. I'll take anyone, so long as they don't cause trouble. Except for Lily Pearce.'

Rian stretched his legs towards the fire, his socks flopping off his feet. 'What is *wrong* with that woman? She seems to have really taken against you. Do you know why?'

Kitty hesitated. 'Well, I suspect she'd like to make you one of her, ah, conquests.'

Rian snorted disparagingly. 'I wouldn't sleep with Lily Pearce if she were the last woman on Earth. And I certainly wouldn't *pay* her!'

'But she is attractive.' Kitty couldn't help pushing Rian a little, if only to give him the opportunity to deny the appeal of another woman and compliment the allure of his own wife. And, she reluctantly had to admit, to reassure herself.

'Well, to some, perhaps, but not to me. Anyway, she's probably riddled with pox.' He left a long, long pause, then grinned and said, 'And she's *nothing* compared with you, *mo ghrá*. Nothing at all . . . Is that what you wanted to hear?'

Kitty went red. 'No, it was not.'

'Yes, it was!' Rian was laughing now.

'No, it wasn't!' Kitty snapped, thinking she was far too old for this sort of thing.

She was saved from further discomfort by

Amber appearing at door and announcing that supper was ready.

Walking arm-in-arm with Rian to the crew's tents, Kitty noticed that, now that the end of October was approaching, the diggings suddenly, and unexpectedly, seemed a little less harsh and unforgiving. The breeze on her face was no longer laced with the icy touch of winter, and the colour green was creeping back into the landscape. She had been so busy with the bakery she had barely noticed the quiet approach of spring.

No one said anything as they dug into Pierre's lamb stew with dumplings, savouring the usual high quality of his cooking. These days he prepared enormous amounts of food: he was feeding thirteen people, and sometimes Patrick and his wife, Maureen, as well as occasionally Binda and her own two grandchildren. There were seldom leftovers.

Mick set his tin plate on the ground, leaned back on his elbows and burped gently. 'Would anyone be thinking of going to the moonlight dance?'

Nods from the crew, but Kitty was mystified. 'What dance?'

'At the Adelphi Theatre, Saturday night,' Mick replied. 'Have you not seen the bills posted everywhere?'

Kitty hadn't. 'And it's a public affair? For diggers?'

'If it wasn't, it would be at the assembly rooms, wouldn't it?' Simon said, referring to the frequent balls held by Ballarat's government officials for themselves, military officers and the town's swells.

'Can I go?' Amber asked eagerly. She'd been to the circus once so far, but a dance would be even better.

'Certainly not. Not by yourself,' Kitty shot back.

'Well, why don't we all go?' Rian suggested. 'It'll do us good.'

Mick sat up. 'Think of all the colleens!'

Don't get your hopes up, Kitty thought; Flora had already told her there were only about 200 single women on the diggings. But that wouldn't deter Mick, and he'd probably visited one of the brothels already. If he had, she hoped it had been Flora's establishment and not Lily Pearce's.

But, she wondered, what do you wear to a dance in a tent in the middle of a goldfield?

★   ★   ★

Anything, apparently. The men all seemed to sport trimmed whiskers and slicked-down hair, and were dressed in ensembles ranging from the simple addition of a waistcoat over clean work clothes, to pressed serge or canvas trousers, jackets and smart hats. The women had also gone to some effort to look their best, wearing a great array of bonnets featuring lace, ribbons and artificial flowers, and even a few fancy straw hats. Practical day dresses had been replaced by 'best' gowns, and drab capes with light shawls in paisley, tartan and good wool.

Kitty chose a dress made for her by Rian's

sister, Enya, a dressmaker in Sydney. It wasn't her most elaborate gown, but its full faille skirts and fitting bodice in soft raspberry complemented her colouring and was not so ostentatious that she would stand out among the other women. Rian hadn't bothered to dress up, despite Kitty's exhortations, but had put on a decent jacket and had condescended to shave, and Amber wore her favourite dress, a checked rust and navy blue taffeta with a high neckline and a full, calf-length skirt. But she had refused to wear the ribbon Kitty had picked out for her hair, 'inadvertently' leaving it on the daybed before they'd come out. As a consequence, her hair was already tumbling wildly about her face.

Ropata and Leena, however, had declined to come. Leena was still smarting over Lily Pearce's unpleasant comments, and was convinced that everyone would point her out as 'that myall'. Realising that his wife's pride had been badly bruised, and feeling for her as deeply as if his own mana had been offended, Ropata acquiesced to her request that they not attend.

The Adelphi Theatre, although only a tent, was vast and already filled almost to capacity with people evidently determined to have a good time. In one corner was a rough stage, on which was jammed a musical ensemble consisting of four fiddlers, two penny-whistle players, two men and a woman with *bodhráns*, a concertina player, and two men who sat with *uilleann* pipes across their laps.

Wooden benches formed a perimeter around the sides of the tent; the centre was cleared for dancing. The fact that there wasn't a bar didn't seem to be a deterrent, and many had brought alcohol with them. The noise level was already high, and the air above the crowd hazy with pipe smoke.

Rian dodged through the throng and found a place to sit that would accommodate them all. Kitty spotted Patrick and his wife and waved, noting at the same time that there were very few Aborigines in attendance, and not a single Chinese person. Rian withdrew a bottle of whiskey from the sagging pocket of his jacket, eased out the cork and took a healthy swig.

Amused, Kitty warned, 'I'm not carrying you home tonight.'

'Ah, there'll be a spare wheelbarrow some-where.'

After a few preparatory fiddle squeaks and a wheeze from the concertina, the band launched into an energetic and not quite synchronised rendition of 'The Daughters of Erin'. Shawls and jackets were immediately discarded, the crowd surged towards the centre of the tent, and the dance floor became a whirling kaleidoscope of movement and colour. Mick, Gideon and Pierre — reeking of the lavender water he habitually wore for 'special occasions' — headed deter-minedly off, on the prowl for partners, leaving Simon, Daniel and Hawk behind.

Observing the great clusters of unpartnered men standing around, Rian muttered, 'They'll be lucky.'

Mick, no doubt, would be, Kitty thought — he usually was — and Pierre would probably find someone, too, his exoticism and immense charm overcoming his short, wiry stature. Gideon might initially find it more difficult to convince someone to dance with him, given his spectacular size and alarming appearance, but his huge smile and lovely manners made him more popular with the ladies than might be expected.

Rian nudged Daniel in the ribs and urged, 'Go on, get out there. But you'd better be quick.'

'No, I'd prefer to just watch,' Daniel replied, trying to ignore Rian's amused look. He stared moodily ahead for a moment, then reached under the bench for his bottle.

Rian shrugged. 'What about you, Hawk? Happy to be a wallflower?'

Hawk scowled, his brows almost meeting in the middle. 'I do not dance, Rian. You know that.'

But Kitty, noting his proudly curved mouth, high-bridged nose and the gleaming fall of his black, waist-length hair, suspected it wouldn't be long before some woman, tipsy with ale, would summon the nerve to ask him onto the floor. And he did dance, just not in this manner. She'd watched him more than once over the years performing the rhythmic, hypnotic and elaborate dances of his people, which required great strength, and he had been beautiful to behold.

'What about you, Simon?' she said.

With exaggerated dignity, he replied, 'I think you are forgetting, Kitty, that I have two left feet.'

Kitty laughed.

Simon added sanctimoniously, 'Anyway, I note

that *you're* not dancing.'

'He's got a point there, *mo ghrá*,' Rian conceded. He took Kitty's hand and said in a beseeching voice, 'Madam, would you care to dance with a lonely old sea captain desperate for the attention of a beautiful and cultured woman?'

Kitty was very surprised — he *must* be in a good mood, as he was almost as reluctant as Hawk when it came to dancing. Accepting with the grace a queen might bestow upon a favoured courtier, which she spoiled by giggling, she followed him onto the dance floor. Glancing back, she saw Amber standing before Daniel, hands determinedly on hips, presumably badgering him into dancing with her. Daniel smiled, put his bottle aside and stood, and Kitty thought, Ah, you're a good man, Daniel Royce.

The band tore enthusiastically through a range of songs, each one greeted with a loud cheer by the convivial, and increasingly drunk, crowd. Kitty and Rian were bumped mercilessly as dancers hurled themselves around in energetic reels and jigs, polkas and hornpipes, accompanied by much loud stomping and shouting.

Kitty watched, amused, as Mick went from partner to partner, spinning giggling, pink-faced women as far out as they would go and whirling them back in again, ignoring sour looks from husbands and hopeful beaux alike. Gideon had indeed found himself a partner, a tiny woman whose head barely reached his chest and who shrieked with delight every time he lifted her in the air and spun her around. Even Simon was up now, mashing the toes of a middle-aged woman who was politely smiling throughout his shuffling efforts.

Finally, the band, clearly requiring a breather, eased into a version of 'Carrigfergus', with which many of the dancers, and the crowds of men left lining the perimeter of the tent, joined in, bellowing with particular gusto the lines 'But I'll sing no more 'til I get a drink, for I'm drunk today, and I'm seldom sober!'

And it was during this interlude in the dancing that heads began to turn like wheat in a gentle breeze towards the tent's entrance. Kitty, craning her neck, just managed to see that Flora McRae, dressed again in elegant black from head to toe, had arrived accompanied by five or six comely young women. They paused for a moment in the doorway, surveying the crowd, heads held high.

'That's Flora,' Kitty murmured to Rian.

'The woman in black? And those are her girls?'

'I presume so. Would you like to meet her?'

'Yes, I would, actually.' Rian laid a hand on Kitty's arm. 'But not just yet, eh? If I go charging up to her, people might think I'm desperate to, er, secure a business transaction.'

'Well, you'd have to stand in line,' Kitty remarked, nodding at the crowd of men already drifting towards the women, their carefully arranged expressions implying that their intentions were merely to dance with the pretty young things.

She led Rian off the dance floor and sank gratefully onto the bench, hot now from her exertions and uncomfortably aware that the fancy boots she hadn't worn in months were pinching her toes.

Amber, strands of hair sticking sweatily to her face, pointed. 'There's Flora over there, Ma. Can you see her?'

'Yes, we saw her come in.'

Amber waved energetically. 'Look, she's seen us.'

Flora approached, weaving her way between couples and small groups who had begun dancing again now that the tempo of the music had increased, and sat down beside Kitty.

'Good evening, Kitty. I trust you're enjoying yourself? Good evening, Mr Bullock,' she added to Simon, then nodded politely at Daniel.

Simon inclined his head. 'Good evening to you, Miss Langford. It's a pleasure to see you again.'

'Mrs McRae,' Kitty reminded him.

'Oh, of course, I beg your pardon.'

Flora shifted her gaze to Rian, where it lingered for some time. 'And this, Kitty, must be your captain?'

Kitty caught Rian's eye and smiled. 'Yes. This is my husband, Captain Rian Farrell. Rian, this is Mrs Flora McRae.'

Rian reached across Kitty and briefly clasped Flora's hand. 'I've heard much about you, Mrs McRae.'

'And I you, Captain,' Flora replied graciously. 'I felt it was time that we met. I don't normally attend these public affairs — my girls are perfectly capable of making their own, shall we say, arrangements — however, I did tonight in the hope that you would both be here.' She paused. 'I felt it would be inappropriate for me to be seen visiting Lilac Cottage. For you, I mean, not me.'

Rian waved away her last comment. 'Thank you for your consideration, Mrs McRae, but I receive whomever I choose at my own hearth. And so does Kitty. You are welcome to visit Lilac Cottage whenever you like.'

'Thank you very much,' Flora replied. Then her mouth made a tiny *moue* of distaste. 'I suspect we are being observed.'

Kitty followed Flora's gaze: Lily Pearce had also arrived, and stood near the door watching them with narrowed eyes. Then she turned haughtily away and clicked her fingers, sending her girls out into the crowd.

'She has them trained like animals,' Flora remarked. 'And I am told, I'm afraid, that that is exactly how they sometimes behave, although I've never had the misfortune to see it myself.'

'Animals?' Rian queried interestedly. 'Rats? Apes? Dingos?'

Flora looked at him, her pale face impassive. 'Oh, no. I'm given to understand that dingos are really quite bright. And apes.'

The corners of Rian's mouth twitched.

'And on that note,' Flora said, rising, 'I have matters to see to, so you must excuse me. Delightful to finally meet you, Captain Farrell. Goodnight, Mr Bullock.' She bent and whispered in Kitty's ear, 'I could arrange something for your quiet friend, if he's amenable. He's far from unattractive and I expect none of my girls would consider it a chore.'

Kitty glanced at Daniel. 'Perhaps you should ask him yourself.' She was shocked to realise that the faint pang she felt at Flora's offer was something close to jealously. 'Actually, there's — '

Flora eyed her with dreadful perception. She smiled knowingly. 'Then I take your point. Goodnight, Kitty.'

Her cheeks burning, Kitty watched as she walked away.

Rian took her hand. 'An interesting woman, your Flora McRae.' Then he burst into laughter. 'What on *earth* is he doing?'

Kitty and Rian stared in bemusement as Pierre, some yards away on the dance floor, executed a series of horribly complicated steps around a woman almost weeping with laughter at his antics.

'That,' Kitty said slowly, 'is his version of a hornpipe. I think.'

'Shall we try our version?'

But as they stood the music changed to a reel, and they were caught up in a group of ten dancers, weaving a lively and complex pattern, and changing partners every few bars.

'Who's she dancing with now?' Rian asked.

Kitty followed his gaze towards Amber, who was laughing and spinning around with a man in a smart blue waistcoat. 'That's Mr Searle. He comes into the shop. I think he's taken a shine to her.'

'Bit old for her, isn't he?'

'Don't worry, she says he has bad breath.'

Rian caught Kitty around the waist, led her

under his arm and turned to face her. She laughed and curtsied and around they went again, swinging in time to the music and ducking between other couples. Then Kitty let go of Rian's hands to execute a spin, and when she turned back Lily Pearce, like a great, bright raptor, had swooped on him and steered him away and into the crowd.

Kitty stood absolutely still, her mouth open, feeling sick. Then Daniel appeared at her side, his hand hovering near her shoulder, and she could see he wanted to take hold of her so she wouldn't look such a fool, but couldn't decide whether it would be the right thing to do.

'Did you see that!' she exclaimed.

'I'll cut in, get her away from him,' he said, looking as offended and embarrassed as Kitty felt.

But Rian was already extricating himself even as Lily, one hand clamped against his back and the other gripping his shoulder, led him deeper into the dancing throng.

'Let go of me,' he warned.

'No.' Lily laughed. 'I think this is awfully cosy, don't you?'

Rian's eyes narrowed and his voice was taut with anger. 'Well, I fucking don't. So get *off me!*'

Lily's lips parted and she breathed rather than spoke the words, 'Make me.'

Dangerously close to losing his temper completely, Rian grasped the hand gripping his shoulder, disconnected it and pushed Lily away.

'I'm not interested, do you understand?' he growled. 'I don't like you and I don't want you.

Keep away from me.'

He turned his back on her, but as he did, he heard her say quite clearly, 'But I want *you*, Rian Farrell. And I *always* get what I want.'

★   ★   ★

'Rian?'

'Mmm?'

Kitty rested her face against his warm, damp chest, surreptitiously inhaling his lovely masculine smell, the scent that always came off him after they had made love. 'I nearly had a heart attack when Lily took you away tonight.'

Rian smoothed her hair with a languid hand. 'Christ, so did I. I wondered what the bloody hell she was doing.'

Kitty was quiet for a moment. Then, 'What did you say to her?'

Rian heard the disquiet in his wife's voice, and it upset him. 'I told her to leave me alone.'

Kitty took Rian's hand and held it, then absently twisted the ring he wore, a heavy gold band set with a milky, grey-blue star sapphire cabochon. She'd had it made for him five years ago and he rarely took it off, not even when he was working. 'In no uncertain terms?'

'Definitely in no uncertain terms.'

But Rian wasn't at all convinced that Lily Pearce had received the message. The damn woman was a harpy, and she was causing trouble, and he would have to put a stop to it.

7

Late October 1854

'There is a man looking for you, Mrs Farrell,' Wong Fu said as Kitty passed him the *baguettes* he had requested. He glanced outside at Amber and Bao sitting on the verandah, giggling together and wiping *macaron* crumbs from their mouths. 'He is giving your name, your husband's and your daughter's.'

Kitty swept a stray lock of hair off her face with the back of her wrist. 'Did he give his own name?'

'No, I have not spoken with him. I have only been told.' A pause. 'But he is a big man and he has dark skin.'

Gideon? But Wong Fu had met Gideon and knew who he was. Then, with a sensation like the warmth of the sun rising on a cold winter morning, Kitty suddenly thought she knew. Her heart thudding with excitement, she asked, 'Is he alone, do you know?'

'I was told he has a boy with him.'

It must be! 'Thank you, Mr Wong! This is wonderful news!' Kitty turned to Pierre. 'Did you hear that?' She pulled off her apron and tossed it over a chair. 'I'm just going up the street to see if I can find them. Will you be all right?'

Smiling, Pierre closed the oven door. 'Course.

121

Just send that girl back in, *oui?*'

Kitty hurried out of the shop. 'I'm going out, Amber. Can you give Pierre a hand?'

Amber, the last *macaron* halfway to her mouth, said, 'Where are you going? Can I come?'

'No, it's a surprise. But I'll be back soon.'

Kitty set off up the street, glancing into every shop, and then, finally, she saw them, walking towards her, waving and grinning madly. She picked up her skirts and broke into a run, oblivious to the stares of passers-by.

'Haunui! You came!' She threw her arms around him and he swung her around, laughing his big, loud laugh.

'Hello, my little Pakeha daughter! We have been looking *everywhere* for you, eh, Tahi?'

The boy at Haunui's side nodded. 'Hello, Aunt Kitty.'

As always, after she had not seen him for a while, Kitty was amazed at how much Tahi had grown. Fondly, she kissed his cheek. 'Hello, love. It's *wonderful* to see you! How are you?'

Tahi shrugged with the characteristic insouciance many boys on the verge of manhood seem to affect, and smiled shyly. 'All right, thank you, Auntie.'

His straight black hair skimmed his shoulders, and in his light hazel eyes, high cheekbones and defined chin lay echoes of his dead mother Wai's lovely face: an image that still tugged painfully at Kitty's heart. At fourteen Tahi was already five foot nine, although his frame did not yet carry the bulk of the muscle he would soon develop. But next to Haunui he still seemed short.

Haunui was in his sixties now, his hair uniformly pewter and his face etched with lines of age as well as those of his full-face moko. But he was still very fit, his muscles greatly in evidence and his broad back straight. He was Tahi's grandfather, a revelation that had not come to light until Wai had died giving birth to Tahi. It had been assumed that Wai was the daughter of Haunui's arrogant and irascible brother Tupehu, a Nga Puhi chief, but in fact she was the result of a long and secret love affair Haunui had had with Tupehu's wife, Hareta.

When Kitty had been sent with her Aunt Sarah and Uncle George Kelleher to a mission station at Paihia in New Zealand in 1839, Sarah had taken in several Maori house girls, one of whom had been Wai. George, a minister in the Church Missionary Society, had forced himself on Wai before he had mysteriously disappeared, and she had become pregnant. When Wai's 'father' Tupehu discovered this, Kitty and Wai had been forced to flee New Zealand, and Rian had taken them, with Haunui, to Sydney. After Wai had died, Haunui had returned to Paihia with the infant Tahi to raise him among his own people. Kitty saw them whenever the *Katipo* sailed to New Zealand, but that had not been for two years now.

'How is everyone?' Haunui asked. 'Are you filthy rich yet?'

'No, we are not,' Kitty replied ruefully, recalling that in her letter to Haunui suggesting that he and Tahi come to Ballarat, she had made much of Rian's conviction that there was a fortune to be made on the diggings. 'But the shaft is almost down to the lead now, so we should see something soon. If it's there,' she added.

Haunui slipped his arm through Kitty's, and they began walking. 'But you have been here almost two months. Has it taken that long to dig down?'

Kitty nodded. 'Two months is quite quick, actually. And it's a deep shaft. But a lot of them are now.'

'And the crew are all here?'

'Yes, and Pierre's opened a bakery! Well, it's my business, I suppose, but Pierre does most of the baking.'

At mention of the word 'bakery', Haunui's eyes lit up. 'Good, we are *starving*.'

Which Kitty knew meant that Haunui hadn't eaten for possibly up to two hours. 'When did you arrive?'

'We got to Melbourne ten days ago, but we have been to Bendigo to see some whanau from home trying their luck on the goldfields. Ah, they are filthy rich now, eh, Tahi? They have a nugget as big as this!' Haunui held his hands apart to illustrate something the shape of a good-sized head of cauliflower. 'But they said it's too cold for them in the winter and they miss the sea.'

'So they'll be going home soon?'

Haunui shook his big head. 'They want some more nuggets.'

Kitty laughed. 'When did you get to Ballarat?'

'Just after midday. We came on the Cobb & Co. Very hard on your arse, those coaches.

Crowded, too,' Haunui added. 'But me and Tahi spread out, eh, boy?'

Kitty laughed again, envisioning the other poor travellers cowering in their seats hour after hour, trying not to come into contact with the large, tattooed, fierce-looking Maori man. 'And the voyage across the Tasman?'

Haunui shrugged. 'Smelly. Came on a whaling ship to Sydney, then caught another ship down to Melbourne.'

'And how is everyone at Paihia? How is Aunt Sarah?'

'Fat and happy.'

Kitty felt pleased; poor Sarah had had such a difficult life, until the mystery of George's disappearance had finally been solved and she had been free to remarry.

Haunui politely tipped his hat to a pair of passing women, causing them to step smartly away in alarm. Then, at the sight of Amber waiting excitedly on the bakery verandah, her face almost split in two by an enormous smile, he stopped and roared in a voice that echoed up the street, '*There she is — my most beautiful mokopuna!*'

Amber launched herself at him, and allowed him to gather her in a tight embrace.

'E hine,' he said in wonder, 'look at you: you're almost a woman!'

Amber stole his hat and put it on her own head, where it slipped down over her eyes. 'Ah, Koro, I am not!'

Kitty felt an immense rush of love for Haunui, her oldest surviving friend from her early days in

New Zealand. No matter what path she had chosen to take since then, even if it had seemed foolhardy, he had stood behind her and accepted her decisions, and the people she had gathered close to her. Amber had regarded him as her grandfather since she was four years old. She had been abandoned by her family, and no one had known who her Pakeha father had been, and Haunui's generous efforts to teach her of her Maori heritage were something for which Kitty was also very grateful to him.

Amber glanced shyly at Tahi. 'Hello.'

Tahi ducked his head and mumbled something in reply.

Kitty shared an amused glance with Haunui. Both the same age, the children had always competed, ever since Amber had shoved Tahi flat on his back in the sand at Paihia the first time they'd met. But two years ago, when they were twelve, something had changed between them and their easy if argumentative companionship had gone, replaced by awkward silences, stolen glances and blushing faces. It appeared that this phase hadn't yet passed.

'Speak up, boy,' Haunui said. 'Where are your manners?'

'Kia ora, Amber,' Tahi muttered.

Another silence.

'Well, then. Did you say you were hungry?' Kitty said. 'Come inside.'

Pierre was waiting for them with a platter of hot pasties and pies, bread and *macarons* for Haunui's sweet tooth, and a pot of tea. He and Haunui embraced, the discrepancy in their heights making them an odd sight, and Pierre solemnly shook Tahi's hand.

'It is very good to see you, *mes amis*. Very good. You eat something, then we go up to the claim and see Rian, *hein?* I am taking the dinner. Leena be here soon.'

His mouth already full of pasty, Hainui said in surprise, 'Leena's here?'

Kitty nodded. 'She arrived at the beginning of the month. Ropata was absolutely delighted.'

'And the children?' Haunui and Leena had met only twice before, but it had been enough to forge the beginnings of a solid friendship.

The bell over the door chimed and several people entered, glancing curiously at the large tattooed man with gravy running down his chin.

Kitty put her apron back on. 'Yes, the children are here as well, having a lovely time running all over the place. Leena has an Aboriginal woman looking after them when she's working here, but I suspect they're running the poor thing ragged.'

Haunui nodded empathetically, having himself had much experience with small, tearaway children.

The bell rang again; Mr Searle came in, smiled, removed his hat and made straight for Amber standing behind the counter. A moment later, Leena arrived.

Slipping off her shawl, she noticed Haunui and Tahi and smiled. 'Hello! You came!'

Pierre cleared his throat. 'I do not want to interrupt, but — ' he indicated an enormous steaming pot and a basket of muslin-wrapped bread, 'the dinner will go cold if we don't take him now.'

Outside, the dinner and Tahi loaded onto the cart, Pierre and Haunui headed off for the claim. They drove to the far end of the street, heading south along the Main Road.

Haunui waved his hand in front of his face. 'It stinks here.'

Pierre sniffed the air delicately. 'Shit?'

'Ae, shit. But there is something else. Something . . . dark.'

His brows creasing, Pierre thought for a moment. 'She is a sour smell?'

'Ae.'

'The earth then. That is the smell of the earth.'

'If it is, then it's the smell of earth that has been *insulted*. Perhaps too much has been taken from Papatuanuku without enough given back.'

'Papa-what?'

'Papatuanuku. The earth mother.'

Pierre *hmmph*ed and flicked the reins across the bullock's neck. 'You and your heathen gods.'

Haunui gave Pierre a sideways look. 'You and *your* heathen gods. And your voodoo magic and your dolls and your snakes!'

Still chuckling, they passed through the Red Hill area until Pierre turned right off the Main Road and onto the track that would take them around the base of the Golden Point Range and towards the Malakoff Lead and Rian's claim.

Missing very little as the cart jolted along, Haunui asked Pierre why the shafts, and tents indicating shafts, appeared to follow such organic but nevertheless distinct patterns. 'They

128

go where the underground rivers go,' Pierre explained.

Haunui looked horrified. 'There are underground rivers? Will the miners not all drown?'

'Some have drowned doing the digging, *oui*. And a few they have fallen down shafts coming home when they are pissed. But the rivers they are not' — Pierre groped for the right word — 'they are not *torrents*. They are ancient, and they seep through the rock and the clay. It is where the gold settles, and where the men must dig.'

Haunui nodded, mollified. After the cart had lurched over a particularly deep rut, he said over his shoulder, 'That kai all right back there?'

Quickly tucking the muslin back over the bread, to which he had been helping himself, Tahi nodded.

'You've got crumbs on your face, boy,' Haunui remarked benignly. Turning back to Pierre, he muttered, 'That boy never stops eating.'

Pierre shrugged. 'He is a boy. That is what they do.'

Haunui settled his bulk more comfortably on the narrow wooden seat. 'So, what has been happening here, my friend? *Will* Rian find riches?'

Pierre waggled his hand in a maybe-yes, maybe-no gesture. 'It is a wager, even though his claim she is supposed to be a *guaranteed* one. Ordinary men like you and me can grow rich overnight, and rich men become paupers if they are not knowing when to stop. It is like the cards and the dice. It is like a fever.'

Alarmed now, Haunui asked, 'And does Rian have this fever?'

Pierre thought about it. '*Non*, you know him, he is not a stupid man. He just like . . . the *challenge*.'

'Must have spent a lot of money on this challenge. And what does Kitty think?'

'I think she be ready to kick his arse when he first tell her.' Pierre chuckled. 'But now she be all right with it. 'Specially now she has the bakery. Her friend Mademoiselle Flora McRae? She is the business partner. Fine woman. *Very* fine woman.'

Haunui's heavy brows met in a scowl. Who was Flora McRae?

'The woman she stay with in Auckland?' Pierre elaborated. 'When she find Amber? Her name Langford then, I think.'

Ah! Haunui did remember, although he had never met Miss Langford himself. 'What is she doing here?'

'She is being a madam.'

'She is married?'

'*Non*, she is the manager of a whorehouse.'

Now Haunui's brows shot skyward. 'And she lent Kitty money?'

'*Non*, she buy the business, Kitty manages it, I cook for it, Leena and Amber take the money off the customers.'

Haunui digested this. 'And it's doing all right, this business?'

'*Oui*, now. We start off very good, then a bad patch, then very good again.'

Without even turning around, Haunui said

mildly, 'Leave that kai alone, boy.' There was a scuffling as Tahi reluctantly moved away from the bread. 'What was the reason for the bad patch?'

Pierre slowed the bullock and eased the cart off the track as a heavily loaded wagon clattered past. 'You know Leena is in the shop? Well, there is another madam on the diggings, a trollop named Lily Pearce. *Mon Dieu*, what a *chatte*.' He spat over the side of the cart, then told Haunui what had happened in the shop.

Protective as always of his honorary daughter, Haunui asked, 'How does Kitty feel about this Lily woman?'

Pierre made an unhappy face. 'Well, it not be a man's place to ask. But Rian don't like her — he know she upset Kitty.'

'But apart from that, everything else is good?'

'*Oui*, it is. Rian say the gold is not far away, Ropata be thrilled that Leena and the children are here, Mick is happy trying to bed all the *jeunes dames*, although there not be all that many *jeunes dames* here to bed, I have to say, and I am having a good time doing the baking. Gideon be happy, Simon is fine, Daniel *seem* happy, Hawk is himself, Bodie chasing the mousies and stealing the chops and chickens, and Amber has made a little friend called Bao.'

Haunui wondered if Daniel had finally managed to forsake his love for Kitty. Daniel obviously believed he kept it well hidden, but Haunui, at least, saw it in the boy's eyes every time they met. Nothing good could ever come of it, but he did understand: he had never ceased loving Hareta, another man's wife, not even after death had taken her from them both.

'This Bao is a girl?' Haunui asked. Behind him he sensed Tahi's sudden stillness, and smiled to himself.

'*Oui*, a Chinese child. Very pretty manners. I approve,' Pierre declared magnanimously. 'She do not have the chance to make many friends, and a girl should have the friends, *non?*'

Haunui nodded. 'I have not seen many children yet. Are they all at school?'

'The schools they open and they close down. Hardly any of the little ones attend.'

'So where are they?'

'Somewhere getting into trouble,' Pierre replied philosophically. 'Fossicking. Scrounging. Stealing, perhaps.'

'There is a lot of thieving here?'

Pierre snorted. 'All I say is you should nail your hat to your head, *mon ami. Oui*, there is stealing here. Life on the diggings, she is not easy.' Then he brightened and his eyes began to gleam. 'Course, in such a place, you get *la révolte!* And, if I am not wrong, she is not far away!'

★ ★ ★

Wong Fu had invited all fifteen of them to share an evening meal at the Chinese village. The Chinese were extremely self-contained and rarely mixed with other communities on the diggings, and so Kitty knew the invitation was an honour.

The camp was located some distance from the

diggings, as the Chinese had no need to protect claims: they fossicked rather than mined for gold. The walk there in the deepening twilight was hazardous, but only because of the prospect of tripping over piles of mullock or falling into holes; Kitty, Leena and the children were surrounded by the protective cocoon of the crew. At the head of the party walked Wong Fu, his outstretched arm bearing a lantern that spilled only a little light across the treacherous ground. The evening air wasn't cold, but Kitty had brought her shawl, aware that on clear nights here the temperature could drop quite markedly.

'How far is it, Ma?' Amber asked.

'I don't know, love.' Amber had made Bao a small cake, and Kitty suspected the icing on it might be melting from the heat of her hands. 'Why don't you ask Mr Wong?'

'Excuse me, Mr Wong,' Amber called, 'but how far is your camp?'

'Not far.'

Soon the ever-present sounds of the diggings diminished somewhat and they came to another settlement of tents and tin and timber buildings, albeit smaller than the town they had left behind. From within dwellings pale lamps glowed, and the people walking the beaten paths in the encroaching darkness stared in open curiosity. Here, it was Kitty and the crew who were in the uncomfortable position of feeling out of place.

They passed a building that, in the darkness, appeared to gleam softly, suggesting to Kitty that its walls might actually be painted, a rare sight on the diggings. Its roof line was ornate, and the door lintel carved. A temple?

Wong Fu led them on through a jumble of tents and huts until they came to a larger structure, its windows covered with oilskin that allowed only a flicker of lamplight to escape.

'Welcome. We will take our meal here,' Wong Fu announced. In the porch, he paused to remove his shoes, prompting everyone else to prise off their boots, and hope their socks weren't too pungent.

Inside, several lanterns hung suspended from a central rafter, chasing shadows to the farthest corners of the room. A long, very low table sat in the centre surrounded by flat cushions. At the head of the table, his bird-like legs crossed, sat an elderly man; on his left sat another, although he was perhaps no more than middle-aged.

'This is my father, Wong Chi-Ping.' Wong Fu indicated the younger man.

Wong Chi-Ping bowed his head. 'Good evening.'

Rian, as captain of his crew, bowed in response, in the manner he usually employed when doing business with the Chinese.

'And this is Wong Kwok-Po, my grandfather.'

Wong Kwok-Po nodded a curt greeting.

'He does not speak good English,' Wong Fu explained, 'but he understands a little.'

'But why has he come all the way to Australia?' Amber asked. 'Isn't he too old to travel?'

'*Amber!*' Kitty coloured with embarrassment.

Wong Fu shrugged. 'He wanted to see the

world before he dies. And why not?'

Rian then introduced his party, and Wong Fu invited them to sit around the table, the men near the top and the women and children at the end nearest the door, Gideon and Haunui grunting as they struggled into unaccustomed cross-legged positions.

Rian gazed around the room. There was a red cabinet, on top of which sat an extensive teaset, against one wall, and a low cupboard in gleaming black against the wall opposite. A large and decorative hanging adorned the wall behind the elderly gentlemen.

'Do you normally take your meals here?' he asked.

'No, we eat in our tents. This is our association's meeting rooms.'

'Where's Bao?' Amber asked. 'I've made her a cake.'

'Bao will be serving shortly,' Wong Fu replied.

'I thought we might meet your wife this evening, Mr Wong,' Kitty said. 'I've very much been looking forward to that.'

'My wife did not come to Australia with us, Mrs Farrell. She has remained in China with our younger children.'

'Oh, I'm very sorry to hear that. Well, then perhaps I may meet some of the other wives?'

'No,' Wong Chi-Ping said suddenly.

Kitty froze, wondering if she had made some awful gaffe.

'There are two only,' Wong Chi-Ping continued. 'And they do not wish to show their faces.'

135

'I'm sorry? Only two *wives?*' Kitty was incredulous.

'There are only two women altogether,' Wong Fu clarified. 'There are four thousand Chinese men here and only two women. And a handful of children.'

There was a long silence. Then Mick, stunned, asked, 'What the hell do you do, then?'

'We work.'

Mick ignored Rian's warning look. 'I was meaning, you know, when you want to relax, let off steam.'

Wong Fu's face lit with understanding. 'Ah, I see. We have our *tong* — our association — through which we meet in this room to talk and drink tea, we play *fan tan* and *pakapoo*, *mah jong* and cards, we smoke opium, and we have visiting Chinese musicians and theatre. We do not become bored.'

It wasn't the answer Mick was looking for, but he had the sense not to pursue the matter further.

'But you must become lonely at times?' Kitty said.

'Oh, yes. We miss our families. And we miss our home.'

The door opened and Bao appeared, almost staggering under the weight of a lacquered tray bearing several huge bowls of steaming rice. Amber jumped up and presented her with her cake. But, her hands full, Bao could only nod her thanks. Amber set the cake aside and took one of the bowls off the tray and placed it in the middle of the table.

'The older gentlemen first, love,' Kitty whispered, aware of protocol. 'That includes your father.'

Amber giggled and moved the bowl nearer to the senior Wongs. Bao disappeared again, and returned a minute later with more bowls containing pickles, salted fish, preserved duck, and dried beans, as well as fresh vegetables prepared in a light, piquant sauce. The food kept coming until there was a feast on the table, including the tiny cups and six decorated teapots with wire handles from atop the cabinet, which Bao filled with fragrant tea. Finally she presented each person with a bowl and a set of bamboo chopsticks, and sat down herself.

'What are we supposed to do with these?' Haunui asked, mystified.

'Watch this.' Pierre deftly chopsticked a small pile of rice into his bowl, arranged some vegetables and duck on top, then, slowly, so Haunui could see what he was doing with his fingers, secured a piece of duck between his chopsticks and lifted it to his mouth. '*Oui*, the sauce she is delicate but *piquante*.'

Haunui fiddled about with the sticks, attempting to set them between his fingers the way Pierre had. Carefully, he reached across the table and dug them into a bowl of rice and scooped out a portion — which, halfway back to his own bowl, exploded, scattering fluffy white grains far and wide. There were roars of laughter, especially from Wong Kwok-Po, then more as Simon did exactly the same thing. It soon became obvious that only Rian, Kitty, Pierre,

137

Hawk and, for some reason, Leena, were adept at managing chopsticks — everyone else's clothing and immediate surroundings were quickly accumulating little deposits of food.

Finally, at a nod from Wong Fu, Bao quietly slipped from the room and came back with a handful of porcelain soup spoons, which she distributed to all those who clearly would be going home hungry without them.

At the end of the meal, Bao rose once again and cleared the table.

Rian thanked Wong Fu and his kin for the fine meal. 'I would like to ask, however, why did you invite us?'

Wong Fu appeared to consider the question. Eventually, he replied, 'We invited you because you personally have shown us respect, because Mrs Farrell has welcomed us as customers at her place of business, and because we think it is important that Bao has a companion her own age, even if that companion is not Chinese. We wished to thank you for that.'

Grimly, Rian met his gaze. 'It is that bad, is it?'

'Yes, it is.' Wong Fu gave a deep sigh. 'You must understand that we are reviled here on the diggings, and indeed almost everywhere, it seems, except in our homeland. Few of us can speak English, and even fewer white men can speak Chinese. Our way of life is vastly different, and we are hated for our frugality and our industry. We work together and threaten the concept of independence, and we are content to scrape our hands raw, scrabbling in old workings. We are called locusts. We are seen as filthy, idolatrous and immoral. It is believed that when we are not mating with each other we will try to mate with white women, therefore contaminating the British character of this fine colony.' Wong Fu paused. 'But I believe we would have to mate with a lot of white women to do *that*.'

'Quite,' Rian agreed. 'I suppose the obvious question is: why do you stay?'

'We make much money here,' Wong Chi-Ping interrupted. 'We send it home to our families. Kwangtung Province is poor, our villages are poor. It is why we come here.'

'I have heard you operate in specific groups, is that right?' Simon asked.

'That is correct,' said Wong Fu. 'Under the credit-ticket system, each group — sometimes they are as small as thirty, sometimes as large as a hundred or more — borrows money from a broker in China to come here. These groups are connected by kinship and community, and they are led by an individual of some standing and wealth. The borrowed money is paid back to the broker from earnings from gold, and the rest is sent home.'

'And who is that individual in your group?' Rian asked.

'My brother, Kai,' Wong Fu replied. 'He is in Melbourne.'

'And how long will you stay here?'

'We do not know.' Wong Chi-Ping shrugged his thin shoulders. 'Perhaps until the gold runs out? How long will *you* stay, Captain?'

★ ★ ★

Good question, Rian thought as he trotted along the Main Road. McCool hadn't been ridden for a week, and pulled at the bit, tossing his head and skittering sideways at imagined dangers in every narrow alleyway. All the signs indicated that they would hit the lead in the next few days. They'd gone reasonably deep now, near enough to forty yards, and had spent some time slabbing and rendering the sides of the shaft for safety. The windlass used to lower and lift the men and buckets had started off flat on the ground, but, during the sinking, the mullock brought up to the surface had gradually piled up until the windlass had finished up sitting on a small hill, packed in place by a retaining wall of logs. If the washdirt proved to be good — if the ore in the lead did actually *contain* gold — the crew intended to build a shelter for whoever was operating the windlass, and for resting in. A sail had already been erected to ventilate the shaft, as the air became foul at a depth of around fifteen feet. And if the lead *really* paid and there was potential for going even deeper, Rian had plans to employ a whip, which entailed buying a workhorse — another expense — which would raise and lower the buckets without everyone having to nigh-on kill themselves slaving over the windlass.

But, of course, if the lead they struck yielded little, or it turned out they had missed the lead altogether, all that time and money would have been wasted.

However, Rian had other business to attend to today, and he wasn't looking forward to it. At the northern end of Red Hill he turned off the road and made his way to what appeared to be a private house set a short distance from the road. He had been told, when he'd discreetly enquired, that 'you can't miss it', and actually you couldn't. The establishment was single-storeyed, of unpainted wood and fronted by a rather precarious-looking verandah, but was catapulted from the ordinary by a huge sign painted across the front wall in red and gold copperplate proclaiming *Lily Pearce's Saloon of Delight*. Rian reined in and dismounted, tying McCool to the verandah rail and hoping that nothing spooked him, or he'd have the whole verandah off and dragging across the diggings behind him.

He stepped up, knocked on the door and waited, but not for long. It soon opened to reveal a girl standing in a short chemise, blue stockings and grey suede boots that laced up to her knees. Her hair was falling out of its clips, her breasts out of her stays, and she smelled as though she could do with a good wash.

'Er, good morning,' Rian said. 'I'd like to see Lily Pearce, if you will.'

'Ooh, yes, an' I *know* she wants to see *you*,' the girl replied, grinning. 'I know who *you* are.'

'Would you just fetch her, please?' Rian said wearily.

The girl disappeared, but was back in less than three minutes.

'She says you're to come in.'

'Tell her I'd rather speak with her out here.'

The girl shook her head. 'Nup. She says come

141

inside or she won't see you.'

Rian sighed and took off his hat. In the hall was a carpet runner with frayed edges and an unpleasant-looking stain in the middle of it. There were several not very well executed paintings on the walls featuring women in various stages of undress, and a hall table on which sat a china bowl containing six dead flies.

'Miss Pearce's office is this way,' the girl said, smirking and indicating that Rian should follow her.

They passed an open door; Rian glanced in and noted three bored-looking young women sitting around. Two were chatting and one was knitting. All were dressed only in their undergarments, and Rian wondered if they were cold. Summer had recently arrived at Ballarat, but its warmth hadn't penetrated the dampness he could feel rising up under the house.

The girl in the grey suede boots knocked on a door and opened it, announcing triumphantly, 'Here he is, Miss Pearce!'

Office my arse, thought Rian as he went in. Lily Pearce had arranged herself elegantly at her desk, a ledger book open in front of her and her legs crossed to show a hint of silk-clad calf.

'Captain Farrell,' she cooed. 'How *delightful* to see you. I knew you'd come to see me sooner or later.'

As well as the desk, the room contained a large, white-painted iron bed draped with a red comforter and matching cushions, a tin bath in one corner, an armchair, and a pair of huge armoires, one of which featured a built-in mirror, bowl and accompanying ewer.

'I'm here on business, Miss Pearce. Personal, but business all the same.'

Lily smiled. 'Yes. Most men who come to see me are after some sort of transaction or another, Captain. Or can I call you Rian?'

'No, you can't.'

Lily rose from the desk and, her hips swaying, walked slowly across to the armchair where she subsided gracefully in a way that caused her low-cut bodice to gape even wider, 'Well, I don't mind calling you captain, Captain. You can be the pirate master and I'll be the slave girl you've captured from some exotic corner of the world.'

'For Christ's sake, I'm not here for that!' Rian said through gritted teeth, valiantly resisting the urge to stride across the room and slap the bloody woman. 'I'm here to tell you to keep the bloody hell away from me. And my wife. And my crew, if it comes to that. You're a troublemaker, Lily Pearce, and there's nothing at all about you I'm remotely interested in.'

'Not even this?' Lily asked shamelessly as she slowly slid her skirts up her legs, past pale pink stockings and white flesh, finally revealing a bush of dark hair nestled between her parted thighs.

A wave of anger and intense frustration swept through Rian, but to his horror he felt his cock, completely independently, begin to swell in his trousers. He thanked God he had his hat in his lap.

'No, not even that. Come on, Lily, why would I be interested in scrag-ends other men have picked over when I have choice tenderloin in my bed every night?'

There was a ringing silence as the belated realisation that Rian truly did dislike her, perhaps even scorned her, cut sudden ugly lines into Lily's painted face. She slammed her legs shut, leaned forward and spat, 'You *bastard!* How *dare* you!'

Rian felt his erection deflate immediately.

'Get out of my house!' Lily's face was white with fury. 'You'll pay for this, Rian Farrell. By Christ, you'll *pay!*'

Rian stood, relieved to be on his way. 'Just so long as you stay away from me and mine, understand?'

Her hand quivering with rage, Lily pointed to the door. 'Go on, fuck off!'

So Rian did.

Part Two

To Stand Truly by Each Other

8

Ballarat, November 1854

Rian had some excellent news for Kitty: this afternoon they had hit the lead, and the very first bucket of washdirt had shown the colour. Not just tiny, barely visible flakes, either, but actual nuggets; most not much bigger than match-heads, but a couple the size of peas. There had only been time to put a couple of buckets through a cradle before the sun started to go down, but tomorrow they would begin working the long tom, sluicing the washdirt as fast as they could dig it out and bring it up.

From now on, one of the crew would be sleeping above the shaft with a loaded shotgun, and tonight Gideon had drawn the short straw. Someone would have to take his supper out to him.

'What's Pierre cooking tonight?' Rian asked as they rattled in the cart towards home.

Hawk, sitting on the seat beside him, replied, 'Pork? He said yesterday he was seeing the butcher about a pig.'

'I thought it was going to be one of his gumbos,' Simon said in a jerky voice, bouncing around in the back.

'I could eat a whole pig meself, so I could,' Mick remarked. 'I'm starving.'

They were almost back at Lilac Cottage now,

in high spirits and prattling on, looking forward to a good supper and a few whiskeys perhaps to celebrate.

'Is that Wong Fu?' Rian pointed towards a shadowy figure dodging between the huts and tents. 'What's he's doing here?'

By the time the cart had stopped outside the cottage, Wong Fu was knocking on the door.

'Mr Wong,' Rian said as he jumped down, 'good to see you.'

But Wong Fu was not his usual calm, inscrutable self. 'I must speak with you, Captain. It is urgent.'

Rian ushered him into house. Kitty, sitting in the rocking chair darning socks, looked up. 'Mr Wong? What are you doing here?'

The Chinese man's hands were pressed against his belly, each gripping the opposite wrist, the skin of both white from the pressure. 'Bao has not come home. I told her to be home before the sun was properly set. When did she leave here?'

Rian and Kitty exchanged a look of dawning horror. 'Amber was spending the afternoon with Bao *at your* camp.'

'No, Bao was coming here,' Wong Fu whispered.

And all three of them, realised that something was very, very wrong.

★ ★ ★

They formed into three search parties: Hawk, Wong Fu, Rian and Pierre in the first; Haunui,

Tahi and Daniel in the second; Ropata, Simon and Mick making up the third. Rian wished Gideon was with them, but there wasn't time to fetch him.

Leena also asked to join the search, but Ropata told her to stay behind and mind the children and the tents. Kitty insisted on coming.

'No,' Rian said as he checked that his pistol was loaded. He stuffed the powder horn, balls and caps into a pocket, half-cocked the pistol and slid the barrel under his belt.

The door was open and everyone waiting outside, but Kitty didn't care as she rushed around looking for her cape and her stout boots. 'But she's my daughter.'

'No,' Rian repeated, very quietly.

'But I can't let her wander around in the dark by herself.'

'Kitty, I said no.'

'But Rian — '

'*I bloody well said no!*' he shouted right into her face, standing over her so she was forced to take a step back. 'No, all right? Stay here!'

Then he was gone, leaving Kitty staring after him in shocked dismay and dizzy with horrible, grinding fear.

Outside Rian exhaled raggedly, experiencing exactly the same emotions as his wife. He had bullied her, and harshly, but he was terrified of what they might find, and the thought of Kitty being there was almost more than he could bear. He caught Hawk watching him and looked away.

'Where should we start?' Hawk asked quietly, calmly.

149

'I don't know, do I?' Rian snapped.

Hawk could see that his friend was in no fit state to lead the search. Normally he was extremely capable and level-headed, but not when it came to his precious daughter.

To Haunui he said, 'You, Tahi and Daniel go along the road towards Red Hill and the Camp. Simon? You men go into the gullies towards Golden Point. And ask everyone you pass whether they have seen them. We will go east out along Navy Jack's Lead and the Canadian, and around the tents there.' He turned to Rian. 'What time do you want to meet up again?'

'We won't. We'll keep looking until we find them.'

Hawk made an arbitrary decision. 'We will meet at eleven o'clock back here. We will eat, then we will go back out again.'

Rian seemed satisfied and turned away, ready to go. But then he paused, and said, 'And if we find them, and they've been — ' he glanced at Wong Fu, wondering if his own face was as awash with fright as the Chinese man's. 'If someone's got them, then *I* want to deal with them. *My* way. Understand?'

Everyone nodded, and set off.

Rian's party had not been walking for more than ten minutes before footsteps came pounding along behind them.

'Rian! Rian, man, stop. Wait!'

Patrick O'Riley was pelting down the track after them, dodging potholes in the rapidly fading light, his gun in one hand, hat in the other. Panting, he pulled up and bent over, his

150

hands on his knees. 'Kitty told me what's happened, so she did. Thought I could lend a hand seein' as I've been here a lot longer. Know more people, you see. Know where they live and that.'

Grateful, Rian nodded. 'Thanks, Patrick. Appreciate it.'

They walked on, looking left and right, in every shaft and pit, behind every mullock pile, and calling out at every tent, hut and shanty they passed. A few hard-hearted bastards shouted at them to shut up and piss off, which made Rian want to pound them to a pulp, but a gratifying number of passers-by stopped and asked who they were looking for, and said they'd keep their eyes open.

'How many friends has the lass got?' Patrick asked after a while.

With a jolt Rian realised that he didn't know, that he had spent so much time lately up to his waist in muddy water that he'd lost touch with his daughter's daily affairs. 'Just Bao, I think,' he said, looking to Wong Fu for confirmation.

The other man nodded. 'Bao has not said anything about another playmate. I would know.'

'So no other friends at all? Not even acquaintances?' Patrick probed. 'Not even to say hello to in the street? Lasses? Adults? Women? I might be after knowing them, you see.'

'No. I'm pretty sure — ' Then Rian remembered something that had happened at the dance. 'A chap named . . . Christ, what was it? Apparently comes into the bakery all the time. Stirling? Sewell? Scurr?'

151

Patrick's face fell. 'Ah, *shite*. Searle?'

'That's it.' Rian's eyes suddenly narrowed. 'Why?'

Patrick looked as though he wished he were anywhere else but standing in front of Rian. 'Josiah Searle. He's, well . . . ah God, how do I say it?' He blew out his cheeks and took a precautionary step backwards. 'I'm sorry, Rian. Some say he's one for the girls. The young girls.'

Rian remained utterly motionless for several seconds, then kicked viciously at a mullock pile, sending gravel and dirt scattering in all directions.

'Steady,' Hawk warned, laying a hand on Rian's shaking arm. 'We do not know whether this man even has them.'

Remembering Searle's cheery smile as he lounged on the counter chatting to Amber, Pierre said, almost to himself, 'I will kill him.'

Wong Fu said nothing, simply stood with his fists clenched by his sides, his face rigid.

'Does he live by himself, this Searle?' Hawk asked Patrick.

'He *was* livin' in a shack out past the end of Navy Jack's, with an eejit called Alfred Tuttle. And he is an eejit — the man's half-witted. But Searle had the shite beaten out of himself back in July, and he might have set up his swag somewhere else by now.'

'Could you find this shanty?' Rian asked.

'I think so,' Patrick replied, hoping he hadn't just signed an innocent man's death warrant. But he didn't think he had.

Rian checked for the third time that his pistol

was loaded. 'Come on then, let's go.'

'Is that a good idea?' Hawk asked, nodding at the gun.

But Rian didn't answer.

They moved in silence now: Rian didn't want to alert Searle to their approach.

After close to half an hour it seemed they had passed the last derelict shacks some time ago; uninhabitable affairs that had collapsed into the mud during the winter. This far out, the sounds of the diggings were muted.

Rian stopped, peering around the now moonlit landscape. 'You're sure this is the right way, Patrick?'

' 'Tis.' He held a finger to his lips and pointed.

A hundred yards away a squat little hut came into focus, a faint line of yellow light spilling from a window. Suddenly a yelping sound ensued from the shanty. Rian raised his pistol, fully cocked now, and felt his heart lurch into his mouth as the door flew open and two figures, hand-in-hand, shot out and raced towards them. A second later he was almost sick as he realised he'd been about to shoot his own daughter.

Amber launched herself at him and he dropped the pistol and gathered her in his arms. 'Amber, sweetheart, are you all right?' But she wasn't — he could see that her lip was bleeding. 'Oh, Christ, love, did he hurt you?'

'They tried. We have to go, Pa. I'm frightened of those men.'

Men? Rian felt an incandescent rage rise up in him. 'In there?' He gestured at the shanty.

Amber nodded, and started to cry.

So did Bao. She had collapsed and was crouched in a huddled heap, keening quietly, her delicate hands covering her face. Wong Fu squatted before her, his hands fluttering helplessly over hers, trying to calm her, speaking to her gently in Chinese. The fastenings on the front of her jacket had been torn and he clumsily tried to do them up again, but she let out an anguished wail and jerked away from him, scrabbling at the fabric and wrenching the garment closed herself. Then she turned her head and vomited a stream of watery bile onto the ground.

Rian, fury making his voice almost unrecognisable, tuned to the Irishman. 'Patrick, take them home, can you? Tell Kitty we'll be back shortly. Tell her we're . . . dealing with it.'

Patrick understood exactly what was going to happen, and condoned it wholeheartedly. He slung his gun over his shoulder and held out his hands. 'Come on, lasses, let's go home, shall we?'

'Wong Fu?' Rian looked at Bao's father. 'Do you want to stay or go back?'

The tears running down the man's cheeks caught the moonlight, but his jaw was clenched when he answered, 'I will stay.'

Bao seemed on the verge of fainting. Patrick offered to carry her, but she immediately shrank from his outstretched hand, so Amber settled an arm protectively around her. The Chinese girl clung to her so tightly that Amber felt the fabric of her dress tear.

As Patrick led the girls away, Rian, Hawk, Pierre and Wong Fu crept up on the shanty.

Then Rian kicked in the door.

Two men sat on wooden crates in front of a small fire. The smaller of the pair nursed a copiously bleeding nose, while the larger, a man with a shock of red hair that obviously hadn't been cut or brushed for some time, was hunched over with his hands clamped on his privates, moaning to himself. What meagre possessions there were lay scattered around the shanty — a single spindly chair on its side, the bedding from two bedrolls kicked about, and the remains of what appeared to be a meal of cabbage, meat and perhaps damper strewn all over the floor.

'Josiah Searle?' Rian demanded, pointing the barrel of his pistol directly at the man's face.

Searle nodded miserably. He seemed to have bite marks across the bridge of his nose.

'Who's this?'

'Alfred Tuttle.' Searle said quickly, clearly keen to share the blame for whatever had gone on in the shanty.

'Did you lay a hand on those girls?'

Searle blinked up at him. 'What girls?'

Rian kicked the crate out from underneath him so that he sprawled on the dirt floor. 'My *daughter*, Searle, Wong Fu's *daughter! Those* girls!'

Searle righted himself. 'I didn't touch them.'

'We didn't do nothing,' Tuttle mumbled. 'She kicked me in the nuts, that one with the pretty hair.'

Rian didn't believe either of them. 'For God's sake, they're children!'

'You were *going* to touch her, Josiah,' Tuttle

accused Searle. 'And you slapped her face.'

'Shut up! *You* tore the Chinkee girl's blouse!'

Rian fired his pistol at the roof to shut both of them up.

'Stop it!' Searle whined, his hands over his ears. 'I can't help it — I've tried, but I can't.'

Apparently not bothered by the noise, Tuttle wiped his nose on the back of his hand and said, 'Got nice tits, the Chinkee girl.'

Pierre stepped over to him and gave his flank a swift, hard kick.

'If you let us go we'll never go near them again,' Searle pleaded.

'No, you won't go near them again,' Rian said, 'and let this be a reminder.'

He reached down, dragged Searle up off the floor and punched him in the face. Then he did it again. And when Searle fell down, he kicked him hard in the kidneys. But when he dragged him back up by the hair, Hawk grabbed his arm.

'No, Rian, leave him. You might kill him. He is not worth swinging for. You, too. Pierre. Let him be.'

Pierre was only two-thirds the size and weight of Tuttle, but such was his rage that he had managed to rip out a chunk of his hair, knock out two of his teeth and bloody his nose.

And through it all Wong Fu stood by the door and watched, his face impassive.

★　★　★

'Did they interfere with her?'

'She says not.'

Rian felt ill with relief. 'And Bao?'

Kitty shook her head. 'Thank God, though it was close.'

'What's she doing now?'

'Having a wash. She'll be out in a minute. Put your hand back in the basin.'

Rian dangled his swollen knuckles in the warm salted water again. They stung where he'd grazed them against Searle's ugly perverted head.

They sat in silence, the lamplight flickering on their dismayed, weary faces.

Eventually, Rian said, 'She lied to us.'

'I know she did. But she shouldn't have been able to. I should have known where she was.'

'You thought you did. You thought she was with Bao at the Chinese camp.'

'But if I wasn't so busy at the bakery, I'd be spending more time with her.'

'And if I wasn't so busy trying to become the richest bloody man in the Southern Hemisphere, *I'd* be spending more time with her.'

Kitty shook her head slowly and blinked back tears. 'God, Rian, she wasn't even safe with Bao. The two of them together, and they weren't safe.'

They gazed at each other remorsefully until Amber appeared and sat down at the table. She had scrubbed herself from head to toe, and her hair was wrapped in a towel and piled on top of her head. Her poor lip was swollen from the slap she'd received and her face was very pale.

Rian folded his good hand over hers. 'What happened, sweetheart? You don't have to tell me

157

the bits you talked to your mother about, but what happened?'

So she told them.

She and Bao had gone to the circus. She had already been once with Kitty, but she'd wanted Bao to see it, too. They'd both known, however, that they would not be permitted to go alone, especially not by Bao's father, so they'd gone anyway. And yes, she was very sorry now that they had lied, but the circus at least had been good.

When the performance had finished just after three o'clock, Amber had seen Mr Searle at the entrance to the tent, standing with his hat in his hand. She had waved and he had approached them, saying he had a message for her from her mother.

'I was at the bakery earlier and she's asked me to take you to pick up some new aprons she's ordered for the shop. Pretty ones with the name embroidered on the pockets.'

And Amber had said, 'But she doesn't know I'm here. She thinks I'm at the Chinese camp.'

Mr Searle had winked at her then. 'Is that where you're supposed to be? I thought the pair of you looked like you were up to something! I saw you after I left the bakery and followed you here, but I didn't want to interrupt your treat. I know how children love the circus. My daughters do, anyway.'

His message had annoyed Amber — surely her mother trusted her to look after herself while she walked into town from the Chinese camp to the draper on the Main Road?

'Which draper?' she had asked.

'They're not at the draper's. Your mother had a seamstress make them up. She lives out on Navy Jack's. Her husband's a digger. Not a very lucky one, by all accounts, so she makes ends meet doing a bit of sewing.'

'We do excellent tailoring at our camp,' Bao had said to Amber. 'We could have made you lovely aprons.'

And Mr Searle had given Bao a strange and not very friendly look.

Amber had wondered why Kitty couldn't collect the aprons herself, but supposed she must be busy, and could see this afternoon's lie unravelling if she didn't do as she was asked, so they had gone with Mr Searle.

'It's a long way out,' Amber had said.

'We're almost there, see?' Mr Searle had said, finally indicating a tiny hut.

Mr Searle had knocked and called out, 'Mrs Dunne, the young lady is here for the aprons!' and opened the door for them.

But as soon as they were inside he had slammed the door shut. And there had been no Mrs Dunne in the hut, just a big ugly man with wild carrotty hair.

'And the hut smelt, Pa. It smelt of *really* dirty bodies and farts. We were nearly sick,' Amber said, screwing up her face at the recent memory.

Bao had run to the door, but Mr Searle had barred the way, grinning and giggling like the monkeys they had seen in the circus. He had pushed Bao and she had fallen down, then the big man had picked her up and dumped her in a corner, and put Amber there as well. The girls had yelled and screamed, but no one had come to help them.

Then the two men had had an argument. The big one, whom Mr Searle had called Albert, had wanted to get straight down to 'doing the business', but Mr Searle had wanted her and Bao to be 'their wives'. He was sick of eating bad cooking, he'd complained, and he'd always wanted a pretty girl for a wife instead of the sour old bat he'd been saddled with in England, and what could be nicer and more fitting than a good meal followed by the conjugal rights owed a man by his loving bride? Albert could have Bao, because he wanted Amber.

In an effort to stall for time, Amber had asked Mr Searle how his daughters would feel about their father pretending to be married to someone who wasn't their mother.

'And do you know what he did, Pa?' Amber said, tears forming again and spilling down her cheeks. 'And this is just about the worst bit. He just laughed and said there had never *been* any daughters! He said he'd made all that up so there would be something to talk about in the bakery! He took me for a fool, Pa. He *tricked* me!'

He tricked all of us, Kitty thought miserably, and wished to hell she'd paid more attention the dozens of times the bloody man had been in the shop.

So Amber and Bao had made Albert Tuttle and Josiah Searle a meal of mutton, cabbage and damper. While they waited for the mutton stew to cook — and, to their delight, it had taken over an hour and a half — they were told to clean up the shanty, which was in a filthy state. All the while, Tuttle had sat on the single chair with his back against the door, watching their every move, and Mr Searle had perched on a crate in front of the fire, smiling to himself and humming happily with anticipation.

Finally, the food was ready. Amber and Bao had been offered a share but had refused.

'That made Mr Searle angry,' Amber said. 'He said it was very rude of us, and a real wife would be pleased to be invited to eat with her husband.'

'What time was this?' Rian asked, wondering how far away he and the search party had been at the time.

'I don't know, but it had gone dark.'

Amber and Bao had sat in the corner growing more and more fearful as the men consumed their meal. Then Tuttle had put aside his plate, wiped his hands on his shirt, burped loudly and ordered Bao to stand in front of him. When she refused, he dragged her across the room to the fire and ripped open the front of her jacket, exposing her golden skin and budding breasts. She struck out at him, but he batted away her hand and tried to press his greasy lips against hers. Horrified, Amber had leapt after Bao and darted around behind Tuttle. His knees were bowed as he bent to accommodate Bao's diminutive height and Amber delivered an almighty, well-aimed kick to his baggy crotch that sent him grimacing in silent agony to his knees, then onto his side on the floor.

Searle, appalled that his lovely evening had gone so suddenly wrong, reached for Amber, grabbed a fistful of hair and slapped her face, opening the cut on her lip. Bao, her normally serene eyes flashing with shame and fury, grasped the front of Searle's waistcoat, launched herself upward, clamped her teeth on his nose and bit down hard. Then, amidst the groaning and outraged squealing, Amber had taken her hand and they'd run for the door.

'And there you were, Pa,' Amber finished. 'I knew you'd come and find us. I knew we'd be all right.'

★   ★   ★

Rian sat at the table nursing a glass of brandy. His *sixth* glass of brandy, if truth be told. Kitty and Amber had gone to bed. Amber had not wanted to sleep out here on her own tonight, and he had offered to take the daybed. His vision was blurring slightly — whether from the brandy or fatigue he wasn't sure — but the more he drank the more he became convinced that he knew who was behind Amber's abduction. And poor little Bao's, although he didn't believe she had been the primary target — she'd just had the misfortune of being Amber's friend. What the hell was he going to say to Wong Fu the next time they met?

No, it had been an orchestrated kidnap, and he knew who had planned it. Who in Ballarat had it in for him — especially him — and for Kitty? And who, in particular, would know about the nasty little proclivities of a man like Josiah Searle?

Lily Pearce, without a doubt. She would have put the dirty shite up to it, he was sure. Probably even paid him to do it.

He drained his glass and poured himself another. Then stood, reached for his hat and left the cottage.

In the bedroom Kitty lay awake, both Amber and Bodie snuggled against her chest, dreading to think what he was off to do now.

★   ★   ★

'Open the door!' Rian shouted, banging on it again. 'Open up!'

A pale face peered out of the window. 'Hold your 'orses, Mister. There's plenty for everyone!'

Inside someone was playing a piano, accompanied by laughter and muted shrieks.

'I want to see Lily Pearce *now*!' Rian demanded.

'You're a keen one, ain't ya?' the girl remarked, looking him up and down.

'Just shut up and send her out.'

The girl, finally realising he was highly irate, not desperate for sex, pulled her head in and disappeared.

Waiting, Rian paced up and down the verandah.

Lily finally appeared in her underwear, a floaty peignoir of some sort draped about her shoulders. 'Oh, it's you,' she disdainfully. 'What do you want?'

'Did you send Josiah Searle after my daughter?'

Lily looked nonplussed. 'Josiah Searle? The one who fancies young girls? No. Why would I do that?'

'My arse, you didn't.'

'Good idea, though. That would have taught you a lesson, wouldn't it?'

Rian leaned forward and breathed brandy fumes in her face. 'He took her and her friend this afternoon and had them holed up in his filthy little shack with some half-wit called Albert Tuttle. Christ knows what they would have done if we hadn't found them in time.'

Raising her arched eyebrows condescendingly, Lily said, 'Still in one piece, are they?'

'Yes, they are. Just.'

Lily made a dismissive gesture with her hand. 'What age is your daughter? Thirteen? Fourteen? That's not that tender, you know. Wouldn't have been the end of the world. I've got girls that young working here.'

Rian glared at her through bleary eyes, running through a range of suitable responses he couldn't seem to coax out of his mouth. 'I'll prove you were behind this if it's the last thing I do.'

Making a show of stifling a yawn, Lily replied, 'Well, I wasn't, so don't waste your time. And rest assured, *Captain*, when I take my revenge, it won't be as simple as giving your daughter a fright. Oh no, it will be much worse than that. *Much* worse.'

'You're full of shit, Lily Pearce.'

'And you're full of booze. Go home to your precious wife,' Lily snapped, and slammed the door in his face.

★ ★ ★

The bell over the bakery door chimed as Flora entered, her face uncharacteristically grim.

'I heard about what happened last night,' she said to Kitty as she set her basket on the counter. 'Is she all right?'

Kitty nodded and inclined her head towards Amber, who was rolling out dough on the table, in a manner that suggested Flora should perhaps mind what she said.

But Flora ignored her. She lifted the hatch in the counter, stepped through and laid a gentle hand on Amber's shoulder. 'I can imagine it was a terrifying experience for you, dear.'

Amber stopped rolling. 'It *was* quite awful.'

'Did they . . . harm you anywhere?'

'No, except I got a fat lip.'

Flora shared a glance of intense relief with Kitty.

'But they were going to,' Amber said, who, after her talk with her mother the night before, understood what Flora meant. 'And the big stupid one tore Bao's jacket and looked at her bosoms.'

'Oh, poor sweet Bao.' The *coque* feathers on Flora's hat fluttered as she shook her head angrily. 'I'll call on her and her father later this morning, make sure she's all right. I heard you kicked Mr Tuttle in the balls, dear?'

'Yes. It was really satisfying.'

165

'*Good* girl! But you have to remember, Amber, that not all men are like that. In fact *most* aren't. There are plenty of fine men in this world, so don't let this put you off. Your father is one of them. So is Pierre.'

Pierre, shaping *croissants* and pretending not to listen, blushed furiously.

'And so are all the other men who work for your father. And once you find a good one, you should keep him, because he'll be worth holding on to.'

Kitty blinked in surprise. Given Flora's, preferences, she had assumed that Flora would have little to say in men's favour — she certainly had no qualms about taking financial advantage of their desire for the charms of women.

Careful not to get flour on her black gown, Flora leant against the table. 'Have you heard yet about what else has happened?'

Kitty and Pierre stared at her expectantly, not even noticing when someone came into the shop.

With far too much cheer for what she was about to impart, Flora said, 'Josiah Searle and Albert Tuttle died in the small hours of this morning. Apparently, they burned to death in their shanty.'

And Kitty's heart thudded wildly as she remembered the door closing so quietly after Rian had gone out last night.

★   ★   ★

Flora accepted the tiny cup of tea that Wong Fu passed to her. Bao was shaken, and feeling

166

deeply ashamed regarding what had happened to her, but physically she was unharmed.

'Do you think she will be all right?' Flora asked.

'I hope so. She takes things very much to heart. She can be very . . . delicate,' Wong Fu replied. For a moment he looked extremely sad and tired. Then he sighed. 'No, I fear she may not be. She has always been frightened of white men. To her they are too big, and too loud and foul-smelling. And for her to have one of them touch her . . . '

'Yes, I can quite understand that,' Flora agreed wholeheartedly.

Wong Fu's face darkened and he struggled to keep the snarl out of his voice. 'Especially such a filthy cretin as Tuttle. She cannot eat, you know. She cannot hold down food. She says she is not hungry, but I know that is not it.' Wong Fu tapped his head. 'I know what she is seeing. In her mind she is seeing the hands and faces of those pigs, and she knows what they — ' He stopped talking, silenced by his own anger. He forced his shoulders to relax and took a long, measured breath. 'I beg your pardon, Mrs McRae.'

'Of course. If there is ever anything I can do . . . '

'Yes, thank you. You have visited Captain and Mrs Farrell?'

'I saw Kitty this morning, yes.'

'How is the child Amber?'

'Shaken, but bearing up. Forgive me for saying so, but she seems to be cut from more resilient cloth than Bao.'

167

'Yes, and that is a blessing for her mother and father.'

'It is.' Flora hesitated. 'You will have heard the news?'

'What news is that?'

'Tuttle and Searle died this morning. An unfortunate accident involving an oil lamp.'

There was a long silence. Finally, Wong Fu said, 'That is unfortunate. Is your tea hot enough?'

'It's fine, thank you. But I didn't need to tell you about that, did I?'

'No.'

'Because you knew about it before anyone else.' A statement, not a question.

Another silence. Then, 'Honour must always be avenged, Mrs McRae.'

9

The inquest into the deaths of Josiah Searle and Albert Tuttle concluded with a finding of accidental death owing to domestic fire. It was not an uncommon occurrence on the diggings, along with fatalities related to disease, accident, and alcohol-related misadventure. They were buried three days after they died, with only the Methodist minister in attendance.

Rian said to Kitty that he wanted to spend less time working on the claim and more with her and Amber. Somewhat taken aback, Kitty told him it was a lovely sentiment but not to let his guilt take precedence over common sense — that was *her* job — especially since the claim now looked as though it might indeed be a good payer, as predicted by the late Mr Murphy, and that minding a child was a mother's responsibility, not a father's. So he continued working with the crew, while she reduced her hours at the bakery to spend more time with her daughter.

Bao still came to visit Amber, and Amber continued to visit the Chinese camp, but Kitty usually walked her there, or sometimes Tahi did, and she was always collected; Bao never again made the trip to or from Lilac Cottage unaccompanied either.

★   ★   ★

169

Kitty, Flora and Amber rode along the Main Road towards Red Hill. Beyond that the ground rose and became the hill that met the road running east towards Melbourne, and on which the smarter stores and businesses had set up in the area known as Bakery Hill, which also included the very busy Lydiard Street. Flora, of course, had shopped on Bakery Hill numerous times, been to the Camp on occasion, and even patronised the handful of exclusive stores in the properly surveyed little grid of streets behind the Camp, but Amber and Kitty had really only visited Bakery Hill when they had arrived in Ballarat in August.

But now it was the beginning of November, and the weather was growing warmer by the day. Warmer, windier and dustier. The wind was hot and came from the north, and the dust, fine as flour, was beginning to drive Kitty mad as it settled on every surface and in every tiny crevice. When the rain had stopped, the mud had dried, leaving for several weeks strange, miniature geological formations that had quickly been eroded by the rising winds, turned into dust and was now adorning the clothes, belongings, skin and, on particularly bad days, the teeth and eyes of all who ventured out in it. The winds would pass, so it was said, and Kitty was praying for the day, and wishing vehemently to be back on board the *Katipo*, with a brisk sea breeze tugging at her hair and sparkling spray from the bow cooling her face.

They rode slowly, as Amber wasn't yet confident on horseback. She'd never really had the opportunity to learn to ride, having spent the latter ten of her fourteen years learning to be a sailor on the *Katipo*, scampering barefooted around the decks, hauling in sails and shinnying up riggings like a monkey. Kitty, on the other hand, had been riding all her life, missed it very much and leapt at any chance to do so, although preferably not side-saddle, as she was having to do now. But Amber, just young enough to get away with sitting astride, was using Rian's saddle.

Flora, perched daintily atop her own coal-black mount, looked, as always, like a fashion plate from a lady's magazine come to life. But Kitty, in a smart day dress and her best boots, knew that she also looked attractive. She wasn't especially vain, but she recognised an admiring glance when she saw one. And it was all, she was sure, because today she wasn't wearing her despised bonnet, which this morning she had given away to Binda.

Flora was taking her and Amber shopping in the fancy stores, but first they were treating themselves to morning tea at Bath's Hotel. Leaving the horses tethered outside, they went in, sat down at a table and ordered. As they waited, a woman passed the window, glanced in, then entered.

Approaching the table, she said, 'Hello, Flora, I've not seen you for some time. How are you?'

'Very well, thank you, Eleanor,' Flora replied. 'We're just about to enjoy a cup of tea. Would you care to join us?'

The woman thought for a second. 'Thank you, but I really must get to the post office before the mail coach leaves.'

'Perhaps on your way back? I imagine we'll still be here.'

'Really? That would be lovely, thank you.'

'That was Mrs Eleanor Buckley,' Flora said when the young woman had hurried off. 'Her husband is a Camp official — well, a clerk — and her brother is a digger. She married 'up' before the gold rush. Or should I say, her husband didn't marry very far down. She's a very intelligent woman, her husband a little less so. A decent man, though, I suspect, constrained by the demands of his job. Eleanor has proved rather helpful regarding certain matters relating to my claims.'

'You own a claim?' Kitty was surprised, then wondered why: Flora was a very astute businesswoman.

'I own several. This is Ballarat, after all.'

Eleanor Buckley returned ten minutes later. A pretty woman in her mid-twenties with pale red hair, hazel eyes, and a smattering of freckles across her nose and cheeks, she greeted Flora properly this time with a kiss.

'Eleanor, this is my friend Mrs Kitty Farrell, and her daughter, Amber.'

'Good morning, Mrs Farrell,' Eleanor said, as she fluffed out her skirts and sat down. 'Hello, Amber.' She untied the ribbons on her bonnet, then set it on a chair at the next table.

Flora summoned the serving girl and asked for extra tea and cakes. Amber, by now bored and fidgeting, said, 'Ma, can I go for a walk along the street?'

'No, you can't,' Kitty and Flora replied in unison.

Amber sighed in weary resignation and pulled a battered copy of *Wuthering Heights* out of her pinafore pocket.

When the refreshments arrived, Flora poured the tea and sat back. 'Kitty, Eleanor is very familiar with what's been happening on the Victorian goldfields over the past few years. If you wanted to know about anything, she could well be a good person to ask.'

Kitty felt awkward, and vaguely embarrassed. 'It's not so much that I have a burning interest in the situation here at Ballarat, Mrs Buckley, it's more that I have a husband who from time to time sees himself as a crusader. He likes to — how shall I put it — champion the underdog.'

'And you don't think he should?' Eleanor Buckley asked. 'Or do you not think that underdogs should be championed?'

'Neither,' Kitty replied. 'I simply like to know what my husband is getting himself into. Forewarned is forearmed, as they say.'

'That's a fair comment.'

'Thank you.' Kitty paused, then said, 'I think you will agree, Mrs Buckley, that it's somewhat unusual for a woman of your station to be knowledgeable about matters such as politics. Please don't think me rude, but may I ask how you find yourself in that situation?'

'Well, that's an easy one to answer,' Eleanor said, grinning. 'My brother Robert has a claim here on Black Hill, and my husband, Carl, is a clerk at the Camp, so I get to hear both sides of the story. Frequently and at great length, I might add.'

She stirred sugar into her cup, then said cryptically, 'Trouble has been brewing on the diggings for some time. I suppose the crux of the matter lies with the licence fee. Well, it certainly started with that. You'll have heard about all this?'

Kitty nodded. She most certainly had — at least half a dozen times from Patrick.

'Well, twenty shillings is still a lot of money, especially if you're not finding any colour. The diggers see it as a tax that benefits the colony, but not necessarily them, and personally I can't argue with that. Carl can, though.'

Kitty cleared her throat. 'Pardon me for saying so, but that must put considerable, er, strain on your marriage, if you don't agree with your husband's point of view,' she said, thinking of the many 'differences of opinion' she and Rian had had.

'Not really,' Eleanor said. 'I just don't listen to what I don't want to hear. Apart from that, Carl is a very good husband.' She reached for the sugar bowl again. 'What the diggers hate even more than the fees are the licence raids by the police. Your husband has a claim, doesn't he, Mrs Farrell? Well, you'd know all about that, then.'

Kitty said yes, and cut herself a small slice of buttermilk cake. Rian complained constantly about the endless police demands to inspect his licence, not to mention the monthly cost. As far as he — and by most accounts every other digger in Australia — was concerned, the continent's gold didn't belong to the Queen, so why the hell should they have to pay her for the privilege of digging it out?

'The gold commissioners are a problem, too,' Eleanor went on. 'They were appointed as soon as the rush in Victoria got under way. Some of them have been good, most have been useless — plainly incompetent, or just not up to the job. Unfortunately, the good ones don't seem to last long. They either find the job too odious or they resign because of the corruption.'

She wrinkled her top lip in distaste. 'Then there are the police and the police magistrates. But there have never been enough police, despite what the diggers might think. Any dross can enlist, and they do, and they're underpaid and overworked.' She held up a hand. 'No, I don't have any sympathy for them, because most are as mean as dogs. All I'm saying is, they don't have the ability or the character to do the job properly. And neither do most of the police magistrates. They're corrupt, the lot of them — they take bribes, they blackmail, and they bully. You know that every fine a policeman collects, he pockets half? They're at the root of most of the trouble on the diggings.'

Flora laughed. 'Eleanor, are you saying that if it weren't for the police throwing their weight around, every digger would be paying his licence fee and refraining from sly-grogging?'

Eleanor rolled her eyes. 'Of course not! But

the Joes have made it worse. And that's why the military have been called in.'

Kitty nodded: they'd been all over the diggings of late. 'Who are they?'

'The 40th Regiment of Foot,' Flora replied. 'We've been seeing rather a lot of them.'

Amber looked up from her book. 'Ma, it says here, 'In vapid listlessness I leant my head against the window'. What does 'vapid' mean?'

Kitty thought about it. 'Well, do you remember when I found you in Auckland and you came to stay at Mrs Fleming's house with me and Flora and Hattie? And how Hattie sighed a lot and said silly things and sometimes didn't understand what we were talking about? Well, Hattie was 'vapid'.'

Flora cackled into her tea.

'Oh,' Amber said, and went back to Emily Brontë.

Kitty squinted at the spine of Amber's book. 'What are you reading? *That's* not suitable for a young girl! Give me that!' She snatched the book from Amber and stuffed it in her reticule.

'You might have heard about the monster meeting in December '51 at Forest Creek?' Eleanor said.

Kitty nodded again.

'Well, there was another one in October the following year at Castlemaine.'

'That's a lot of monsters,' Amber remarked.

'Read your book, dear.'

'That started the Red Ribbon Rebellion. You know about that?'

Kitty did.

'Anyway, the whole thing ended in acrimony, the petition was turned down, and La Trobe blamed everything on what he decided were gold miners with no real grounds for protest, foreigners with anti-monarchical ideas, and secret associations of subversives.' Eleanor gave a small smile. 'I wouldn't say that myself. What's happening on the diggings is hardly revolutionary. It's simply the beginnings of political consciousness, of an awareness of what constitutes the proper rights of a citizen.'

Kitty blinked. 'Really? That sounds like the rhetoric of a Chartist, Mrs Buckley.'

'Yes, I suppose it does, doesn't it?'

That must sit well with Carl, Kitty reflected.

'But after the Red Ribbon Rebellion, things quietened again, except that the police seemed to become even more obnoxious. Even though the licence fee went down, the system stayed more or less the same, and the diggers' rights remained withheld. By early this year they seemed to have lost heart.' Eleanor sat back, toying with a sugar cube, tapping at it until a corner broke off. 'It was sad to see, really. Then Hotham arrived and stirred things up, James Scobie was murdered and we had that farce of a trial. And then there was the fire. And you must be aware of how restless everyone is about the Scobie inquiry?'

At Hotham's instigation a new trial had begun eight days earlier, and the diggers were fully expecting a verdict of justice for the murdered man. God help Hotham if there wasn't one. On top of that, Thomas Fletcher, Andrew McIntyre and Henry Westerby had been arrested several days ago and charged with rioting and burning down the Eureka Hotel, which had further enraged the diggers.

'So what's next, do you think?'

Eleanor shrugged elegantly. 'The Bendigo diggers started up what they've called the Goldfields Reform League last month, so they're organising again, and something might come from that. But I rather think that any significant change is more likely to be the result of something more spontaneous, some more . . . *inflammatory* event.'

'Rian, my husband, was talking about the Bendigo League the other night. He was saying there should be something like that here. Perhaps there should, but I'd rather he left it to someone else to organise. He wouldn't make the most diplomatic of politicians.'

Eleanor's eyebrows had risen in amusement. 'Is your husband *Rian* Farrell? *Captain* Rian Farrell?'

'Yes. Why?'

'It's just that Carl told me an interesting story about someone named Captain Rian Farrell. At least *I* thought it was amusing. He was accidentally arrested instead of Thomas Farrell, wasn't he?'

'Yes, he was,' Kitty replied, bristling slightly. 'And actually, it wasn't particularly amusing. Amber and I were very upset.' Well, somewhat concerned. Rian had been arrested dozens of times, and had always somehow managed to wriggle or buy his way out of the more dire of the consequences.

'And didn't it turn into a brawl involving upwards of thirty men?'

'I believe there were nine policemen versus Rian and his crew of seven.'

Eleanor grinned and drank the last of her tea. 'Your Rian sounds like a very interesting man, Mrs Farrell. I believe he and my brother Robert would get on very well. Perhaps one day they should meet? I have some shopping to do, but is there anything else you'd like to know before I go?'

'I don't think so, Mrs Buckley. It's been very nice to meet you.'

Eleanor reached for her bonnet. 'I have to say it's been very nice talking to you. We live in the town proper behind the Camp and, to be truthful, I don't find conversation with the women there to be terribly stimulating. All they ever seem to talk about is who will be hosting the next dinner party. Carl and I are more or less on the bottom of the social ladder and we rarely get invited to anything, but he insists that we behave as though we should be. It's very tiring. Excuse me, Amber, dear?' Amber looked up from her book. 'Have you read *The Heir of Redclyffe* by Charlotte Yonge yet? It's really very good. I think you'd enjoy it. You can probably order it through one of the general stores.'

When she'd gone, Kitty remarked, 'You do know some interesting people, Flora. How did you meet Eleanor?'

But Flora only smiled.

★　★　★

179

While Kitty was having morning tea with Eleanor Buckley, Rian and the crew were slogging away on the Malakoff Lead. Just before dinner time, Tahi, squatting several hundred yards away atop a huge mullock heap keeping an eye out for police, shouted, 'Coo-ee! Joe! Joe! Licence hunt!' and ran towards the shaft, his bare feet kicking up small puffs of dust as he slid down the hill. All around him, diggers on nearby claims burst into feverish activity like disturbed ants in a nest, either disappearing down holes or departing alto-gether if they were not in possession of the required licence. Tahi vanished into a gully, and when his head popped up again Rian called, 'How many?'

'Three!' Tahi breathlessly shouted back.

Rian, fed up to the back teeth with being threatened at least twice a week by roving bands of bullies and extortionists calling themselves policemen, decided he was in the mood to cause as much trouble as he could. So while other men hid or scrabbled in pockets for crumpled and dog-eared licences, he stood with his arms crossed, waiting.

Eventually the Joes made their way along the meandering line of claims until they reached him. To Rian's grim satisfaction, he recognised Sergeant Coombes. His eyes narrowed, and Hawk, at Rian's side, knew from experience what would inevitably happen next.

Coombes scowled, grunted and stuck out his hand. 'Licence.'

'My *miner's* licence, do you mean?' Rian

queried, as though he hadn't quite compre-
hended the question.

'Yes, your miner's licence,' Coombes replied
impatiently.

Rian patted the pockets in his trousers, his
shirt, and his vest. Then he went back to his
trouser pockets and dug around in them, the
expression on his face becoming progressively
more alarmed. He emptied them, stuffed
everything back, said, 'I know it's here
somewhere', then returned to his shirt pockets.
Nothing. 'I left my jacket at home this morning,'
he explained. 'It's getting so warm of a day now.'
Behind him, the crew smirked. Rian called for
his knapsack, but Coombes interrupted him.

'No! Not good enough. You know the rules.
You've to carry the licence *on* you.'

To hell with you, Rian thought, remembering
the fear on Amber's face when Coombes and his
accomplices had burst into Lilac Cottage. He
scratched his head, '*I* know where it is!' He
removed his hat and upended it, feeling about
the lining, but, it became obvious, to no avail.
Grimly, he put his hat back on. 'I'm afraid I
don't seem to have my licence on me, Sergeant
Coombes. You'll have to arrest me.'

'I'm not arresting you, Farrell, I'm fining you.
Five pounds.'

'*Another* five pounds?'

'Aye. Pay up.'

Rian knew Coombes wanted to avoid taking
him into town so he could keep the entire fine
for himself, rather than just half, which was the
unofficial arrangement if the case went up in

front of the magistrate. Very deliberately, he said, 'No, I don't think so, Sergeant. I'd rather be arrested.'

Coombes's face grew thunderous as his patience ebbed. 'I don't need to arrest you. Unless you contest the fine or assault me or my men.'

The assault option was very tempting, but could prove costly. 'Then I contest the fine.'

Shaking his head in disgust, Coombes arrested Rian and led him roughly over to the wagon, on which already sat six long-faced, licenceless diggers. His hands manacled, Rian climbed aboard and greeted his fellow miscreants with a terse nod.

Hawk sighed, beckoned to Gideon and said quietly, 'Start walking. Go to the Camp and meet him there, just in case there is trouble.'

Coombes and his men searched the remainder of the crew, continued along the Malakoff Lead, then headed back into town. The trip seemed to take ages, as Coombes stopped to bully other parties of diggers into producing their licences — or not — and loaded five more unfortunates onto the wagon. On the diggings, some refused to pay the fee to make a point; some simply couldn't afford to. Most of these men were in the latter category; their clothing was no better than rags, they were thin to the point of emaciation, and defeat hung about them like the stink over an offal pit.

At the Camp it was the same procedure: in through the gates, off the wagon, and in front of Magistrate d'Ewes.

When it was Rian's turn, d'Ewes looked up from his papers, sighed, and said, 'Oh no, not you again.'

'I'm afraid so.'

'First licence offence?' d'Ewes asked Coombes, who nodded unenthusiastically, clearly wishing he could say no. Repeated licence offences could attract a gaol sentence.

'The fine for not producing a miner's licence when required is five pounds,' d'Ewes said to Rian.

Rian let almost half a minute go by. 'But I have a licence.'

Magistrate d'Ewes closed his eyes. When he opened them again, he settled his gaze on Sergeant Coombes. He looked pained. 'Sergeant?'

The colour had drained from Coombes's normally florid face and he had pressed his lips together until they'd turned white. He forced them apart. 'He couldn't produce one earlier, sir.'

Rian withdrew his licence from his trouser pocket and displayed it so d'Ewes could see it.

'You can't have carried out your search very efficiently, Sergeant,' d'Ewes remarked, sounding almost amused.

The blood flooded back into Coombes's face.

'Get him out of my sight, Sergeant,' d'Ewes continued, and waved his hand in dismissal. 'Damned troublemaker. And be a bit more diligent next time. I haven't got time for this sort of tomfoolery.'

Tight-lipped again, Coombes saluted and

herded Rian out of the room. Outside, he whirled and shoved Rian against the wall of the building, twisting a handful of shirt in his fist. A small chorus of hoots and jeers arose from the line of diggers waiting to go in before the magistrate, and out of the corner of his eye Rian saw Gideon watching from the Camp gates.

'You made a fool of me in there, Farrell,' Coombes breathed, his bad teeth tainting his breath.

Rian returned the shove and stepped away, mindful that he wasn't armed. 'You made a fool of yourself, Coombes. Perhaps that'll teach you for frightening women and young girls.'

Coombes spat, barely missing Rian's boot. 'I'll be watching you. One foot out of line and I'll have you.'

10

A couple of days later Kitty was hanging wet
sheets outside Lilac Cottage, hoping they would
dry in the warm air before the wind arrived,
bringing the detested dust with it, when
Maureen emerged from the shanty next door.
For some minutes she stood by the door,
watching Kitty wrestling with the linen. Kitty
waved, and eventually Maureen came over.
'Would you be wantin' some help?'

'Yes, thanks, Maureen, if you don't mind,'
Kitty replied, and handed her the end of a sheet.
Together they slung it over the length of rope
that Rian had stretched between the cottage and
the privy, pegged it securely, and hoisted the
laden line higher with a notched eucalyptus pole.

'I hope the dust don't come up,' Maureen
remarked.

'So do I — I really don't feel like washing it all
again.'

'You wouldn't, no.' The sheets were all hung
now, but Maureen continued to stand there,
nervously winding a corner of her apron around
one rough, red finger.

Kitty looked at her, and Maureen glanced
back, then dropped her gaze, blushing fiercely.

'Is there something amiss, Maureen?' Kitty
picked up the empty washing basket.

'Sure there isn't! Nothin' at all!' Maureen
swallowed, then nodded reluctantly, a strand of

hair falling across her face. 'Well, happen there could be.'

Kitty eyed her uneasily. 'What's wrong, Maureen?'

Maureen let out a resigned sigh. 'There's no easy way to say this, Kitty, but I think you should know. Not that I believe it meself, so I don't.' She rolled her eyes to reinforce the ridiculousness of what was coming next. 'Here it is. Colleen O'Hara, she as is married to Patrick's syndicate partner Liam O'Hara? She said to me the other day that your Rian has been seen at the house of that Lily Pearce. At her actual, you know, house of work. At least twice. I told her not to spread such filthy lies. Gossipin' skivvy.' She fell silent for a moment, then added, 'I'm sorry. I thought you should know.'

The pulse of blood surging through Kitty's ears had all but drowned out Maureen's last words, but she understood that her intent had not been malicious, and that she was genuinely insulted and concerned by the gossip. Kitty heard herself thanking Maureen, then saying that she must put her washing basket away. She felt her heart thump wildly as she walked back to the cottage, closed the door behind her, and slowly sat down at the table. Bodie hopped off the daybed and ducked beneath Kitty's skirts, weaving between her ankles, then sharpening her claws on the toe of one boot.

Kitty felt sick. She thought back to all the sly, suggestive little comments Lily Pearce had made to her about Rian, to the moonlight dance when she had snatched Rian away, and, most stomach-lurching of all, to the night she had heard him, full of brandy and anger over Amber's abduction, quietly letting himself out of the cottage.

Slowly she twisted the thin band of gold on her wedding finger, then rested her elbows on the table and covered her face with her hands. A large fly buzzed somnolently against a window pane, and outside a bullock in harness rattled past. Then, unbidden, into her mind crept an image of Rian coming in dirty and exhausted from a day's work on the claim and collapsing into the rocking chair, only a few feet from where she sat now. They would exchange pleasantries, and she would mention, in a casual way, what Maureen O'Riley had told her the O'Hara woman had said. Rian's face would go still — he might even have the grace to look ashamed or embarrassed — and he would admit that yes, he had been with Lily Pearce. That lust had driven him to lie between her pale legs and plough into her and drip sweat on her and spill himself all over her. And in just a few horrific seconds Kitty's life would be irredeemably shattered and she would fly at him and punch him and rake his face with her fingernails and —

She sat up and said aloud, 'Oh, for God's *sake!*' Shifting her skirts, she scooped up Bodie, plonked her on the table and said to her, 'He just wouldn't do that. I know he wouldn't.' And, as simply as that, she knew that he wouldn't.

Bodie licked a paw and washed her greying face, an action which suggested a distinct lack of interest in Kitty's domestic affairs. Then she stood, presented her bum, and jumped off the table.

Kitty remained sitting a while longer, but when she did rise, her knees felt wobbly and the beat of her heart hadn't quite returned to normal. Maureen's news had given her a fright, and she was even more alarmed that she had allowed herself to imagine it might even be true. She felt annoyed with, and ashamed of, herself. Rian would never betray her, especially not with someone as awful as Lily Pearce. But she did need to talk to him about it, especially if his movements around the town were becoming the subject of common gossip. It wouldn't bother him, and gossip didn't unduly concern her, but there was Amber to think of.

She busied herself letting down the hem of one of Amber's dresses — she'd grown what seemed to be at least an inch in height in the past few months — until she heard Rian and the others arriving on the cart. Putting in the last small, neat stitches, she tied a knot in the thread and cut it, then slipped the needle back into its mother-of-pearl case.

Letting a swirl of warm, humid air into the cottage with him, Rian banged the dust off his hat, wafting it all over the room. He kissed Kitty hello, collapsed in the rocking chair, bent to untie his laces and toed his boots off.

'God, what a day! Where's Amber? How was yours?' His face was streaked with dust, and it had caked at the corners of his mouth and eyes, which were red and irritated.

'At the Chinese camp with Bao. Mr Wong's

bringing her back later.' Kitty frowned at the small piles of dust trickling off Rian's boots onto the freshly swept floor, then gave a mental shrug of resignation.

She rose from her chair and set a bucket of water near Rian, then fetched him a facecloth and a towel. He scooped up a handful of water, rinsed it vigorously around his mouth, then spat into the fire. Kitty dipped the cloth into the bucket, wrung it out, then began dabbing at the dust around Rian's eyes. It had mixed with tears coaxed forth by the afternoon winds and formed tiny crusts.

'Damn dust,' he grumbled. 'People are going blind.'

'They say the winds will die down soon,' Kitty murmured. Dabbing carefully but efficiently, she wondered how to broach the matter of Colleen O'Hara's gossip. Rian's eyes, only inches away, stared deeply into hers.

'What?' he asked.

Her hand stilled. 'What do you mean, 'what'?'

'You're getting ready to say something. I can tell.'

'No, I'm not.'

His mouth flickered in a half-smile. 'Come on, Mrs Farrell, out with it.'

She wiped the last smudge of dust from the corner of his eye with a little more force than was really necessary.

'Ow!'

'Sorry.' Kitty handed the cloth to Rian and settled back on her haunches, watching as he removed his shirt. Agitated though she was, she noticed she was still managing to feel aroused by the sight of his muscled arms and chest, and the trail of dark gold hair that ran down his flat belly and disappeared beneath the waistband of his dusty trousers.

'Is this the good soap?' he asked, sniffing the bar she'd set next to the bucket.

'Yes. Why? Are you going out somewhere?'

Rian waggled his eyebrows at her suggestively. 'Actually, I was planning on spending the night with a rather sexy woman I know.'

Kitty couldn't summon the smile she knew he was expecting. She stood, one knee cracking like a pistol shot, and sat on a chair. 'I need to talk to you, Rian.'

He saw that she was serious, and suddenly he was, too. 'Do you mind if I wash first, or is it urgent?'

She waved him on, and watched as he washed his face, neck, hands and forearms, then fetched him a fresh shirt as he towelled himself off. As he fastened his buttons, Kitty told him, bluntly, what Maureen had said.

Then he sighed. 'And you want to know if it's true?'

'Yes, Rian, I do.' It felt bad all of a sudden — frightening — and it was because the jealousy had come rushing back.

He rolled one sleeve up to his elbow, then the other. 'Actually, it is true.'

Kitty's heart gave a single, nauseating lurch. But the expression on Rian's face was soft, and she knew he couldn't be about to hurt her. So she held her breath and waited for him to offer her the explanation that would make things right again.

'I did go to see her twice. The first time was after the moonlight dance. I went to her house and we spoke in her room. I told her to leave me alone and to stay away from you and from Amber. I insulted her, and she swore I'd pay for it.' Rian rubbed his hand over his face, and Kitty could see on it regret for his misguided efforts. 'When Amber and Bao were abducted, I thought she was behind it. So I went to see her again. But I didn't go inside this time; I stood on the verandah and shouted at her. So, yes, I have been to see her, but not for the reason the O'Hara woman was implying.'

A sense of wellbeing and relief surged in Kitty like a spring tide. 'But why didn't you tell me?'

Rian thought about it. 'I didn't want you to know. You wouldn't have wanted me to even try to discuss the matter with her, would you?'

'No,' Kitty agreed. 'I would have preferred you to just keep out of her way.'

'Well, I thought I had to make myself clearer than that. So I did, and I do believe she got the message. And the second time, well, I was drunk.'

'I heard you go out that night. I've been wondering where you went.'

Rian's eyebrows went up. 'Did you? Then why didn't you say something?'

'Because I thought that if it was important, you would eventually tell me.'

Recalling what a loud-mouthed nuisance he'd made of himself on Lily Pearce's doorstep, Rian scowled. 'Well, as it turned out, it wasn't. I made a mistake. It wasn't Lily Pearce at all.'

Kitty let out a long, slightly shuddery breath. 'Do you know where I thought you'd gone, that night?'

Rian shook his head.

'I've been thinking for weeks that it was you who burned down Searle and Tuttle's hut. That you might have killed them, then set the hut alight to hide the evidence.'

'Ah, Kitty, *mo ghrá*.' Rian crossed to Kitty's chair, enfolding her in his arms and pressing her face against his belly. 'My poor love. That's a terrible thing to be carrying around with you all this time. Why the hell didn't you just ask?'

She shook her head but said nothing, content just to listen to the sound of his strong heart beating, and a gurgling rumble as his innards demanded their evening meal. He stroked her hair and rocked her. After a minute, she sat back.

'In a way, I don't think I would have minded if it had been you. They certainly deserved it. It wouldn't have changed anything between us.'

Rian cupped her cheek with a hand and looked down at her, at the complete lack of regret in her dark eyes for what had happened to the two men who had dared to hurt Amber. 'I understand. You killed for her, and it made me love you even more.'

'That was different: I had to.'

'Well, clearly whoever killed Searle and Tuttle thought they did, too. If I knew the man I'd shake his hand, wouldn't you?'

'Yes, I would. *Now*. But when I thought it was

you I was worried the police would get involved. I was worried . . . ' She blew out her cheeks on a big, weary sigh. 'Oh God, Rian, I don't know, it's all just becoming so fraught here with the hotel burning down and the meetings, and then Amber and Bao and now the soldiers coming and everything. I was frightened that if you had been involved in their deaths, you could have been found out. I mean, there are people everywhere and someone could have seen. And something really awful is going to happen soon, I know it is.'

Rian reached for the brandy bottle and two glasses. 'Is it? How do you know?'

'Well, can't you . . . sense it?'

Pouring them each a small nip, Rian said, 'I can't deny there's *something* in the wind. I think everyone's aware of that. Is it worrying you?'

'Yes, of course it's worrying me!' Kitty replied a little more tersely than she'd intended. 'There are soldiers everywhere! What if there's some sort of clash? I saw enough fighting in the Bay of Islands, thank you very much.'

'They wouldn't dare,' Rian said, knocking back his brandy in one go. 'There are too many diggers. They'd have to get in hundreds more troops.' His gaze met Kitty's and he frowned. 'Wouldn't you think?'

⋆　⋆　⋆

Kitty stood in the doorway of the shop, waiting for her eyes to become accustomed to the gloom inside, when an unpleasantly familiar voice behind her drawled, 'Shouldn't you be at home darning your husband's socks, Mrs Farrell?'

Kitty knew she should ignore her, but she turned anyway, feeling the muscles in her jaw tighten as she did so. Bloody woman.

Lily Pearce stood a short distance away, smirking up at her. She looked supremely self-satisfied, and Kitty wondered if she had heard what people were saying about Rian and his visits to her whorehouse. If she had, no doubt she was delighted. In which case, Kitty knew she should walk away immediately, but she stepped across the verandah and down onto the street. 'I'm not sure that it's any business of yours what I do, Miss Pearce.'

'Rian told me you're quite the homebody,' Lily said conversationally, twirling her parasol and watching Kitty closely for a reaction. 'During one of his visits to my house, this was.'

Kitty tightened her grip on her shopping basket. 'Miss Pearce,' she said loudly, mindful that several people nearby were now happily listening, 'this is a charade. We both know that my husband has never visited you for the purposes of engaging your . . . professional services. And please do not refer to him by his Christian name.'

Lily laughed gaily. 'Oh, dearie me. I don't know what he's told you — nothing, I expect, since most men don't discuss such matters with their wives — but he most certainly did visit me for the purposes of engaging my professional services.' She tapped her painted lips with an index finger and her gaze shifted skyward as if trying to remember something. 'Mmm, what was it he said? Oh yes, that's right. He said he was tired of scrag-ends in his bed every night and had a hankering for choice tenderloin.'

There was a gasp from the small but growing knot of spectators. Kitty felt her breath catch in her throat, even though she knew damned well Rian would never have said any such thing. She made an almighty effort to rein in her rapidly inflating anger and said, with icy dignity, 'Are you sure he didn't say that the other way around, Lily? You are a *lot* older than I am, after all.'

Lily's assurance slipped momentarily, but she rallied quickly. 'The fact is, your husband came to my house, Kitty Farrell, and spent time with *me!*' She shook a triumphant finger at Kitty. 'And you can't deny it. How do you feel about that!'

'Very little,' Kitty lied through gritted teeth. 'We've sailed around the world many times, my husband and I, and seen women whose beauty and exoticism defies description. If he was ever going to be tempted, I can safely say that it wouldn't be by someone the likes of you.'

A low *oooh* emanated from the onlookers.

The blow clearly found its mark, and Lily retaliated with a sneer that didn't quite conceal her discomfiture. 'Ah, yes, I'd forgotten about your little sailing ship.' She left a long, calculated pause. 'Your daughter must be very busy, with all those sailors on board.'

A single second of silence ensued, at the end of which Kitty swung back her hand that gripped the shopping basket and aimed it at Lily's head.

Lily dodged, but the basket caught her tiny hat and knocked it off, taking with it her wig of dark red ringlets. Beneath it, her rather sparse and patchy hair was an ordinary brown colour, pulled into a bun at the back of her head.

Lily screeched, torn between retrieving her wig, which was lying like a small, furry animal in the dusty street, and fighting back. Anger and humiliation won out and she lunged at Kitty. Still incensed with rage at Lily's vile insinuations, Kitty dropped her basket and struck out with a closed fist, remembering to keep her thumb on the outside as Mick had once shown her. She missed altogether and the force of her punch put her off-balance, and she stepped forward into a stinging slap from Lily's right hand.

Around them the number of onlookers increased almost instantly, attracted by the fascinatingly awful spectacle of women fighting, especially as one appeared to be a respectable lady. The scandal!

Dimly aware of the crowd forming a circle around her and Lily, Kitty blinked at the vicious slap, mentally shoved aside her mortification at such a demonstration of common vulgarity — fighting in the street, for God's sake! — and concentrated on the task at hand. She knew Lily would not permit her to walk away from this now; she, Kitty, had thrown the first punch and had humiliated Lily horribly. There would be no civilised apology; it had gone too far for that now.

So, knowing that she was covering herself in a

shame she would never live down, she ducked another well-aimed slap from Lily and struck out again, grunting with satisfaction as she knocked the other woman completely off her feet.

★   ★   ★

Not far down the street, Rian leaned on a shop counter contemplating the piece of jewellery he'd had made. The jeweller, a Russian Jew named Mr Rabinovich, had been delighted to accept the commission — as a master craftsman he'd grown bored over the past year polishing vulgar gold nuggets to be worn on watch chains or making nugget pins to fasten pretentious cravats.

The finished article was lovely. Made from Ballarat gold, naturally — in the new twelve-carat — the brooch was fashioned in the shape of a spray of three forget-me-not flowers. The petals were made from Persian turquoise cabochons, with small but brilliantly sparkling diamonds at their centres. The leaves were of green enamel. Rian didn't know much about jewellery, but he'd chosen the forget-me-not motif in the hope that Kitty would recognise the sentiment behind it. He knew he was woefully inadequate when it came to putting into words how he felt; and how he felt was guilty, for spending all their money on the claim, even though it was paying out now, and for dragging her all the way out here. She had shown a remarkable degree of tolerance for this latest in a succession of — and even he had to admit this — sometimes ill-considered schemes, and he wanted to do something that demonstrated his appreciation of her patience and her faith in him. And his love for her. He had commissioned the piece a month ago, but the gift was probably even more timely now.

'It's very pretty, isn't it?' he said appreciatively. He was no connoisseur, but even he could see that the jeweller had done a very fine job.

Mr Rabinovich allowed himself a small smile of self-satisfaction. 'I think so.' He tilted the brooch so that the diamonds caught the sun streaming through the shop window. 'It was a very satisfying piece to make. However, I had to go to Melbourne to visit a colleague for the glass powder for the enamel. I did not have the perfect colour here.'

Rian flapped his hand dismissively. 'I trust you've added the expense to the fee. And were you able to attend to the other matter?'

Reaching under the counter, Mr Rabinovich retrieved a slender, muslin-wrapped package, and carefully opened it to reveal a single sprig of freshly cut ivy. 'I did not pick it myself, you understand. It transpires that the only source of ivy in this town is in somebody's lovingly tended garden, so I paid an urchin to steal it.' He rewrapped the ivy, placed the brooch in a red velvet case, wrote the final figure for the work on a scrap of paper and handed all three to Rian. 'I hope your wife enjoys her new jewel, Captain. It has much style and elegance, as I'm sure she does herself.'

Rian paid the bill, slid the case and the ivy into his jacket pocket and said proudly, 'Yes, she has *considerable* style, my wife. Good day to you, Mr Rabinovich.'

Outside, Rian mounted Finn and set out along the street, heading back towards Malakoff's Lead. A short distance on he noticed a crowd of about fifty people, and as he approached he saw that in the centre of it two women were rolling on the ground, kicking and slapping the hell out of each other. God almighty, he thought with distaste as he steered Finn around the ruckus.

But something suddenly made him stop. Christ! That hair — it was the exact shade of raven black he woke next to every morning. Leaping off Finn, he thrust the reins at a spectator and elbowed his way into the circle.

It was Kitty, all right. He reached down, grabbed her elbow and hauled her to her feet. 'What the *hell* do you think you're doing!'

'What does it look like!' she hissed hysterically. Her hair had come out of its customary chignon and was tangled and dishevelled, one sleeve of her dress had torn under the armpit, and there was a large smear of dirt across her cheek.

Rian glanced at Lily, sitting on the ground glaring at them. 'That bloody shrew of a wife of yours started it!' Lily accused in a pathetic whine, pointing a finger at Kitty.

'For God's sake,' Rian said, and angrily led Kitty away. But a second later he was almost knocked over as Sergeant Coombes barged through the crowd, his nightstick in his hand.

'What's going on here?' he demanded.

'That woman assaulted me!' Lily shrieked, having suddenly rediscovered her voice, and pointing again at Kitty. 'I want her locked up!'

'Ah, you probably deserved it, Lily,' Coombes replied wearily. He put away his stick and hauled Lily up off the ground.

'My wig, my wig!'

Coombes retrieved Lily's wig. It had been severely trampled on, and would require a fair bit of ministering to restore it to its former glory.

Rian, watching the interaction between the two of them, suspected a familiarity born of more than just a casual acquaintance. He gripped Kitty's arm more tightly, propelling her out of the crowd. 'Come on, I don't want to tangle with Coombes.'

But Kitty jerked her elbow out of Rian's grip. '*Don't* push me around like a wayward child!'

'Why not? You were behaving like one. For God's sake, woman, what were you thinking?' Rian snatched the reins off the goggle-eyed man with whom he'd left Finn. 'What are *you* staring at?'

Correctly assessing Rian's filthy mood, the man shook his head mutely and stepped smartly away into the dispersing crowd.

'She was absolutely *beastly* about Amber, Rian! She said the most *awful* things!' Kitty protested, the memory sending her blood pressure soaring again. 'Bloody *witch!*'

'Calm down, calm down,' Rian said to both Kitty and the horse, as Finn, one rolling eye on Kitty, skittered away.

'But what was I supposed to do, Rian? Just walk away?'

'Kitty, I said *calm down!*'

Kitty stood still, glaring at Rian, and breathed deliberately in and out through her mouth until she felt her heartbeat begin to slow. Rian watched her, noting the tension drain from her jaw, neck and shoulders as she gradually gained control of herself. He felt his own anger begin to slide away. He couldn't blame her, really. Lily had obviously said something pretty nasty to make Kitty lash out at her. His wife, Rian knew from personal experience, had quite a temper, but she was only ever moved to violence after extreme provocation.

They started to walk.

'Feeling better?' he asked after some minutes. Kitty's hands had stopped shaking and her breathing seemed to be returning to normal.

She nodded, then gave a watery sniff. 'I've lost my shopping basket.'

'I'll buy you a new one. Do you still have your purse?'

Kitty patted the pocket concealed in her skirts, and nodded.

'Well, that's something, then,' Rian said gently. Looping Finn's reins over his arm, he dug around in his own pockets until he located a slightly grubby kerchief. 'Stop for a minute, will you?' Moistening a corner with spit, he gently wiped the smear of dirt from Kitty's cheek then swept her hair back over her shoulders. 'There, now you don't look like you've just got out of bed.'

'I don't go to bed with dirt all over my face!' Kitty protested. They looked at each other, then burst into smothered giggles. 'Oh God, Rian, I'll never live it down! What are people going to think?'

He put his arm around her shoulders and pulled her to him. 'They'll think whatever they're going to think, love, and there's not a thing you can do about it. So forget about it. Come on, I'll take you home, shall I?'

'No, I'm working in the bakery this morning. I'm only supposed to be out buying a pound of salt.'

'Well, I'll escort you to the shop, then.'

Together they walked along the street until they reached the bakery, their boots clattering on the floorboards as they entered.

Pierre and Leena looked up, their jaws dropping when they saw the state of Kitty.

'Ma! What happened?' Amber cried as she lifted the hatch in the counter and darted through.

'Your mother became involved in a bout of fisticuffs,' Rian said matter-of-factly, exchanging a look with Pierre.

'*Fist*-icuffs? Who with? Ma, are you all right?' Amber demanded, picking a twig out of Kitty's hair.

'I'm fine, sweetheart, don't fuss. I'm sorry, Pierre, I didn't get the salt.'

'Lily Pearce provoked her,' Rian explained.

Pierre spat, taking care to avoid the bowl in front of him. 'That *chatte!*'

Kitty took Amber's hand and moved through to the back of the shop, grateful that there were no customers at the moment. 'Don't make excuses for me, Rian. I started it. I'm completely at fault.' She turned to her daughter and said sharply, 'And don't ever let me catch *you* behaving like that, Amber, do you hear me?'

'But you had the chance to get in the boot?' Pierre interrupted.

Rian said, 'Shall we say, Kitty came out of it looking a lot more attractive than Miss Pearce did.'

Leena laughed out loud, and Pierre smirked into his *croissant* dough.

'Anyway, it's time I got back to work,' Kitty declared briskly, anxious to put her embarrassment behind her. 'Amber, love, lend me one of your ribbons, please.'

Amber was happy to oblige, as it meant she could spend the next half-hour pretending to rebraid her hair instead of almost breaking her forearm beating an enormous bowl of butter and sugar for Pierre.

Kitty pulled back her hair and secured it with the ribbon. She looked at Rian. 'Why were you in town anyway?'

'What? Oh.' In all the excitement, he'd forgotten. Neither the setting nor the audience was ideal, but the occasion was probably quite appropriate. He reached into his pocket. 'These are for you.'

Kitty looked at the velvet case and muslin package he'd placed in her hands, then up at his face. 'For me?'

'Yes. Go on, open them.' He watched as first she unwrapped the muslin, then opened the case, and smiled as he saw on her face that she understood exactly what his message was.

Forget-me-nots and ivy: true love and fidelity.

11

If Kitty hadn't been so preoccupied with defending the good name of her family, she might have paid more attention to the events happening around her — events that, coming so soon after what had already taken place at Ballarat in recent months, provided yet more fuel for the unrest that was steadily building on the diggings, gaining more and more energy until some sort of explosion must surely be inevitable.

On 11 November, a meeting of almost 10,000 convened at Bakery Hill, directly and some said deliberately opposite the Camp, during which the Ballarat Reform League was established. Its goals, based on Chartist principles, included the right for all men to vote (by secret ballot), abolition of diggers' and storekeepers' licences, reform of goldfields administration, and revision of laws relating to Crown land. Nothing new, Kitty noted, when news of the meeting did finally filter through to her, but it would no doubt please many people.

Five days later, the Colonial Secretary dismissed John d'Ewes from his position as police magistrate, much to the delight of many, and Governor Hotham appointed a Goldfields Commission to look into conditions on the diggings. Two days after that, on 18 November, James and Catherine Bentley, Thomas Farrell and William Hance were finally convicted of the manslaughter of James Scobie, and many at Ballarat celebrated that justice had at last been done.

But only three days later, in Melbourne, diggers Henry Westerby, Thomas Fletcher and Andrew McIntyre were tried, convicted and gaoled for the destruction of James Bentley's Eureka Hotel. Rian gave voice to the opinion of many when he remarked to Patrick over a glass of brandy that it was absurd; dozens of men had tossed brands at Bentley's hotel and bowling alley, so why had Westerby, Fletcher and McIntyre been singled out and punished so harshly?

It seemed that many at Ballarat wanted that question answered, so the league sent a delegation, carrying a copy of the league's charter, to Hotham in Melbourne with a demand for him to release Westerby and his two compatriots. Hotham, however, took exception to the use of the word 'demand' and sent the delegation on its way. The miners departed for home, not realising they were trailing contingents of the 12th and 40th Regiments of Foot already dispatched to Ballarat to reinforce the Camp.

Patrick saw what happened as the soldiers marched into town on the night of 28 November, and told Rian, and anyone else who cared to listen, about it the next morning.

Rian, sitting on a mullock heap eating one of Pierre's pasties, said, 'And what were you doing all the way over on the Eureka Lead at that hour of the evening?'

Patrick looked shifty. 'Conferrin' with me colleagues.'

'Stirring shit, more likely,' Mick commented, wiping pasty juice out of the beard he hadn't bothered to shave for a week.

Patrick gave him a look. 'It might behove you to stand up for what you know to be right, me lad. You might be a sailor by trade, so you might, but you're a digger as long as you're here. Have some pride. Where's your Irish spirit?'

'In me Irish arse,' Mick replied benignly. 'I don't go looking for fights, so I don't.'

'It's all right for you, boy. You'll be sailin' away after this.'

'I will,' Mick agreed.

Patrick scowled into his mug.

'So what actually happened?' Simon asked.

Cheered at the prospect of telling the story, Patrick slurped the last of his tea. 'Well, it was a sight to behold, I can assure you. The 40th come stridin' along, swords drawn and bayonets fixed like they're marchin' on Sebastopol, and them that's linin' the route — and there was plenty of us, make no mistake about that — start shoutin' and jeerin', because what are they here for if not to cause trouble, I ask you?'

'Were you expecting them?' Rian asked. 'Is that why you were at the Eureka diggings?'

Patrick looked surprised by the question. 'No. I was there for a meetin'. I think they might have gone the wrong way and it was such a spectacle everyone came out.'

Daniel said, 'I heard a drummer boy was shot.'

'Hold your horses, I'm *comin'* to that.' Patrick

produced his pipe, tamped in a plug and lit up. 'Anyway, we're yelling and goin' on and generally demonstrating our displeasure, but I have to say they were steady, those lads, they just kept on marchin'. But not ten minutes later, just when we think there's nothin' else to see, here come the bloody 12th! Well, they're armed to the teeth as well, not to mention they're haulin' ammunition wagons and drays loaded with God knows what else. So we want to know from their officer in charge if they're bringin' in heavy ordnance, and it all starts gettin' a bit out of hand, so it does.' He paused and made a vaguely rueful face. 'I suppose it *might* have looked like we were mobbin' him. Anyway, the officer pipes up and says he'll have 'No communication with rebels!' — *rebels!* — and all hell breaks loose, and he turns tail and disappears! The soldiers look like they're going to open fire, so we start throwin' stones and bottles and anything we can lay our hands on. And somehow two or three of the soldiers get the bejasus beaten out of them, and two drays get pushed over and everything ends up in the ditch. Then the shootin' *does* start and that's when the drummer boy gets hurt.' He frowned. 'It's not right, that, is it? Puttin' a lad in the line of fire.'

'Who started the shooting?' Rian asked.

Patrick began, 'Who do you think? It was the bloody . . . ' He faltered, then gave a weary sigh, as if reluctantly coming to terms with an unpalatable truth. 'I'd like to say it was the soldiers, but in truth it could just as easily've been a digger.'

'Did he die, the drummer boy?' Simon asked.

'Can't tell you for a fact, but I heard he was only wounded. And so was a shopkeeper and an American fellow.'

Hawk upended his mug and knocked the tea leaves out of it. 'So, the first blood has been shed. How many extra troops have been brought in now? Four hundred? Five hundred? You surely cannot be expecting a peaceful resolution to your grievances at this late stage, Patrick. What do you think will happen next?'

Sunday, 3 December 1854

'It might never have come to this, you know, if Rede hadn't insisted on that final bloody licence hunt.'

Rian and Hawk were inside the Ring, a barricaded area of heavily mined ground abutting the northern side of the Melbourne Road, east of Bakery Hill and just west of the Eureka Lead. It was cool but not cold, and the sun hadn't yet begun to rise. Fires inside the Ring sent smoky ashes swirling into the dark sky on a gentle pre-dawn breeze.

Hawk, ever the voice of reason, said, 'I expect he thought he had to do something to try to reassert his authority.'

Patrick shifted on his log to ease his thin buttocks, and said grumpily, 'Whose side are you on?'

'We're not on anyone's side, Patrick,' Rian reminded him. 'We're here because you asked us to help.' And because I owe you a debt for finding Amber.

'That's true,' Patrick agreed, for once sounding as old as he looked. 'I did, too. And I appreciate it. You didn't have to come. You could be asleep in your beds.'

Yes, we could, Rian reflected ruefully, thinking of Kitty in her nightgown, the gauzy fabric moulding enticingly to her curves. He suppressed a smile as he wondered if she was wearing her brooch — she'd hardly taken it off since he'd given it to her. 'Sorry, Patrick, what was that?'

'I said: and the reason I *did* ask you was because you said you'd done a bit of fightin' against the Queen's men yourselves, and I thought the experience'd come in handy.'

'Well, not exactly. More observing, really,' Rian replied.

'Still, the more the merrier,' Patrick remarked.

But events at Ballarat over the past few days had developed into a situation that was far from merry.

After the 12th's inauspicious arrival, another monster meeting had been held at Bakery Hill, at which the future direction of the Ballarat Reform League had been energetically discussed. Ideas of direct action were very popular, especially the proposal to burn licences. The next morning, Commissioner Rede had instigated a licence hunt on the largest scale ever seen in Ballarat. He chose the Old Gravel Pits, the closest lead to the Camp. Stones were thrown, a riot soon developed, troops fired on the diggers,

Rede read the Riot Act and a handful of miners was arrested. By then word had reached even the most outlying leads, and diggers had come into town by the thousands to protest the latest government outrage.

That evening another meeting was called on Bakery Hill. When the league's leaders failed to appear, Peter Lalor mounted the stump, proclaimed 'Liberty', and called for volunteers for companies. A council of war was chosen and the blue and silver Southern Cross — newly designed, and hurriedly sewn by a tentmaker — was hoisted. Diggers knelt, heads bare and hands raised, and swore by the new flag to stand together and fight for their rights and liberties.

Although they were in the crowd, neither Rian nor any of the crew followed suit. After so many years, they had come to accept that in practice they were soldiers of fortune: they bought, sold and traded — and fought — wherever and whenever it suited them. They owed allegiance to no one, and never would.

The following morning a crowd of 1500 armed and angry diggers again gathered at Bakery Hill, then marched on to Eureka, where they spent the day preparing for a clash with soldiers and requisitioning arms and ammunition. The military was on high alert, and had been since the 12th's arrival: the cavalry were sleeping with their bridles in their hands, and the wooden buildings of the Camp were surrounded by bales of hay, sacks of grain and logs. The townspeople had been warned that their properties were also in danger. The tension was almost unbearable.

The previous morning, Saturday, work had begun on the Ring, with the Southern Cross as its proud centrepiece. Rian had watched some of the activity, and despite words such as 'stockade' and 'fortification' being bandied about, he knew no one could pretend it was anything more than a fenced-off mustering place. The area, an acre or so, was encircled by a waist-high barricade of slabs, logs and rocks. Inside were close to twenty tents, whose occupants included women and children, perhaps double that number of shafts with accompanying mullock heaps, and a smithy, which was busy turning out rough weapons such as pikes and the like.

The night before, there had been around a thousand men inside the enclosure, many organised into companies based on nationality to make communication easier. But now, very early on Sunday morning, Rian was nervous: there were nowhere enough should the soldiers attack. Some diggers had gone back to their tents and shanties — either for a decent night's sleep, or permanently because the fire of rebellion had burned out of them. Others were drunk and had wandered off down to the Main Road. There were perhaps ten dozen men left. Not even Peter Lalor was here. And security was non-existent: people were coming and going from the compound constantly.

Rian glanced over his shoulder at the others, who were reheating last evening's stew and toasting bread over a fire. Pierre, Ropata, Gideon, Daniel, Mick and Haunui had also agreed to come. Patrick hadn't asked Simon, and Rian knew he had been relieved.

Daniel stood, stretched and turned away from the fire.

'You off?' Rian asked, even though he very much doubted it.

'Going for a piss.'

'Don't go outside the fence. If I were Rede, I'd be planning to attack quite soon.'

Daniel headed off towards the nearest tree as Patrick said, 'Not on the Sabbath, he won't.'

Hawk scowled, his heavy brows almost meeting in the middle. 'Where is Mick?'

'Drunk,' Ropata replied matter-of-factly. 'Gone to look for more whiskey.'

Patrick swore disgustedly and spat on the ground.

Rian laughed. 'He'll be back when we need him, Patrick. He's a good man.'

Patrick made a disparaging noise. 'I have me doubts.'

'I don't,' Rian replied with a hint of coolness. 'I'd trust my life to Mick Doyle. In fact, I have.'

There was a prolonged silence. 'Sorry, fellahs,' Patrick said, 'but there's spies everywhere, I know it. I'm shittin' meself, to tell you the truth. You're right. If Rede is goin' to attack, it'll be tonight while half of us are in our cups and the other half have gone home for a decent night's sleep.'

The Irishman sighed and shook his head. 'Holy Mother of God, what a feckin' shambles. We're not just rebels, you know. We tried to get things changed the right way. We *tried* to get

Hotham and all the rest of them to listen.' He waved a dispirited hand towards the hundred or so men sitting by fires and the sad little fence surrounding then. 'And now it's come to this, so it has. And all them others who pledged support? Where are they, eh? I ask you. And what's happened to the Americans?'

'Ae, what *has* happened to them?' Haunui asked. Yesterday afternoon, the contingent of American miners had taken the horses and gone to search out expected government reinforcements, and had never returned.

A lone kookaburra cackled raucously in the same gum tree Daniel was presently pissing against, and Rian realised that a wash of grey was seeping into the sky from the east. He dug out his watch, flipped open the lid and angled the face towards the fire: almost five o'clock.

He nearly jumped out of his skin as a shot sounded, followed a second or so later by a bugle call; then an unbroken line of flame lit up the western side of the compound as Her Majesty's troops opened fire with a deafening volley of musket fire.

'Ah, shite, here they come,' Rian muttered as he checked that his pistol was tucked into his belt, and reached for his rifle.

Daniel came running back, fumbling with his flies, Pierre kicked dirt over the fire, Patrick scuttled back to his cronies, and the others scrambled for their weapons.

Rian stuck his head up just in time to see a wave of red-coated troops surge over the barricade. The noise of musket fire was ear-splitting, men shouted, women screamed and chaos reigned as diggers and soldiers met and fought hand to hand and Rian lost sight of everyone but Daniel, whom he noted was acquitting himself impressively.

Something crashed into Rian and he went down. A moment later Daniel dragged him back up, and shouted into his face.

Rian spat out dirt. '*What?*'

Daniel pointed to the far perimeter, and when Rian looked his heart almost stopped as he spied through the smoke and turmoil Kitty determinedly making her way towards them, followed by Maureen and Leena.

He exchanged a horrified glance with Daniel.

'I'll go!' Daniel shouted.

Rian ducked a blow from a soldier and shook his head. Daniel looked as alarmed as he felt, but nowhere near as angry. 'Tell the others where I am,' he said through lips that barely moved.

He ducked and weaved through knots of fighting men, and felt a ball go past so close it nicked the skin off a knuckle. Every step he took towards an unsuspecting Kitty raised his temper another notch, and when someone snatched at his arm he hit out with enormous force.

Whoever it was hit back. 'Hey, I'm your mate, so I am.'

'Patrick? Ah, I'm sorry.'

Patrick looked at Rian with beseeching eyes. There was a cut on his temple, and the dark blood had run down his cheek and into his beard. He put his mouth to Rian's ear. 'Maureen's over yonder with your Kitty. Will you take her out of here?'

Rian gave a curt nod.

Patrick grabbed Rian's arm. 'Take yourself out, too, Rian, and your men. It's goin' bad. We're not goin' to win.'

Rian looked at his friend's tired and defeated face. 'My men will come when they're ready, Patrick.' But he knew they would leave the battle as soon as they realised that he, Rian, had gone.

Patrick touched his arm in thanks, then disappeared back into the fray.

When Rian reached Kitty he said nothing, and saw by the look on her face that she knew better than to attempt to say anything herself. He also saw that she was terrified. He grasped her arm, spun her around and marched her in the direction from which she and her companions had just come. Leena and Maureen followed.

Shepherding Kitty out through a gap in the barricade, he led the group onto the Melbourne Road and far enough away from the Ring to be safe from flying bullets and the battle-inspired loutishness of both soldiers and diggers.

'*What* are you doing here?' he demanded in as controlled a fashion as he could manage.

Kitty met his gaze steadily, although her fear was still, very evident. 'I came to see that you were safe. We heard there were other women here.'

'On a field of battle?' Rian asked, his voice so low now it was almost inaudible.

Leena and Maureen exchanged a nervous glance.

215

'But there are women in there, aren't there? I saw them.'

'They're *trapped*, Kitty. They can't get *out*.'

'*You* got out,' Kitty snapped, fear making her shrewish. 'But are you all right? We heard the muskets open up and we thought . . . Well, we were worried,' she finished lamely. To be truthful, they hadn't expected the soldiers to attack the Queen's own subjects with such determined vigour, and in such numbers, but once they'd made their way into the compound they'd decided they might as well keep going.

'I'm fine,' Rian said shortly. 'And so are Patrick and Ropata.' This last was directed at Maureen and Leena, although he hadn't actually seen Ropata once the fighting had started.

To Leena, he said, 'Does Amber have the children? Kitty, you shouldn't leave Amber by herself at night.'

'I'm not by myself.'

Kitty, Rian and Leena all stared, varying degrees of shock registering on their faces.

Behind them, Amber stood against a barrel some yards away, Tahi at her side.

Kitty demanded, 'Amber, why aren't you at home!' at the same time that Leena said, 'Amber, where are Molly and Will?'

'I'm not at home because I wanted to see what was going on,' Amber replied with more than a hint of defiance. 'Binda has Molly and Will, out at her camp. I hope you don't mind, Leena. She said it would be safer for them out there.'

Leena relaxed a little; Binda was probably right.

216

Rian said, 'How many times have you been told *not* to go out alone?' God, why could the women in his family *never* behave?

'I *said*, I'm *not* alone,' Amber insisted, as Tahi's arm settled around her shoulders.

Oh dear, Kitty thought, something's definitely changed there, while Rian said to himself, Christ, I'll have to have a word to Haunui about this. Then he sighed. Perhaps it was time he accepted that his days of trying to control his wife, and clearly now his daughter, were long gone. He wasn't sure, either, that he could be bothered fighting other people's fights any more. Perhaps it was time, too, to concentrate on extracting as much gold as they could from the claim, then move on. He missed the sea so much that he could physically feel the ache in his bones.

Out of the corner of his eye he saw Ropata, then Pierre and Haunui emerge from the smoke drifting over the compound, and knew the others wouldn't be far behind.

He slipped his hand into his wife's. 'I'm starting to get tired of this, *mo ghrá*. I think we'll take what we can, then go home.'

Kitty turned her face to him and her eyes held a glow he hadn't seen there for some months. Then she blinked and coughed, as a wreath of gunpowder and smoke enveloped them. 'You mean, home to the sea?'

Behind her, several tents in the compound burst into flame. They all ducked and Rian nodded. 'Not now, but soon.'

And Kitty squeezed his hand, hard.

217

The fighting had lasted little more than twenty minutes. The soldiers tore down the Southern Cross and trampled it into the dust, then the police systematically hunted the insurgents and arrested over a hundred not quick enough to flee, including Patrick. More than twenty diggers had died, some from wounds received after the battle had ended, and six soldiers and police had been killed. Rian and the crew, who had left Eureka before the fight was over, kept their heads well down.

Now, later in the morning, Amber, Leena and Kitty walked north along the track out past the Old Gravel Pits towards Black Hill, where Binda's people, the Watha Wurrung, were currently camped. Although the upper reaches of the low mountain were densely timbered, the lower slopes were now almost bare, denuded by the miners. The morning was already glaringly hot and the sky cloudless, and Kitty was deeply regretting so cavalierly giving away her bonnet. She might well be forced to purchase another one, or perhaps she would start a new mode and wear a panama hat like Rian.

'We must be nearly there,' Leena said hopefully. She hadn't been to Binda's camp before, but Amber had.

'Not far,' Amber confirmed. 'I hope they haven't gone walkabout,' she added, then instantly wished she hadn't.

Leena stopped. 'But they were here last night?'

'Er . . . '

Kitty looked at her daughter. 'Amber, you did bring the children here yourself last night. Didn't you?'

Amber made a face that was part defiance, part discomfort. 'I saw Binda in town. She had some other children with her. White children. She looks after them sometimes, like she does with Will and Molly, and she said she was bringing them out here because it would be safer. And I . . . well, I wanted to see what was happening at Eureka so when she asked if I wanted her to take Will and Molly as well, I said yes.'

'You just *gave* them to her?' Leena was outraged. 'You just gave her my babies!'

'Yes, but Leena, you *like* Binda! She minds them all the time!'

'But not to take away! Amber, you do not even know where she has taken them!'

Kitty knew that Leena liked Binda, but could see on her face that somewhere inside her, perhaps not even on a conscious level, she did not quite trust the older woman.

'I do know!' Fear was beginning to replace indignation on Amber's face. 'She brought them out here. To her camp!'

Kitty could also see that this was getting them nowhere. Deserving though she thought Amber was of Leena's ire, she urged, 'I think we should wait until we get to the camp before anyone gets upset, don't you? I'm sure there's nothing wrong. Will and Molly are probably having a lovely time.' But, mentally, she crossed her fingers. God help them all if anything had happened to Leena's children.

Leena stalked off ahead, and soon they came to the camp, an open patch of ground on one side of the track in the shelter of a high bank of rocks. A semi-circle of five *mia mia* — shelters made from sticks jammed in the ground and hung with bark and branches — stood around several low fires, and the camp clearly hadn't been abandoned. Three elderly men sat around one of the fires, even though the morning was so hot, turning something that had been alive not long ago on a green stick. They stared as the women approached.

'They're not here,' Leena said dully.

'They will be,' Amber countered, slightly desperately.

Kitty addressed the men; 'Good morning, my name is Kitty Farrell and — '

'I'll do this,' Leena interrupted, and launched into a short speech in her own tongue. There was no response, so she tried what sounded to Kitty like a slight variation. Still nothing. Leena rolled her eyes, sighed in irritation and said in rapid but diluted pidgin English, 'Me Leena from Cadigal Sydney. Your woman Binda got my kids Will an' Molly. Where they be at? I want 'em back.'

The three men looked at her, then at each other. Then one said, 'Up the hill. In the cave, eh?' He pointed.

Leena looked at the narrow track that wound up through the rocks behind the camp and disappeared into the trees. 'Who you be?'

'Barega of Watha Wurrung.'

'They safe?' she asked, meaning the children.

He nodded. 'They all safe.'

Visibly, Leena relaxed somewhat.

'Big fellah business in town last night? Or sorry business?' the man asked.

'Sorry business,' Leena replied.

He shrugged. 'Well, not ours, eh?'

Leena led the way past the camp and up through the rocks.

'Why are they the only ones down there?' Kitty asked, lifting her skirts so she wouldn't trip herself up. She had been perspiring before, but now she could feel the sweat trickling freely down her back and sides. 'And where are the young men?'

'Out hunting. Probably been out before dawn,' Leena replied over her shoulder.

Kitty noted her voice was still tight with worry, and knew she wouldn't relax completely until she had seen her babies with her own eyes. She couldn't blame her. Sometimes she could happily throttle Amber.

After half an hour of what was turning into a thigh- and buttock-torturing climb, they finally moved into the shade of a canopy of pungent eucalypts and blackwoods, with wattle and other shrubs growing beneath them.

Leena stopped, parked her backside against a rock and rubbed her sleeve across her sweating face. She stared accusingly at Amber, who looked away, her bottom lip beginning to tremble.

Then Binda herself stepped silently out of the bush. 'They in here. No worry, they safe.' She wore her usual faded old dress, which barely skimmed her thin calves, her dusty feet were bare, and her customary wide, white smile was in place.

Kitty watched as Binda and Leena locked eyes. Something passed between them, then Leena's shoulders slowly subsided and the suspicion and guarded fear drained from her face.

Binda beckoned, and they followed her into the cool dimness of the eucalypts. Soon they came to the mouth of a cave, a tall, narrow crack in the side of the mountain. They all fitted through it comfortably, but a really corpulent person, Kitty reflected, could run the risk of becoming stuck. For some reason the image struck her as immensely funny and she stifled an inappropriate snort. Maybe she was more tired than she thought.

Inside the cave, which opened out some fifteen feet into the mountain, it was light enough to see quite easily, owing to a natural skylight formed by a fissure in the roof, through which dangled the roots of several bushes.

But the real surprise was the children. As well as three other, presumably, Watha Wurrung women and their little ones, there were also eight white-skinned children, as well as Will and Molly, all playing a game. Around them were heaped possum-fur rugs, on which they had clearly spent the night, and the detritus of a morning meal.

On seeing their mother, Will and Molly jumped up and ran to her, gripping her skirts but appearing perfectly happy and hale. Leena knelt and spoke to them in her own tongue, and, apparently satisfied that they were indeed unharmed, said to Binda, 'They be good, Binda. You did right bringin' 'em here.'

Binda inclined her head in acknowledgement, then stooped to lift her small grandchild and perch him on her ample hip, where he clung to one of her flat dugs beneath her dress in a manner that looked very painful to Kitty. 'Better safe than sorry, eh?'

Amber had the good sense not to look too vindicated.

'The fighting all done?' Binda asked.

Kitty said, 'It seems to be, but things are still very on edge.'

Binda looked across the cave at the children playing on the sandy floor, oblivious to what had happened overnight. 'But better take 'em back, eh? Nannie Binda can't keep 'em for ever.'

Everything was packed up, and twenty minutes later the whole party snaked its way down the mountain to the Watha Wurrung camp, where the three old men still sat by the fire, a small pile of picked-clean bones on the ground in front of them.

The younger men were back now, a dead wallaby evidence of their hunting expedition. They carried spears and the boomerangs Kitty had previously seen used to such spectacular and lethal effect. As if reading her mind, one of the young men withdrew a boomerang from his belt, cocked his arm and, with what seemed to be little more than a flick of his wrist, threw it so far that it disappeared from view. The visitors present all waited open-mouthed — Amber, in particular — for almost a minute, until it came spinning back and landed only inches from his feet. The young man turned and grinned hugely in a manner that suggested he knew full well how impressive his throw had been and the effect it had had on his audience. Show-off, Kitty thought.

Reading her mind, Binda snorted and said, 'That Warrun, he throw good, he hunt good, he track good, and he think he be so clever.'

Kitty laughed out loud. It was time to go home.

12

When Kitty and Amber got back to Lilac Cottage, there was a note on the table saying: *Gone out, keeping low. Mr Wong would like you to visit him at the Chinese camp. Will see you tonight. Rian xxx*

Kitty was vaguely annoyed: she had wanted to talk to him about exactly how soon they could leave Ballarat, She did realise, however, that it wouldn't be particularly prudent of him, or the crew, to sit around waiting to be visited by the police. They wouldn't be at the top of Commissioner Rede's list of insurgents to be arrested, but they had been in the compound the night before, and Rian, especially, was known to Sergeant Coombes.

She showed the note to Amber, whom she had decided to forgive now that it was clear that Leena's children were safe. 'I wonder what he wants?'

'I don't know. But it might be about Bao.'

'Why would it be about Bao?' Through the window, Kitty watched Bodie stalk a bird.

'Because she hasn't been very happy lately.'

'Bao hasn't?' Although, now that Amber had mentioned it, Kitty did recall that Bao had been even quieter and more reticent than usual. She had lost weight, too, her hair had lost its lustre, and shadows darkened the delicate skin beneath eyes that now appeared perpetually dull. Kitty had assumed the child was simply not sleeping well, perhaps because of the heat, but had not, to her shame, given the matter much thought beyond that. 'Do you want to come with me, then? To the village?'

'I do, but I want to go and see Patrick as well.'

'I'm sure you do, love, and it's a nice thought, but you can't.'

'We can't just leave him in the lock-up by himself.'

'He's not by himself, and I'm sure Maureen will have been to see him by now.'

Amber kicked the leg of a chair so that it shunted across the floor in grating increments. It was rather annoying. 'Will they hang him, Ma?'

'What? No, of course they won't!' But Kitty mentally crossed her fingers for the second time that day.

'They might, you know.' Silence for a moment. 'Will Pa be arrested, too?'

Ah. Kitty sat down. 'Oh, I really don't think so, sweetheart. Is that what's worrying you?'

'But he's already been arrested here twice. And he was right in the middle of the fighting last night.'

'Yes, he was, but he's going to do his best not to be arrested for this.' Kitty realised how weak her words sounded, and saw that they weren't doing much to bolster the girl's confidence. She took Amber's hands in hers and looked her daughter in the eye. 'I know your father gets into some scrapes from time to time. Some quite bad ones, occasionally.' They both allowed themselves a little giggle. 'But nothing is going to happen to him here, I swear.' She looked towards the door as Bodie trotted in, a recently murdered willie wagtail in her mouth, dragging it between her front paws. 'I swear on Bodie's life, all right? Your father will be fine.'

Amber regarded her for a moment, then nodded in acceptance and ducked under the table to shoo the cat outside.

Kitty, however, didn't feel quite so convinced by her own words.

★   ★   ★

Wong Fu passed her a tiny cup of the aromatic green tea he always offered her when she came to visit, and perched on the tea chest that served as a stool.

'Forgive me for insisting that we talk in my tent, but I wish this conversation to remain private. You are not discomposed by being alone with me?'

It was a very frank comment, but Kitty had become accustomed to such ingenuousness. Out of the public eye, at least. Around those he did not count as friends, Wong Fu could be extremely circumspect.

She settled herself more comfortably on the cot which was presumably his. Its twin — just as narrow and no doubt equally unforgiving — sat against the other side of the small tent, the worn fabric doll on the flat pillow confirming that it belonged to Bao.

'No, I'm not, Mr Wong. Thank you for asking.'

Wong Fu sipped his tea and looked uncharacteristically ill at ease. And very tired, the shadows beneath his eyes accentuated. 'How is Amber?' he asked.

'She's well, thank you.'

He nodded. Another silence. Kitty waited. Then: 'The clash at Eureka last night. You witnessed it?'

'It was more than a clash, Mr Wong, it was a rout, and it hasn't stopped yet. The soldiers and police are still out and about causing havoc, and the town's reeling. Have you not left your camp today?'

'No. And we will not until this has settled. It is nothing to do with us.'

It wasn't, either, Kitty reflected. The Chinese would go on working the edges and the dregs of the goldfields regardless of the politics of the other diggers, silent, inscrutable and unpopular.

Wong Fu set down his cup and sighed. 'Bao has been terrified. She has spent the past four nights cowering on her cot, the blanket over her head, weeping.'

Kitty looked at him aghast. 'But . . . why?'

His shoulders rose, then slumped again in defeat. 'I have asked her, of course, but she will not tell me. Not directly.' He sighed again, the creases at the corners of his mouth betraying his anxiety. 'I fear something has happened to her mind. With our continued persecution, and the growing tension over the past months and the soldiers coming, she has been . . . not quite with us.' He picked up the end of his queue, examined it momentarily for split ends while he gathered his thoughts, then let it drop. 'And since the terrible business with Tuttle and Searle, she has become so much worse. I am very worried, Mrs Farrell. I wish her mother were here.'

Now Kitty knew why he had asked her to call, and her heart ached for him. 'Would you like me to talk to her, Mr Wong?'

'Thank you for your kind offer, Mrs Farrell, but I do not think talk will help.'

Kitty blinked at his bluntness.

'Please do not be offended. What I believe she needs most is to leave Ballarat for a time. My brother in Melbourne has his wife with him. I would like her to go there. I will be forever in your debt if you would take her there for me.'

'Me?'

'Yes. I cannot go myself as I have commitments here, and she has told me she will not travel in the company of any other man unchaperoned, and I will not force her to. You must understand what lies behind her insistence about that.'

'Yes, of course I do.'

'I will pay all your expenses, of course, and compensate you for your absence at the bakery.'

Kitty waved away such silliness. 'I will need to speak to my husband. The situation is a little delicate at the moment. He managed to become involved in the battle last night and Rede's men are still trying to track down the participants. If I were to go to Melbourne I'd want to make sure he's avoided arrest before I leave. When were you thinking of sending her?'

'If you are amenable, at the end of the week?'

Kitty thought; it was Sunday today, five days should be long enough. Unless Sergeant Coombes decided to play out a vendetta. 'I would be honoured to escort Bao to Melbourne, Mr Wong. We've become very fond of her over the past few months, and I'm extremely sorry to hear that she's not well. But I do need to speak to Rian first.' She stood and smoothed her skirts. 'Can I give you my answer tomorrow?'

Wong Fu rose too, his face almost slack with relief. 'Of course, of course.' He bowed deeply. 'I am *most* grateful, Mrs Farrell. *Most* grateful.'

Kitty felt herself going pink, and turned away. But at the flap of the tent, she paused. 'Mr Wong: Searle and Tuttle — did you kill them? Because I thought Rian had done it, but he says he didn't.'

Wong Fu regarded her, the teapot and little china cups stacked in his hands. Then he shrugged. 'What choice did I have, Mrs Farrell? She is my daughter.'

* * *

Kitty walked through the Chinese camp until she found Amber and Bao, engrossed in playing with a litter of possibly the sweetest kittens Kitty had ever seen.

'No — before you ask,' she said to Amber.

'But Ma — '

'No, love.'

'But — '

'No.' Kitty crouched in front of Bao. 'How are

230

you feeling, sweetheart?'

'Very well, thank you. Have you been speaking to my father?'

'Yes.'

Bao just nodded, and stared at her feet in their little slippers.

Kitty felt awkward. 'Well, he did say you haven't been feeling your best lately. So, if there's anything you might ever like to talk about . . . '

'I will remember. Thank you very much,' Bao murmured, politely but effectively cutting her off.

Kitty exchanged a glance with Amber, then stood up. 'Well, come on, love, we'd better be going.'

Amber gave Bao a little wave, and they left her where she was, her lap full of wriggling kittens.

Kitty suddenly gave her daughter a quick hug.

Amber looked at her. 'What was that for?'

'Because I love you.'

As they walked briskly back into town, they began to encounter newly posted bills featuring advertisements offering substantial rewards for the apprehension of various 'rebels'. To Kitty's enormous relief, Rian's name was not on them.

★ ★ ★

The next day, Friday, they would be off to Melbourne, and Kitty was very pleased to be going. Two days ago, 800 troops led by Major-General Sir Robert Nickle had arrived in Ballarat and martial law had been declared. The mood in the town had quickly transformed from one of stunned shock to anger, and the authorities were responding accordingly. Rian had decided to stay behind, but had insisted that Amber go with Kitty and Bao, and that Simon and Haunui chaperone them, and, because Amber was going, Tahi demanded to go, too.

As of the afternoon before, Daniel was also going, as he had fallen in the shaft and was nursing what he was insisting was a sprained arm. It was very obviously more than sprained, however, which is why he, Simon and Kitty were at the doctor's surgery now. And while he couldn't work, Rian reasoned that he might as well make the trip to Melbourne alongside Haunui and Simon, given the many rumours of bushrangers, and check on the *Katipo*.

Rian, too, was at the surgery, slightly drunk from the whiskey he'd imbibed to dull the ache of a troublesome back tooth. But not as drunk as Daniel, who could barely stand up, such was the pain caused by his arm. The door opened, the doctor beckoned, and in they all trooped. Once the various maladies had been explained, the doctor told Daniel to remove his shirt then lie on a sturdy table, both of which he achieved with difficulty.

Doctor Hurley, his white sleeves held above his wrists by garters, grasped Daniel's lower arm and proceeded to manipulate it rather energetically. When Daniel began to retch, the doctor gestured to Simon to retrieve a bucket from beneath the table.

'You've broken it,' Doctor Hurley diagnosed as he gave the arm an extra hard prod. 'Not through the skin, though, that's a bonus.'

Daniel turned his head and vomited into the bucket. Mostly.

'Go easy, for God's sake!' Simon exclaimed. 'You're hurting him!'

'Yes. Unavoidable, I'm afraid.' As though Daniel might be deaf as well as drunk and in possession of a broken limb, the doctor said loudly: 'When did you sustain the break?'

Daniel, his eyes bleary and half-closed, mumbled, 'Yesterday.'

Doctor Hurley nodded. 'That's all right, then. Not too late.' To Simon, he said, 'I'll need your help, if you will. I want you to grip his upper arm while I pull the hand and align the bones, then I'll apply a splint. How much did you say he's had to drink?'

'I didn't,' Simon replied, 'but quite a lot.'

'Yes, I can see that. I hope it's enough.' Doctor Hurley turned to Kitty. 'You might like to leave the room, madam.'

'No, I don't think so. I've seen worse,' Kitty said.

'Are you ready?' Doctor Hurley asked Simon. Simon nodded and the doctor gave a firm, steady pull on Daniel's hand, who passed out as pieces of his radius grated past each other and slid back into alignment.

'Well, that was easy!' the doctor said cheerfully. 'Madam, would you mind?'

Kitty kept the tension on Daniel's hand while the doctor fitted a pair of splints from his elbow to his palm and bound them tightly with layers of bandage.

'There, that should do it.' To Simon, he said, 'Presumably, you work with this man? Yes? Tell him, then, not to remove the bandages for six weeks. Should they become loose, simply apply more over the top. The bones should have knitted by then and the arm be functional. With luck.'

Daniel's eyes fluttered, then he coughed and let out a watery burp. Simon whipped up the bucket, but Daniel pushed it away. Instead, he almost but not quite focused on Kitty and slurred, 'Kitty, angel, please: it hurts, make it go away.'

Kitty and Simon exchanged a horrified glance, and Kitty shot a look over her shoulder at Rian, who, scowling and worrying at his bad tooth, fortunately hadn't heard.

'Get him out!' she whispered to Simon under her breath. Simon helped Daniel off the table and hastily escorted him from the room.

'Next,' Doctor Hurley said, eyeing Rian.

Reluctantly, Rian approached the table, but the doctor redirected him to a high-backed, upholstered chair. When the doctor depressed a pedal, the chair back lowered, affording him a better view into Rian's mouth. He dug around for a minute, murmured 'Mmm', then reached for a large pair of pliers.

Hovering nearby, Kitty said, 'Excuse me, if you don't mind', and gestured at the instrument.

Doctor Hurley looked at it. 'Oh, I beg your pardon.' He wiped the business end of the pliers with a piece of muslin and dropped the cloth into a tray.

234

Kitty inspected it distastefully. As she had suspected — chestnut-coloured horse hairs.

After a deft flick of the wrist and a muffled curse from Rian, the offending tooth was out a moment later. It was indeed rotten, and brought with it a clot of blood and foul-smelling pus.

'*That's* much better out,' Doctor Hurley remarked, and pinged it into the bucket into which Daniel had vomited.

Rian spat, rinsed his mouth with the whiskey he'd brought with him, and said, 'What do I owe you?'

'Are you paying for the other chap as well?'

'Yes, he's one of my men.'

As Rian handed over the money, Doctor Hurley said, 'Are you sure he did it yesterday, and not last Sunday?'

With his tongue, Rian probed the hole where his tooth had been. 'Would it have made a difference?'

Doctor Hurley looked as though he might be going to lie. Then he shrugged. 'He wouldn't have been the first. Ask Peter Lalor. What difference is it to me? I'm a doctor, not a politician.'

★   ★   ★

Kitty lifted the lid and peered into the oversized picnic basket. 'They look lovely, Pierre, thank you, but we're only going to Melbourne, not England.' He must have risen especially early this morning, because he'd made them a selection of really tempting pastries, speciality

235

breads and pies for the journey and arranged them in a snowy white cloth. 'We'll never eat them all.'

'*Mais oui*, Haunui is with you.'

'That's true,' Kitty agreed.

At her elbow, Haunui chortled.

The sun was only just up, but it was already obvious it would be another scorching day. They had gathered outside Bath's Hotel, and were waiting for the horses to be backed into the shafts of the Cobb & Co coach. Currently three coaches were leaving Ballarat for Melbourne every day, and they had booked the earliest as they wanted to arrive at their destination before sundown.

Rian said, for at least the tenth time, 'Are you sure you're happy about doing this?'

Struggling to keep the exasperation from her voice, Kitty replied, 'Yes, of course I am. Really, what can go wrong?'

Plenty, actually, and they both knew it. Delivering Bao to her relatives *should* be a straightforward exercise, but the Chinese were a very closed society not known for welcoming those it did not recognise or trust. However, Kitty would, of course, have Bao with her, and a letter from Wong Fu himself should she be unable to locate Wong Kai immediately in Melbourne. She had also been warned by Wong Fu that Wong Kai could be a difficult man, but Kitty had elected not to share this particular piece of information with Rian. The other undertaking on the agenda for Melbourne did have the potential for trouble, but Kitty was confident that, with the help of Haunui, Simon and Daniel, she would manage.

The livery man fastened the final buckles on the harnesses, then signalled the driver that he was clear to start loading. Pierre passed the picnic basket to Haunui, who heaved it onto one of the bench seats inside the coach.

'We won't all fit, Ma,' Amber said, peering in after it. 'Can me and Bao sit outside with the driver?'

'Bao and *I*,' Kitty corrected. 'No, you can't. You'll sit inside with me.'

'But that'll be boring,' Amber complained.

'I'm sure it will,' Kitty countered, 'but there will be plenty of stops.'

Amber was right, though; the interior of the coach would only seat six comfortably, and now just five because of the picnic basket — two people *would* have to sit outside. She raised her eyebrows at Haunui.

'Suits me, as long as you keep passing up those pastries. You want to sit up with the driver, too?' Haunui asked Simon.

Simon said yes, even though he knew he wouldn't be next to the driver — he'd be perched on the little seat behind and slightly above him, because Haunui certainly wouldn't be travelling all the way to Melbourne on it with his knees up around his ears.

'I will,' Daniel interjected quickly. 'Could do with the fresh air.'

He did look peaky, which was no surprise after the amount he'd had to drink the day before. Kitty wondered if he remembered what he'd said. Since he wouldn't meet her eyes, perhaps he did.

As the last of the luggage was loaded, Rian squeezed Kitty's hand and said, 'You'll be very careful, won't you?'

'I will. And you be careful, too. Watch out for Sergeant Coombes — and for God's sake, Rian, steer clear of Lily Pearce.'

Rian grimaced as he handed Kitty into the coach. 'Don't worry, *mo ghrá*, I intend to.'

Wong Fu embraced Bao, then watched sadly as she climbed on board the coach, followed by Simon. Tahi hung back to wait to see where Amber sat, then settled himself beside her. Observing this, Haunui leaned into the coach and tapped him on the shoulder. 'Hey, boy, how do you know she wants you to sit next to her?'

Tahi reddened.

'It's all right, Haunui, he can stay,' Amber decreed graciously.

Kitty suppressed a smile, and shuffled over so that Simon and Bao, next to her, had more room.

Haunui winked at Kitty, then disappeared, and the coach gave an ominous groan as he climbed up onto the seat next to the driver. A more subdued lurch signalled Daniel's arrival on his perch and then they were off, Kitty, Amber and Bao leaning out the window waving at Rian and Wong Fu until they went around a bend and could no longer see them.

★　★　★

They struck trouble just after Bacchus Marsh, a little more than halfway into their journey. The horses were fresh because they'd been changed less than an hour earlier, so at first Kitty wondered why the coach was slowing.

Then it stopped altogether. For perhaps ten seconds nothing could be heard but the horses snorting and the rattle of harnesses, then Haunui's upside-down face appeared at the top of the window.

'Trouble. Stay inside.' He disappeared again.

Kitty, her heart sinking nauseatingly, looked at Simon.

'Bushrangers?' he whispered, his face paling.

Beside her, she felt Bao stiffen with fear.

'Bushrangers!' Amber repeated far too loudly.

Her exclamation must have travelled, because there was a subtle but unmistakable warning tap on the ceiling of the coach. Kitty lifted her reticule from the seat and nestled it in her lap under a fold of skirt, thankful she had left her lovely brooch back at Lilac Cottage.

Outside, she could hear murmured voices. Knowing she shouldn't, she leant as far to the right as she could manage and looked out the window. From her vantage point she could see two men on horseback in front of and slightly to her side of the coach, their shotguns aimed at the driver, and presumably at Daniel and Haunui. No doubt they had emerged from the stand of bush bordering the road. By straining her neck and looking up, she could just see the barrel of a gun aimed back at them. A stand-off. She pulled her head back in.

'Can you see anything?' she whispered to Simon.

He looked. 'Two on this side. Armed.'

'Could we rush them?' Tahi suggested, suddenly looking far more mature than his years. The hairs on Kitty's arms began to stand up.

Bao let out a whimper, and, very slowly, she lifted her feet up onto the seat, put her head on her knees, and folded herself into a tight ball. Kitty felt her heart constrict with compassion, but there was nothing she could do for the girl right now.

'One's dismounting,' Simon said hoarsely.

Footsteps approached, crunching through drifts of dry eucalyptus leaves on the road. Kitty tugged off her wedding ring and slipped it down the front of her dress. Tahi's hand moved to the hilt of his knife.

'Steady,' Simon warned.

A bearded face peered in at the window and inspected them, then its owner stepped back and called, 'Man, woman an' three kids.' Then, still aiming the barrel of his gun at them, he opened the door and leant in, bringing with him the rancid stink of someone who had lived rough for a very long time.

Bao gave a barely audible whimper.

The bushranger had a good peer around the interior of the coach, presumably looking for potential valuables. He lifted the lid of the picnic basket, frowned at the remains of the pastries, then helped himself to one and stuffed it in his mouth. Chewing, he gestured at Kitty's hands clasped in her lap, which she held out, revealing bare fingers. But he had seen her reticule beneath the folds of her skirt.

'Gimme that,' he said, pointing.

Kitty picked up her reticule, slipped Rian's pistol out of it, cocked it and aimed it directly at the man's forehead. His startled eyes comically round in his sunburnt face, he stared first at the pistol then at Kitty, before retreating from the coach so rapidly that he hit his head on the door lintel. Tahi rose in a half-crouch, snatched the pistol from Kitty's hand, took aim and fired it at the bushranger. The ball hit the man in the arm; he let out a bellow, turned and ran.

Instantly a shot rang out, then another followed by a flurry of hoof beats.

'*Tahi! I could have shot you!*' Kitty shrieked into the ensuing silence.

'Have they gone?' Amber asked, her voice squeaky with fright.

Cautiously, Simon put a foot outside, then almost leapt out of his skin as something very large jumped down from the top of the coach.

'Everyone all right?' Haunui asked. 'What happened?'

The driver followed him a moment later, his face parchment white. 'No one hurt? God help me, I didn't even see them. Usually they'll have someone in the middle of the road, but this time they just came straight out of the trees.' He mopped his sweating brow with a large red kerchief. 'I don't know: I got off the escort carts to get away from this sort of thing.'

Daniel climbed down, his rifle hooked over his good arm, his face like thunder. 'I think I might have missed.' He sounded disgusted with himself.

'Good shot, though, eh, for one arm,' Haunui said.

'I still missed.'

'They missed, too,' the driver pointed out.

'Why did they give up so easily?' Tahi asked.

They were all standing around the coach now, except for Bao, who had refused to come out. Kitty thought a drop or two of laudanum might be in order; it wouldn't do her any harm to sleep the rest of the way to Melbourne, and it might help to settle the poor child's nerves.

'Busy road,' the driver said, and just as he did, a wagon they had passed several miles back appeared around the bend. He flagged it down to warn the occupants of the danger.

But the rest of the journey was uneventful, and they arrived at Melbourne safely, as did the 752 troy ounces of gold from Rian's claim carefully packed into the bottom of the picnic basket.

★   ★   ★

The following morning, Kitty rose early. The night before, they had taken rooms at the Criterion Hotel on Collins Street, and at breakfast shared a table in the dining room. Haunui presented an odd sight, sitting regally with a table napkin tucked into the neck of his shirt beneath his grizzled and heavily tattooed face. Judging by the agitated stares of the waiting staff, Kitty suspected they would have liked to have tossed him out, but were too frightened to do so.

Today he and Daniel were off to inspect the *Katipo*. It was a very good thing that Rian's claim had proved to be so profitable: God knows how they would have paid for the well-overdue work on the schooner otherwise. Amber and Bao were to be left in Simon's care, while she would attempt to find Wong Kai.

Breakfast over, Kitty stepped out onto Collins Street and walked until she came to a cab stand. When the driver dismounted from his seat to open the door for her, she told him she wanted to go to the area of Little Bourke Street that fell between Swanston and Russell Streets.

'Chinatown? Are you sure?' he asked, frowning. 'That's no place for a lady.'

'Yes, I am sure,' Kitty said as he handed her into the cab.

'No shopping there, you know. Not for the likes of . . . well, people like us, if you know what I mean.'

'I'm not interested in shopping. I have business to attend to,' Kitty said as she sat down and arranged her skirts.

The cab driver shrugged; after all, he'd had much stranger requests. He closed the door and climbed back onto his seat.

The cab moved off and Kitty watched as the wooden and brick buildings of Collins Street went past the window. The streets here were not yet paved, but they were remarkably wide, the main streets at least, and, as it was approaching the height of the Australian summer, they were now also dry and dusty, a marked change from the mud and puddles she and Amber had dashed through in August. The town was no less busy, though. There were people everywhere — on foot, on horseback, and riding in carts and cabs and carriages.

The cab driver turned into Elizabeth Street, then Little Bourke Street, but stopped as he came to Swanston and slid back the covered window behind his head. Through the gap he informed Kitty, 'I'd rather not take me horse in. Too hard to turn around. Will this do you, Missus?'

Kitty grinned to herself. 'This will be fine, thank you.' She let herself out, paid the driver and walked into Chinatown.

For people unaccustomed to the Chinese way of life, she supposed, this particular area of Little Bourke Street might seem a little disconcerting, but she had visited Shanghai and Canton many times and was familiar with the mystery and exoticism. Here, as there, the street was lined with all sorts of merchants, and provisions stores with their wares extending in orderly piles onto the street, and eating houses and Chinese apothecaries and doctors. Upstairs and behind the scenes, Kitty knew, would be the lodging houses and the premises of the *tongs* — the clan and district benevolent societies. And the opium dens.

The faces she passed were all Chinese, and they were neither friendly nor hostile. Some were curious, no doubt wondering what a white-skinned woman was doing wandering alone in the middle of the Chinese quarter.

Kitty caught the eye of a man who was trying not to let her see he was observing her, and stepped in front of him. 'Excuse me, could you please tell me how to get to Celestial Avenue?'

The man stared at her, appeared momentarily flustered, said something in what Kitty thought might be Cantonese, then shook his head.

'I'm sorry, do you not speak English?'

The man shook his head again, the oil dressing his queue gleaming in the sun, then hurried away, clearly embarrassed.

There was not a single woman in sight.

Kitty thought for a moment, then entered a shop. It was packed from floor to ceiling with goods in bales and baskets and boxes, on pallets and in packets and hanging from poles. There were foodstuffs, clothing, tools, fabrics, household goods and all things required for daily living. In short, it was exactly like a European general store, but with a very oriental flavour and the distinct, sharp and spicy smell that came with it.

At the rear stood a man behind a counter, watching Kitty with a gimlet eye as she approached. He was Chinese, but did not wear the usual queue; his hair was cut short, and he was dressed in well-cut grey trousers, a precisely pressed white shirt with a high collar, and a buttoned grey waistcoat. Kitty was fairly confident that he would speak English.

'Good morning,' she said. 'I am looking for an address on Celestial Avenue. I wonder if you could tell me how to get there?'

The man appeared to consider the request.

Then he spoke. 'Who is it that you are looking for, may I ask?' His English was very good.

'I have business with a man named Wong Kai.' The man's face remained impassive, but an unguarded spark of interest — and unease? — flared in his eyes. 'Do you know him?' Kitty asked.

'I know *of* him.'

Kitty suspected he was obfuscating. 'I have been told that he resides on Celestial Avenue, although I have not been given the exact location of his residence.' She withdrew Wong Fu's letter from her reticule. 'I have a letter of introduction from his brother. Perhaps this may help you to decide whether you wish to assist me?'

The storekeeper seemed to be engaged in some sort of internal debate. Finally, he said, 'This is not my business, Mrs, er . . . '

'Mrs Farrell.'

' . . . Mrs Farrell, and I do not know what *your* business is with Wong Kai, but I do know him. I know him well and I warn you that he is not a man with whom you should involve yourself. He is a powerful man and — '

'Yes,' Kitty interrupted, 'but I am here on family business, among other things, and I'm sure he will want to see me.'

'He is a family man, I agree, but I fear you may not be as welcome as you seem to believe you will be.'

Kitty was getting sick of this. 'Look, Mr . . . Shopkeeper,' she said, moving closer to the counter and making the most of the fact that she was taller than he was.

'I am Wu Chun-Kit,' he said tartly.

'Mr Wu, I have Wong Kai's niece with me and I need to deliver her to him. She is not well. I appreciate your concern for my welfare, but I would like your help to find him. Can you oblige me or will I have to go somewhere else?'

Mr Wu took a moment to adjust his shirt cuffs, and Kitty could see that he had been somewhat startled by her outburst. 'Mrs Farrell, I will be blunt. I have to say that I admire you, and for that reason I will help you. Your character and fortitude seem to be fashioned from some material that is not common to most European women. But it is not your welfare about which I am concerned: it is *mine*. Wong Kai is a business associate, but he is also ... what is the appropriate English word? The *overlord* of the Chinese quarter. I will not endanger my business, or indeed my own health,' he added with unexpected dryness, 'just to fulfil your request.' He wrote something on a scrap of paper and handed it to her. 'So please do not say where you came by this information. Celestial Avenue is the second lane on your left.'

Kitty read the address on the paper, memorised it and gave it back. 'Thank you, Mr Wu. I am most grateful.'

Mr Wu bowed. 'Good luck, Mrs Farrell,' he said, and allowed her a small smile, but behind it Kitty saw a ghost of real fear.

13

Haunui and Daniel picked their way across the cracked, barren flats bordering the Yarra, trying not to turn their ankles on the treacherous clods the sun had made of the winter's mud. Down here it stank almost more than it did in the town — the shit, animal carcasses and unnameable scum collecting along the river's edge testifying to the reason. There were perhaps a hundred vessels at anchorage, and Haunui and Daniel made a game of guessing their ports of origin as they tottered along, swearing energetically, until they came to the wharf at which the *Katipo II* was moored, a short distance below the falls. She was off her hull now, and standing proud against a backdrop of dozens of other masts and furled sails. Their boots on solid boards, they clomped out over the evil-smelling water and boarded the schooner, Daniel calling out as they did so.

Charlie Dunlop appeared from below a minute later, sucking on a pipe and drinking something the colour of crude oil from a mug.

Haunui sniffed the air suspiciously, but it didn't smell like rum.

Charlie Dunlop's empty left sleeve was neatly pinned just below the shoulder. A seaman himself, he had lost his arm to a shark off Fiji, and it had broken his heart not to be able to return to the life he loved. Hanging around ships in port was the next best thing.

'Coffee?' he offered, raising his mug.

Daniel declined, and introduced Haunui.

'Aye, I met fellows like you in New Zealand. And in Hawaii and the Marquesas. You related?'

'In the past.'

'How's the prospectin' going? Made your fortune yet?' Charlie asked Daniel.

'We're doing all right.'

'Thought about giving it a go meself, but, well . . . ' Charlie waggled his stump, then emptied the dregs of his coffee over the side of the schooner. 'You'll be wanting to have a look around. Thinking of going back to sea, are you? I'd give my right arm to go with you.' He laughed uproariously at his own joke, although it was obviously one he'd told many times. Glancing at the splint on Daniel's forearm, he added, 'What a pair of cripples, eh? What did you do? Get caught up in the stoush at Eureka?'

'Fell down a mine shaft,' Daniel confessed sheepishly.

'Well, at least you'll get yours back. Come below and have a look at what they've done with the cabin. Nothing flash, mind, but it's exactly what Captain Farrell asked for, all nice and new. And that Frenchie fellow that does the cooking, he'll be pleased with his new galley.'

'Cajun,' Haunui corrected.

'Eh?'

'He's Cajun, not French.'

They had a good look around, and the ship's fitters had indeed done a fine job. Back on deck, Daniel inspected the repair work and the new masts, and the coils of bristly, fresh rope.

'Sails shouldn't be far away,' Charlie said. 'Sailmaker said he could salvage a few, but that they were all mostly on their last legs. Said it's a wonder you actually got to Melbourne.'

Daniel nodded. 'When does he think they'll be ready?'

'Another month? A few navy ships are in and wanting work, and they pay better, of course. And he says he don't do ensigns, so you'll have to get your own.'

'Can you send us a message when they've been fitted?'

'I can,' Charlie said agreeably.

Daniel thanked him, gave him the money Rian had sent, and he and Haunui trudged back to town, Daniel holding his splinted arm against his belly to ease the ache.

'Rian'll be pleased,' he remarked.

Haunui decided that now was as good a time as any. Without turning his head, he said, 'He won't be if you keep on saying silly things to his wife.'

Daniel's pace faltered, but he kept walking. He didn't say anything for almost a minute; then, 'Who told you? Kitty?'

'No, Simon.' Haunui glanced at Daniel out of the corner of his eye to gauge his reaction, but saw only a resigned acceptance. 'He wasn't telling tales. He's worried, eh? For Kitty and for Rian. And for you.'

'I was drunk, I didn't mean to say it.'

'Ae, I know you didn't *mean* to say it, but you did. And Rian could have heard you. He would have had your balls for ear pendants. And, boy?

How do you think it made Kitty feel, eh?'

Daniel blew out his cheeks, lifted his hat and swept his hair back off his face. 'I know, I've been thinking about it and I feel like a shit. I've never said anything like that before. I've always, well, I've never said anything at all.'

'Ae, I know. Simon said.' They'd come to a public house, and Haunui stopped and gestured at the door. Daniel nodded and they went inside, waiting for a moment while their eyes adjusted to the gloom.

They each bought a pint of ale and sat down. 'It's been ten years, boy,' Haunui said, as though there hadn't been a break in the conversation. 'There's nothing you can do about it. Nothing is ever going to come between those two. Certainly not you.' He knew he was being blunt, and that Daniel wouldn't appreciate hearing it, but it was probably better for the lad coming from someone he didn't know particularly well.

'Look, I know that,' Daniel said, his mood fraying slightly now, although Haunui sensed that the anger was only masking a bone-deep hopelessness. 'And, well, there's nothing else to be said, is there?'

'Not really.'

'No.'

Haunui took a long draught of his ale, then stifled a burp. 'Good, 'cause you can't have her, boy, and that's that.'

Daniel stared stonily into his drink; Haunui knew exactly how he felt.

*   *   *

Kitty rapped on the door and waited. After more than a minute, a small slot opened and a pair of dark, suspicious eyes peered out at her.

'Good morning, I'm looking for Wong Kai,' she said. 'Is he here, please?'

The eyes stared for a second, then the slot snapped shut.

Damn, Kitty thought. But she waited.

The slot opened again and the eyes reappeared. 'Who is speaking?'

'My name is Mrs Kitty Farrell. I am here on business relating to Mr Wong's family. I have a letter from his brother, Wong Fu.'

The slot closed again.

Kitty crossed her arms and looked around. Celestial Avenue, which came off Little Bourke Street, was a very narrow lane not even wide enough for a cart to enter. It sliced between wooden buildings that stood two and three storeys high and barely allowed the sun to reach the ground. Where it did, several skinny dogs sunned themselves in the dust. The doors that opened off it were featureless, and the windows, some glazed and some shuttered, unwelcoming. The distinctly pungent smell of dried fish lingered in the air.

The door opened to reveal a man in tunic and trousers, and an embroidered skullcap. 'He says he will see you for five minutes.' He stepped aside, which Kitty took as a signal to enter.

Immediately in front of the door was a steep set of stairs. The man went up first, his slippers making a whispering sound on the bare wooden treads. Behind them, the door swung shut, closing out most of the light. At the top a dimly lit hall stretched ahead of them, its closed doors leaking muffled sounds as they passed. But one room was open, revealing two large tables occupied by Chinese men intent on, at one, the counters and bowl of *fan tan* and, at the other, the character-covered paper tickets of *pakapoo*. Several glanced up as she passed, perhaps startled to see a European woman in their midst, but most were too preoccupied with their gambling to notice her.

The man led Kitty to the end of the hall to another closed door; the air was laced now with a musty, sweet smell, and Kitty thought she knew what would be behind it. When the door opened, he took Kitty's elbow and escorted her inside.

She had never been in an opium den before. Rian had, in Shanghai, and she suspected that some of the crew had as well, and not just on business, but Rian had never allowed her to visit one. She imagined he would be rather cross if he knew she was here now. Perhaps she just wouldn't tell him.

There was one small window, draped with a fall of red cloth, in the comparatively large room, and two lamps on the wall, but no other light. Six wide divans lined the space, each occupied by two people. They lay propped on large cushions, a tray of opium-smoking paraphernalia between them. Some slept; some chatted in quiet, relaxed tones. The only reaction to her presence seemed to be mildly curious glances. The room was clean, the carpet of good quality, and the linens on the divans appeared fresh. The air was thick with smoke and Kitty fancied she felt it going straight to her head. If Mr Wong was on one of the divans, she didn't think they would be having much of a conversation.

'This way,' her escort urged, and led her through yet another door concealed behind a wall-hanging.

In this next room, the air was much less redolent of opium. Wong Kai — and it surely must be him, as the resemblance to Wong Fu was very strong — sat in a velvet-upholstered, high-backed chair, buffing his fingernails. His long robe was of deep blue silk, and his hair hung unbraided down his back. He was clean-shaven and Kitty thought he looked remarkably benign for a man with such a fearsome reputation. To one side was a desk piled high with what appeared to be invoices and receipts and various ledger books, and an abacus.

Wong Kai gave his thumbnail a final, careful pass with the buffer and looked up. 'Ah, thank you, So-Yee. You may go now. Mrs Kitty Farrell, I presume?'

'Yes. I am pleased to meet you, Mr Wong,' Kitty replied, hoping it was indeed him. 'You are not an easy man to locate.' Wong Kai smiled, and she had the distinct impression that he knew full well she had been looking for him.

'And I am pleased to meet you.' He set his nail buffer aside and indicated a chair with an ornately carved dragon climbing up its back. 'Welcome to the Chinese quarter. Please, do sit down.'

Kitty did so, and instantly regretted it because the seat was very close to the ground and now she had to look up at him.

'May I offer you tea?'

'Yes, thank you,' Kitty replied with genuine gratitude. She was parched.

When So-Yee had been summoned and the tea served, she said, 'Mr Wong, I am here about your niece Bao.' Wong Kai's face stilled and his brows lowered a fraction; Kitty noticed, but she went on. 'Your brother Wong Fu is a friend of both me and my husband, Captain Rian Farrell. A good friend. Bao is also a companion of our daughter, Amber. Bao has not been well of late, and Wong Fu believes she needs time away from Ballarat, so he has asked me to escort her here to stay with you and your wife.' Kitty paused to allow Wong Kai to make some general sort of comment about Mrs Wong, but there was none. 'That I have done. She's presently at my hotel with my daughter — I did not wish her to accompany me this morning in the event that I couldn't locate you. I'm not convinced that this is an altogether safe town.'

'It is not. And yet you have ventured out alone?'

'I have.' Kitty looked pointedly at the teapot and Wong Kai poured her another cup. 'Thank you. I will bring her here this afternoon.'

'No, not here. Not even my wife comes here. I will arrange to have her collected.' Wong Kai contemplated Kitty unblinkingly, then inclined his head in a small bow. 'Thank you, Mrs Farrell. I am indebted to you. I am very fond of my niece. But tell me, what has been the nature of her illness?'

Kitty explained what had happened to Bao, from the persistent persecution on the Ballarat goldfields, to the fear generated by the Eureka uprising. Wong Kai nodded, indicating his understanding that such things could be unnerving for a young girl. Then, not bothering to conceal her own anger over the affair, she told him frankly about Searle and Tuttle.

For some time Wong Kai didn't utter a word. His face was expressionless, except for a small muscle that began to spasm beneath his right eyelid, but his eyes hardened until they seemed to resemble glittering, smoky quartz. Even though he sat some distance from her, Kitty felt the rage roll off him in silent waves, and she involuntarily pressed herself back into her chair.

'These . . . *men*,' he said eventually, his voice taut. 'Justice was dispensed?'

'Do you mean were the authorities alerted?' Kitty asked, even though she was fairly sure he didn't.

'No, I mean were they made to pay.' Each word came out of his mouth like a ball from the barrel of a musket.

'I believe your brother attended to it.'

Wong Kai relaxed, just a little. 'Then we must see what we can do to set poor Bao on the road to recovery. Fu has done the right thing.' He gave himself a little shake and his anger seemed to get sucked back into him, like smoke disappearing up a chimney. 'Now, Mrs Farrell, I also hear that you may have other business to discuss.'

Kitty nodded. How could he have known that? She hoped Mr Wu wasn't in trouble. 'Yes, I have a certain amount of gold I am in the market to sell. I don't wish to go through the official channels, or to approach a gold buyer,' she waved her hand vaguely at Wong Kai's window, 'on the street. I wondered if you could help.' Gold purchased by Wong Kai, if he was indeed in that line of business, would not go back to England, but to China, and therefore would not be subject to certain duties and taxes. The price Kitty might get for it could well be better than the £3 normally on offer.

'Are you sure that I buy gold, Mrs Farrell, or are you guessing?'

Kitty smoothed a crease from her skirt. 'I'm guessing, Mr Wong. But I think it's a reasonably educated guess.'

Wong Kai leaned back in his chair and made a steeple out of his fingers. 'How much gold do you have? If I was in the business of buying gold, I would not be interested in a kerchief knotted around a handful of paltry little flakes.'

'On this trip, 752 troy ounces. There will be more in the near future. Quite possibly a lot more. My husband believes his claim has nowhere near bottomed out. Our intention is to take out all we can as quickly as we can, as we wish to return to sea.'

Wong Kai looked thoughtful. 'And your husband wishes to mine this claim himself?'

'Well, yes, he does.' Then Kitty understood what Wong Kai was thinking. 'He doesn't wish to sell it, no.'

'Mmm.' Wong Kai appeared to put that possibility aside. 'As it happens, Mrs Farrell, I am in the business of buying gold, and I will buy yours. Here are my terms.' He wrote a series of figures on a sheet of paper, placed it on a small lacquered tray and passed it to her. 'And those are my best terms, given the panic the recent uprising at Eureka seems to have caused. They are not terms I am prepared to offer everyone with whom I do business, but you have been of great assistance to my family, so I am offering them to you.'

Kitty considered his offer; his terms were not spectacular, but certainly better than those she would encounter on the street or at the bank. 'Yes, I believe we can do business, Mr Wong. I will deliver the gold to you today.'

Wong Kai finally smiled. 'And how will you carry forty-seven pounds of gold through the streets of Melbourne, Mrs Farrell? In your dainty reticule? Under your arm?'

Slightly insulted by the silly picture of her his words had just painted, Kitty replied brusquely, 'I have several of my husband's men with me, Mr Wong. They will bring the gold.'

'No. It will be collected from your hotel this afternoon along with Bao. You will receive the money then. After the gold has been weighed, naturally. Is that acceptable to you?'

'Yes, it is.' Kitty rose to take her leave. 'Thank you, Mr Wong, it has been a pleasure doing business with you.' Well, she had achieved everything she had come for.

Wong Kai stood himself, and bowed. 'And

thank you again for your service to my family. I hope I may one day return the favour.'

Wong Kai rang a bell, and So-Yee appeared and escorted her downstairs and out into the warm, fish-tainted air.

★   ★   ★

Mr Wong's people arrived at The Criterion as arranged that afternoon, all three attired in smart European clothing. One, a bespectacled gentleman who introduced himself as Mr Chen, carried a case in which was packed a set of elaborate measuring scales, which he assembled in Simon and Daniel's room, before weighing Rian's gold ounce by ounce. The money was then handed over and the gold taken away, along with Bao. She wept a little and said she would miss Kitty and Amber, and that she would return to Ballarat as soon as she felt rested. It was obvious to Kitty, though, that the child was relieved to be away from the brutality of the goldfields. Here in Melbourne, Bao would benefit from the familiar and comforting company of her aunt, and, in the rabbit warrens that made up the Chinese quarter in Little Bourke Street, would perhaps also find the physical security she needed.

★   ★   ★

The following day Simon went to visit Patrick in the Melbourne gaol, where he'd been transported from Ballarat along with the thirteen other insurgents arrested after Eureka who had been charged with high treason. Daniel had gone off somewhere after breakfast, and following the midday meal Haunui, Tahi and Amber had set out on a mission to find an Irish ensign for the *Katipo*.

Having spent the morning happily browsing around the shops with Amber, Kitty was now packing, ready to return to Ballarat the following day. She had made a few purchases for Amber, including a new dress, and bought Rian a beautiful white lawn shirt and herself a panama hat — which she was going to wear in the sun whether people laughed at her or not — and was struggling to close the lid on the trunk she was sharing with Amber when a discreet rap came at the door. Distracted, she crossed the room.

'Oh, hello Daniel. Are you looking for the others?'

'No, actually, it's you I'd like to speak to, Kitty. If that's all right,' Daniel replied, hoping he didn't sound as nervous as he felt.

He'd been standing in the hall for ten minutes trying to pluck up the courage to knock, and praying she didn't suddenly open the door and see him hovering there like a fool.

'Oh. Yes, of course.' She stepped aside. 'Come in, please.'

His heart gave a silly little lurch. 'Into your room?'

Kitty smiled. 'We'll leave the door open, shall we?'

He hesitated, then removed his hat and followed her inside.

'Please, sit down, Daniel.' Kitty indicated a chair.

'No, thank you,' he replied, then cursed himself for sounding so pompous. He crossed the room, averting his eyes from the lace-trimmed chemise that lay folded on top of the open trunk on the bed, and stood by the window, his heart thudding with a combination of nerves at what he needed to say and exhilaration at being alone with her. He closed his eyes. This had been a mistake.

'Daniel?'

He turned away from the window and saw that Kitty had decided to take the chair herself. She was gazing at him in that patient, slightly amused and genuinely attentive way she had that always made people think they were special, that she was listening just to them. And she looked lovely. She always looked lovely. He cleared his throat. 'I wanted to apologise.'

Kitty inclined her head quizzically, but said nothing.

'For saying what I did in the doctor's surgery. When I was drunk. I didn't mean to. It just . . . came out.' He held her gaze for a moment, then looked away, knowing he still hadn't told the truth. Because what he was truly sorry for was that he hadn't also told her he loved her. 'And I'm sorry if what I said embarrassed you, Kitty, I truly am.'

He felt himself reddening, and turned back to the window. Outside, in the street, a wagon had lost a wheel and there were barrels all over the road.

Behind him, Kitty was silent for almost a minute. Then she said, 'Thank you, Daniel. There was no need to apologise.'

He waited — hoped — for her to say something else, but she didn't. Finally, he faced her. 'Well, that's all I wanted to say. I'll leave you in peace now.'

Kitty rose and came to stand next to him. She touched him on the back of his hand, and he thought the skin where her fingers had rested might catch fire.

'I appreciate it, Daniel. I appreciate . . . everything. But you do understand. Don't you?'

And he saw then that she knew it all — everything that he felt for her, everything he wanted, and everything he wasn't going to get. In her face he saw genuine empathy, and friendship, and affection, and even respect, but nothing that gave him any hope of anything else — no hint of love, and no desire. And there never had been.

He nodded, picked up his hat and left.

For a long while Kitty stared at the empty doorway, feeling upset and inexplicably guilty, then she went back to her packing, jamming the lid of the trunk down and banging on it with somewhat unnecessary force.

Part Three

The Lamp of the Wicked

14

Ballarat, late January 1855

'Bao says she's feeling much better,' Amber relayed, holding the letter in one hand and wafting a palm-leaf fan across her face with the other.

'Does she say it's hot in Melbourne?' Kitty asked.

'Roasting,' Amber confirmed. 'She says people are swimming in the Yarra.'

I don't blame them, Kitty thought as the sweat trickled down her sides and pasted the fabric of her chemise to her skin. If she could be granted a single wish right now, she would chose to be on the *Katipo*, in delicious, cool, full sail.

Since their return from Melbourne seven weeks ago, the temperature on the diggings had soared. Every morning, the sun rose and beat a relentless path into the sky, wilting everything it touched and fraying the tempers of even the most benign of characters. In the bakery the heat was unbearable, but customers still wanted their pasties and their savoury pies in spite of the height of the mercury in the thermometer. The price of ice had become prohibitive and, as butter became rancid within hours unless kept packed in the precious commodity, she and Pierre had temporarily ceased making *croissants*. Customers complained at the disappearance of their buttery French treats, but there was nothing for it.

Things had changed in Ballarat after the uprising. The clash between the diggers and the Queen's men at Eureka had been more or less impromptu, but the outcome seemed as though it might finally, eventually, clear the path towards the goals for which the miners and shopkeepers of Victoria's goldfields had been striving for years. Licence hunts had been suspended, and Major-General Nickle, who had arrived with the 800 reinforcements on 5 December, had turned out to be not such a martinet after all. In fact, he had immediately gone about actually listening to the diggers' complaints, then restrained the behaviour of the police, and within days had lifted the decree of martial law. The diggers charged with high treason, however, were still awaiting trial in Melbourne, although word was that the Crown would have a tough job making the charges stick, given the findings the Goldfields Commission was likely to deliver in its report expected in March.

Soldiers were still at large in Ballarat, although in smaller numbers, and the police continued to roam, but the respite in the licence hunts reduced the impact of their presence markedly. There were far fewer opportunities for bullying and extortion, and Nickle's men had been ordered to keep an eye on such activities anyway, which, as Rian remarked to Kitty, must be severely clipping Sergeant Coombes's wings. All the same, Rian had continued to keep his head down after Eureka, concentrating on extracting as much gold as possible from the claim as quickly as he and the crew could manage.

Christmas had been a quiet, strange affair. They were more accustomed to celebrating the holiday at sea, and not usually in temperatures of almost 100 degrees. But the crew had knocked together a long table from pieces of packing crate and arranged tea chests around it for chairs, Kitty, Leena and Amber had spent all afternoon decorating and laying it for an evening feast, and Pierre had cooked himself into a lather. True, the ox-tail soup was actually kangaroo tail, and several parakeets had given their lives to stand in for pigeons in the game pies, the plums in the puddings were tinned, and Ropata broke a tooth on a small gold nugget hidden in one of them, but the general opinion was that the meal was superb.

Maureen was invited, and even though she said she had a lovely time, she kept blotting her eyes and blowing her nose because of Patrick's absence. She cheered up only when Rian assured her that, in his opinion, as soon as the commission's report was released, the 'Eureka fourteen' would be released and on their way home before she knew it.

Flora also came, in spite of Christmas Day being a very busy time for her: so many lonely men missing home and their womenfolk, she explained in a voice designed not to carry as far as Amber's ears. As gifts she brought, for the women, scent in pretty crystal bottles, and for the men a choice of either a bottle of best single malt whiskey or an hour with one of her girls.

Poor Mick was in a terrible quandary.

Kitty gave Rian the shirt she had bought him in Melbourne, and he gave her a beautiful nightdress of pale green silk he'd had one of Wong Fu's men tailor, and which made her go the colour of a tomato when she opened it in front of everyone. As usual Amber received extravagant gifts from every member of the crew, and in return she'd made them biscuits in the bakery oven. These were a bit flat and overdone, but they swore to a man that they were the best biscuits they'd ever tasted.

The new year arrived with little fanfare, the temperature increased even further, and Kitty began to look forward in earnest to the day they would pack up, leave Lilac Cottage and head back to Melbourne, the *Katipo* and the glorious sea. Since she had been to see Wong Kai, they had sent another two shipments of gold to him, and their stockpile of cash was now accruing very nicely. The dust from the Eureka uprising was settling, the licence hunts had stopped, she had only caught sight of Lily twice in the street and had been given a wide and wary berth, and Sergeant Coombes appeared to be too busy avoiding the eye of Major-General Nickle to pay any attention to Rian.

Now, if only the terrible weather would break, they might be afforded some relief from the appalling heat.

Kitty pushed herself out of the rocking chair and propped open the door with a lump of quartz Rian had carted all the way back from the river because he liked the way it sparkled in the

268

sun. A tiny breeze meandered in, but did little to dissipate the stifling heat. Bodie lay on the cool stone hearth, her mouth open, panting. Outside the sky was an ominous ochre colour, staining everything beneath it vaguely yellow. Brooding clouds hovered above the hills to the south-east, constipated with rain.

Amber put Bao's letter aside, picked up her skirts and flapped them in an effort to circulate some air around her legs. 'God, Ma, when's the rain going to come?'

'Language, please,' Kitty said automatically, as she looked up at the sky. 'I don't know, love, but I hope it's soon.'

First week of February 1855

Rian gripped the soggy rope with both hands and hung on as he spun slowly upwards towards the watery sunlight, his head down against the fat drops of water falling from the lip of the shaft. At the top, Gideon reached out a huge hand and hauled him out of the bucket and onto solid ground.

Rian was relieved to see that the rain had stopped — at last — but the sky was still a strange, pale, washed-out grey. Weak blue was breaking through to the south, but the dark clouds still sat to the north of Black Hill and purpled the sky beyond, where rain continued to fall, accompanied by muted thunder. It had been raining almost solidly for five days now, and everyone was heartily sick of it. Where once was hard ground there was now mud, reminiscent of winter but without the freezing cold, and many shafts had flooded to the point that mining had ceased, so dangerous had the soft, waterlogged walls become.

Fortuitously, however, Rian's claim was not situated in the path of a new underground watercourse, and had been spared the worst effects of these unexpected subterranean springs. So they had kept on mining, hauling out buckets of washdirt all day and well into the night until they became too tired to work safely. In Rian's estimation, another three weeks would take them to the bottom of the lead and to the outer boundaries of the claim. By then, they would have taken all the gold they could without encroaching on neighbouring claims. Not a bad investment, as it had turned out, and he expected there to be a tidy sum more before they scraped the bottom. But he knew he had to return to the sea soon — he felt that part of him was slowly dying. They all did. This mining lark had been an adventure, but his feet belonged on a deck above rolling waves, not knee-deep in mud or dust. And there was Kitty to consider: she was pining desperately for her beloved high seas, and he hated to see her unhappy. Anyway, he'd promised.

Gideon handed him a mug of coffee enhanced with a liberal splash of whiskey; he downed half in one go, and glanced up at the sun. It was around three, so he'd been underground for four hours. 'When did the rain stop?'

'About two hours ago,' Gideon replied,

peering down the shaft and waiting for Mick to appear.

Rian nodded, and eased his aching back and shoulders. The heat certainly hadn't abated, and the steam rising off the ground and the mullock heaps surrounding the neighbouring shafts gave the landscape a rather unearthly effect. As Mick's dirty face appeared over the lip of the shaft, Gideon halted the horse on the whip, held it until Mick decanted himself, then detached the rope from its harness. The horse, having done the same thing thousands of times, turned itself around; Gideon reattached the rope, the horse plodded off along the worn path and the bucket descended, on its way back down to Ropata to be filled.

A creaking of harnesses announced Daniel's arrival with the cart, Haunui and Simon rattling around in the back. The splint had come off Daniel's arm a week ago but it was still weak, so he'd been put in charge of driving the bullocks, a pair of docile, semi-somnolent beasts. Haunui and Simon jumped out, reached for their shovels, and began tossing arcs of washdirt into the cart. Rian watched for a few minutes, finished his coffee, then picked up his own shovel and set to. In twenty minutes the cart was full and they set off for the river, leaving Gideon behind to supervise Simon's descent into the shaft. Hawk and Tahi were already at the Yarrowee's edge working the long tom.

Because of the rain the Malakoff Lead wasn't as crowded as usual, but not everyone had been flooded out and the diggings were still

271

reasonably busy. Rian nodded in response to hands raised in greeting, and wondered what Pierre was preparing for supper. He'd been bringing it out to the claim lately so they could keep working, and Kitty and Amber, and Leena and the children, often came with him to share the evening meal.

Ahead he could hear the Yarrowee, in summer normally little more than a meandering stream, hissing and gurgling along, swollen and extended beyond its banks after the week's downpour. The day before yesterday they'd had to move the long tom back from the river's edge: instead of leaving the gold in the riffles, the current had simply swept it away, along with the washdirt.

As they rounded a bend the river came into sight, a dirty brown snake of water bringing with it debris and foam from upstream. As usual its edges were lined with diggers bent over cradles and long toms, and the odd low flume temporarily abandoned over water that was for now far too deep and swift. Daniel brought the bullocks to an untidy halt, and everyone got off, boots sending up small dollops of mud.

Rian plodded across to watch as Hawk shovelled washdirt into one end of the long tom and Tahi walked along its length, picking out any large pieces of gravel carried along by the water that might damage the sieve. What collected in the tray at the other end was clean gold.

'Much in this lot?'

Hawk grunted without looking up. He'd removed his shirt, and his skin was glistening with sweat. 'No sign of bottoming out yet.'

'Shall I take over?'

Hawk glanced at the pile of washdirt at his feet still to go into the long tom. 'After this.'

Rian took off his hat and fanned his face. The leaden clouds beyond Black Hill had darkened even further and it was raining again to the north, the smell of it travelling on the warm wind.

Soon, the cart was empty and Tahi and Daniel were ready to return to the shaft. Hawk sat on the riverbank to rest his aching back, Mick began the delicate job of removing the washed gold from the riffles in the collection tray, and Rian took a long draught of unpleasantly warm water from his bottle, then started on the heap of washdirt. The long tom was set parallel to the river's edge, a foot or so into the water to catch the current, which meant he had to stand at the head of it with his boots submerged, but he didn't mind because at least his feet were cool. He began to establish a rhythm, bending first to the left to scoop up a shovelful of washdirt, then swinging it to his right and dropping it neatly into the long tom, being careful not to overshoot the mark and tip any of the precious gold-bearing ore into the river. After a while he became aware of little more than the fluid movement of his muscles and his clothes sticking sweatily to his skin.

Which is why he got such a shock when the ground suddenly began to vibrate beneath his boots and a rumbling noise seemed to rise straight out of the earth. Alarmed, he looked up to see Hawk and Mick staring at him. Earthquake?

273

Then the rumbling grew to a roar, and a torrent of water, mud and small boulders burst around the narrow bend in the river, and swept away everything in its path.

★ ★ ★

Hawk felt himself tumbling over and over, but still he held his breath, feeling the skin on his torso and arms rubbing raw as he scraped against rock and riverbed and branch, praying that he would find air before his lungs burst. Then his scalp felt afire and he was hauled upwards by his hair and out of the watery maelstrom. He reached out and grabbed at whatever had saved him.

'Jaysus, mate,' Mick gasped, as Hawk wrapped a muscular arm around his throat.

Hawk let go and pulled himself further out of the torrent, draping himself over the overhanging bough to which Mick was clinging.

'Where — ' Hawk exploded into a fit of coughing, then vomited up a ribbon of dirty water.

'He should have been just behind us.'

Hawk coughed again, and spat. The water level was beginning to subside now, and rapidly. A minute ago it had reached his armpits — now it was only waist-height. A flash flood.

'He'll have got out further downstream,' Mick said, sounding more hopeful than confident, and cleared his nose into the water. 'Be walking back by now.' He glanced at Hawk's shoulders. 'You've a few good scrapes on your back, so you have.'

274

Hawk wasn't even aware of them. 'Did you see him after we went into the water?'

Mick shook his head. Despite his positive comments, his face was white with shock and dismay. He pushed his dripping hair back off his face. 'Take a look?'

Hawk slid off the bough and dangled his legs until his feet had safely touched solid ground. Mick followed and, without letting go of the branch, they made their way towards the bank until they were out of the pull of the current. As they stood and watched, the water level dropped another foot, leaving the ground strewn with branches, small rocks, plant matter, bits of broken cradle and diggers' gear, and scummy foam. Around them diggers themselves were hauling themselves from the water, stunned at what had just occurred. Two bodies were visible, one face-down on the far bank, and one floating down the river towards them.

Hawk estimated that he and Mick must have travelled with the wall of water at least 500 yards down the river, as they were now nowhere near where they had set up the long tom. With cold dread settling in his belly, Hawk raised a hand to his eyes and peered across at the body lying on the bank. It was hatless and shirtless, but from here he couldn't tell anything more.

A handful of bedraggled diggers stood gingerly in the shallows, apparently waiting for the body in the river to wash up. Hawk watched as Mick strode past them, up to his knees in water, then turned the body face-up. He signalled a negative to Hawk, then dragged it by one limp arm out of the river and onto the muddy bank.

He shook his head as he approached Hawk, who pointed across the river at the other body.

'Current safe in the middle yet, do you think?' Mick asked.

Hawk shrugged, and together they made their way carefully across, armpit-deep in water that was filled with mud and floating debris.

The body was lying on its face but the head was turned to one side, and before they even got close Hawk and Mick saw that it wasn't Rian. They both let out deep breaths of relief. This unfortunate digger had been bearded, although he possessed only part of his beard now, as his right lower jaw had been torn off. His eyes were open, staring sightlessly at the mud that had become his final resting place. Near his nose was embedded a small nugget of gold. Mick crouched, dug it out and slipped it into the man's trouser pocket.

They recrossed the river, and Hawk sent Mick running back to the claim to fetch the others while he began to walk back along the bank searching for Rian, but before Mick had gone far he met everyone else, piled into the cart, coming the other way.

Daniel reined in the bullocks, and Simon called out, 'Is it true, there's been a flash flood?'

''Tis,' Mick shouted, 'and we can't find Rian!'

All around them streams of diggers were heading for the river, and several stopped to listen while Mick gave a very abbreviated version of what had happened, until Daniel told him to get in and finish telling them while he drove on.

'He will just be further downstream,' Gideon said. 'You say there are men pulling themselves out of the water everywhere. He will just be walking back.'

'He might not even have gone down as far as you and Hawk,' Simon suggested. 'He might even have only gone a few yards and then managed to get out.'

'Ae, he might just be sitting there on the bank where the long tom was, wondering what is taking you so long,' Ropata added.

Mick looked at them, staring back with hopeful faces and trying to reassure themselves that nothing bad could have happened to Rian, and he couldn't tell them. He couldn't tell them how incredibly powerful the torrent of water had been, and he couldn't tell them that it had carried within it rocks that could smash a man's head open like a rotten pumpkin, and he couldn't tell them how once it had dragged you under it was only luck that spat you out again.

But he felt Haunui gazing directly at him, and saw that somehow Haunui knew, and he suddenly couldn't meet the older man's eye.

Haunui turned to Simon and said quietly, 'Go and let Kitty know what's happened. Stay with her. Don't let her come out here.'

By the time they reached the river it seemed that every man on the Ballarat diggings had arrived. They couldn't get near the water's edge, and Hawk was nowhere to be seen. When they located him an hour later, two more bodies had been recovered from the river. Nobody had seen a man answering to Rian's description, dead or alive.

At five-thirty, Hawk said, 'We need to tell Kitty.'

★   ★   ★

She sat at the table at Lilac Cottage, a cold cup of tea in front of her, her back as rigid as though a rod of iron were lashed across her shoulders. Simon sat opposite, pushing around a slice of the spiced fruit billy bread that Maureen had brought across and which Kitty had refused to touch. Amber was huddled on the daybed cuddling Bodie, who for once was allowing herself to be excessively petted.

Kitty had repeatedly made Simon tell her what he knew, but as it wasn't much they'd been silent for some time, Kitty sitting white-faced and tight-lipped. Initially, as predicted, she had wanted to go to the river and help with the search, but Simon had convinced her to stay by telling her that she needed to be at the cottage in case Rian staggered home under his own steam, exhausted and disoriented. He thought this highly unlikely, but it was preferable to the idea of her witnessing the extraction of Rian's pale, lifeless body from beneath some overhanging bank miles downstream, or from several feet of stinking, sucking mud. But he wouldn't be dead, of course. He could well be lying hurt somewhere, but he wouldn't be dead.

Amber leapt up and opened the door. 'They're here, Ma!'

Kitty hurried to the door and moved Amber aside, then mutely stepped out of the way to let in Hawk, Daniel and Haunui. A quick study of their faces told her that the news wasn't good, and her heart felt once again gripped in a fist of ice. For a short while, sitting at the table, she had managed to convince herself that everything that was happening was nothing more than an exceptionally unpleasant and unwelcome dream, that if she sat still enough and said nothing, it would eventually stop and she would wake up. And that had worked for a little while, but then Simon had started pushing around his piece of cake and the tines of the fork had made irritating, intrusive noises on the plate, and then she'd begun to think she could hear the bits of dried fruit in the cake squeaking and scraping over the porcelain, and by then the bubble she'd fashioned around herself had been punctured and little snippets of what he'd said had started creeping into her thoughts again. And now here were Hawk and Haunui and Daniel, and they'd never been able to hide anything from her when it came to Rian.

They all looked exhausted. Hawk had someone else's shirt on. It was too small for him, and he must have hurt himself because the back was stained with watery blood.

He touched her shoulder. 'Kitty, you should sit.'

'No.'

So Hawk sat instead. 'We have searched thoroughly up and down the river bank for two miles from where we were working. There is no sign of him.'

'So he must have been swept farther down than that,' Kitty said simply.

'Yes, he must. We will go back soon, and keep searching.' Hawk blinked up at her, and Kitty could see how terribly tired he was. 'But Kitty, we cannot search tonight. It is overcast and there will not be enough light.'

'I'll do it,' she said, and even she heard the desperation in her voice. 'I'll take a lantern.'

Haunui and Daniel exchanged an uneasy glance; she was not going to be rational and calm about this, but then none of them had expected her to be. They hardly felt rational and calm themselves, but searching in the dark would be unlikely to help find Rian. Next, she would get angry, as she often did when she was frightened or upset, and Kitty angry could be extremely daunting.

'E hine,' Haunui said gently, 'there are new . . . puddles? What do they call them?'

'Billabongs,' Hawk said.

'Ae, from the flood, and some of the shafts near the river have filled with water. It's too dangerous in the dark. You can't search tonight.'

Kitty stared at him. Suddenly she blurted, 'He's not dead, you know. Just because you haven't found him yet, don't start thinking that.'

Slowly, Amber uncurled herself from the daybed and stood, her hair an untidy halo and her arms loose at her sides. In a very quiet voice, she said, 'No one said anything about Pa being *dead*.'

'No, Amber, dear,' Simon said hurriedly, 'He's not dead, we just haven't been able to find him yet.'

Amber's gaze swept from Kitty to Simon, then back to her mother.

'Ma?'

'We will find him, love, I promise.'

But Amber's face crumpled. She marched up to Kitty and punched her arm. 'You swore on Bodie, Ma. You said Pa would be fine!' Her voice shot up an octave. 'You swore on Bodie's *life!*'

And she hit Kitty again. And again, until Haunui stepped in and picked her up and carried her away.

★   ★   ★

The following morning, they were all out at the river just after dawn. Pierre had propped a sign in the bakery window saying *Closed Until Further Notice*, even though he, Leena and Maureen were inside cooking furiously to feed the search party, which had grown as word had spread overnight about Rian's disappearance.

Flora would have to be consulted some time during the day, but he had arbitrarily decided to dedicate himself to supporting the search, rather than baking for their usual customers. Anyway, he was too distraught to piddle about making fancy little breads and confectioneries — now was the time to be throwing meats and spices into pots to create hearty Cajun dishes that would line the bellies of searchers and give them the energy to find his beloved Rian.

The men from Patrick's syndicate had taken the day off to help search, and so had about two dozen other diggers whom Rian had become acquainted with over the past months. Wong Fu, too, had arrived with a dozen men from the Chinese camp. And even the majority of diggers on the Malakoff Lead who couldn't spare the time removed their hats in a show of support as the search team moved towards the river.

They searched all day until sundown, wading along the river, which had returned to a level only a little higher than normal for that time of year, risking bites from eels and stings from catfish spines while feeling under banks, poking about in the debris that had piled up along the river's edge, and wading through the billabongs and tiny, shrinking tributaries the flood had left behind. The only places they didn't — couldn't — check were the flooded shafts close to the river. The water in those would eventually drain, but, according to old hands, that could take more than a fortnight.

The following day they searched again, and the day after that. The river gave up two more bodies, grotesquely bloated and nibbled by fish and eels, but neither was Rian. Funerals were held for the dead, the undertaker's black and glass-panelled hearse busy for two days in a row, ferrying its increasingly stinking cargoes along the Main Road to the cemetery on Creswick Road.

Haunui kept a very close eye on Kitty. He had half-expected her to begin to wilt with grief as it became more and more obvious that Rian might

282

never be found, that he might have been swept away to some secret little place where Hine-Nui-Te-Po would hold him in her arms for ever. But she wasn't wilting. Instead she was angry, and she seemed, to Haunui at least, to be using her anger to drive herself on. She wasn't eating enough, she was refusing to rest — according to Amber she was barely sleeping at night — and her distress was certainly showing on her face, which was pallid and drawn, her eyes underlined by deep purple shadows. She was making herself sick, and for once he didn't know what to do.

On the fourth morning after the flood, the search team was noticeably smaller, as most of the diggers who had gathered to help had gone back to work. But the *Katipo*'s crew naturally all mustered, and Wong Fu and three or four of his people also stayed on.

They were eating one of Pierre's hearty breakfasts outside the crew's tents just after the sun had risen when Kitty emerged from Lilac Cottage and marched across the dew-damp ground towards them. She was wearing her panama hat, had a rolled-up tube of some sort under her arm and a wild look in her eye. Amber trailed after her, and in the rear came Bodie, picking her way delicately through the wet grass. Without Rian, Haunui thought with a stab of sorrow, the three of them looked somehow diminished, even the bad-tempered cat.

Kitty sat down and unrolled the tube. It was a map. Haunui passed her a plate of stew, which she put aside.

'Eat,' he ordered.

'In a minute.'

'Now!' Haunui countered in a voice that made everyone flinch.

Reluctantly, Kitty dipped a spoon into her stew and ate a tiny morsel. Then several more as Haunui stared at her menacingly. Then, defiantly, her gaze daring him to challenge her again, she put down the plate and went back to her map.

'I've divided the whole area up into squares, see?' she said, pointing with her finger. 'And if we break into groups and each group takes a square on this side of the river, then we do the same on that side of the river, and cross each square off my map when we've done it, then nothing will be missed. We will have covered every inch. That way, if he's tucked away somewhere we might not have checked until now, we'll find him. And I think we should start going further downriver. I don't think five miles is far enough.'

Haunui nodded, but said nothing. He'd sent Daniel and Ropata ten miles downriver on the horses yesterday and they'd found nothing. And he had told Kitty that last night.

Kitty rolled up her map, stood up and said, 'Right. Let's set out.'

The others, still eating their breakfast, looked at her, embarrassed. No one knew how to manage this new, strange Kitty. It was deeply upsetting seeing her so distraught, deliberately domineering and demanding. Hawk, who had finished his stew, crossed to the scrap bucket and scraped his tin plate. Then he approached Kitty and laid a compassionate hand on her arm.

Looking at her with empathy and doing what he believed to be the kindest thing, he said, 'Kitty, you must prepare yourself. You know I love Rian as a brother, and my heart is bleeding for him. But you must accept that he is probably dead. You must be prepared for that.'

Haunui winced, because so far no one had said it aloud; certainly not within earshot of Kitty.

She glared at Hawk, then slapped him so hard that a red handprint immediately appeared on his cheek. 'How *dare* you say that, Hawk! How *dare* you! He is *not* dead!'

Hawk stood his ground, and when her hand came up to strike again he took hold of her wrists and simply waited.

'I will *not* give up, do you hear me? I will *not* give up!' Kitty's face turned scarlet. 'We're going to look and look until we find him — all of us. And if you won't, then I'll do it myself. Because he is *not dead*, do you hear me? *He's not dead!*'

Horrified, Simon and Wong Fu stepped in, but Haunui beat them to it. He wrapped Kitty in his arms and squashed her to his chest, nearly smothering her. She struggled for almost a minute, then she began to cry softly, saying over and over into his shirt, 'He's not dead, Haunui, he's not dead.'

Over her head he regarded his companions, and saw in their grim expressions that their discomfort and dismay were extreme.

Pierre, perhaps, summed it up. He was bent over the fire, stirring the pot viciously, and

Haunui could hear him asking himself what in God's name was happening to his precious *Katipo* family, and weeping into what was left of the breakfast stew.

15

Haunui nodded his thanks as Flora placed a cup of tea on the small table at his elbow. He felt slightly silly jammed into one of her elegant little silk-upholstered armchairs, but if he remained standing he would tower over her, and that would be impolite.

Flora sat down opposite, her own cup and saucer balanced on the arm of her chair. 'No luck with the search, Mr Haunui?'

Haunui shook his head. 'It has been seven days now. And it is just Haunui.'

'As you wish. Forgive me for being blunt, but you know that after this amount of time, it's highly unlikely that Rian will be found alive.'

Flora tapped her fingernails against the side of her teacup: people disappeared in the bush frequently, victims of accident or foul play or a misread compass, their remains found years later, or more likely never at all. 'And the flooded shafts, when are they expected to drain?'

Haunui took a careful sip of his tea, and had a bad moment when he thought he might not be able to get his finger out of the delicate handle. 'The ones farthest from the river have emptied already.'

'Nothing, obviously?'

'Only mud. The rest are expected to drain in another four or five days.'

'Mmm.' Flora set her tea aside and sat back.

'And Kitty? I assume it's Kitty you've come to talk to me about.'

'Ae, it is.' Haunui told Flora about Kitty's strange, driven behaviour, and her outburst at Hawk, and her continued refusal to accept that Rian might have died. 'I thought she would understand that, well, even the ones we love die.' He sat in contemplative silence for several seconds. 'And she's getting sick. She's getting too thin. I'm very worried.' He eased himself forward in the armchair. 'I know you and I don't know each other well, Mrs McRae, but Kitty is as a daughter to me. She and my tamahine Wai were very close. I know that you and Kitty are also good friends. I was wondering whether . . . I was *hoping* that you would speak with her.'

'I've been to see her already, you know.'

'Ae, she said that.' Haunui paused, hoping he wasn't about to sound too callous. 'But I would like you to make her understand that . . . Rian has more than likely gone.'

A deep, vertical line appeared between Flora's pale brows, and she said disbelievingly, 'Do you mean you want me, as her friend, to tell her to give up hope?'

Haunui looked at Flora for a long time, then said simply, 'Ae, I do.'

'Why?'

'Because this holding onto hope is hurting her too much.'

'And you think having no hope at all is a preferable state?'

Haunui's face settled into an expression of miserable obstinacy. 'Ae. Better that she lets go of it. Then she can start to get well again.'

Flora gave him an utterly scathing look. 'You stupid man. If having hope is hurting her, what do you think having no hope at all will do to her?'

Haunui ignored the insult. 'She will survive it. Kitty is a strong woman.'

'Not strong enough, according to you.' Flora narrowed her eyes and fixed Haunui with a stare that even he found disconcerting. 'You are a selfish man, Haunui. You can't bear to see her in such pain, and you just want it to stop. You think that if you can get her to accept that Rian's dead, she'll eventually stop grieving and then *you'll* stop feeling so dreadful. Well, you might be right, but is what you're *doing* right? Yes, Rian might be dead — probably *is* dead — but who are you to interfere in the natural course of things? Who are you to interfere in the way another person grieves?'

Haunui's face had gone from brown to dark red, the lines and whorls of his moko standing out in stark relief. There were a long six or seven seconds during which he glared at Flora, the muscles in his big jaw tense, then he slumped, deflated, against the back of the chair.

Wearily, he said, 'He wouldn't want her to suffer like this. He would want her to get on with her life.'

'No doubt he would. But that's still for her to decide, isn't it? So give her the opportunity to do it the way she chooses to. The poor woman has just been robbed of her husband, Haunui. Don't also deny her the chance to hope.'

He sat for a while, thinking, then inclined his

head in acknowledgement of Flora's advice and eased himself out of the chair. He stood and collected his hat. Perhaps he was a selfish man. Perhaps these days he was just an old fool who shouldn't be interfering in other people's business. But he loved Kitty dearly, and watching what was happening to her was killing him. He caught Flora's eye and saw that she knew very well what was going through his mind.

'It was nice speaking with you, Mrs McRae. Thank you for the tea.'

'My pleasure, Haunui.'

At the door he turned and offered her a rueful smile, and the one she gave him in return was almost affectionate.

★ ★ ★

Kitty sat on an upturned crate, watching as the bucket was laboriously winched up over the lip of the shaft and the contents dumped into a waiting cart. Cornelius Powell and his syndicate weren't financially fortunate enough to own a whip — and certainly wouldn't be in the near future now that their claim had been inundated by the flash flood — and therefore used a windlass to haul everything up from the depths, so the process of clearing out the mud had begun very early this morning, twelve days after the flood.

Being closest to the river, Powell's was the last shaft to drain. The other shafts had revealed nothing except a collection of diggers' gear and the swollen carcasses of eight drowned dogs.

Kitty had not been unduly surprised that Rian had not been at the bottom of any of them — how could he be when he was still alive somewhere?

'How much more, Mr Powell?' she called.

He shoved back his hat and scratched at his sweaty head. 'Another dozen buckets? Once they're up we'll get a good look at — ' He shut up, remembering to whom he was talking. Everyone knew why Mrs Farrell had been sitting here since dawn. Such a shame, and such a pretty widow. 'Anyway, not long now.' He hesitated. 'You're sure you . . . ?' He gestured vaguely at her, then at the shaft. He had no idea how he or his men would be able to go back down if it turned out her husband *was* floating around in there.

'I'm sure, thank you, Mr Powell,' Kitty replied, adjusting her panama hat.

Another hour passed, the last bucket of mud came up, and not a sign of Rian.

'Thank you very much for your help and your patience, Mr Powell,' Kitty said, and walked across to the cart where Haunui was waiting. 'What did I tell you?' she said as she climbed onto the seat next to him.

Haunui held his tongue. All it meant was that Rian's body wasn't at the bottom of any of the shafts, not that he was still alive. 'Can you drop me off at the bakery, please?' Kitty asked.

'You want to go back to work?'

'Yes. Pierre and Leena can't run the shop by themselves.'

Haunui was relieved. The strain of the military

291

precision with which she was insisting they go about the search, and the disconcerting possibility of her being present if they did actually find Rian's body after all this time, was beginning to tell. He turned the cart around and headed for the Main Road.

'You didn't bring Amber this morning,' he said eventually.

'No, I thought it best she stay away.'

Haunui noted the slightest hesitation in her reply. He glanced at Kitty out of the corner of his eye, and saw that she was sitting rigidly on the seat, staring straight ahead, doing her very best to ignore him.

He opened his mouth, then shut it again.

'That's right, Haunui, I don't want to talk about it,' Kitty said, still not looking at him.

They drove the rest of the way in silence.

Leena and Pierre were busy preparing for the midday crowd at the bakery. While the crew were still searching every day for Rian, they weren't working the claim and there was no money coming in, so Pierre, with Kitty's sanction, had reopened for business.

They both looked up in wary surprise when she swept in. Pierre, knowing where she'd been, steeled himself for bad news.

'Nothing!' Kitty said gaily as she opened the hatch in the counter and stepped through.

Pierre's heart sank. He needed a body. He couldn't bear the thought of the soul of his beloved friend and boss wandering the earth for ever, without a consecrated grave in which to settle.

Kitty pulled an apron over her head and rolled up her sleeves.

'*Chérie*, what are you doing?' Pierre exclaimed, alarmed. She had that look in her eye again.

'I'm working in my bakery.'

'No more of the searching?'

Kitty put her hands on her hips and turned to face him. Why was she constantly having to explain herself to everyone? 'Pierre, I believe now that the men are quite capable of locating him without my help. Or he'll come back under his own steam, which I think is more likely. Why can't everyone else see that? We can't give up hope. We *mustn't* give up hope. And in the meantime, as you well know, we're running out of money and, according to you, your fingers are nothing more than ragged stumps of bone.'

Pierre looked at his hands, recalling his complaint last evening about being short-staffed. '*Oui*, but — '

'So here I am. And Amber will come in, too, if necessary, although I'd rather she didn't.' She glanced at Leena, who nodded in understanding.

Amber was supposed to be looking after Will and Molly, now that Leena had forgiven her, but in actual fact Binda was looking after the children *and* Amber, who was behaving as though her father really was dead. Kitty couldn't understand this at all. It was as hurtful and bewildering as not knowing where Rian was.

'*Non, non,* she cannot come,' Pierre said, vehemently shaking his head. 'She be grieving — ' He stopped himself.

Kitty looked at him shrewdly. 'Go on, say it.'

'Say what?'

'Whatever it was you were going to say, but decided you shouldn't.'

This had been going on for days now, with Hawk and Haunui and Simon and the others. Even Wong Fu. They all thought she was going mad.

Finally Pierre's ratty, weathered little face was overcome with an expression of profound sadness and his eyes watered as he struggled to contain his emotions.

'*Chérie*, I say this with love, so hear me, please. I know you think Rian he is still alive, but how can he be after this time? The men, they love him, but they know. Mick, he is getting drunk every night and being sick on the searches, and Daniel he is not even speaking any more. Gideon's face be extra ugly, and Simon do nothing but pray. Hawk, even I am too scared to say things to in case he be biting my head off!' He patted his pockets, withdrew a handkerchief and wiped away a trickle of tears. 'So it is all right for you to believe he has gone, Kitty. You will not be alone. You will never be alone. Always you will have us.'

Kitty heaved a great sigh of exasperation. 'But you just don't understand, Pierre, do you? He *isn't dead!*'

But Pierre just wept harder for a few embarrassing minutes, then blew his nose vigorously, turned back to his work table and began kneading a pile of dough as though he wanted to kill it.

Kitty tried to catch Leena's eye, but she'd

turned away and had her head down as she sieved flour into a bowl.

They worked in awkward silence for the next hour, Kitty serving and blankly accepting condolences from customers who left the shop feeling bewildered at such a lacklustre, and, yes, even ungrateful, response from the new widow.

At half past one the bell over the door chimed and a smartly dressed man entered. Removing his top hat, he tucked it under his arm and stepped up to the counter, then moved discreetly away again as another customer bustled into the shop. When they'd made a purchase and departed, he approached the counter once again.

'May I ask, would you be the wife of the late Captain Rian Farrell?' he inquired in an obsequiously polite tone.

'No, I would not be,' Kitty replied icily.

'Oh. I beg your pardon. I was informed that this establishment was owned by Mrs Kitty Farrell.'

'It is.'

'Then may I speak with her, please?'

'You are.'

The man frowned deeply, then an expression of dawning understanding crept across his face, which was immaculately shaven except where his fashionably bushy mutton chops sprouted from his temples to his lower jaw. Clearly this poor woman was deluded by her grief, and would obviously require delicate handling.

He withdrew a black-edged business card from the interior of his smart black cloth coat and placed it reverently on the counter, next to his hat, as though it were a precious gift. 'My name is Jeremiah Grimstone, Mrs Farrell, and I am the local undertaker. I hope to be able to offer you assistance and succour during this terrible time.' He whipped out a small brochure. 'There is our hearse, of course, with sides of etched glass, carved mouldings along the top and five classical urns, pulled by a magnificent black four-in-hand adorned with black ostrich feathers. We also have two mourning coaches pulled by — '

'Get out.'

Stunned, Mr Grimstone gaped at Kitty. 'I beg your pardon?'

'I said: get out. My husband is not dead, and your behaviour is disgusting. Now get out of my shop.'

The woman was *deranged*. 'Well, I'm very sorry, but if that's the way you feel — '

'It is. Get out.'

Mr Grimstone settled his hat on his head, but on second thoughts left his business card on the counter, turned smartly on his heel and strode for the door.

As he opened it, Kitty grabbed a *baguette* from a nearby basket and hurled it, smiling with grim satisfaction as it bounced off the back of his head and sent his top hat spinning out through the open doorway. Through the window she watched him retrieve his hat from the street, dust it off and scowl at her darkly as he jammed it back on and hurried off.

Behind her the silence from Pierre and Leena was deafening.

★　★　★

The supper things were cleared away, and Pierre, with great reluctance, had laid his special cloth out on the ground. Around him the others sat at a respectful distance, close enough to see what he was doing, but far enough away not to be 'tainted', as Mick had described it, by what he was about to do with his bones and stones and 'smelly little bags'.

Kitty, though, sat very near to him. He hadn't wanted to do this, she knew that, but she had been on at him for days now.

'Does any of this tomfoolery really work?' Mick asked, as far away as he could get without disappearing into the evening's darkness altogether.

'Mick,' Hawk warned. 'Have some respect.'

'You must think so,' Simon remarked, amused. 'I'm surprised you can see anything from way over there.'

Pierre ignored them all. From a worn velvet bag he decanted a small collection of items: a two-inch-tall statue of a monkey and a rooster carved from pale marble, a string of brightly coloured beads, a handful of highly polished dark red stones, and what appeared to be a dried chicken's foot. He arranged the items in a square then opened a smaller bag, green in colour and tightly closed at the neck with a purple silk cord. From this he poured a heap of small bones, about the size you would expect to find in a human hand.

Finally, from his jacket pocket, he produced a

crude doll and placed it in the centre of the square. It was five inches tall and clothed in simply constructed moleskin trousers and a shirt held together with the tidy, firm stitches of a lifelong sailor, and wore a miniature hat made from a folded and tucked piece of eucalyptus bark.

Kitty leaned forward to touch it, but Pierre stilled her hand.

'Is it Rian?' she asked wonderingly.

'*Non*, but it represent him.'

Mick, who in spite of himself had moved a little closer, said, 'I thought you were after needin' a snake for all this?'

'*Oui*,' Pierre said, and upended a flour bag at his side, liberating a slender brown snake about a foot long.

There was a collective exclamation of alarm, but Pierre picked up the snake by its tail and waggled it. 'See, he is not poisonous.' Then he dropped the snake and casually put his boot on it so it couldn't get away.

He bowed his head and was quiet for so long that Kitty wondered if he'd gone to sleep, then she realised he was praying and, as his voice rose steadily in volume, she recognised the peculiar version of French which was his native tongue.

When he finally finished, he quickly swept up the bones, dropped them back into the green bag, breathed into it, then tipped them out again at the feet of the Rian doll.

Then he grasped the snake behind its head, stuffed it into the bag the bones had been in, and placed the wriggling bag on the cloth.

The bag became motionless.

Kitty held her breath, although she had no idea why.

The snake did nothing for a long, tense minute, then its head emerged from the bag, tiny tongue flickering, and it slithered towards the bones where it hesitated, then wriggled into the little heap and became still again.

Was it thinking? Kitty glanced up and saw that everyone was watching it raptly.

It began to move again, smoothly, like a fine rope of brown silk, until several of the delicate bones had been nudged to one side of the pile. Then it turned, knocked aside two more, then another. It lay inert for almost a minute, then slithered rapidly across the cloth and disappeared. All the Catholics in the circle of onlookers crossed themselves, as did Simon, even though he was Anglican.

'It's getting away!' Kitty cried.

'*Non*, he has finished,' Pierre said, gathering up the bones the snake had isolated.

He set them out in a straight line and studied them for what, to Kitty, felt like an inordinately long time.

Finally, he sighed and said, 'I am sorry.'

All the bones were from different fingers, and one was from the thumb, but he was just not skilled enough as a practitioner to decipher the message the snake had delivered. The finger bones meant that Rian was no longer here, but the inclusion of the thumb bone meant something else altogether, and he didn't know what that was.

'I am sorry, Kitty,' he said again. 'I can only tell you he is gone.'

Pierre had a lot of faith in his charms, dolls and *gris-gris* bags, which he somehow managed to fit neatly alongside his Catholicism, and Kitty had a lot of faith in Pierre, so she was bitterly disappointed that Pierre's spirits or whatever they were couldn't tell him that Rian was alive somewhere, perhaps wounded but safe, or even on his way back to them. She stood and wiped her hands on her skirts. 'Come with me, Amber, it's time you went to sleep.'

Amber stayed where she was, sitting next to Leena. 'No, I'm staying with Will and Molly. I don't want to sleep in the house tonight.'

'Amber, I'll thank you to do as you're told!'

Kitty heard her words through what felt like someone's else's ears, and winced inwardly. She sounded exactly like her own mother, Emily Carlisle, whenever she had reprimanded Kitty for some petty misdemeanour as a child. She'd sworn she would never allow that to happen. Without Rian she felt utterly adrift, like a tiny vessel afloat on the Pacific Ocean without sail or rudder or oar, and now she was pushing her own daughter away from her. It hurt like a knife in her belly.

And then she made it worse. She took hold of Amber's hand and tried to pull her up off the ground.

But Amber jerked out of her grasp and shouted, 'No, Ma! Leave me alone, I don't *want* to!' She started to cry. 'I *hate* the cottage now. I wish Pa was here. And we can't even have a funeral because *you* won't let us!' Then she leapt to her feet and disappeared into Leena and Ropata's tent, leaving a shocked silence in her wake.

Kitty stood with her eyes closed, feeling dismay surge through her veins with such force she thought she might be sick. When she opened them again, she saw that no one would meet her gaze. She turned and walked away.

★   ★   ★

Kitty gave Amber's chemise a good shake in case a spider had crawled into it while it had been on the washing line, then folded it loosely and dropped it into the laundry basket. As she bent to pick up the basket, she noticed that the crew were returning early.

But the cart didn't stop at the tents, and neither did the horses. She waited until they were almost upon her, and it was then that a thread of dread began to unravel inside her.

Haunui and Simon climbed off the cart and walked towards her.

She took a step back, feeling dizzy, a rush of blood beginning to echo in her ears.

Haunui reached for her and took hold of her upper arm. She saw from his reddened eyes that he had been weeping.

'E hine,' he said in a voice rough with emotion, 'we have found him.'

Black spots danced across Kitty's vision. A monstrous roaring noise filled her head, to her left the washing line swept upwards in a graceful arc and a second later her face was pressed against the hard ground, dry brown grass tickling her cheek.

Dimly she heard a voice saying something about air.

Distractedly, a tiny part of her mind wondered why she wasn't delighted now that he'd been found, then the much larger bit she'd so determinedly been battling since Rian had disappeared sixteen days ago finally gained ascendency, and she understood that it had been evidence of his *death* that had been discovered, not him. A horrible ragged chink opened in her heart and the shock caused her to drag in such a great choking breath that a mechanism in her chest jammed.

More snippets of voices came to her. Someone said, 'She can't breathe!' and she was pushed up into a sitting position. Another voice, panicked, suggested, 'Bang her on the back!' while someone else said wretchedly, 'Ah, shite.'

She jerked forward as someone did indeed bang her on the back, and it enabled her to draw in enough breath to let out a wail that raised hairs on the arms of all who heard it. Then she began to cry. She sobbed and sobbed and almost choked herself again as it roared out of her — all the fear and the horrible worry and the nightmare imaginings and now the realisation that Rian really was dead. She was vaguely aware that Maureen had arrived, and that she was shooing the men away but they wouldn't go. She didn't care. Snot ran down her upper lip in rivulets and her face felt horribly swollen and her head hurt, and then someone was lifting her to her feet and pressing her face against their chest. It was Hawk, and he was weeping — and he never cried. Then Maureen had one of her arms and Haunui had the other and then she was in the cottage, lying on the daybed.

She rolled onto her side, pulled her knees up and covered her head with her arms and wept. And then it occurred to her.

She stopped crying.

She sat up. 'I want to see him.'

Haunui blew his nose into a large kerchief, shoved it into his trouser pocket and cleared his throat.

'We didn't find a body.' Seeing hope inevitably flare in Kitty's swollen, red eyes, he shook his head sadly. 'There is no doubt. We found these.'

He gestured to Hawk, who was sitting awkwardly in the rocking chair. At Hawk's feet lay a sack.

'Is this wise?' Simon asked.

'Ae, I think it's necessary,' Haunui said sadly.

Hawk passed over the sack; Haunui opened it and pulled out several items. Maureen gasped and clapped a hand over her mouth. One was a brown leather belt, and the other a blue flannel work-shirt. The shirt had ragged rents in one sleeve and on the back and the buttons had been torn off, and the belt looked chewed. Both were liberally smeared with blood.

'Are these Rian's?' Haunui asked gently, even though he knew they were.

Kitty took the shirt from him and tried not to

303

see the little darned patch where she had reattached the pocket a month ago. Harder to barricade from her mind was Rian's scent. It was very faint but it was still there, and it sent a lance of anguish straight into her heart.

'What happened?' she asked dully.

At the last second Haunui hesitated. 'This is not going to be nice to hear, e hine.'

Kitty waited. None of this was nice. It hadn't been nice since the afternoon of the flood.

'We think it might have been dingos, eh?'

Stunned, Kitty stared at him. 'That killed him? *Dingos* killed him?'

'No, not killed him,' Simon interjected quickly, 'We think he was already, well, that he had already passed away by then. We think the dingos . . . took his remains.'

Haunui glanced at Hawk, and the lie they had all agreed upon earlier was cemented. It was a much less upsetting way of explaining it to her, but it didn't really account for the blood on Rian's shirt; if he had already been dead, he wouldn't have bled when the dingos attacked him.

Kitty smoothed the shirt across her knees, seeming not to notice the dried blood all over it. She reached for the belt and laid it across the shirt. 'Where did you find them?'

'On the far side of the river, about three miles downstream,' Hawk replied. 'Daniel and Tahi did.'

Kitty frowned, and wiped her nose on the back of her hand. 'But we looked there, every day.'

'This was nearly two miles farther west than we've been before.'

Kitty was quiet for a long time. 'And you think he might have been washed up and then the dogs found him? But why was he so far west of the river?'

'Kitty, we're only guessing,' Simon said despairingly. 'We'll probably never know.'

'But where are his boots?'

'In a dingo's den somewhere,' Haunui said as bluntly as he could, hating himself for it. But she was going to start questioning the story, he knew it, and then she would realise that Rian might have been alive when the dingos had found him.

Kitty jerked backwards, her eyes full of pain.

'I say, Haunui!' Simon was appalled at his friend's cruelty.

Haunui silenced him with a quelling look and Simon belatedly realised what Haunui's intention had been.

But it was too much for Maureen. Hands on hips, she shook an outraged finger at Haunui. 'That's enough from you now, so it is! The poor woman's had a terrible shock and you're only after makin' it worse. Dens, I ask you! Have you no idea how to behave in times of bereavement? Now be off, all of you, and leave the poor soul to get some rest.'

Kitty, though, had other ideas. She pushed herself shakily to her feet. 'No. Thank you, Maureen, but there are things I have to do. I need to tell Amber.' Her voice cracked, but she said it anyway: 'And I need to organise a funeral.'

Rian had been a Catholic, but Simon took the service because Kitty knew it was what Rian would have wanted. Around a hundred people gathered in the open air on pews borrowed from the Catholic chapel, and there was food afterwards and plenty of alcohol, as befitted an Irish wake. Kitty refused to wear either black or a mourning veil, but she did concede to wear a dark-blue dress she already owned, with the forget-me-not brooch Rian had given her pinned to her breast. Throughout the proceedings she sat holding Amber's hand, her back straight and her head up, willing herself not to reveal the gut-twisting grief that consumed her. She accepted the condolences of the mourners graciously and, as soon as was polite, escaped to Lilac Cottage and closed the door behind her. Inside, where there were no prying eyes, she lay down on her empty bed and cried and cried until, finally, she slipped into merciful sleep.

16

Amber woke her at dusk and lay beside her on the bed, and together they dozed in each other's arms, the angry words between them forgotten, until Pierre tapped on the door with two plates of food. Sitting at the table, they ate little and discovered that, for now at least, there wasn't much they needed to say to each other.

Kitty noted the dark, puffy shadows beneath her daughter's eyes and the pallid cast to her normally lustrous skin, and the knowledge that she could do nothing to alleviate it felt like yet another vicious kick to her stomach.

She pushed her plate away. 'Would you like to go and play with Will and Molly?' she suggested gently, knowing that the children always brought a smile to Amber's face.

Amber half-heartedly shunted a piece of meat around with her fork. 'What will you do?'

'Stay here. Tidy up a bit.'

'And think about Pa?' Amber asked perceptively.

Kitty's eyes filled with tears yet again. 'Yes, love, and think about Pa.'

So Amber went off to visit, but Kitty didn't tidy up. She left the supper things to the flies, and instead took all of Rian's clothes out of his trunk and from the rail across one corner of the bedroom, and sat on the bed, holding each piece to her face and sniffing it, trying desperately to extract the last little bit of his essence and fix it in her mind and in her heart.

When Leena appeared an hour later to tell her that Amber had fallen asleep with the children, Kitty was sitting in the dark.

'Shall I wake her and bring her over?' Leena asked, ignoring the fact that her friend was surrounded by a jumble of clothing.

'No, don't. She must be exhausted. Can she stay with you?'

'Of course. Shall I take these plates away?'

'Please.'

When Leena had gone, Kitty carefully folded and rehung Rian's things, then poured herself a brandy and sat down in the rocking chair, its familiar creak for once a comfort rather than an annoyance. After a while, she refreshed her drink and lit a lamp, its flickering yellow light and oily smell permeating the small room, deliberately allowing it to smoke a little to deter mosquitoes.

As the brandy loosened the tension in her body, she dozed, and when she woke someone was tapping at the door. She sighed, but called out, 'Come in.'

Nothing happened, so she got up and opened the door.

It was Daniel, standing in the darkness with his hat in his hand. 'I'm very sorry, Kitty. I hope I didn't wake you.'

'No, you didn't.'

'It's just that I need to talk to you.'

He looked so desperate and ill at ease that Kitty stood aside and let him in, indicating a chair at the table. Hesitantly, he sat down.

'Brandy?'

'Yes, please.'

She fetched a glass and poured him a drink, then sat across from him. In the lamplight his blue eyes appeared almost black and his dark hair gleamed. He needed a haircut and hadn't shaved for a day or two, and looked as though he could sleep for a week. But now he seemed unable to say whatever it was he had come to impart. Instead, he half-emptied his glass in one draught and stared at her.

Kitty stared back. Finally, she prompted, 'You said you needed to talk to me?'

Daniel cleared his throat. Then he took a big breath and said in a rush, 'I know that Rian was the only man for you, but if there's ever anything I can do for you, you only need to ask. It doesn't matter what it is, I'll do it. It would mean a hell of a lot to me, because I — '

Oh God, Kitty thought, don't say it, not now.

' — owe him so much. You realise that, don't you?'

Kitty blinked in surprise.

'I mean, he took me on as a crewman when he knew I'd murdered someone, even if it was only Walter Kinghazel, and he took me on when he was aware of my feelings for you. And he kept me on all these years, Kitty, knowing that that's never changed. What other man would do that? So I owe him my life, and I intend to honour that debt even though he's gone.'

To Kitty's horror Daniel's voice wobbled as he fought to retain control of his emotions, and she felt her eyes sting with sympathy and fresh grief.

He put his hands over his face and made a noise that was half-grunt, half-sob, then raised his head and stared at the cobwebby ceiling for a few moments, calming himself. He gulped the rest of his brandy and stood. 'I'm sorry, I've made a mess of this. You know how I feel about you, Kitty, and that will never change, but it's Rian I'm thinking of at the moment.'

He stepped towards the door, but Kitty moved in front of him, tears trickling down her face.

'Oh, and me, Daniel, and me, and I can't stop it! I can't get the thought of him dying alone out of my mind! It's as if those dogs are in my heart and tearing at me and, oh *God*, it hurts!'

And then his arms were around her and her face was pressed against his chest, the tangy scent of his sweat in her nostrils. He was taller than Rian, and leaner, not quite as compactly muscled, and she felt his chest hitch as he tried hard to wrestle his own tears into submission.

They remained that way for some minutes, their breathing finally quieting in unison, leaning on each other physically and emotionally, until Kitty became aware that Daniel was growing stiff against her belly.

'Ah, Jesus, not now,' he said very quietly over the top of her head, but he didn't step away from her.

And nor did Kitty move.

He looked down, and his lips descended to hers and she tasted the salt of his tears as he kissed her, gently at first but then with rapidly rising passion. His hands closed over her breasts and briefly cupped their fullness, and she knew that this was not going to be an act of love or even finesse, but an urgent and greedy coupling to blunt the pain of a shared grief. And she also knew that, at this moment, she would accept it.

She raised her arms and settled them firmly around Daniel's neck as their mouths hungrily tasted each other, his groans increasing in urgency and his erection jabbing at her. He slid his hands down to her buttocks where they squeezed her flesh almost hard enough to hurt, then she felt the warm night air on her calves as her skirts were lifted to the small of her back. One hand held them there while the other slid between her legs through the gap in her drawers, and into the silky wetness there.

Daniel gasped raggedly, let the skirts fall and hurriedly, clumsily undid his flies. He gathered up Kitty's skirts again, this time from the front, shoved them out of the way, then bent his knees and picked her up. Guessing what he intended, she wrapped her legs around his waist and, her arms still clamped around his neck, slid herself onto him. He let out a strangled groan and, his knees close to buckling, pushed her against the wall and began to thrust powerfully into her. Almost immediately, the flimsy partition let forth an ominous splintering noise.

'Oh God. In here?' Daniel panted, indicating the bedroom.

Kitty murmured her assent against his shoulder and he carried her in and laid her on the bed.

As he drove in and out of her she closed her eyes, and soon his hair became dark gold with just a touch of grey at the temples, his eyes steel grey, his body a little more muscled and dusted with copper, and his touch the one she so desperately longed for. She felt the familiar sensation build deep within her, and when it had passed, she realised she was crying again.

So was Daniel. He rolled off her, tugged up his trousers and lay staring at the roof, tears trickling into his hair.

'I'm so sorry.'

Kitty didn't look at him. She was too, now. 'I know.'

'I didn't mean . . . I mean, that wasn't what I wanted. Not like this.'

'I know. I really do. But perhaps you should go now.'

He got off the bed and made a half-hearted effort at tucking in his shirt. At the door he said, 'Don't hate me for this, please.'

'I don't.' And she didn't. 'But it might be best if you didn't . . . if you kept away for a while.'

He looked wounded, but she could see he saw the sense in it. She listened as he opened, then closed, the cottage door, and then he was gone.

She lay back and covered her eyes with her arm.

She could smell him on her. It wasn't unpleasant, and Daniel hadn't been unpleasant, but for the first time in her life she had the scent of a man on her who wasn't Rian.

Oh God, what had she done?

⋆　⋆　⋆

312

Pierre wouldn't let her return to the bakery the following day — Amber had gone in her stead — so she was at home when Flora and Eleanor Buckley called.

'Thank you for coming to the service yesterday, Mrs Buckley,' Kitty said as she stood aside to let them in, wishing that people would simply leave her alone.

'You look awful, Kitty,' Flora said, pulling off her black kid gloves and dropping them on the table. 'Have you any brandy? You look like you could do with some.'

Kitty started guiltily, wondering if what she had done last night was somehow evident on her face. 'Would you like a drink?' she asked as she reached for the bottle at the back of the shelf.

'It's rather early but, now that you mention it, a tot would be agreeable,' Flora said as she sat down.

'Mrs Buckley?' Kitty offered.

'Perhaps just a drop. Thank you.'

When they were settled at the table, Flora said, 'I know you're wishing we would just go away, Kitty, but Eleanor has something to tell you that might prove to be very important. Eleanor?'

Eleanor, her eyes watering from the brandy, dabbed at her lips with a lace-edged handkerchief. 'You may recall that the first time we met I told you that my husband Carl is a clerk at the Camp?'

Kitty nodded.

'Well, he's not supposed to discuss his work with me, but he does, because like most people

313

he's not averse to a bit of gossip. And that's all this is, Mrs Farrell, but I do so hope it has at least a grain of truth to it. Anyway, this morning Carl told me that yesterday, just before he finished his duties for the day, he was in the records room and inadvertently overheard a conversation outside the door in which the name Rian Farrell was mentioned.'

Kitty went very still, her brandy glass halfway to her mouth.

'Carl, of course, knows who your husband is,' Eleanor went on, 'because Captain Farrell had been up in front of d'Ewes twice before d'Ewes was moved on, and he also knows that I'm acquainted with you and attended your husband's funeral, so his ears pricked up. He thought you would want to know. Not that he makes a habit of listening at doorways, you understand.' Eleanor frowned. 'Actually, he's a civil servant, so he probably does.'

'Eleanor, will you get on with it!' Flora reprimanded.

'What was being said about him?' Kitty demanded. 'About Rian?'

'Well, please don't get your hopes up, and I've no idea what this means, but, according to Carl, the person speaking said something about not being surprised that there wasn't a coffin at Rian Farrell's funeral, and that his band of merry men could have searched for a body until the cows came home and not found one, because Rian Farrell was nowhere near Ballarat.'

'Were those the exact words?' Kitty asked, her heart beginning to pound with something that

314

was almost, but not quite, hope.

'Those were Carl's exact words to me,' Eleanor replied.

'Would your husband tell me what he heard, do you think?'

Eleanor shook her head. 'I'm sorry, Mrs Farrell, I don't think he would, no. He's happy for me to pass the information on to you, but I think he would regard talking to you as some sort of betrayal of his role as a government clerk. I could ask him, but I'm sure he won't.'

Flora said, 'Eleanor, tell Kitty who Carl believes he overheard.'

'Oh, yes. He couldn't be sure, but he thinks it was Sergeant Coombes.'

★　★　★

Kitty arrived at the Camp just before eleven in the morning, and told the guards on the gate she had urgent news for Sergeant Coombes about one of the rebels still in hiding after the Eureka uprising. When she asked to speak to Coombes at the office, however, she learned that he had departed first thing that morning for Bendigo and would not be back for a week. Swallowing her disappointment and frustration, she rode out of the gates again, but instead of heading back to Lilac Cottage, she went north through the Old Gravel Pits towards Black Hill.

Soon she came to Binda's camp, where the three elderly Watha Wurrung men still sat around the fire as though they hadn't moved since the last time she was there. This time, however, the women and children were also present, except for Binda, who was busy looking after Will and Molly. She dismounted inelegantly from her side-saddle and looped Finn's reins over the branches of a wattle. Two of the old men were staring morosely into the flames, while Barega was painting a pair of sticks red and white while at the same time ignoring a small child attempting to climb onto his thin shoulders.

'Good morning, Barega,' Kitty said as she approached the fire.

He glanced up from his work and gave a perfunctory nod. 'Mornin', Missus.'

'I'm looking for Warrun. Is he about?'

'Hunting. Be back soon.'

Kitty stifled a sigh of frustration; 'soon', she knew, could be anything up to a week.

Barega grimaced as the child gave his wiry grey hair a particularly energetic yank, and barked something to the group of women sitting a short distance from the fire. A girl hurried across, giggling, and snatched up the infant. 'Can wait if you want,' he offered.

Kitty brightened: Warrun couldn't be that far away, then. She gathered her skirts around her legs and perched on a log, wrapping her arms around her knees and wishing she had the guts to go about in her chemise like these women did. The heat today was abominable.

Presently Barega said, 'Binda say your man gone to the Dreamtime.'

Kitty looked at him. 'Perhaps not.'

Barega nodded, as though this sort of ambiguity concerning a man's corporeal and

316

spiritual status were perfectly normal.

'I mean, I'm not sure if he really is dead,' Kitty elucidated.

'But maybe lost?'

'Yes.'

Barega dabbed at a splodge of red paint in his beard. 'And you want Warrun to track?'

'If he will.'

'You pay him, he will.'

'I'll pay him whatever he asks.'

What Warrun asked, when he turned up an hour later with three possums tied together and slung around his neck like a fur stole, was five pounds and Kitty's panama hat. Kitty gave him the money immediately, but, in the interests of staving off sunstroke, promised him the hat at the end of the day.

She had to wait, doing her best to hide her impatience, while he ate a meal, then put a bridle on one of the two rather sinewy horses hobbled in the shade of a stand of eucalypts, but finally they were off and heading back into town.

Passing by Lilac Cottage they saddled up McCool, whom Kitty then led out to Malakoff's Lead and the claim, on which the crew had now returned to work. Telling Warrun to wait out of sight, she rode along the lead until she came to the shaft, and Gideon and Mick who were sitting on the mullock heap surrounding it, apparently taking a break from shovelling washdirt. Daniel, thank God, was nowhere in sight.

Clearly surprised by her appearance, Mick skidded down the heap and took hold of Finn's bridle. 'Is something wrong?'

'No, everything's fine, Mick. But I do need to see Tahi.'

'He's down the shaft.' Mick squinted up at her. 'You sure nothing's wrong? You look . . . I dunno. Fidgety?'

Kitty thought, no, Mick, try reinvigorated. Resuscitated? Galvanised? Desperate with hope? She tried to compose her features. 'No, it's Amber. She's upset and she'll only talk to Tahi. You know what she can be like. I'm sorry, but I'll have to borrow him for a little while.' She winced inwardly at the lie, but there was no way around the subterfuge.

Mick signalled to Gideon, who halted the whip horse and shouted down the shaft for Tahi to come up to the surface. He slapped the horse on the rump, it set off again and a few minutes later Tahi appeared riding in a half-full bucket. His face and arms covered with grime, he climbed out looking mystified. His hair was tied back with a leather thong and he was shirtless.

'Kitty wants to talk to you,' Mick explained off-handedly, now that it was clear there was no real emergency.

Tahi dipped his cupped hands into a bucket of water and tipped some over his head, then scrubbed at his face, hands and arms.

'I hope you don't mind, Tahi,' Kitty said, 'but Amber is upset. She said she will only speak to you.'

Tahi tried valiantly not to look thrilled. He pulled his shirt on over his head, shoved the tails into his trousers, and took McCool's reins from Kitty. 'Is she at Lilac Cottage?'

'Yes, she is.' Kitty replied blandly.

As they mounted, Kitty said to Mick, 'I'll have him back as soon as possible.'

Mick shrugged, said, 'Don't worry if it's too late. No point,' then picked up his shovel and went back to filling the cart with washdirt.

'Is Amber upset about her father, Auntie?' Tahi asked as he and Kitty trotted back along Malakoff's Lead towards the Main Road.

Kitty felt an unpleasant pang of guilt at using him like this, but deliberately squashed it. 'Actually, Tahi, I'm sorry, love, but I lied. Amber's fine. She's working in the shop. It's you I need to talk to.'

At the word 'lied' his head whipped towards her, and Kitty glimpsed in his eyes a reflection of all the angry and frightened things Amber must have said to him about her mother. But there was something else in Tahi's eyes, too. Guilt?

'It's all right, I haven't lost my mind,' Kitty assured him. 'Hawk told me you and Daniel found Rian's shirt. Is that right?'

Warily, Tahi concurred.

'Do you think you could take me there? To where you found it?'

Smarting at not being able to ride to Amber's rescue, Tahi became slightly sulky. 'Probably. But why, Auntie?'

Kitty reined Finn to a halt, and McCool automatically followed suit. 'I need this to be a secret between us, Tahi. I don't want anyone else to know, not just yet. Can you do that?'

Tahi nodded, opened his mouth as if to say something, then shut it again.

'Good.' Kitty raised her hand and waved at Warrun, waiting at the turn-off to the Malakoff Lead. He kicked his horse into a trot and approached, bouncing sloppily up and down like a sack of spuds.

'Who's that?' Tahi asked suspiciously.

'Warrun, Binda's nephew or grandson, I'm not sure which. He's going to track for us,' Kitty replied.

She inspected Tahi's face for signs of censure, or at the very least indications that he thought she had lost the balance of her mind, but to her surprise there were none. Instead he said, 'You still believe he's alive somewhere?'

'I do, yes.'

Tahi simply nodded again, inclined his head in a gesture of greeting towards Warrun, then started off in a southerly direction.

They crossed the Yarrowee about a mile further downstream. Diggers still lined the banks with their cradles and long toms, but did not cluster there like flies as they did closer to the township to the north. The trio followed the river for two miles more as it turned slightly to the south-west, then, where a small tributary branched off and almost immediately disappeared into the ground, left its shallow gurgling and splashing behind and struck out west.

Finally, after they had ridden — according to Warrun — exactly one and a half miles directly into the sun, Tahi reined in and said, 'I think this is it.'

There was nothing to see, so far as Kitty could tell. Low scrub, a few rocks, tinder-dry grass, dirt — nothing to suggest that a man's life had ended here beneath a pack of scrapping dogs.

Warrun slid off his horse. 'Whereabouts?'

Kitty looked questioningly at Tahi, who also dismounted and began to walk carefully about until he came to a bare patch of dirt. 'It was here, I think.'

Warrun joined him, then hitched up his trousers and squatted, inspecting the ground as though reading a book. He rubbed his fingers in the soil and raised them to his nose. 'Blood,' he said, and stood up.

Kitty's heart lurched.

Warrun closed his eyes and sniffed again, then prowled about, his bare feet making no sound at all as he stepped on grass and dried leaves and small branches. Eventually he declared, 'Dingo shit, but old.'

Kitty found she was holding her breath, and made herself let it out lest she faint and fall off Finn. She removed her panama and fanned herself with it vigorously as sweat trickled down her face. There was no noise out here, save the buzz of flies and the odd bird call.

'Tracks, Warrun, are there any tracks?' she prompted.

'Hold your horses, Missus,' he replied tersely.

Tahi shot Kitty a look to see if she was going to object to the blackfellah's rudeness.

But she didn't. She would wait for him all afternoon and night if she had to.

There was no need, however, as he soon raised his hand and beckoned to her. She dismounted and walked across to him. Tahi followed.

'See?' Warrun said, pointing. 'Feet marks.'

Kitty couldn't see anything.

'Ours?' Tahi suggested. 'When we were here the other day?'

'How many days?' Warrun demanded.

'Four.'

'Then not these ones. These older, eh?'

'How many feet?' Kitty asked.

'Six,' Warrun said after a moment. 'No, eight.'

'Eight people?'

'Eight *feet*. Belong four people. Three good, one sick.'

Kitty started to feel sick herself, from excitement and from fear of what might have happened to Rian. 'Can we follow them, the tracks?' she asked, and was startled at the harsh, raw sound of her own voice.

Warrun didn't reply, but returned to his horse, grazing un-enthusiastically on parched grass, and jerked on its reins to make it follow him.

In single file they walked, leading their horses, in an easterly direction, and it became clear they were heading back towards the Yarrowee. They met the river about half a mile further downstream than where they had left it. They crossed, and Warrun picked up the trail on the other side until it turned into tracks left by the wheels of a cart.

The cart tracks were fairly obvious, but Kitty had been able to see nothing at all of the tracks made by foot.

Warrun vaulted onto his horse and announced, 'That's it. Give us me hat?'

'What?' Kitty was shocked. For some reason

she had imagined that Warrun would lead her all the way to Rian. But of course he wouldn't. He was a tracker, not a clairvoyant. In truth the tracks could belong to anyone and could have been made at any time since the rains had stopped. She felt her heart, and her hopes, plummet.

'Follow this track long way 'til it join with the Melbourne Road. They gone to Melbourne, eh?' Warrun said cheerily.

Kitty passed him her panama, and watched dispiritedly as he trotted off.

★   ★   ★

'Auntie?'

Kitty hoisted herself into her hated saddle and hooked her knee around the pommel. 'What is it, Tahi?'

'Warrun just said they went to Melbourne.'

'I know he did, Tahi, but he doesn't know that, does he?'

Tahi was quiet for a moment. Then, 'Those tracks we've been following, did you think they were Uncle Rian's?'

'I had hoped so, yes.'

'And do you think someone found him after the flood and took him?'

'I heard something recently to suggest that may have happened.' Kitty frowned at him, trying to fathom what he was getting at. 'Why?'

Tahi fidgeted in his saddle. He gathered up the reins, dropped them, then rubbed at a dirty mark on his trousers. He looked eight years old again.

Then he said in a rush, 'Because I saw what happened. And I might know where Uncle Rian is. I think Warrun was right.'

Kitty gaped at him. 'You *saw* it!'

'Not in real life,' he said quickly. 'I saw it in here.' He tapped his head. 'When I was asleep. You know, like when you brought my mother home from Sydney.'

Swallowing, Kitty thought back to 1845, when they had returned Wai's bones from her burial place in Sydney, and the beach at Paihia in the Bay of Islands had been crowded with Wai's people because Tahi, not even five at the time, had dreamed she would be returning that day. 'When? When did you see it?'

'Two nights after the flood. But Koro told me years ago that whenever I have the visions I should keep them under my hat, so I do. But when you said that you thought that Uncle Rian might still be alive somewhere, I thought maybe I should tell you, but I wasn't sure. And now Warrun said that about Melbourne.'

'What about Melbourne, Tahi?' Kitty urged Finn closer, her stirrup clinking against Tahi's. 'What about Melbourne?'

'In my vision I saw that great building with the big arches and all the horses in it — '

'Tattersall's Horse Bazaar?'

'I don't know what it's called.'

'On Lonsdale Street?'

'I don't *know*, Auntie!'

Kitty realised she was frightening him. 'I'm sorry, love, really. Just tell me what you saw.'

'There were other buildings on the street with

the horses, and I saw Uncle Rian in one of those. In a little room.' He gave Kitty a wary look, as though he wasn't sure how she was going to react. 'I think he was sick. Or hurt.'

'Which building was it, did you see?' Kitty pressed eagerly.

Tahi saw how bright her eyes had become, and the excited anticipation on her face, and, desperately wanting to please her, said, 'Beside the horse place, one of those.' He regretted it the moment the words left his mouth, but already it was too late to take them back. He *had* seen Uncle Rian in a little room in one of those buildings, but then, in the same vision, he had seen the room again, and it had been empty, and he didn't know what that meant. He hardly ever knew what his visions meant, except for the one about his mother coming home.

'Was he alone, Tahi?'

'No, there was another man there.' This, unfortunately, had been crystal-clear. He had been a very bad man: just the feel of him in the dream had given Tahi a horrible, creeping sense of dread.

'What were they doing? Were they talking?'

'They weren't doing anything.' Tahi struggled to put into words how he saw things in his visions. 'They were just . . . there. And so was I, but I wasn't.' He shook his head in frustration. 'I'm sorry, Auntie, I just see things. I don't often know what they mean.'

'But how did he get there? How did he get to Melbourne?'

'They took him, after he came out of the river. I saw them pick him up off the ground.' And beat him until he bled.

'Who picked him up? Who was it?'

'I don't know. Just some men.'

'So it wasn't dingos at all? Why didn't you say something at the time, Tahi? Even if it was only to me?'

Tahi hung his head. 'I was too scared. Koro said if I went around telling people about my visions, the missionaries at Paihia would think I was possessed by a demon and send me away. I didn't want you to think I was possessed.' He paused. 'Or Amber.'

Ah, Kitty thought with dawning realisation. She reached out and touched his arm. 'Well, *I* don't think you're possessed. I think you've just given me the best gift I've ever received. But we still have to keep it a secret for now, do you understand?'

And Tahi, desperate for Amber to remain ignorant of his unusual talent, nodded in vigorous agreement.

★   ★   ★

They rode back towards town and parted ways at the turn-off to the Malakoff Lead. By the time Kitty reached Red Hill, she had made up her mind. Tying Finn's reins to the rail outside a draper's, she went in and bought a hat to replace the one she had given Warrun. Next, she paid a visit to a gunsmith's and brought extra ammunition for Rian's pistols and shotgun.

Lastly, she purchased a capacious set of saddlebags.

She did all this with a single purpose of mind, concentrating on the enormous and daunting task ahead of her and barely noticing those around her, which is why she walked straight into Lily Pearce as she was leaving the saddlery. The saddlebags were knocked out of her arms and fell to the ground. Kitty was on the verge of apologising when she realised whom she had banged into. Instead, she stood very still. Lily, overdressed as usual in an array of flashy finery and too much jewellery, found herself literally backed into a corner between a verandah post and a rain barrel. She glared venomously at Kitty.

'You want to be careful who you bang into, Kitty Farrell,' she snarled.

'You want to be careful yourself,' Kitty replied in an equally poisonous tone.

The saddler looked worriedly through the doorway; he had several expensive saddles on display on the verandah and had visions of them being scuffed and thrown in all directions should an altercation break out. He stepped outside, raised his hands in what he imagined to be a placatory manner and said, 'Ladies, ladies, please, if we could all perhaps calm down?'

But both women ignored him, practically hissing and spitting at each other and putting him in mind of two tigresses he had once seen at the London Zoo.

Lily smiled nastily. 'Or should I say *Widow* Farrell?'

Not taking her eyes off Lily's, Kitty bent and retrieved the saddlebags, forcing every fibre of her being to refrain from swinging them at Lily's head. She stepped down off the verandah, slung the bags across the pommel of her saddle, mounted Finn and rode off.

It wasn't until she reached Lilac Cottage that she realised she recognised the stone in the pendant Lily Pearce had been wearing around her neck.

It had been a milky, grey-blue star sapphire cabochon.

★   ★   ★

She was ready. She had dressed in her new hat and the trousers she wore on the *Katipo*, Rian's shirt and jacket — still smelling comfortingly of him — and her boots, and had tied back her hair and tucked it under the hat. Her 'lady' clothes had been rolled and packed in the saddlebags, along with a little food, the pistols, money, a small lamp wrapped in a cloth, oil, matches and a few other necessities she thought she might need; and Rian's shotgun was loaded and ready to go into the saddle holster. Finn, whom Kitty preferred over McCool, had been watered, rested and resaddled. Amber was spending the night with Will and Molly again, and all Kitty had to do was finish her letter to her, and leave it on the table where she would find it in the morning . . .

My dearest Amber,
Your father, I believe, is alive, and by the

time you read this letter, I will have left Ballarat to find him. I want to tell you not to worry about either of us — or at least try not to worry too much.

I am so very sorry that you have been angry with me these past few weeks, and I know that it has been just as hard for you as it has been for me. I couldn't bear to think that your father had left us forever, and I know you couldn't either.

The crew will look after you. Talk to Haunui or Pierre, or to Leena if you need 'women's' advice. They all love you almost as much as your father and I do.

She sat with the end of the pen in her mouth, knowing there was something else she wanted to say. Finally, she dipped the nib into the ink and added:

I will be back with you as soon as I can, whether your father is with me or not. Even if it turns out that we have lost him, you will always have me, Amber, and I will never, ever abandon you.
All my love always,
Ma

She reread what she had written, blew on the paper to dry the ink, and glanced around to see if she had forgotten anything.

Through the window she could see the shadows thrown on the inside of Leena and Ropata's tent some distance away as Amber and the children moved around, preparing for sleep. Leena and the men themselves had all gone into town, leaving their tents in darkness. The moon was bright but occasionally obscured by scudding cloud.

Kitty closed the cottage door behind her and walked quickly across the grass to where she had tethered Finn, and shushed him as he welcomed her with a soft whicker. She slid Rian's shotgun into the saddle holster, untied the reins and swung herself up, relishing at last the comfort and ease of being able to sit astride.

She patted Finn's neck, leant forward in the stirrups, and whispered as near to his ear as she could reach, 'Come on, Finn, let's see if we can make it to Melbourne by sun-up, shall we?'

★ ★ ★

As she trotted off towards the track that would take her around and behind Red Hill and up onto the Melbourne Road, Hawk and Haunui emerged from their place of concealment in their darkened tent, and watched her until she disappeared into the shadows. All afternoon they had had a suspicion that Kitty was up to something.

His arms belligerently folded across his chest, Hawk scowled and grumbled, 'I still do not think we should be permitting her to do it. Rian would not have allowed it.'

Haunui scratched his head. 'Ae, but it is not a matter of permitting, is it? She just does things.'

Hawk grunted. 'I thought she had begun to accept his passing.'

Haunui glanced at Hawk's sharp profile. 'Have *you*?'

A short pause. 'No. Not in my heart.'

'So why are you expecting Kitty to?' Haunui asked.

'But I am not riding off to Melbourne on a wild-goose chase,' Hawk countered. 'I suppose she is going to Melbourne?'

'But is it a wild-goose chase?'

It was Hawk's turn to shoot a look at Haunui. 'I do not know. Is it?'

Haunui recalled Flora's counsel. 'I don't know, either. But I do know we have to let her do it, whatever she's up to. Ae, we could follow her and bring her back, and then what? Lock her in the cottage? For how long? Do you want to be the one to deliver her kai, eh?'

'No, thank you,' Hawk said quickly.

'And do not forget, Kitty owns the claim now that Rian has gone. And all the equipment and the livestock. And the *Katipo*. She is my daughter in spirit, but now she is *your* boss for real. We can't lock up your boss.'

Hawk was unusually silent, even for him. Perhaps, Haunui thought, this hadn't occurred to him.

Finally, Hawk said, 'No, but she still should not be venturing out alone.'

'I don't think she will be alone,' Haunui replied, and pointed across the grass to where the bullocks and McCool were hobbled several hundred yards away.

As they watched, a figure crept stealthily from behind a canvas-and-iron hut, using the clouds crossing the moon as cover, and cautiously approached McCool. An arm was extended, the horse took something, and while he ate the figure slipped a bridle over his head and laid a saddle across his back. The hobbles were removed and left on top of a tree stump, then the thief mounted McCool and trotted off into the night.

'Hmmm,' Hawk said.

'Ae,' Haunui agreed.

The thief was Daniel Royce.

★   ★   ★

But Kitty and Daniel weren't the only travellers to ride out of Ballarat that night. A little over two hours later, Lily Pearce also left for Melbourne.

17

Melbourne, late February 1855

Kitty arrived in Melbourne just after dawn. Her eyes were gritty and sore, her backside was tender, and the skin on the inside of her legs raw from rubbing against the stirrup leathers. She was hungry and desperately needed a hot drink and a wash.

Fighting the urge to ride straight to Lonsdale Street and start knocking on doors around Tattersall's Horse Bazaar, Kitty instead headed for Collins Street and the Criterion Hotel, where she knew she would find a comfortable room. Forgetting she was dressed in men's attire, and grubby men's attire at that, she received a startled and disapproving look from the publican's wife as she arranged her accommodation.

Finally in her room, having been left to haul her saddlebags upstairs unaided, Kitty washed her face and hands in the bowl on the night stand and lay on the bed for a few minutes to rest her bleary eyes.

She woke four hours later, stiff and sore, to the realisation that the sun was high in the sky and she had wasted almost half a day sleeping when she should have been looking for Rian.

Groaning and easing herself off the bed, she tugged the bell pull and, when the house girl arrived, ordered bread and cheese and a pot of tea. While she waited she peed in the chamber pot, then emptied her saddlebags onto the bed, changed into her dress, brushed her hair and put it up in a chignon. Her late breakfast arrived, and by the time she'd eaten it and had two cups of tea she felt a little more refreshed.

Downstairs, she asked that Finn be saddled and brought around from the hotel's stables, but it wasn't until he appeared that it suddenly occurred to her that she couldn't ride him astride in long skirts.

'Shite,' she said under her breath, feeling suddenly deflated and more than a little overwhelmed by the task ahead of her.

The boy leading Finn, an undernourished ginger-haired lad of about eleven wearing a uniform clearly too big for him and notably baggy in the arse, glanced at her in momentary astonishment, then smirked.

'I don't know what you're smiling at,' Kitty snapped, 'especially if you're expecting a tip, which you certainly won't be getting now. Take him back and unsaddle him, go on.'

But the boy turned out to be a lot more wily than Kitty had given him credit for. 'Would ya be wantin' a lady's seat, then?'

'Why? I suppose you happen to have one, do you?' Kitty said, without much hope.

'I might,' the boy said, squinting up at her. 'For the right price.'

Kitty rolled her eyes. 'Go on, then — let's see it.'

'Hold this,' the boy said, handing Finn's reins

to Kitty before scampering off on bare feet.

He was back less than five minutes later, almost staggering under the weight of a very fine side-saddle in cinnamon-coloured tooled leather with a suede seat and double pommels.

'Have you just stolen that?' Kitty asked reprovingly.

The boy's freckled countenance took on an expression commensurate with Kitty having just accused him of murdering his entire family, including his grandmother. 'I did not! I borrowed it.'

'Borrowed. I see.'

'Yeah, and ya can rent it if ya like.'

'How much?'

The boy named an extortionate fee, which Kitty considered only because she might have days of riding around Melbourne ahead of her.

When the deal had been concluded and the saddles transferred, Kitty asked, 'And with whom have I had the pleasure of entering into this transaction?'

The boy scratched a scabby shin and said, 'Wot?'

'What's your name?'

'Oh. Israel.'

'Israel what?'

'Israel ya-little-bastard,' the boy said, making a joke of it, but Kitty could see the veiled sadness in his hazel eyes.

'All right, Israel, when I've finished with this saddle I want mine back, and I don't want to discover that it, too, has been 'rented out', do you understand?'

'Aye aye, missus,' Israel said, saluting smartly. 'Ya don't want a gig as well, do ya? Or a dogcart?'

Kitty pulled herself up onto Finn and gathered the reins. 'Not just now, thank you.'

Israel waved cheerfully as she rode off, then his smiled faded as he noticed a dark-haired man standing in the shadows on the other side of the street, watching the lady as a circling hawk in the sky watches a rabbit on the ground.

★ ★ ★

Kitty rode straight to Lonsdale Street and began systematically knocking on doors to the buildings on either side of Tattersall's Horse Bazaar. Some were dwellings and some were business premises, but none was empty. A few curious owners and tenants allowed her inside to look about, but most would not, simply shutting the door in her face when she asked. But Kitty had a plan: the buildings were rambling but no taller than double-storeyed, and festooned with narrow drainpipes and very flimsy ladders to comply with at least the letter of the law regarding fire escapes. A small boy, say around eleven years old, would easily be able to scale them under the cover of darkness and peep through shutters and windows, especially if he had a pound coin nestling comfortably in his trouser pocket.

In her heart, though, she suspected that Rian wasn't here, regardless of what Tahi had seen in his dream. She was sure that if he were this close to her she would know — she would *feel* it, somehow.

She went next door to the horse bazaar in case Tahi's vision had somehow been geographically askew. In the summer heat the huge stone building reeked, despite the lofty arches designed to funnel breezes through the complex, and flies buzzed thickly around piles of horse shit in the stalls, and floated along channels of urine like tiny mariners bound for voyages across Melbourne's open sewers. There were carriage stands, tack rooms and stables on the ground floor, and haylofts and granaries above, but no sign of Rian, and, apart from an offer to buy Finn, Kitty came away with as little as she'd taken in.

But she wasn't unduly despondent: she believed Tahi — Rian must be in Melbourne somewhere.

She rode back along Lonsdale Street and turned into Elizabeth Street until she came to the offices of a printer, where she dismounted and went inside. Twenty minutes later she emerged, having ordered 150 posters asking for information leading to the whereabouts of Captain Rian Farrell, and including his description, where she could be contacted, and the fact that she was offering a sizeable reward for any genuine leads. The posters, she had been assured, would be ready by nine o'clock the next morning.

It was suppertime by the time she returned to the Criterion Hotel. Israel was sitting on the boardwalk a short distance from the front door, pretending he wasn't looking out for her. As she approached, he leapt up and trotted over, taking Finn's reins and grinning up at her.

'How was the saddle, eh? Nice an' comfy?'

'Very, thank you, Israel. For a side-saddle.' Kitty lifted her leg and slid to the ground. 'Can you see to Finn, please?'

Israel nodded enthusiastically but didn't move, obviously waiting for his tip.

Kitty didn't move, either. 'Israel, I would like you to do a job for me.'

Israel looked shifty. 'There money in it?'

'If you do it well.'

'I will, I promise.'

Kitty looked at him through narrowed eyes. 'You don't even know what it is yet.'

Israel shrugged, clearly confident of being able to carry out any task asked of him.

'Do you think you can climb up drainpipes and narrow, rickety ladders and possibly look through some windows?' Kitty asked, trying not to roll her eyes.

'If I pushed meself, I think I could, yeah.'

'Well, that's what I'd like you to do.' And she told him exactly where and when, and what to look for.

'Easy. How much?' He didn't even ask who the man Kitty was searching for might be.

'A pound. I'll have to trust you, though, Israel,' Kitty said. 'You could just go around the corner or sit in a pub for two hours then come back and tell me you've done it, and I wouldn't know any different, would I?' She waited, watching him until she knew he was paying her proper attention. 'But this is my husband I'm looking for, the man who means more to me than anything else in the world. I thought I'd lost him, but now I've been given a second chance, if only I can find him. Now, I'm too heavy to get up those pipes and what-have-you, so I have to rely on you. You can deceive me if you choose to, but I'll know, Israel. I'll know. So take your pound now, and if you do decide to cheat me, just don't come back, all right?' She handed him a gold coin. 'Otherwise, my room is number twenty-two.'

And she turned and walked into the hotel, leaving him staring after her, the pound coin cool and heavy in his hand, and thinking that the dark-haired man called Mr Royce had been right — she *was* a very decent person, and not at *all* like other so-called ladies who promenaded around Melbourne thinking they were that much better than everyone else.

And now he had *two* pound coins in his pocket!

⋆   ⋆   ⋆

Israel had come back with a large scrape down his back from slipping off a drainpipe, and a bruise blooming on one scrawny buttock as a result of being caught peering into a window, but with no news of Rian. Kitty had been disappointed, but she had learnt long ago to trust her heart, and her heart had told her that Rian had not been in those specific buildings. She didn't blame Tahi — no doubt even visions could be fallible when it came to details — but it did leave her in a quandary about where to start looking next. The posters, she hoped, would help.

She rose early, and as she opened the door to her room she almost fell over Israel, who sat up yawning and rubbing his eyes.

Astonished, she asked, 'Have you been here all night?'

Israel nodded, farted gently, and scrubbed his hands through his untidy mop of hair.

'Don't you have anywhere else to sleep?' Kitty said, concerned.

'Yeah, hayloft.' But Mr Royce didn't pay me to sleep there, Israel thought, he paid me to keep an eye on you. But perhaps not this close an eye, he reflected ruefully as he eased his tender buttock off the meanly carpeted floor, and scrambled to his feet. 'We puttin' up them posters this morning?'

'Are you not supposed to be tending the hotel stables today?'

'Day off.'

Kitty doubted that, but it wasn't her affair. Israel followed her downstairs, then stood outside the dining-room window, gazing longingly in as Kitty ate her breakfast. Finally, she could stand it no longer. Going to the door, she beckoned him over.

'Israel?'

He shuffled towards her, hands clasped in front of him, huge eyes blinking up. 'Yes, missus?

'Go and break that pound coin I gave you. You're putting me off my food.'

Israel laughed and skipped off, knowing his bluff had been called.

By midday they had put up all the posters, mainly in store windows and public houses, and on fences and notice boards, and Kitty went back to the Criterion to await news.

By three o'clock in the afternoon she realised the folly of her plan. Sitting in her room, with nothing to do but let her mind run amok with terrible imaginings, was possibly the worst pastime she could have devised for herself. So she went downstairs, found Israel who had literally been dragged back to work by his boss, paid for his time for the rest of the afternoon, and made him sit on the sofa with her in the hotel lounge and talk.

Israel, it turned out, was not the orphan she had assumed — and he had certainly implied — he was. He was originally from Rotherhithe, London; his father had left for the Bendigo goldfields two years ago and had simply never returned, and the last time he had seen his mother she had been senseless from gin underneath some sailor behind a pub on Flinders Street. That had been about six months ago.

'So where do you live?' Kitty asked, disquieted, but not entirely sure she believed him. She knew, though, that he was quite possibly telling the truth, or at least some version of it.

'In the hotel stables. I get me meals there and all. It's all right.' He shrugged with the stoicism of someone much older.

'And your name?'

Another twitch of the shoulders. 'Me father read the Bible a lot.' A pause. 'Dunno what he reads now.'

Kitty found herself telling him about all the exotic places that she and Rian and the crew of the *Katipo* had been, how Amber had come to be part of the family, and the events that had led up to Rian's disappearance. An hour later, she realised she had been talking about Rian almost constantly, and that Israel had sat through her monologue barely even fidgeting.

She smiled ruefully. 'I'm sorry. It's just that I miss him.'

But Israel wasn't listening now, his attention snared by an approaching figure.

'Mrs Farrell?'

Kitty turned; the man standing before her was vaguely familiar, but it took her several moments to retrieve his name.

'It's So-Yee, isn't it?' she said, rising and offering her hand.

The Chinese man stared at it for a moment, then shook it reluctantly. 'Yes. Wong Kai has sent me. He wishes that I escort you to speak with him. On a matter he believes will be of great interest to you.'

Kitty's heart quickened and the blood rushed from her head as she realised with dismay that for nearly two days she had been completely ignoring a prime source of information: if anyone knew about secrets in this town, it would be Wong Kai.

She snatched up her reticule. 'Of course, yes.

Thank you, So-Yee.'

She followed him outside to a waiting cab, but when Israel made to climb in after her, So-Yee leaned out and pushed him back onto the street.

'Hey!' Israel exclaimed indignantly, his hand on the cab door. 'I'm her chaperone! I have to go everywhere with her.'

'Could he not just — ?' Kitty began.

So-Yee gave a single, sharp shake of his head. 'No. Only you.' He slapped Israel's hand away, shut the door, then rapped on the roof of the cab.

His mouth set in an angry line, Israel watched the cab lurch away up the street, then ran off to find Mr Royce.

⋆ ⋆ ⋆

'And he didn't say where they were going?' Daniel asked, scowling and trying to ease the awful crick he had in his neck from the boarding-house cot he'd slept on the night before. Tonight he might try his luck in the stall he'd rented for McCool — it certainly couldn't be any less comfortable.

Israel shook his head hard enough to make the straggly ends of his hair fly about. 'He just said this Chinkee cove wanted to see her.'

'And he was Chinese himself?'

'Yeah, he had this long pigtail down to here, and one of them little caps on and them baggy suits they wear.'

'What was his name?'

'Which one?'

343

Daniel suppressed a sigh of exasperation. 'The man Kitty was going to see.'

Israel made a face as he concentrated on remembering. 'Wonky? One key?'

'Wong Kai?'

'That were it!'

Daniel was silent for a moment, drained the glass of ale he'd been nursing half the afternoon, then said almost to himself, 'Then I presume they'd be heading for Little Bourke Street.'

'Well, they don't live nowhere else round here, those Chinkees,' Israel remarked, and stole the pickle Daniel had left on his plate. 'Good job, too. Don't want 'em stinkin' up the whole town.'

Daniel clipped him sharply across the side of his head. 'They're called Chinese, boy. I paid you a pound to be my eyes and ears, not an ignorant little shit, so keep your prejudices to yourself.'

Rubbing his stinging ear, Israel mumbled, 'Sorry, Mister Royce. Do ya know the way to the *Chinese* quarter? I can show ya.'

'Not necessary.'

'Can I come with ya, then?'

Daniel looked at Israel's dirty, eager little face. 'Why?'

''Cause she's nice, that Mrs Farrell. I like her.'

Oh God, so do I, Daniel thought desperately, his stomach performing a lazy roll at the thought of her. 'I'm not paying you any more money.'

'Don't care. I'll do it for nothing,' Israel declared and darted out of the pub.

Daniel followed, wondering how much longer he could keep tailing Kitty without her seeing him. He spared a guilty thought for Tahi: he'd

344

browbeaten the lad until he'd finally confessed to what Kitty had wanted from him that afternoon out on the Malakoff Lead. All Daniel had had to do was follow her to Melbourne and make sure he kept out of sight. Then she'd taken a shine to the young stable boy, and his job had become a little easier. But now it seemed the boy was falling under her spell as well.

★   ★   ★

The same sickly-sweet smell hung in the air as Kitty sat in Wong Kai's office, fanning her face with the painted silk fan So-Yee had given her. He'd also left her a jug of water, and a facecloth wrapped around an ice cube to hold against her forehead. Very thoughtful, Kitty reflected. If only So-Yee had managed a smile, Wong Kai's hospitality could even be considered gracious.

The door from the opium room opened and Wong Kai himself entered. He sat down in his velvet-upholstered chair, made a steeple out of his fingers, looked over them at Kitty, and said, 'So, your husband has disappeared.' A statement, not a question.

'Yes.'

'My men saw your . . . ' his hand fluttered as he searched for the correct English word ' . . . advertisements? Would you care to tell me how this came about?'

Kitty complied, grateful that Wong Kai didn't even blink when she came to the parts about Pierre's snake, Tahi's vision and Warrun's tracking skills. Evidently, the Chinese were comfortable with matters concerning mysticism.

'And you suspect that this Sergeant Coombes is working with the woman Lily Pearce?'

'I don't know.' Kitty folded the fan and laid it on the low table at her elbow. 'Rian did say once he thought there might be some sort of arrangement between them, but whether it was just business or something more intimate he couldn't say. Or didn't say. I don't think he cared to speculate.'

'But why would they kidnap your husband?' Wong Kai asked.

'I don't know! All I know is that I saw that *woman* wearing the sapphire from Rian's ring around her scraggy neck, a ring that *I* had made for him and would know *anywhere!*'

Wong Kai waited for Kitty to calm herself. 'So,' he said when she had, 'Rian was arrested twice by Sergeant Coombes, and both times made a fool of the man, and was also involved in the Eureka uprising but was never arrested for it, is that correct?' Kitty nodded. 'Also, he was approached several times by Lily Pearce and spurned her, once publicly. Is that also correct?' Kitty again concurred. 'Finally, you and Lily Pearce were involved in a catfight in the street, resulting in her public humiliation. Again, am I correct?'

'Well, her wig came off,' Kitty admitted.

Wong Kai stared at her with a faintly disbelieving air. 'And you do not know why the pair of them would wish to cause you harm?'

Kitty sat stunned. The relief at having so recently discovered that Rian probably wasn't dead was now replaced by the dismaying knowledge that, in all likelihood, their own actions had caused the awful predicament in which they now found themselves. 'But surely retribution on this scale is completely out of proportion?'

'Would that not depend, Mrs Farrell, on the extent of their humiliation? Also, if your husband is not dead, you must ask why not. Kidnap is usually accompanied by a demand for ransom.' Wong Kai was silent for several beats. 'And, of course, there is the possibility that they may not be working alone.'

'What makes you say that?'

'Nothing in particular. I am simply considering all possibilities.' He picked a thread off the sleeve of his robe and let it fall to the floor. 'Now, I assume you do want my assistance in this matter? I am indebted to you regarding the matter of Bao, and I am happy to discharge that debt by helping you to locate your husband.'

Kitty said that this sounded extremely fair.

'Good. Now,' Wong Kai went on, 'you will discover that all manner of fools and confidence men will approach you as a result of your advertisements.' He shook his head regretfully. 'You should not have bothered. You should have come to me first. Mr Chen will return with you to your hotel to discourage any such unwanted attention, since it is unlikely that you will learn anything useful through such channels.'

Kitty frowned. Wong Kai was always so sure of himself.

'How do you know that?'

Wong Kai smirked, as though he knew exactly what she was thinking. 'Because already I have my people out and about, and any information you are likely to receive, even if it has not been fabricated, will probably be redundant by the time you receive it.'

Kitty shot forward in her seat, her heart hammering. 'Why? What have you heard?'

'Nothing concrete — a rumour here, a word there. But with a touch of persuasion, and the calling in of several debts owed to me — '

'But you said 'redundant'. Was he here, Mr Wong? Was he here and now he's gone?'

Kai inclined his head in partial agreement. 'Your young friend with the gift of second sight was correct. He was here, I can assure you of that, but I have not yet discovered where he is now.'

It was Kitty's first real proof that Rian was still alive. Her heart soaring with relief and her throat aching against a torrent of tears that sprang from both gratitude and fury, she put her elbows on her knees and her hands over her face so Wong Kai couldn't see her livid expression. Why, why, couldn't you have told me that as soon as you walked in?

'He may still be in Melbourne,' Wong Kai continued, addressing the top of her head, 'or he may have been taken somewhere else. I am awaiting further information.'

Kitty straightened, smoothed a crease in her skirt, and studied his face. He looked . . . amused almost, as though he knew she was angry with him and he found it entertaining. She composed herself to the best of her ability.

'I am extremely grateful for your assistance, Mr Wong. I'm sure you know how disadvantaged I would be without it. When are you expecting to receive this further information?'

Kai shrugged, the stiff silk of his robe making a soft whispering sound against the back of his chair. 'I am hoping sometime tonight, but who knows? When the quarry is information, the hunt cannot always be measured in time.'

Oh, what a lot of shite, Kitty thought. 'Well, I would very much appreciate being told as soon as you hear anything. Any hour of the day or night.'

Wong Kai nodded beneficently. 'Of course. It will be my pleasure.'

So-Yee escorted Kitty downstairs, where she was met by Mr Chen, and together they walked along Little Bourke Street, hailed a cab and headed back to the Criterion Hotel.

Concealed uncomfortably behind a stack of empty barrels in an alleyway, Daniel and Israel watched as the cab rattled off.

'What do ya think he had to tell her?' Israel wondered aloud.

Daniel had no idea, but she certainly looked brighter than she had for some weeks — and that could mean only one thing. He leant against the wall behind the barrels and closed his eyes, expecting to be overcome by a surge of jealous despair, or hopelessness, or even possessiveness now that he'd actually, after all these years of longing, made love to Kitty.

Then he gave a mental sigh of despondency,

because it hadn't been love, had it? Certainly not on her part. Kitty had been seeking comfort, at best. And he had been left profoundly regretting what he'd done — and when she was at such a low ebb. Her lips had silently formed Rian's name at the peak of her passion, and he'd pressed his face into her throat so he wouldn't have to see it, and so he could keep pretending it was him she was loving, and not her dead husband. And now that it seemed that Rian might be alive after all, Daniel felt . . . what? He rubbed his hands over his unshaven face and then nearly smiled, because the closest he could come to it was . . . joy.

'Why don't you go back to the hotel and ask her?' he said to Israel. 'Christ almighty, boy, it's what I'm paying you for.'

⋆ ⋆ ⋆

The bespectacled Mr Chen, attired in his smart suit and a beautiful panama hat, had brought with him a *mah jong* set, and he and Kitty spent the remainder of the afternoon and the evening in the hotel lounge drinking tea and playing. The tiles were exquisitely crafted and decorated, and from time to time a small crowd gathered, enjoying the novelty of watching such a skillful Chinese game. Initially, the Criterion's proprietor inquired privately of Kitty whether she and Mr Chen intended to embark upon a marathon gambling session and, if so, could they please hie themselves elsewhere as the Criterion prided itself on its genteel and sober reputation, but a very tart reminder from Kitty that she was a paying guest, and entitled to use the facilities and receive visitors, soon shut him up.

Mr Chen perched on a sofa while Kitty sat opposite in an armchair, enjoying the opportunity to relax a little and use the skills she'd learnt occasionally playing *mah jong* with Wong Fu at Ballarat. Israel at first refused to sit next to Mr Chen, but after an hour he had drawn closer, attracted by the bright colours on the tiles and the distinctive sounds they made as they were moved about, until finally he was almost on the Chinese man's knee.

Amused, Mr Chen began to explain to him how the game was played, and by the time Israel dashed outside to use the privy, he was moved to remark, 'He is quite intelligent, is he not, for an uneducated, snot-nosed, white-skinned boy?'

Kitty laughed, but when Israel had not returned almost an hour later she began to wonder where he was. By the time he did come back, several men had called at the hotel, each asking to speak with Kitty. Mr Chen dealt with them on her behalf, saying little to her afterwards except that they did not have anything to offer except deliberate falsehoods manufactured to separate Kitty from her money, and tenuous sightings that would have proved erroneous had they been pursued.

At eight o'clock they ate supper, and Kitty noticed that Israel had again disappeared.

18

Kitty cautiously opened her door, peering out at Israel through the small gap. 'Oh, it's you. Where have you been?'

'Out an' about.'

He'd been sitting in yet another pub with Mr Royce, who'd turned out to be not such a bad-tempered bastard after all. In fact, he'd told Israel not to call him Mr Royce because, he reckoned, it made him feel like he was a hundred years old, and to call him Daniel instead. And he'd bought Israel two glasses of ale and a lovely steak-and-kidney pie, so Israel had sat there calling him Daniel and chatting away and having a high old time. Actually, Daniel had done most of the talking — and a fair bit of drinking. So Israel had gone back with him to his shit-hole of a boarding house and made sure he'd got to bed — well, on it, at least — then come back here.

When Kitty told him there had been no news, Israel heard the weariness and disappointment in her voice, and had no idea how to make her feel better.

'Will you sleep out here again?' Kitty asked.

Israel nodded.

'Look, why don't you come in and sleep on the chair inside. I don't mind.'

Israel felt a very disconcerting stirring in his loins, and quickly shook his head. 'Nah, I'll be all good out here.'

'I'm not entirely sure why you're sleeping on my doorstep anyway, Israel,' Kitty remarked.

'Well, 'cause I've — ' Israel stopped himself just in time. He'd almost said because he'd been paid to, but that wasn't actually it, not anymore. He was doing it because he wanted to. He wanted to know what was going to happen to Kitty Farrell, and he wanted to help her if he could. And, to tell the truth, he wanted to help Daniel Royce as well. The pound coins were neither here nor there now, although he certainly wasn't giving either of them back.

★   ★   ★

At a quarter to four the next morning, someone stood on Israel's arm. Jerked out of a moderate sleep, he yelped and rolled out of the way.

'Boy, wake up!' a voice ordered. Its owner gave him a light kick in the ribs.

Israel staggered to his feet, saw that his attacker was the Chinkee who had barred him from riding in the cab with Kitty, and struck out with a fist.

'Stop that,' So-Yee said, casually blocking the punch with the side of his hand. He rapped on the door. 'I am here to see Mrs Farrell.'

Kitty answered in less than a minute, and Israel wondered whether she had even been asleep.

'So-Yee! Is there news?'

'Yes. May I enter?'

Kitty stepped back. 'Of course.' She let him in,

not minding when Israel slipped in behind him.

So-Yee stood in the middle of the room. Kitty noted that he looked very grim, but then she had never seen him look anything else.

'I have news,' he began. 'It is both good and bad.'

Kitty's stomach began to churn.

So-Yee continued: 'Your husband was indeed held captive in premises in Lonsdale Street, incapacitated from wounds. The day you yourself arrived in Melbourne, and for that reason, he was taken from there and transported to Geelong — '

'Geelong!' Kitty gasped.

'Yes, where he is presently incarcerated in a building near the Corio Bay waterfront.' He slid a hand into his tunic and passed Kitty a folded square of paper. 'This is a drawing of the location of the building.'

Kitty opened the paper and studied it. 'But I don't understand, So-Yee. Who is holding him prisoner? And why?'

So-Yee looked even more grave, if that were possible. 'Wong Kai has not been able to ascertain why, Mrs Farrell, but he has discovered who.'

And when So-Yee told her, Kitty felt fear settle on her like an icy, black cloak.

★ ★ ★

'I'm slipping!'

Astounded that someone who had worked in a stable since they were nine had never ridden a

354

horse, Kitty reached an arm behind her back, grabbed a handful of Israel's shirt and yanked him upright again.

'For God's sake, will you hang on! We're nearly there!'

His arms tightened around her waist and she felt him tuck his bare feet between her calves and the saddle flaps, holding on for all he was worth. She could see the docks not far away, and the long finger of Australia Wharf where the *Katipo* was berthed. A few minutes more and they would be there.

It would take a day to travel to Geelong overland, but only four hours by sea, perhaps as little as three if the winds were good — *and* if the *Katipo* could be sailed at something close to her maximum speed.

* * *

Daniel sat on the edge of his cot, scratching viciously at a row of flea bites down his leg, and cursing a noisy bloody bird outside his window that was insisting on heralding the approaching dawn with unnecessary cheer.

He'd been awake since two o'clock and had finally decided he would talk to Kitty. He was tired of skulking around after her, and paying good money to a boy who smelt of horse shit to find out what was going on when he should be doing that himself. And if she refused to see him, then he would simply slip back into the shadows and wait.

He opened the lid of his watch — half past

four. It was early, but now that he'd made up his mind, he realised he couldn't wait. He splashed his face with cold water from the cracked ewer, cleaned his teeth with powder and spat it out the window at the irritating bird, pulled on his boots and walked the quarter-mile to where McCool was stabled. Even at this hour and with the sun not quite up, the streets of Melbourne were busy, fruiterers and fishmongers and butchers setting up stalls for the day's markets, and carts and barrels and yapping dogs blocking alleyways and lanes.

Outside the Criterion Hotel he looped McCool's reins over a rail and went inside. Here, too, the staff were already afoot.

'Help you, sir?' someone asked Daniel as he stood in the foyer.

'No,' he replied as he turned and walked up the stairs. He knew which room Kitty occupied because Israel had told him.

He located the room, although the boy wasn't sleeping outside the door as he'd been expecting, knocked gently and waited. He knocked again, loudly this time. Still nothing. He pushed the door and it swung open.

Kitty wasn't there. Feeling faintly guilty, he went in and looked around. Some of her things were scattered about — the dress she had been wearing the last time he'd seen her, a chemise, a pair of button boots, some toilette articles. A nightdress was tossed across the unmade bed, and a few bits and pieces abandoned on the floor. Everything, in fact, suggested she had gone somewhere in a hurry.

He stared briefly at the tableau for a moment, then hurried out of the room, along the hall and down the stairs, almost knocking over a housegirl coming the other way carrying a teetering armful of sheets. The stables were behind the hotel, and he accosted the first person he saw, a fat-bellied man sitting on a barrel enjoying a pipe in the first rays of the morning sun.

He seemed to take an irritatingly long time to formulate his answer. 'A good-looking woman with black hair, you say? On a chestnut mount? Aye, 'twas less than an hour ago. Wearing trews, she was. Quite a sight to behold, and not one ye see often, I have to say. Trews and a man's jacket. Very nice fit, too, the trews. Took off on a man's saddle, to boot — '

'Where was she going, did she say?' Daniel interjected.

The man appeared not to hear him. 'Had my young stable boy with her, too. Or should I say, ex-stable boy. Had to inform him he no longer has a job here. Can't be doing with unreliability, can I? Didn't seem to give a bugger, I have to say.'

'Yes, but where were they *going*!' Daniel demanded, wanting to strangle the fat fool.

The man screwed up his face, thinking. 'The wharves? Aye, that's what she said. Rapido? Something like that. I weren't really listening, ye see.' He shook his head in wonderment. 'Them trews!'

Katipo. Daniel was already running back towards the street and McCool. Why on earth was Kitty heading for the wharves? Where would she be going? And surely she couldn't be intending to actually launch the *Katipo?*

★ ★ ★

'We can't sail her by ourselves.'

Kitty said, 'You're not sailing her at all.'

They were standing on the wharf next to the *Katipo*, Kitty holding Finn's reins and Israel's face beginning to go a deep, obstinate red colour.

'Ya said I could come with ya!'

'I said you could come along to look after Finn after I've gone. That's all.'

'But I know where I can put him!' He pointed vigorously. 'Me mate works at them stables just down the way there, see? Ya can't sail a whole ship all on your own!'

'I won't be on my own,' Kitty replied calmly, even though her heart was racing and her stomach felt as though it contained two dozen sparrows all madly flapping their wings. She handed the reins to Israel and walked up the gangplank onto the *Katipo*, calling, 'Charlie? Charlie Dunlop!'

There was a clatter and a curse, and Charlie's grizzled head appeared at the top of the cabin steps.

'Mrs Farrell? Aye, it is, too! Good day to you, Mrs Farrell!' He clambered up on deck and hurried towards her, his remaining arm offered in greeting.

Kitty shook his hand. 'Good morning to you, too, Charlie.'

358

Charlie glanced around. 'The captain not with you? Still making millions out at Ballarat?'

'No, he isn't.' And Kitty explained very briefly what had happened, and what she wanted to do.

Charlie stared at her, aghast. 'And you want to sail her by yourself?'

'Er, not exactly, Charlie. I want you to captain her; I'll work the rigging.'

Charlie's face went from white, to red, back to almost bloodless again, then erupted in an enormous, gap-toothed smile. 'You want me to captain her! Old one-armed Charlie Dunlop? With just one rat in the ropes? Lord above! Be a bloody risky business,' he added, although the prospect didn't diminish his delight any. 'Course I will.' He couldn't seem to stop grinning. 'And thank you for askin'. I'm that honoured.'

And I'm that desperate, Kitty thought. But Charlie had a reputation as a sea dog — he would know what he was doing even if he could no longer physically manage everything.

'What about me?' Israel called plaintively from the wharf. He hooked Finn's reins over a bollard and ran nimbly up the gangplank. 'I can climb ropes and do all that. I can help.'

'Who's this?' Charlie asked, regarding Israel down his nose.

'Israel.' Kitty took her purse from her pocket and withdrew a handful of coins and gave them to the boy. 'Take Finn to your friend's stable, then find the tugmaster and tell him to be here in thirty minutes. I don't care if there are other ships ahead of us in the queue, pay him whatever it takes. Bribe him if you have to.'

Charlie's eyes had almost popped out of his head. 'You're never givin' that much money to the likes of *him*?!'

'I trust him,' Kitty replied simply.

Charlie made a disbelieving face. 'Anyway, tugmaster won't take heed of a scrap of a boy in bare feet. I'd best have a word with him.'

He whipped some of the money out of Israel's hand and marched off.

Thinking furiously, Kitty walked about, checking that the new ropes were neatly coiled and those sails she could examine from the deck correctly furled, feeling Israel's eyes boring beseechingly into her. Turning on him so quickly he gave a little start, she said, 'If I let you come with us, will you promise to do exactly as you're told?'

An enthusiastic nod.

'And you will stay on the *Katipo* at all times, understand?'

More energetic nodding.

'No running off?'

Vigorous head-shaking this time.

'No deviating from the plan because you think you know better?'

Shaking of the head so rigorous that Israel's eyes almost crossed.

'Good. Now promise me.'

'I promise,' Israel said, and snapped off a smart salute.

Kitty contemplated his dirty, exuberant face, hoping she was doing the right thing. 'Right, then, you can come. Off you go and sort out Finn.'

Israel trotted happily across the deck to the gangplank, then stopped so quickly he almost lost his footing: Daniel was on the wharf below, sitting on McCool, staring up at him.

Israel glanced over his shoulder at Kitty, who was shifting a coil of rope closer to starboard.

'Um . . . ' he said.

She didn't look up. 'What is it?'

'There's someone here.'

She raised her head. 'Who?'

Daniel had dismounted and was on the gangplank; she'd see him in a second. Israel stood aside.

Kitty straightened, a look of confusion on her face. She took a few hesitant steps forward. 'Daniel? What are you doing here?'

He stepped onto the deck and clipped Israel across the ear.

'Ow! What was that for?' Israel wailed.

Unable to decide whether she was delighted to see Daniel, or angry at what he'd just done, she exclaimed, 'Don't hit my ship's boy!' then slapped Daniel's face.

Daniel put his hand to his cheek and had the gall to look aggrieved.

'What's he ever done to you?' Kitty demanded.

'He neglected to tell me you were coming down here to the wharves. I had to find out from that fat fool at the hotel stables,' Daniel added accusingly to Israel. To Kitty he said, 'You've had news?'

'Yes, Rian is being held prisoner at Geelong.' She stopped, feeling quite a sense of mental dislocation, realising that Daniel didn't know anything. 'Daniel, he isn't dead after all! He was kidnapped after the flood and he was here in Melbourne but — '

Daniel raised a hand to quiet her. 'Kitty. Kitty, I know. I know Wong Kai has had his people out looking for information and I know nearly all of it except for the bit about Geelong, and I'll sail with you if you'll have me — and I'll do anything I can to help get Rian back.'

'But how do you know?'

Then she understood. Her head slowly swivelled and her gaze settled on Israel.

In very clipped tones, she said, 'I'd like you to take the horses along to your friend's stables, Israel. Now.'

★   ★   ★

Israel ran with a pair of reins in each hand, his arms outstretched so that the horses trotting behind him wouldn't clip his heels, his rasping breath tasting like metal filings in his throat, and praying that it wasn't his mate's day off. It wasn't and he managed to get a good deal, then raced back along the waterfront to Australia Wharf, terrified that Kitty would be so angry that she might have sailed away without him. But, to his immense relief, he arrived just in time to see the paddle-wheel tug preparing to tow the *Katipo* out of her berth and into the middle of the Yarra.

The gangplank was still down and Israel ran up it, pleased to see that Daniel was still on board. Charlie Dunlop was back, too. No one was talking, but that, even Israel knew, was because they were all too busy running around doing the sorts of things sailors did before they sailed. There was a bump and then quite a violent lurch as the tug pulled away from the schooner and the slack between the two was taken up, and Daniel shouted to Israel to pull up the gangplank.

He stooped and grabbed the end of it, then something made him look up, and freeze. A hundred yards away, near the land end of the wharf, was a line of scruffy, nefarious-looking Chinkees, and they were trotting straight towards the *Katipo*! Even worse, he could see the one they called So-Yee! He let out a squeak of terror, dropped the gangplank and darted across the deck into the safety of the cabin.

'*He* didn't last long,' Charlie remarked to himself.

But Kitty, who was fifteen feet up the mainmast, had spotted the group and climbed down as the first of their number stepped onto the gangplank. Mystified, she crossed the deck, then relaxed as she recognised the figure leading the party, although in a black cotton shirt tucked into worn, knee-length trousers he looked notably less dapper than usual. Gone also was his smart hat, and his feet were bare, but his spectacles remained firmly in place.

Without preliminary, he said, 'How many hands do you have at your disposal?'

Kitty, feeling protective of her people, but also deeply apprehensive regarding what they were about to attempt, replied stiffly, 'Me, Mr Royce who is normally a crewman, Mr Dunlop who, as you can see, has the use of only one arm but is a very experienced sailor, and a boy whom I must admit is not entirely accustomed to the sea.'

Mr Chen made a *pffft* noise. 'Do not be silly, Mrs Farrell. You cannot sail a schooner with only one real sailor. Wong Kai has sent us to assist you.'

The *Katipo* lurched again and swung around into the Yarra's current. The gangplank tipped up of its own accord and slid onto the deck with a clatter. Daniel closed the hatch and stowed the gangplank, hoping Kitty hadn't seen the look of relief on his face. He'd never met this Wong Kai, but he was deeply grateful to him for sending seven of his men to help sail the schooner. Between them, he and Kitty and Charlie Dunlop might — *might* — have got away with sailing out into Port Phillip Bay, with the perfect intensity of wind to drive them and nothing amiss with the new gear, but as all sailors knew, there was no such thing as wind with perfect intensity and gear always broke, whether it was brand-new or not. But for him to have suggested to Kitty that they travel to Geelong by horse or coach instead would possibly have earned him another slap across the face, or, far worse, the misery of having to watch her reduced to weeping yet again. And he didn't think he could bear that.

★   ★   ★

The tug cast loose once the *Katipo* had moved into the deeper waters of the bay, tooted once, turned in an arc and headed back up the river.

The sun, well above the horizon now, was almost behind them, and the wind, in spite of Daniel's pessimism, rose to a sharp northerly that filled the new sails until they snapped and cracked. The comforting roll of the deck beneath her feet delighted Kitty, lifting her heart and replenishing her spirit. At this rate they would be dropping anchor in Corio Bay in a little over three hours.

Mr Chen's people — including So-Yee, who had greeted Kitty with his usual charmless nod — were swarming all over the schooner, sailing her as though they had been born to the sea. This had intrigued Kitty, and when she'd asked Mr Chen where these mariners' skills had come from, he had explained that the region in Kwangtung Province from which they hailed was not far from the coast, and that they were as accomplished at raising a sail as they were using a hoe or guiding a plough across ground ripe for breaking.

Charlie was at the helm having the time of his life, Israel had been coaxed out of the cabin, and he and Daniel were tying down ropes as sails were unfurled to their fullest extent. The wind had picked up from sharp to almost brutal, and the *Katipo* was approaching her top, and legendary, speed of twelve knots.

Kitty took a few moments to lean on the ship's rail and watch the waves skim past below. Then she lifted her gaze to the bright shoreline little more than a mile away, the force of the wind coaxing involuntary tears from her eyes. Very soon, she would finally be with Rian again. She felt elated beyond words that he was alive, and sick to her stomach with fear that by the time she reached him he might not be, or that it would all go horribly wrong and they would perish in their attempts to rescue him. Daniel had insisted she was not, under any circumstances, to go into the place where Rian was being kept prisoner, but she had made her views on that subject very clear. He'd glowered, but she knew he hadn't the power to stop her, except perhaps by physical force, which she strongly suspected he might use if necessary. So she had glowered back at him, then Mr Chen had intervened, suggesting that as both himself and Mr Royce were armed with pistols, they should all three go, as no doubt the captain would want to see Kitty as soon as possible. And if he was as incapacitated as had been reported, they would all be needed to carry him out once he had been liberated.

Daniel had grumbled but agreed, and Kitty had also thought it was an excellent idea, especially as she, too, was armed: Rian's pistol was tucked neatly out of sight in the back of her waistband beneath her jacket.

She felt desperately sorry for Daniel. She knew he must feel awful after those few short minutes of sweaty, grasping pleasure they'd shared in the cottage only four nights ago. She certainly did. She'd felt guilt and embarrassment and shame at her passionate abandonment, and yet she was grateful to him because he'd given her comfort. He was the only man apart from Rian who could ever have done that.

What must he be thinking now he knew Rian was alive? Rian was his good friend, and his boss. He must surely be feeling he had betrayed him. Will he tell Rian what he and I did? she wondered.

But what would *she* say to Rian? Because Daniel hadn't committed the worst kind of betrayal — she had.

★   ★   ★

The *Katipo* changed course slightly as she followed the curve of the shoreline, turning more due west towards the narrow channel into Corio Bay. Her sails deflated a fraction as the wind was deflected by a promontory of land, and Charlie gave the signal for several to be lowered to half-mast, slowing the schooner and settling her hull a little deeper into the waves.

Four or five dozen ships were already anchored in the outer harbour, and perhaps several dozen more notably smaller vessels on the other side of the channel in Corio Bay itself.

'Do you want to chance it?' Charlie asked, coming to stand next to Kitty.

'The channel? How deep is it? Will she do it?'

Charlie shrugged. 'Wouldn't put money on it. Only thirteen feet at high tide. Many a ship's had her arse torn out, and the channel's only been open a year.'

'Then we'll anchor out here,' Kitty decided, turning away from the rail.

The *Katipo* weighed anchor and the ship's boat was lowered. Kitty, Daniel, Mr Chen and two of the Chinese sailors climbed down the rope ladder and seated themselves at the oars. A second later So-Yee followed, landing lightly in the boat.

Mr Chen looked at him, and said something in Chinese.

So-Yee replied in kind, sat down and took the last oar.

Mr Chen spoke again, this time much more sharply.

Daniel and Kitty exchanged a mystified glance. The two Chinese sailors stared at the shoreline, apparently deaf.

Very quietly, So-Yee uttered a few further short words. Mr Chen bowed his head in reluctant acquiescence, but his mouth settled in a compressed line and the knuckles wrapped around his oar were white.

They pushed off and were soon over the sand bar and pulling towards the shore, Kitty with the drawing of Rian's prison safely folded in the pocket of her shirt. Israel, who had begged to be allowed to come ashore, had been left behind to hang over the *Katipo*'s rail, waving forlornly, Charlie at his side.

There were plenty of people about, unloading cargo brought through the channel via the smaller vessels and by barge across the bar. Wharves reached seaward above the lapping waves and the town's buildings encroached almost as far as the beach. There was no major river in Geelong running to the sea to provide a dumping ground for effluent, but the town still stank in the summer heat. It was almost, in fact, a replica of Melbourne with its wide, dusty streets and pockets of grand architecture next to rows of wooden buildings hastily thrown up to service hopeful miners arriving from the four corners of the world.

They reached the beach and hauled the boat up onto the sand.

'Do you know what you're looking for?' Daniel asked, pulling his hat low over his forehead to reduce the sun's glare.

Kitty handed him the map, tattered now at the edges.

'Someone must have really been in debt to this Wong fellow,' Daniel remarked, then squinted down the beach. They should almost be able to see the place from here.

They trudged across the sand and up onto the street that ran parallel to the beach until they came to the building depicted in the drawing. It looked abandoned, and the back of it extended out over the water on wooden poles encrusted with barnacles, just visible below the green-stained high-water line. A jutting lattice of crooked poles and splintered planks suggested that there had once been a short jetty there, but that it had been torn down or had decayed beyond repair.

Deeper than it was wide, the building was two storeys high and bereft of paint, there were weatherboards missing, all the windows had been boarded over, and the single narrow door visible from the road looked barely wide enough to squeeze through. The waves beneath the rear of the building lapped against the pilings, sending up tiny plumes of spray and the smell of invisible sea creatures dying in the shade.

Kitty's heart sank: surely no one would keep a wounded man prisoner in such a ruin? But, yes, one man would, and she knew it.

She approached the door and pushed on it, stifling a gasp as it creaked open an inch or two. 'It's not even locked!' she whispered to Daniel.

'Could he know we're coming?' Daniel knew better than many what sort of man they were dealing with, and he wouldn't put it past him to have prepared a particularly unpleasant welcome.

Kitty beckoned So-Yee. 'Mr Wong's informant: is there a chance he could have double-crossed him?'

So-Yee gave her a look that could have frozen water at the Equator. 'No. It is common knowledge that Wong Kai does not tolerate turncoats.'

Daniel pushed the door all the way open. The small foyer inside was bare, except for a narrow, straight staircase directly ahead. Leading off the foyer in both directions was a mean hallway, its ceiling sagging and its floor holed, revealing shadowed views of the sand below. Daniel unholstered his pistol and crept along the hallway to the left, followed it around behind the staircase, peering into each dank, smelly room he came to, then reappeared again having gone full circle.

He shook his head and whispered, 'Nothing.'

Above them, something made a faint creaking sound.

Convinced that the pounding of her heart

must surely be audible above the whisper of the waves beneath the building, Kitty began to inch up the stairs, then was jerked indelicately backwards as Daniel clamped a hand on her shoulder.

'*I* will go first!' he hissed directly into her ear. 'You stay right at the back, do you hear?'

She glared at him, but stayed where she was until Mr Chen and So-Yee had squeezed past her.

At the top of the stairs a wall barred their way; it seemed to completely intersect the top floor. Behind them, a small landing appeared to lead onto a series of small rooms, but all that stood in front of them was the wall. There was, however, a door in the wall, and the door was closed.

Pushing her way to the front, and feeling Daniel grab a good handful of her jacket as she went past, Kitty carefully put her ear against the door and listened. And as she did, she felt her fists involuntarily clench. A moment later she abruptly pulled away.

Daniel raised his eyebrows.

Through clenched teeth she mouthed, 'A man. And a woman.'

He frowned, both at the very unlikely prospect of a woman being in there, and at the thunderous expression on Kitty's face.

Her features suddenly softened. 'Daniel?' she whispered, her fingers as light as a butterfly's wing on his cheek.

He loosened his grip on her jacket and leant closer to hear her better, and just like that she was gone.

19

Kitty burst through the door. The room before her was neither large nor small. The windows on either side were boarded over, and the one at the far end of the room, through which a view of Corio Bay could be glimpsed, was part-shuttered and part-glazed, its dirty glass cracked but letting in enough light to illuminate the tableau within. Something smelled bad.

Lily Pearce stood with her back to the window, a glass halfway to her mouth, which was open in an 'o' of shock.

To one side, a man sat at a table facing away from Kitty. His coarse, grey hair hung loose to his shoulder blades. It had been groomed until it gleamed, and he wore no hat. His light summer coat and trousers were of a good cut, and his boots shone with recently applied polish. He laid aside the pen with which he had been writing in a journal, picked up a pipe propped next to a burning oil lamp, and, in a leisurely fashion, turned to face her.

'Miss Carlisle,' he said in the cultured, gravelly voice Kitty recalled so clearly, and which still made the hairs on her neck prickle nastily. 'Or I should say Mrs Farrell, now, shouldn't I? How wonderful to see you.' He appeared perfectly composed, but his voice bore a trace of surprise and annoyance.

Avery Bannerman had not aged well — he was

probably approaching sixty by now, Kitty guessed — but year upon year as an inmate in Hyde Park Barracks did that to a man. His bloodhound features had sagged even further, the hoods over his eyes sunk deeper, and his jowls were now pendulous. His full lips, however, had retained their somehow shocking sensuality, and his watery blue eyes were as sharply intelligent as ever. He smiled at her with his big, tobacco-stained teeth.

Kitty felt Daniel and the others move cautiously into the room behind her. A quick glance told her that they had not yet drawn their weapons.

'Aha!' Bannerman exclaimed. 'Sergeant Royce! So that's where you disappeared to! We all wondered, you know. Especially after that Kinghazel business.'

Kitty ignored his outburst. 'I understand you have my husband.'

'I do, indeed,' Bannerman said, and waved his pipe at a filthy heap of bedclothes in the far corner of the room.

Kitty walked, then ran across to the dishevelled pile, and fell on her knees. Rian was lying flat on his back, so insubstantial among the tangle of old blankets that she hadn't even seen him. His eyes were closed, and beads of sweat had collected on his brow and upper lip. He had a beard and he stank, and he seemed to be unconscious. But he was breathing.

She bent close to his ear and whispered his name, but there was nothing. So she shook him, hard; this time he moaned faintly, but she saw no sign that he recognised her, or even that he was awake.

'You'll have to do more than that if you want some sort of a response, Kitty, my love!' Bannerman called jovially from across the room. 'Try pulling his trousers down!' And he laughed.

Bannerman loved riddles, Kitty knew — he wasn't *just* a dirty old bastard — so she lifted a blanket off Rian's legs, and recoiled in horror and revulsion.

His right thigh was a reeking, festering mass from a point three inches below his groin to his knee, crawling with maggots and oozing pus and watery blood. She gagged, swallowed, gagged again, and closed her eyes and waited until her gorge had subsided.

'Daniel?' she called weakly.

Not taking his eyes off Bannerman or Lily, Daniel crossed the room. 'Christ almighty,' he said quietly, feeling the red heat of rage start to burn in his belly.

Slowly, Kitty pushed herself to her feet, trying very hard not to cry. She walked away from Rian, Daniel at her shoulder.

Dully, she said to Bannerman, 'What do you want?'

Lily Pearce interrupted, her voice strident. 'Just a minute. How did you know where to find us? Who squealed, Avery? What are you going to do about it?'

'Yes, that's a point, isn't it?' Bannerman mused.

So-Yee, standing near the door, said in a tone so sanctimonious that Kitty flinched, 'Who squealed? Mr Bannerman, you sell goods on the black market, you are a money-lender, you are a dishonest landlord, you launder money and you finance houses of ill repute. You must surely be a man with *many* enemies.'

Kitty looked at Lily. Was that the connection? Had Avery Bannerman paid for her whorehouse in Ballarat, and now she owed him a debt?

And at that, Kitty's vision, just for a second, became disconcertingly bright and sparkly with shock as the realisation hit her like a blow to the head.

Rian owed Bannerman a debt! If Bannerman hadn't provided Rian with forged documents, Rian would have been hanged in Sydney in 1840 — and the debt had never been paid!

'Very good, Kitty!' Bannerman said delightedly, watching her face. 'I knew you'd work it out in the end.'

'But what about the traitor, Avery!' Lily whined.

'Oh, shut up, Lily. I know who the traitor is,' Bannerman replied, allowing his gaze to wander casually about the room until it settled deliberately on one particular person. 'Don't I?'

Kitty flicked an appalled glance at Mr Chen. His expression remained inscrutable, but a slight clenching of his fists at his sides gave away his mortification.

Mr Chen's lips barely moved. 'I had expected you would accord me anonymity, Mr Bannerman, and a little honour.'

'Oh, dearie me, no, Mr Chen, there's no honour among thieves.' Bannerman gave another of his oily laughs. 'You should know that.'

So-Yee stepped forward, flicked his wrist and a flash of brightness tumbled through the air. Mr Chen's eyes widened, he made a little burping sound, then slumped forward onto his knees where he remained for several seconds. Then he collapsed onto his side and lay gasping quietly like a recently landed fish, as a small pool of blood spread beneath him. After half a minute, he stopped breathing altogether.

So-Yee retrieved his knife, wiped the blade clean on Mr Chen's shirt and resheathed it in his belt.

'Well then!' Bannerman exclaimed gaily, as though they'd all been treated to a particularly good parlour trick but now it was time to get down to business. 'Your husband, Mrs Farrell, owes me a debt, and as payment I want his claim at Ballarat. I was told by reliable sources,' he said, pointing at Mr Chen's body, 'who sadly couldn't pay their gambling debts and had to trade useful information in lieu, that it's paying extremely well. At first, to be honest, I wasn't entirely sure how I was going to convince your husband to sign his claim over to me, but what a godsend that flash flood turned out to be! Then he got sick and now he *can't*. But you can. Really, it's a good thing you *have* come along, isn't it?'

Kitty eyed him and thought, You can have the damned claim. But she didn't trust Bannerman at all. 'No. I want Rian taken out of here first. *If* he survives, I'll make sure he signs the claim over to you.'

Bannerman shook his head. 'Oh, no, no, no. I'm afraid you've misheard. I said I want you to sign it over now.'

'I don't have the authority, not while Rian is still alive.'

Bannerman's sleekly groomed eyebrows went up. 'Really? All right, I'll kill him.'

He withdrew a pistol from inside his coat, cocked it and aimed at Rian.

Daniel started to move and by the time Bannerman pulled the trigger, Daniel was between Rian and the pistol. The bullet hit him in the side and he crumpled, sliding across the floorboards into the pile of bedding, shunting the whole lot against the wall.

Kitty drew her own pistol and fired it at Bannerman. To her surprise, her shot hit him in the left temple. He leaned back in his chair, a bemused look on his face, then very slowly his head tipped farther and farther back until he was gazing directly at the ceiling. His hand opened, his pistol clattered to the floor, and his bladder let go.

At the instant that Kitty fired at Bannerman, Lily whipped a small handgun out of her skirt pocket, but before she could even cock it, So-Yee threw his knife. It went through her forearm, the tip of the blade protruding from one side and the handle from the other: staring at it goggle-eyed, she was so mesmerised with shock that she didn't even notice Bannerman was dead.

So-Yee ran past Kitty, crouched and pressed his fingers against Daniel's neck.

'He is breathing. Help me.'

Kitty, her heart thudding behind her ribs and her bowels feeling alarmingly watery, took hold of Daniel's boots and hauled him, weakly coughing blood, onto Rian's blanket. She and So-Yee took an end each and began to drag the two men towards the door. They felt as though they weighed at least a ton, and the blanket kept catching on splinters in the floorboards, and by the time they got across the room she was weeping openly.

'Stop it, girl,' So-Yee said; and for once, Kitty noted, he didn't sound bad-tempered.

There was a crash as behind them a chair fell over, then Lily's voice, harsh with pain, rang out.

'Stop, or I'll shoot you!'

Both Kitty and So-Yee froze.

Slowly, they turned.

Lily stood only yards away, her feet set apart for balance, the arm with the knife protruding from it held stiffly across her body, the hand holding the pistol resting on it and aimed directly at them. Fat, dark drops of blood splattered steadily onto the wooden floor. Her face was as white as flour.

'Sign the claim over, Kitty. Sign it over to me.'

Kitty straightened, careful not to move too quickly. 'No, you'll just kill us if I do that.'

'I'll kill you if you don't.'

'My men know where we are, Lily.'

'They do not. You would have said that to Avery.'

Kitty shot a glance at So-Yee, trying to ascertain whether he was carrying another knife. He understood, and with the merest narrowing of his eyes managed to convey to her that he was not. On the floor, Daniel groaned.

'It won't work,' Kitty said. 'What do you think our men will do if you return to Ballarat with a deed saying you now own Rian's claim?' She took an almost imperceptible step towards Lily.

'Stay where you are!' The pistol in Lily's hand shook and her fingers tightened around the grip. 'I'll dismiss them all. I'll say that their precious captain has finally repaid his debt to Avery Bannerman, and that Avery Bannerman owed me a debt.'

'You're mad, Lily. They won't believe you.'

Anger and pain twisted Lily's face, and she moved her wounded arm so that it rested against her chest. 'Why won't they? Why shouldn't they believe someone like me? They always listen to you, don't they? I'm as good as you are. Why shouldn't they believe me?'

Her voice rose higher and higher until she was almost shrieking. Spit flew from her paint-smeared mouth, and her wig had slipped so that strands of someone else's hair stuck to her pale, sweating face.

Behind her Kitty could feel So-Yee tensing. She hoped he wasn't about to leap at Lily because she could see that the hammer on the pistol was cocked. Her own gun was useless now, the chamber empty.

Suddenly, but without taking her eyes off Kitty, Lily bent, staggered slightly and righted the chair she had knocked over. She sat down in it heavily, resting her arms on the table. The tableau was surreal — Lily with the glint of metal protruding from her bloodied, swelling forearm, and the corpse of Avery Bannerman slumped next to her, ruined head back, mouth gaping open, urine-stained trousers already drying in the heat.

'My arm hurts,' Lily whined, and beneath the truculence Kitty heard a chilling whisper of rising madness. 'I have to take the knife out.'

Before she'd even thought about it, Kitty cried, 'No! You'll bleed to death!'

Lily raised the pistol at Kitty again. 'You're lying.' She looked at So-Yee. 'Is she?'

'Yes. Remove it,' So-Yee said.

'Bitch,' Lily swore at Kitty.

She laid down the pistol, grasped the handle of the knife and gave it an almighty tug. The blade stuck for a moment, then slid out, releasing a fountain of blood that splattered across Lily's face and down the front of her fancy dress.

She cried out, leapt to her feet, staggered and collided with Bannerman's chair. Bannerman's head fell forward and knocked over the oil lamp, the contents of which spilled across the table top and onto the floor. The oil ran along the grooves in the floorboards and soaked into the hem of Lily's skirts, then caught alight, turning her within seconds into a human lamp.

Kitty let go of the blanket and clapped her hands over her ears to drown out the terrible sound of Lily's screams as she careened around the room, her clothes and wig alight and her skin bubbling and blackening.

Then So-Yee jerked her through the door and shouted at her to take hold of the blanket again.

Somehow, as smoke began to curl down the stairs and fill the building, they managed to get Daniel and Rian outside and onto the sand. The ship's boat was waiting and it took less than a minute to settle both men in the bottom and push off into the outgoing tide.

Melbourne

Flora sat in the chair, her hands folded in her lap, and watched as Kitty packed the last of her things into her trunk.

'And the claim? What have you done with that?'

'I've sold it to Wong Kai, and Wong Fu is going to manage it,' Kitty replied. 'And all the gear and the livestock and the cottage. There's probably a little more gold down there before it bottoms out.' She stopped what she was doing and made a rueful little face. 'I'm sorry, Flora. If I'd thought about it, I'd have offered it to you. But I just wanted to be rid of it.'

Flora nodded; she did understand. Her friend looked pallid and exhausted. The last few weeks had been a terrible ordeal for her, which was why she, Flora, had come to Melbourne with the *Katipo* crew when they'd heard from Wong Fu via a message from his brother about what had been going on. Haunui and Hawk had been preparing to come to Melbourne anyway, having regretted allowing Kitty to ride off in search of Rian with only Daniel as a sort of shadow chaperone. What must they both be feeling now?

381

Flora wondered grimly, given the consequences.

'I still don't quite understand everything that happened leading up to this, Kitty.'

Kitty laid a pair of Amber's drawers on the bed and folded them with unnecessary precision. 'You already know about what a crook Avery Bannerman was.' Kitty had told Flora years ago when they'd first met in Auckland. 'Apparently after he received his certificate of emancipation he started up a few businesses in Sydney, then moved here to Melbourne where he established a few more, mostly illegal. One of those ventures, I'm fairly sure, was to lend money to Lily Pearce to set up — '

'Ah, yes, I knew someone had backed her, but I never found out whom.'

'So that put her in debt to him. And did you realise she was doing personal favours for Sergeant Coombes in exchange for a blind eye?'

Flora nodded and made a face. 'I much preferred to pay cash.'

'We were selling our gold to Wong Kai because he gave us a better rate than anyone else, and Mr Chen was Mr Wong's accountant. Unfortunately Mr Chen had accrued huge gambling debts and had borrowed from Avery Bannerman and couldn't pay him back. Bannerman offered to wipe some of the debt in exchange for information he might find useful, and Mr Chen happened to tell him about the gold coming from our claim at Ballarat.' Kitty sighed heavily and sat on the bed. 'And this is where Rian had no one to blame but himself. And neither did I. I was just as responsible for repaying that debt to

Bannerman as Rian was.' Her throat was suddenly tight and she swallowed painfully. 'Bannerman told Lily he wanted Rian. She must have thought she could get him into bed and somehow get the claim that way, but it didn't work.'

Flora snorted.

'And then the river flooded, and by chance Coombes found Rian and brought him to Melbourne.'

Flora said, 'So what Carl Buckley heard was actually Coombes describing what he'd done?'

'Yes — so I have Eleanor to thank for that. When you next see her, could you please explain to her that we're not going back, that we've sailed for Sydney then New Zealand? And would you please give her my thanks?'

'Of course.' Flora had two more questions. 'Did you discover who drew the map?'

'No. I suspect only two people do know who drew it, and that's probably for the best.'

'And you say So-Yee just took it upon himself to kill Mr Chen?'

'Yes. It turns out he isn't Wong Kai's butler after all, he's his . . . lieutenant, I suppose you'd call him. And apparently what Wong Kai detests more than anything is disloyalty, so when So-Yee realised what Mr Chen had been up to, he killed him, knowing that Wong Kai would sanction it.' Kitty made a regretful face. 'I felt a little sorry for Mr Chen. I think he was so shamed by his gambling debts he couldn't tell anyone about them, and his pride only got him into even more trouble.'

'Wong Kai, however, clearly values loyalty over ego.'

'Yes. I nearly went back to Lily, too, when she was on fire.'

Flora rolled her eyes. 'Don't say you felt sorry for her as well!'

Kitty tapped her throat. 'No, I wanted Rian's sapphire back. But it was too late.'

She stood, placed the last of her things in the trunk and closed the lid. When a boy arrived to collect the luggage, they followed him as he wrestled the trunk down the hotel stairs on a wooden hand-truck.

In the foyer, Flora took Kitty in her arms and embraced her tightly.

'I know you'll be back one day, Kitty, and I'll see you then. Or perhaps our paths will cross somewhere else. Take care. You're a strong woman: I know you *will* survive this.'

Her face against Flora's lightly scented cheek, Kitty said, 'Thank you so much for being my friend.' They kissed, then Flora walked out of the Criterion and into the sunshine on Collins Street.

Kitty waited until she'd blinked back her tears, then entered the hotel salon. Mick lounged by the window, Simon was in an armchair reading the paper, and Rian and Amber sat side-by-side on the sofa, playing with the *mah jong* set Mr Chen had left behind.

Simon smiled, then folded the paper and put it aside, Amber ran over to her, and Rian glanced up, then went back to pushing the *mah jong* counters about.

'Are we going to get Daniel now?' Amber asked eagerly. 'Has Flora gone?'

'Yes to both,' Kitty replied, her eye on Rian.

Over the past ten days his physical health had been improving as well as could be expected, thanks to the medicines and treatments the doctor was administering — remarkably, in fact, given the severity of his blood-poisoning when they had brought him back from Geelong — but otherwise he'd been feeling fairly grim. Daniel was so ill, yet Rian himself was still recovering from the shock of his ordeal. He hadn't been savaged by dingos, but he had been whipped about the back and arms by Coombes's men when they'd found him crawling dazed in the wrong direction one and half miles from the Yarrowee, and he'd lost a lot of blood when he'd gashed his thigh in the river. Then Bannerman had denied him medicine, and deliberately kept him thirsty and underfed.

And since Kitty had told him two nights ago of what had happened between her and Daniel, his mood had darkened dramatically. She didn't blame him, of course, but she had had to tell him. She couldn't look at him all day long, have him smile at her and touch her, while she knew she'd given herself to another man. So she'd told him in just a few, short, unembellished sentences what she'd done and why, and there had been no angry outburst from him, no histrionics. He'd just said 'Thank you for telling me,' and had his things moved to another room in the hotel. He'd barely spoken a word to her since. Kitty didn't know what to do about it, and now there were other things on her mind.

Daniel was dying.

The bullet that had been meant for Rian had lodged in his lung and his time was drawing near. He had expressed a wish to die at sea and they were on their way to collect him from the hospital. The others were at the docks now, preparing to sail, and they all knew they probably wouldn't see Melbourne again for some time.

Rian grasped his cane and pushed himself to his feet, suppressing a grunt of pain. Outside, the coach they had hired was waiting to take them to Swanston Street.

Kitty moved to take his elbow, but he kept his arm clamped firmly against his side, refusing to meet her eyes.

Simon and Mick exchanged a look, but said nothing. The crew knew exactly what had happened between Kitty and Daniel, as Daniel had become less than discreet in his fevered ramblings, but no one blamed either of them. Or Rian for his current foul demeanour. What they blamed, in spite of the buckets of gold they'd extracted from its long-dead rivers, were the soulless, land-locked acres of dirt and clay that made up the Ballarat basin. If they hadn't set foot on the Victorian goldfields, none of this would ever have happened. They were sailors, not miners, and the sooner they returned to the sea the better.

★ ★ ★

Rian became even more taciturn after the *Katipo* sailed. He spent his time up on deck, and in Daniel's tiny cabin, the little round window open to let fresh air in, and the smell of the rot consuming Daniel's chest out.

Kitty wondered what Rian and Daniel talked about, but she never asked.

They each took turns to sit with Daniel so he was never alone — even Bodie, who had always loathed him, but who now slept curled on the end of his bunk.

Israel, whom Pierre had convinced Rian to take on as a cabin boy to replace Daniel, slept on the floor next to his friend at night, quietly snivelling into his sleeve.

There was little talk on the *Katipo*, and even less laughter. They were all waiting, and only the normal, necessary shipboard chores helped the time to pass.

On the second night, Gideon told Kitty that Daniel wanted to see her.

She went into his cabin and sat down on his bunk. The air stank, as though death itself rode on his breath. There were terrible shadows and hollows in his face, which less than a fortnight ago had been so handsome.

He fumbled for her hand and his fingers felt like the bones Pierre kept in his velvet bag. 'I'll be gone by morning,' he whispered.

His teeth were sticking to his lips and Kitty dampened a cloth and dabbed at his mouth.

Swallowing with great difficulty, he whispered. 'I've loved you since that first day at the barracks.'

'I know.' She kissed his clammy brow. 'And if it hadn't been Rian, it would have been you, Daniel. I promise.'

Daniel closed his eyes, and the corners of his mouth moved in a tiny smile.

★   ★   ★

Daniel died at a quarter to five the next morning.

Mick and Pierre wrapped him in a sheet, then sewed him into a piece of sailcloth. Haunui and Gideon carried him carefully up on deck and as the sun rose, Simon prayed:

> *We therefore commit their body to the*
>   *deep,*
> *looking for the general Resurrection in the*
>   *last day,*
> *and the life of the world to come,*
> *through our Lord Jesus Christ;*
> *at whose second coming in glorious maj-*
>   *esty to judge the world,*
> *the sea shall give up her dead;*
> *and the corruptible bodies of those who*
>   *sleep in him shall be changed,*
> *and made like unto his glorious body;*
> *according to the mighty working whereby*
>   *he is able to subdue*
> *all things unto himself.*

Then Daniel was lowered over the side. He floated on the bright waves for a minute or two, as though not quite ready to leave the world of air and light, then as the sailcloth began to take in water, sank slowly until he was no more than a shadow beneath the surface, and then he was gone.

Israel wept uncontrollably, sobbing until he was puce in the face, so that Pierre had to take him under his arm and almost smother him into comforted silence.

Rian, standing near Kitty, took her elbow and drew her closer. His eyes, she saw, were wet with tears.

Leaning awkwardly on his cane, he said so that only she could hear, 'He told me you would always be mine.'

Kitty drew back and studied her husband's face for a long, cautious, hopeful moment.

Rian added, 'I hope he was right.'

And Kitty smiled.

AMBER

Deborah Challinor

When Kitty Farrell is offered a trinket by a street urchin, her impulsive response will change both of their lives forever, and place an unexpected strain on Kitty's marriage. For the past four years, she has sailed the high seas on the trading vessel *Katipo* with Rian, her wild Irish husband; but when they return to the Bay of Islands in 1845, they find themselves in the midst of a bloody affray. Their loyalties and their love are sorely tested, and Kitty's past comes back to haunt her when she encounters the bewitching child she names Amber. As the action swirls around them, Kitty and Rian must battle to be reunited as they fight for their lives and watch friends and enemies alike succumb to the madness of war and the fatal seduction of hatred.

KITTY

Deborah Challinor

When eighteen-year-old Kitty Carlisle's father dies in 1838, her mother is left with little more than the possibility of her beautiful daughter making a good marriage. But when Kitty is compromised by an unscrupulous adventurer, her reputation is destroyed, and she is banished to the colonies with her dour missionary uncle and his wife. In the untamed Bay of Islands, missionaries struggle to establish Victorian England across the harbour from the infamous whaling port of Kororareka, Hell-Hole of the Pacific. There Kitty falls in love with Rian Farrell, an aloof and irreverent sea captain, but discovers he has secrets of his own. When shocking events force her to flee the Bay of Islands, Kitty takes refuge in Sydney — but her independent heart leads her into a web of illicit sexual liaison, betrayal and death . . .